Savannah Law

Savannah Law

a novel

by

WILLIAM ELEAZER

ELEX PUBLISHERS, INC
St. Petersburg, Florida

ISBN: 978-0-9824747-6-1

Library of Congress Control Number: 2009905872

Published by Elex Publishers, Inc.
5 Crescent Place South
St. Petersburg, Florida
www.elexpublishers.com
Call 800-546-3539 for ordering information.

Cover art by Jeslyn Cantrell, www.jeslynsart.blogspot.com
Book design by Susan Leonard, www.otgbookdesign.blogspot.com

Printed in the United States of America

Dedicated to the citizens of Savannah.
Your law school:
Savannah College of Law

Acknowledgments

My special thanks to Shelly Wilson, Sheila Colón, Sally Waters, Marie Miller, Barbara Samford, Toni Knott, Lisa Bacon, and Jill Sokol, for editorial assistance and advice, and to my wife, Jan, for more than I can explain in many words. And to Christopher Marlowe, who explained it all in just a few.

. . . Where both deliberate, the love is slight:
Who ever loved, that loved not at first sight?
Christopher Marlowe (1564-1593)

CHAPTER 1
Savannah, Georgia
Friday, August 18, 2006

It was Friday night and the Library was overflowing with students. Glasses of beer lined the wooden tables, and backpacks filled with newly purchased law books were scattered on the floor. Jaak Terras, owner of the Library, stood near the front entrance, welcoming everyone back after the summer break.

"Jaak's Library—Bar and Grill" was the name on the neon sign hanging over the double oak doors that opened onto the sidewalk six steps below, but to most of its patrons, it was simply the "Library." For the students at Savannah College of Law, it was the most popular gathering place, especially on Friday nights. And this was a special Friday night—the first of the new semester.

"Welcome back, Sid. Got your postcard. Thanks."

"Hello, Liz, hello, Wes—one more semester for both of you, right?" Jaak would shake their hands and greet them by name, at least those he remembered, and he remembered most of them.

Jaak Terras was as popular as his bar and grill. Fifty-eight years old, he stood six feet, two inches tall and had broad shoulders and a full head of silver hair with a matching and neatly trimmed mustache. As always on such special occasions, he was flawlessly dressed: dark gray wool trousers, cordovan loafers of fine Italian leather, navy wool blazer, light-blue shirt with French cuffs, and a colorful Jerry Garcia necktie.

Jaak had been in the restaurant and bar business for most of his adult life. The exception was the four years he spent with the U.S. Marines, followed by two years at the University of Georgia, and another two and a half years in his hometown—Springfield, Georgia—helping out after the death of his mother and the lengthy illness of his father. Jaak dropped out of college at the beginning of his junior year to help raise his fourteen-year-old brother—his only sibling—and assist with his father's welding business. After his father passed away, Jaak remained in Springfield until his brother graduated from high school. He then closed the welding business and sold the family home. He found a job as an assistant manager of a popular bar and restaurant in downtown Savannah and moved there, taking his brother with him. That was his first employment in the restaurant and bar business and would lead him to his crown jewel, the *Library*.

The Library opened the same year that the law school moved onto its new campus in south Savannah. The building, just one block from the edge of the campus, had been part of the Chatham County Public Library system. Built in the 1920s, it was abandoned and boarded up when a larger, modern, computer-friendly library was built just a few blocks away. The old library was a large, granite-faced building with arched windows, heart-of-pine floors and heavy wooden doors. Inside were broad eight-foot-long tables, wooden chairs, and book shelves on all walls—all solid oak. This was a building built before air-conditioning, designed with twenty-foot ceilings throughout to make Savannah's hot summer days bearable inside. It had been vacant for almost five years when Jaak purchased it from the county. The county was glad to see it go, and Jaak was glad to take possession at a price he considered a steal.

Jaak spent the next year painting, repairing, and renovating. When the renovations began, Jaak impressed upon everyone working on the project that he wanted to recognize the historical significance of the building by incorporating into it as much of the original furniture and fixtures as possible.

One small room was converted into a private lounge, furnished with a large leather sofa and chair and a custom-designed poker table with seven side chairs. This was Jaak's favorite place to relax and entertain close friends.

The large L-shaped room was divided into two rooms, the smaller one serving as the restaurant segment, the larger room as a bar and lounge. The first year the Library opened, the students dubbed the larger area the "Study Hall," and the name stuck.

Summer was a busy season, despite the absence of most of the law students. Local visitors, tourists, and regular customers kept the staff of servers and cooks busy, but Jaak missed the students. Yes, they were loud and messy, but he enjoyed hearing their laughter and watching their pranks. They brought vigor and excitement to the Library, and Jaak was anxious for the new semester to begin. So there he stood, as he did at the beginning of each new semester, greeting all the old-timers and welcoming the new ones.

"Hi, Manny, how was Atlanta?"

Manny Morgan was a senior and one of the Library's regulars for the past two years. Jaak knew Manny had been offered a summer clerking job in Atlanta with one of its most prominent civil defense firms.

"I'm not sure, Jaak. I never got to see Atlanta," Manny responded as they shook hands.

"Don't tell me you gave up that clerking offer you were promised!"

"Nope, took it, worked my ass off twenty-four, seven for six weeks. Never saw the outside of my Peachtree office building during daylight and never once visited Underground Atlanta. Had a blast!" Manny said with a broad smile.

"You ol' dog!" said Jaak, as he slapped him on the back and pointed to the bar. "Juri will be glad to see you."

Juri was the Library's bartender, assistant manager, and Jaak's brother. He resembled Jaak in facial and physical features but was not quite as tall, and being ten years younger, his hair had not turned silver like Jaak's. Their parents, Jaan and Ingrid Terras, were Estonian immigrants who settled in Springfield, a small town twenty-seven miles north of Savannah, immediately after World War II. The Lutheran Church in Springfield had sponsored them as war refugees, and Jaan quickly developed a successful business as a welder, the trade he learned while growing up in Estonia.

Jaak, the oldest child, was given a common Estonian name. The Estonian pronunciation was YA-ak, but his childhood friends all called him "Jake," and "Jake" he remained.

Juri was named for Jüri Uluots, a World War II resistance fighter who later became prime minister of Estonia. Unlike Jaak,

Juri insisted his name retain the Estonian pronunciation, YER-ee. The name prompted questions of its origin from customers, and Juri enjoyed retelling the stories about his freedom-fighting namesake, embellishing them as he saw fit. Juri was a great storyteller and was always ready to hear or tell a new joke, or pop an impromptu trivia question to the law students sitting at his bar.

Jaak made the decision to serve only beer and wine at the Library as part of his business plan. He would apply for a full-service license, a bigger money maker, if he later changed his mind. So far, he had found no need to apply, as the Library was doing quite well financially.

Beer on tap, served in frozen mugs, was the most popular beverage for the young crowd. The wines were moderately priced, with a few superior California wines available for patrons celebrating special occasions. Juri was in charge of wine purchases and took his position seriously, becoming absorbed in Robert Parker's writings on the subject and occasionally taking a business trip to Napa Valley for an on-site personal study. He considered himself a "Sommelier"— and could even pronounce the word, which he frequently did, just to irritate Jaak, who considered it pretentious.

As Jaak stood at the door, greeting the Library's patrons, he could see a reddening sky filtered by dark clouds, foretelling an early evening rain. He loved the salty smell of the wind blowing in from the expansive marshes southeast of the city. The thunder was still far off in the distance, but the constant rumblings warned that rain was fast approaching. He could see that the law school's east parking lot, a couple hundred yards away, was now half empty. The new-students' orientation program, the only class in session that day, had already ended. Most of his student customers had arrived and were busy sharing stories of their summer vacations or internships.

Nearby residents found the Library a welcome place to unwind after a busy day's work. There were several large apartment and condominium complexes within a mile of the Library. These housed many of Savannah's young professionals, who mingled well with the students. Quite a few faculty and staff members from the law school stopped by regularly. The dean, Winston Adams, occasionally stopped by, and Professor Denis Nolan was a regular player at the poker game hosted by Jaak on Sunday nights, the only day the Library was closed. Professor Nolan had called earlier that day to inquire if the game was on for this Sunday, and Jaak assured him that it was.

The band arrived and began setting up in the Study Hall. Live bands were not an every-night, or even an every-week, occurrence at the Library, but quite often a local band was hired for Friday or Saturday nights and special occasions. Jaak was not much into music of any kind, and he left the selection of music and hiring of bands to Juri, whose taste extended to a wide variety of musical styles: big band, blues, popular, country, and vocal jazz. Juri especially liked female blues and jazz singers. His favorites were Tierney Sutton and Norah Jones. He was also a fan of Amy Winehouse—her voice, not her reputation. He had all of these singers' albums, or at least those he could locate. He had over a thousand CDs featuring artists of various styles and an expensive Numark DJ system that he personally commanded.

Jaak's only demand was that the volume be kept low enough for his customers to converse. To Juri, that meant the volume should not shatter the beer glasses, and this was often a bone of contention between the brothers. Tonight it was the Bank Notes, a local band of four young Savannah bank executives on the instruments and a young female vocalist with a wide-ranging voice that went well with the band's selections of blues and country-western music. The bankers neither asked for nor expected compensation; they just enjoyed having an appreciative audience and an occasional cold beer. However, Jaak insisted that Juri compensate the vocalist. He knew her salary was well below those of the bank executives.

CHAPTER 2

Scott Marino sat at one of the large oak tables on the south wall of the Library, surrounded by a half dozen other students, all joining in a lively conversation about classes, professors, and summer adventures.

". . . yeah, clerked in Boston . . . four thousand a month making coffee . . . pot of Folgers every two hours . . . got damn good at it . . . ."

". . . I just signed up for that new seminar, 'Art, Love, and the Constitution.' Should be sweet!"

". . . took my first cruise ever . . . big luxury liner out of Miami. Arrived in the Caymans just as Hurricane Alberto—and salmonella—hit . . . ."

". . . have you seen that new R & W professor? Hot, man, hot . . . !"

For Jennifer Stone, seated next to Scott, it was all new and exciting. This was her first semester, and she wanted to hear it all. She listened attentively to the spirited conversation. The anticipation of this new adventure, law school, was intoxicating.

Jennifer's bright blue eyes darted around the table as she reveled in the animated tales of each speaker, her curious mind soaking up every word. She wore her blonde hair in a casual, breezy cut, a hair style she had worn since high school. She was five feet, six inches tall, trim and shapely, with a flawless complexion. The only makeup she used was a gloss on her lips that made them sparkle like her eyes. Her uncommon beauty came naturally.

Scott, her escort, was a handsome young man himself. Years of outdoor sports had toned his muscles and maintained his skin in a healthy Mediterranean hue. He kept his dark hair clipped fairly short but long enough for a slight wave to be visible. Slightly over six feet tall, he had an athletic build, hazel eyes, and a winning smile. Jennifer had met him earlier that day at the orientation program. Scott was Student Bar Association president and had overseen the third day of orientation. The first two days dealt with administrative and academic matters. This day, Friday, the last day of orientation, was devoted to student activities of the extracurricular kind: law fraternities, student government, intramural athletics, pro bono activities, and anything else that would occupy a Savannah College of Law student's time away from classes and the study routine.

Scott presided over the entire day's orientation schedule, addressed the new students on several of the topics, and answered their many questions. The new students were invited to a four o'clock barbeque in the school courtyard, hosted by the Student Bar Association. Jennifer was impressed with Scott's knowledge and gentlemanly manner throughout the day, so when he invited her to join him afterwards at the Library, she quickly accepted.

Jennifer had a lot of questions. Her primary interest, at least for now, was to learn as much as she could about courses and scheduling. Her career goal was to be a trial lawyer. What kind of trial lawyer, she wasn't sure. She just knew she wanted to be in the courtroom. She could not imagine spending her life as a lawyer preparing real estate closings, wills, estate documents, and business contracts. This was not unusual for an entering law student, before being exposed to all the varied careers a law graduate might pursue. But it was the intensity of the desire that set Jennifer apart. Scott was just beginning to tell her about some of the clinic and mock trial opportunities she would have at "Savannah Law," as Savannah College of Law was called by students and faculty alike, when he was interrupted by a voice behind him.

"I believe I have met the suave gentleman seated on your right, but to my extreme disappointment, I have not had the pleasure of meeting you or learning your name," the voice recited in feigned sincerity.

As Scott and Jennifer turned, they spotted a tall young man, with light-brown hair hanging in ringlets to his shoulders. Towering over Jennifer, and looking directly into her eyes, he said, "I'm Jeffrey Swenson, and I am at your service if this gentleman is bothering you. I'm third-degree black belt and would commit second-degree manslaughter for you, just say the word. This guy looks like trouble."

Noting a repressed smile on Scott's face that assured her this was all in jest, Jennifer decided to play along, replying, "Is that your pickup line? Surely you could do better."

"Not good? How about this: If I told you that you had a beautiful body, would you hold it against me?"

"That's so old," responded Jennifer.

Faking a hurt expression, the young man said, "Then this: Your eyes are the color of my Porsche."

"Not quite, but better."

"Say, that's a nice dress; can I talk you out of it? I can see it in your eyes—the answer is 'no' to that one also."

"You are so perceptive."

"OK, I'm Irish. Do you have any Irish in you? Would you like some?"

With that, Scott quickly broke in. "Jennifer, please excuse this degenerate. He's lost all of the gentlemanly qualities that were present when he was admitted to law school two years ago. Believe me, he was once a normal, respected citizen of our campus, but this past summer he enrolled in the Public Defender Clinic, and the exposure to so many miscreants and felons has left him without any moral, social, or ethical sense of responsibility. He's hopeless and depraved. But I love him like a brother. Jeffrey, sit down and meet Jennifer Stone, entering Savannah Law student. Jennifer, this is my former roommate, Jeff Swenson. He's a senior but unlikely to ever graduate. And now you see why he is my *former* roommate. Jeff, your conduct tonight is deplorable, like all other nights."

"Glad to meet you," Jeff said, moving to a vacant seat directly across from the two. The band had begun to play, and the other students who were seated there had either departed for the evening or were on the dance floor, leaving only the three of them at the table. Looking at Scott, Jeff added, "You said you loved me. Does that mean you'll dismiss those charges against young and innocent Charles Vandera?"

"I said I loved you like a brother, not a mother," Scott said, and then added, "We're going to trial Wednesday. No more continuances, no more BS, no more of your delaying tactics. Time he does the time."

"What's this all about? Dismiss charges? Going to trial?" Jennifer turned and looked at Scott.

"Jeff and I are in our second semester of the Criminal Law Clinic. Jeff is in the Public Defender Clinic. I'm in the Prosecution Clinic—the good guys. We get to try criminal cases in the Chatham County courts, and we're on the same case, involving one Charles Vandera, who burglarized a CVS drug store in Savannah."

"*Allegedly* burglarized the store," interrupted Jeff.

"OK, *allegedly* burglarized the store. Anyway, we were in the summer clinic when we first got the case. The case is ready for trial. I'm prosecuting the case; he's defending the creep. And that's why we're no longer roommates."

"You had a falling out over the case?"

"No, not a falling out. We just thought it might be an ethical problem: client phone calls to the shared apartment and the necessary phone conversations with witnesses, supervising attorneys, and so forth. We decided it best to find other housing arrangements. Besides, Jeff's a slob and a lousy cook and always late paying his rent. Right, Jeff?"

"Well, I never thought of myself as all that bad of a cook, but a slob and deadbeat . . . yes. But Scott is a snorer, loud, really loud, so I was glad to get out of that apartment. Have you ever tried to sleep with him?"

"Jeff, you're out of order. Jennifer, I apologize again for my degenerate ex-roommate. Jeff, you also apologize to Jennifer."

"Right; sorry, Jen. I'd better be going. Got work to do. Scott, old buddy, I'll see you in court—Wednesday, unless you're willing to grant me a two-week continuance in the name of justice and fairness and whatever. We still need some witness round-up time."

"That's up to the judge, but I'll oppose it. You've already had a continuance and you've had plenty of 'round-up time.' Be ready and beware," Scott said, as Jeff was getting up to leave. Then, as an afterthought, he added, "Not too late to take the pretrial."

"Not my choice, but I can tell you, no way. He still claims he's innocent. He said to take that pretrial and stuff it up your . . . oops, sorry, Jen. I'm outta here." With that, Jeff pushed his chair back under the table and walked out.

Scott turned to Jennifer. "I'm going to have a draft. What would you like?

"I think I'll have some iced tea," said Jennifer.

Scott called a waitress over, and they ordered.

"You actually are going to try a felony case before you even graduate from law school? I thought the clinic students only tried DUIs and such . . . misdemeanors. You have to tell me about this."

"About 'this'? You mean the clinics?" asked Scott.

"Yes. You're already doing what I can only *hope* to do after graduation."

"So, you already have the bug. Good. And that's the beauty of our clinics. You get a chance to go to the ball early on and see if you can dance. Some can't. No rhythm. Or don't have the stomach for the pressure. A clinic semester gives you time to head in another direction when job interviews and summer clerkships come up."

"OK, true, maybe I'll find out that I don't have 'the rhythm,' as you call it—or the stomach for it. But right now that's what I want to do. So, are you going to tell me about that burglary trial?"

"Of course. If you really are interested. I don't want to bore you. Would you have some time Sunday afternoon? I'm going to be working on the case in one of the campus courtrooms. I'll be practicing the opening statement. You could listen and give me a critique."

"I don't claim to know enough to critique, but I really would like to listen. Tell me when and where."

Scott was intrigued. She seemed sincerely interested in this trial. But what was he thinking? He was seated next to the most beautiful woman he had ever met, and he had allowed the conversation to drift into work, school, and careers. Dumb. He wanted to know more about Jennifer.

The waitress brought their drinks. "I have Thomas Courthouse reserved from four to five on Sunday," Scott said. "That's the white-columned building by the school fountain. Can you make it then?"

"Sure."

"Now, with that settled, tell me about Jennifer Stone," said Scott. "We've been talking about me and my trial. And I apologize. I want to hear about you. Where is home? Family? Where did you go to undergrad? How did you end up at Savannah Law?"

Scott and Jennifer were now sitting alone at the end of the table. Before Jennifer could answer, Scott saw Jaak walking toward them. Jennifer looked up and gave Jaak a big smile.

"Hi, Jaak," she said.

Astonished, Scott looked from one to the other. "You two know each other?"

"Of course; we go back quite a way," Jaak replied, with a grin. And with that, Jennifer got up and gave Jaak a hug.

Rising quickly to his feet and extending his hand to Jaak, Scott said, "Jaak, no offense, but please, no hug." And then, with eyes shifting from one to the other, he added, "What gives?" Scott had known Jennifer for less than a day. She had been at Savannah Law less than a week. He had spent all day introducing first-year students to the law school and its surroundings. Only by accident had he now the good fortune to be spending the evening with this charming young lady. He hoped he wasn't being set up for some joke, but it did briefly cross his mind.

Still standing, and with one hand lightly resting on Jennifer's back, Jaak replied, "Jennifer and I are sworn to secrecy, but if she wants to share it with you, it's OK with me. You and I go back a way too, Scott."

"Then sit down and join us, Jaak." As soon as they were seated, Scott said, "Jaak, I would offer to buy you a drink, but this place sells only watered-down beer and jug wine, and I know you have more sophisticated tastes."

Jaak laughed.

"I'd just asked Jennifer to tell me about herself and her family and how she came to Savannah Law. But now I learn that you already know her."

Jaak smiled, looked over at Jennifer and nodded, indicating the missing story was for her telling.

"Hometown, St. Louis. My dad was a high school teacher and principal, and my mother ran an art studio. I was an only child—came along late in my folks' marriage. They thought they couldn't have children, and then I arrived. I was their 'miracle,' so they spoiled me rotten."

Scott smiled. "You admit to being 'spoiled rotten'?"

"Absolutely. They catered to my every whim. And they gave me the best of everything they could afford—private school, piano lessons, art lessons, voice lessons, tennis lessons—you name it. But I recognized early on how lucky I was to have them as parents. They really sacrificed for me. A child can be spoiled and still be grateful. I was determined not to *act* like a spoiled child."

"Did you succeed?" asked Scott.

"Probably not, but I'm still trying."

"Good. Law school's not a place for a spoiled child. Just how did you end up here at Savannah Law?"

"Location. Decided to stay close to my parents."

"You said they were in St. Louis."

"But they're at Hilton Head now. They went there for their honeymoon. They fell in love with the island and returned every summer, eventually purchasing a lot to build on. That was over thirty years ago, before real estate at Hilton Head was priced out of reach for those like my mom and dad. They built a house and moved there the week after my high school graduation."

"And you . . . where did you go?"

"I went with them that summer, trying to decide what to do about college. I had been admitted to Washington University in St. Louis, but I couldn't decide what I wanted to study. I enjoyed art but wasn't much of an artist. My mother was—had her own shop. I worked in it in high school and thought I could be satisfied and successful, managing an art studio. So, when they moved to Hilton Head, I enrolled at Savannah College of Art and Design."

Scott interrupted. "You came to law school from an *art school*? Right here in Savannah?"

"Yep, that's right."

"How did that quirky turn in your career choice come about?" Scott asked.

"Quirky? Well, I suppose it *is* a bit unusual, from an art school to law school. Do you really want to know? I don't want to bore you with the details of my *quirky* change of careers."

"Poor choice of words, good choice of careers," replied Scott. "And I stand chastened. But, yes, I'd like to hear about your, shall I say, 'refreshingly unusual,' path to Savannah Law."

"Well, that's where Jaak enters the picture. During my first year in the basic architectural history course, we were divided into teams to visit at least three historical churches or synagogues in Savannah. We had to submit a team report on the architectural significance of each. The first one on our list was Ascension Lutheran on Wright Square. We called the church, asking permission to visit. Jaak was a member of the church council and volunteered to be our tour guide. Oldest church elevator in the country, right, Jaak?"

"That's what the elevator company says—1928."

"But apparently you've seen each other since then," said Scott.

"Yes, Jaak told us about his 'Library' and invited our team to come see the building. He said it would be a good study for our class. It was. We visited several times, and I later wrote a report on it for my class."

"So that's what Jaak meant when he said you and he go back a way?"

"Well, yes and no," replied Jennifer. "What he meant was more than that. Remember, I said Jaak was indirectly responsible for my being in law school rather than running some art shop in Hilton Head. I'll just have to tell you later. It concerns a visit I had to an old courthouse, and it's a bit involved. Well, 'involved' is not the right word, but it does take a bit of explanation. It's been a long day, and I need to be heading home."

"Fuck you, you fucking asshole," roared a young man in a faded denim jacket several tables away. He was standing, fists clenched, staring at another young man in a Chicago Bears T-shirt who had his right arm extended as if to offer a hand shake. Several young men were standing around the two.

"Excuse me," Jaak said, as he got up and left the table.

All eyes were on Jaak as he approached the confrontation. The regulars knew what was coming. They had seen Jaak defuse such situations before.

"Let's all have a seat," said Jaak.

All those standing immediately took a seat in one of the oak chairs at the nearby table. All except the young man in the faded denim jacket. He remained standing, but the intensity of his gaze was now a bit diminished and scattered.

"I said, take a seat."

Jaak was staring straight into the young man's eyes. As if hypnotized, he immediately sat. Whether it was from the force of Jaak's voice or the absence of any support system from those who had already taken a seat, his strident attitude immediately became one of compliance. He looked around for a friendly eye and found none.

"You are a student here at Savannah Law?" Jaak asked.

The young man nodded.

"Is this your first visit to our Library?"

The young man looked around, furtively. Again he found no sympathetic eye. "Yes," he answered.

"First semester here at Savannah Law?"

"Yes, sir." This was his first "sir," but sooner or later it always happened at these encounters between Jaak and an unruly customer.

"Did you see the sign at the entrance, 'Profane or obscene language is prohibited in the Library'?" Jaak was not just making idle chatter; there was indeed such a sign in the alcove, over the door leading into the bar.

"No, sir."

"Can you think of any reason there should be such a sign?"

The young man shifted uneasily in his seat before answering, "Because there may be ladies present, I suppose."

Jaak responded sharply, "No, sir, wrong answer. Not because there may be *ladies* present, but because there may be *ladies* or *gentlemen* present."

The young man raised his eyelids then quickly lowered them.

"Did you come to the Library with the person who was the target of your outburst?"

"Yes, sir."

"Then I can only assume he's a friend." Jaak sought and found the eyes of the man in the Bears T-shirt. "I believe you were extending your hand in a gesture of friendship earlier. Would you care to do so again?"

"Sure, no problem." He extended his hand.

The young man in the denim jacket, embarrassed and still a little angry, reluctantly put his hand out to end the confrontation.

"I don't care about the reason for your disagreement, nor your names," said Jaak. "I would just prefer to meet you again under more agreeable circumstances." Then, addressing no one in particular, he added, "All of you are welcome in the Library. I just ask that you acknowledge the sign at the entrance. I can assure you that when we are open, there will always be a gentleman present."

Jaak motioned to a waitress who had been listening at a safe distance. "Millie, come and take their orders."

As he turned to leave, Jaak was pleased to hear the young man in the denim jacket ask his friend in the Bears T-shirt, "Ben, what will you have? I'm buying."

When Jaak arrived back at Scott's table, Jennifer was absent, having just left for the ladies' room. "Glad to see you haven't lost your touch, Jaak," Scott said.

"No, I guess I haven't. Defusing testosterone-spiked egos is getting old. But you know, Scott, I'm a bit disappointed in the latest crop of foul mouths. They are so uninspired—they lack creativity. I saw in the newspaper, just a day or so ago, an account of an interview with Dean Adams. He said the average LSAT and GPA at Savannah Law had increased significantly over the past three years, but that guy's simple obscenity was no improvement. He's using 'fuck' as a verb and an adjective. Three years ago, near that same table, we had a first-semester student deride his drinking buddy with, 'Fuck you, you fucking fuck!' Now that was a classy obscenity—a verb, adjective, *and* a noun, and only two extraneous words. Admittedly, hard to improve on that, but this latest crop of foul mouths don't seem to be trying."

The twinkle in Jaak's eyes was soon replaced with a solid and deep laugh, joined by Scott's.

Jennifer returned to the table and asked about the disturbance.

"It appeared to be quite minor," Jaak replied. "I doubt if either will remember it tomorrow."

"Speaking of tomorrow," said Jennifer, "I've got a full day of class preparation. If I read every case I'm assigned to read, it will take me until midnight—and that assumes I'm up at six. This is fun, but I really must be going."

"A law student's life, Jaak, early to bed, early to rise," said Scott. "Time I headed out, too."

"There's still a bit of moisture in the air," Jaak said. "Scott, grab an umbrella on your way out. You are responsible for getting Jennifer home, safe and dry."

Jaak had an ample supply of umbrellas in the Library alcove, stored in two large antique copper milk cans. A sign on each milk can read:

Take as Needed but Please Return

Jaak started this service with a half-dozen umbrellas, purchased just for that purpose. Over time, more umbrellas were brought in than were taken, and now the supply had grown to a couple dozen. Scott grabbed one as he and Jennifer walked out onto the street.

CHAPTER 3

The sky was pitch-black, and although the heavy rain had subsided, a light rain was still falling. A gusty breeze made Jaak's admonishment to keep Jennifer dry difficult. Jennifer had parked in the school's main parking lot, several blocks from the Library. Scott wished he had a flashlight, as visibility was severely limited despite street lights on each corner. Two years on the campus had given Scott a perfect sense of direction, but he couldn't navigate around every puddle that the earlier heavy rain had left.

Holding the umbrella in his left hand and mostly over Jennifer's head, he placed his right arm around her waist—not an intentional gesture but merely a reflex as he sought to protect her from the wind-driven rain that was whipping against them. Maybe it was his imagination, but she seemed to move closer against his body as they walked. He could feel her warmth, and he became oblivious to the moisture that was beginning to cover his shirt. The summer night's rain brought a respite from the day's sweltering heat, and the short walk in the rain was invigorating. They made light conversation about the uniqueness of Jaak's Library, and one or the other, with a laugh, would point out an approaching puddle to avoid. At each puddle, Scott would demonstrate his "chivalrous nature" by pulling Jennifer toward him to avoid the obstacle. Jennifer found it easy to oblige. Neither minded that they were slowly but surely getting drenched.

The parking lot had a single halogen light in the center, and with the rainy overcast, it provided only limited illumination. Jennifer's 2004 Toyota Camry was on a dimly lit far side. When they finally arrived at the car, Jennifer quickly slipped into the driver's seat and rolled down her window. Scott reminded her of their agreement to meet Sunday at Thomas Courthouse.

"I'll be there," she said, as she began to adjust her seat belt.

Scott stood with the umbrella over his head, protecting the open window. "Drive safely, Jen—as your mother would say. See you Sunday."

Jennifer smiled, looked ahead, and turned the key. Nothing. Not even a cough from the engine. She tried again with the same result.

"Is it in park?" asked Scott.

"Of course, it's in park!" said Jennifer.

"Put it in neutral."

She did and turned the key again. Only the sound from the click of the key was heard.

"I'm going over to my car and get some jumper cables. It may be your battery."

Scott was pretty sure it was *not* a battery problem, because her headlights appeared strong. Still, it was a prudent next step. He quickly crossed the lot to his 1984 Chevrolet Camaro, a black, eight-cylinder Z28 that he had owned since his senior year in high school. It was his pride and joy. It was spotless, inside and out, and the engine was strong and always well maintained. Nevertheless, he kept a pair of jumper cables in his trunk, just in case they were ever needed. In a few minutes, he had returned in his Camaro, opened its hood, and attached the cables between the two cars.

Jennifer turned her key again. Nothing. She moved the gear back into park and tried once more. Nothing. Scott left his motor running and went to Jennifer's vehicle.

"Did you hear any cranking noise?" he asked.

"No."

"I'm no mechanic, but I believe it's the starter. Could be the solenoid, could be a wire, could be most anything, but it's not your battery. We're going to have to call a tow."

"I have Triple A." Jennifer looked in her wallet and found her card.

"I'll call from my cell phone. It's in my car," said Scott.

He took her card, went to his car, and made the call. He was told he could expect a tow truck in about half an hour, but Scott knew that on rainy weekend nights, the wait could be an hour or more. He went back to Jennifer's car. Both were wet and cold from the walk in the rain, so Scott invited her to join him in the Camaro where they could enjoy the warmth of his heater.

"Wow, that feels good," said Jennifer, as the warm air enveloped them.

Scott looked over at Jennifer and said, "Earlier in the evening, you said something about an old courthouse leading you to Savannah Law. You said it was a bit involved and would take time. Looks like we have time now. Fill me in."

"Sure. And I'll give you the long version. One of my instructors was especially interested in courthouses, their history and their architecture. He planned Saturday tours to the courthouses in Valdosta and Moultrie—they have two of the most historic and beautiful courthouses in Georgia." Jennifer paused, and then added, "Did you know that Georgia has more courthouses than any other state, except Texas?"

The question caught Scott by surprise. He wasn't exactly listening to her every word. He was thinking, "Here I am, on a rainy night, alone with the most beautiful girl I've ever met. Car trouble, so I immediately call a tow truck to come get her and then ask her to fill me in on the details about some frickin' old courthouse in Effingham County! What the hell's wrong with me? Do I really care how she got to Savannah Law? She's here with me, it's nighttime, it's raining, there's no school in the morning and . . . ."

He saw Jennifer looking at him, apparently waiting for his response. Scott tried to regain his composure, smiled, and said, "Well, Jennifer, we have some pretty classy courthouses in Tennessee, too." He wasn't sure that was an appropriate response, but judging by her expression, it was in the ball park. And since her exact question was beyond his recall, he just waited.

Jennifer seemed to accept the answer Scott had thrown out and continued. "When I told Jaak about the planned visits to those courthouses, he was surprised that Effingham County wasn't on the list. He said its courthouse was historic also. He grew up there, knew the clerk of court, and would arrange a visit if our team wanted to go. Springfield is only about twenty-five miles from Savannah. Have you been there, Scott?"

Scott's mind had drifted again. He was listening but wasn't hearing. Or perhaps he was hearing but not listening. In any case, his eyes were focused on Jennifer. She was leaning against the passenger door, facing Scott, silhouetted in the window by the single light in the distance. And she was alone with him, not in his arms, but only an arm's length away. She smiled as she talked, and her eyes sparkled even in the dim light.

Scott woke from his momentary reverie to the flashing light of a tow truck turning into the parking lot. He flashed his lights twice to signal the truck. The rain had stopped, and both Jennifer and Scott stepped outside. Scott pointed to Jennifer's car, and the tow-truck driver stopped beside it. He was a muscular man, about six feet tall, dressed in dark Levi's and a dark blue T-shirt. He was wearing a biker's skull cap designed with bright stars and stripes. He looked to be in his early thirties. The biceps of both arms were encircled with one-inch armbands—a series of multicolored Xs tattooed into his skin.

He introduced himself as "Craig" and was all business. He quickly checked the Triple A card for eligibility and asked for the specifics of the problem. Scott filled him in with what he had done, stating that he suspected it was more than battery trouble. He added that it might be best to check it again, as the tow truck would provide a stronger jump-start. Craig agreed; he hooked the cables and went through the procedure that had failed earlier. His efforts were no more successful than Scott's.

"Gotta be the starter," said Craig. "I've got a Camry just like this one, except it's black and two years older. I could fix that starter if I had the parts, a ramp, the right tools, and the time . . . and a good mechanic." He paused and laughed at his joke. "But, sorry, I guess I'll just have to tow it."

"I really need it fixed tomorrow," Jennifer said. "Do you know a repair shop that could get it completed tomorrow?"

"Sure. There are a lot of shops working on Saturday. Marvin's Foreign Auto in Garden City could do it. I've often taken cars there for Saturday work. They are usually open until ten, often later on week nights. They let me work on my car there when they have an empty stall late at night. They may be open now, but I doubt they can get the parts until tomorrow."

Jennifer quickly agreed to have the car towed to Marvin's, and Scott offered to drive her there to pick it up when the work was done. They watched as Craig hooked the Toyota behind the tow truck for its trip to the garage.

When Craig was finished, he said, "Let me have your phone number and address for the garage. They will call you when they know something about your car."

When she gave a number on West Taylor as her address, Craig said, "I know where that is. That's about a block or two from the Mercer House."

Scott was familiar with the location of the Mercer House, made famous by John Berendt's book, *Midnight in the Garden of Good and Evil*. He had visited the gift shop that was located there. He walked over to his car to get a pen to write down the address and phone number before he forgot it.

"That's right on the way to the shop in Garden City. I'll drop you off, right at your door. That's no problem. Come on," said Craig.

Jennifer hesitated but then followed him around to the passenger side of the truck, and Craig opened the door.

Scott had been gone less than a minute, but when he returned, he found Jennifer already settled in the truck. He walked to where he could speak to her through the window.

She rolled the window down and smiled. "Craig's going to drop me off on his way to the repair shop. Please call me about noon tomorrow. By then, I should have word about my car and, if you don't mind, I hope you will drive me over to pick it up."

Scott was a bit perplexed. He had expected—and hoped—to drive Jennifer home. But there she was, already in the cab of the truck. "Sure. But let me make sure I have the right number." He glanced at his paper, repeated the number, and Jennifer verified that he had it right. "Then I'll see you tomorrow," said Scott.

By this time Craig was behind the wheel, and the tow truck started slowly moving from the parking lot.

The truck cab was dusty and grimy, and papers were scattered across the dash. But the thick, vinyl-covered seat was comfortable, and Jennifer rested against the back of the seat, looking at the road ahead. Craig was the first to speak.

"You go to the law school?"

"Just started this week."

"Where you from?"

"I finished college right here—Savannah College of Art and Design."

"Yeah? I used to date a girl from there. Sarah Houston. Know her?"

Jennifer did not. She merely answered, "No." She did not feel like initiating any further conversation. Her mind was on Scott and her class assignments for the coming week. She had six books on her kitchen table waiting for a full day of study, beginning in the morning.

They drove a couple of miles and turned onto Drayton Street, heading north. Traffic was light, and the tow truck, with the Toyota suspended behind it, was traveling only about twenty-five miles per hour. Jennifer wished he would go faster. She was already tired, and the cab was noisy and reeked of burnt motor oil.

Craig broke the silence. "How about us stopping for a bite to eat. I'm hungry; how about you?"

"No, I need to get home. I've got a busy day tomorrow."

"What kind of plans?"

Immediately Jennifer wished she had merely said, "No," rather than opening the discussion. She paused, wondering if she really needed to explain. She merely replied, "Studying for the first week of law school."

"Well, that's great, but you need a little fun before that begins, don't you think?"

A bit troubled by the question and not wanting to continue the conversation, she remained quiet. The tow truck proceeded north on Drayton at about the same speed. Just a few more minutes, and she would be home.

As the truck reached the south end of Forsyth Park, Craig turned to Jennifer and said, "You can open up with me. I'm a fun kind of guy. It's dark, rainy, and, like that insurance company says, 'You're in good hands.' It's Friday night—early on Friday night— hell, ain't even midnight, and like you say, you got all day tomorrow. I know a cool place just over Talmadge Bridge. It has a great band and food as good as the Pirate House. You can sleep at your place tomorrow and at my place tonight." Craig was smiling and looking over at Jennifer.

Jennifer saw where this was going and decided to quickly spike it. "You just pull this truck over. You can let me out on the next corner and continue your little joke with someone who might appreciate it."

"Hey, gal, I'm sorry your bad-starter problem caused you and your guy not to get it on. Not my fault. Calm down. I'm serious. We go across the bridge to this nightclub, we have a drink, if you're unhappy, we leave and I take you home, no hurt feelings. That simple." Craig grinned, and stared at Jennifer for an expected answer.

"Stop this truck right now. I'm getting out."

"I can't let you out here; it wouldn't be safe. Company policy, you know. I'll let you out at your house like I promised. But I know you were expecting something big tonight, and I can give it to you."

Jennifer drew herself upright, stared directly at him, and said through clenched teeth, "I beg your pardon. You are way out of bounds. Stop the truck *now*."

"You'll be begging for something before this night's over, but not my 'pardon.'"

By now, they were within two blocks of Taylor Street, where Jennifer lived. It was a one-way street and would be entered with a left-hand turn. But Craig was in the right lane.

As they approached Taylor, Jennifer ignored Craig's crude comment and commanded, "Get over; you need to turn left at the next street!"

The truck merely increased its speed and continued north on Drayton. Jennifer now saw the situation for what it was, and she was terrified. She continued to shout for Craig to stop, to let her out. Talmadge Bridge, which crossed the Savannah River into South Carolina, was only a mile or so away.

"What are you doing?! Where are you going?! Stop this truck! Let me out!" she screamed, but the truck rumbled on. She continued to shout at the driver, to no avail. Then with all the force she could muster, she hurled her right arm and closed fist across his chest.

Her action caused a momentary loss of control, and the truck, with the Toyota elevated behind, swerved onto the sidewalk, crossed back into the left lane, and then into the right lane again.

Craig looked angrily at Jennifer. He reached beneath his seat, took out a heavy metal rod, and shook it at her. She was too frightened to speak; her alarm and terror increased with each street they passed. The truck rumbled on across Liberty Street and Oglethorpe Avenue, at times catching green lights, and at times running reds. Where were the police? Surely, she thought, a truck towing a vehicle through several red lights would be seen. But no police vehicles had been visible anywhere along the route.

Jennifer knew the area well. Bay Street, which paralleled the river, would be coming up, and Drayton Street would end. The truck would have to turn left or right on Bay Street, and from there she could only guess where they would go. Once they were out of the city, she knew there was little chance of a police vehicle seeing and stopping this runaway truck. She knew her chances of being rescued were dimming by the minute.

Craig remained hunched over the wheel, ignoring her demands to stop. It was as if the two were in separate worlds. As the truck approached Broughton Street, the light was red, and there was traffic in both directions. It would not be possible to go through the light without a collision. The truck slowed, and it was obvious it would have to soon stop. As it slowed, Jennifer saw the chance she had been praying for. She found the door handle, and even before the truck had completely stopped, she leaped from it. As she did, a vehicle pulled ahead of it and then turned perpendicular across Drayton Street, completely blocking it. The driver of the vehicle got out and ran toward the truck.

Jennifer landed on her feet and began to run. When she reached the corner, she recognized that it was Scott's Camaro that was blocking the intersection. She rushed to it and got in. Scott was at the truck driver's door when he turned and saw Jennifer as she was entering his Camaro. Even in the poorly lighted intersection, he could see the terror on her face, and he ran to her.

"Take me home! Take me home! Scott . . . Scott, take me home!"

"Jen, I'll take you home as soon as I settle something with the guy in the truck."

As he turned to leave, Jennifer called out, "No, Scott! Please! Please, take me home now. Let's go! Now! Please!"

Scott heard the urgency of her voice; he put his car in gear and cleared the intersection. As he did so, he recalled the last words from Jaak: "You are responsible for getting Jennifer home safe and dry." And he had done neither. Perhaps those words were why he had followed the tow truck.

In minutes he found Jennifer's house on West Taylor Street. Parking was quite limited on West Taylor, but he found a space in the same block. She was now breathing more easily, but her eyes still reflected her fear. Jennifer got out of the car, and Scott followed her to her front door. She found her keys and unlocked the door.

Her apartment was on the street level in a three-story townhouse. As soon as they entered, Jennifer sat down on the sofa. Scott joined her with his arm around her shoulder, holding her close. He knew it was not a time to ask questions.

In a few minutes, Jennifer looked at him with a forced smile. "I'm OK, but I'm so glad you were there. I was so afraid."

"I'm glad I was there, too, but I'm sorry I let you leave in that truck. And now, I'm going to call the police." Scott looked around the room, searching for the phone.

"Scott, no, I don't want you to do that. I'm safe now. I wasn't physically hurt. I wasn't even touched."

"Jennifer, that guy abducted you. Kidnapped you. He tricked you into his vehicle. He terrified you. We should call the police, now."

"He will deny it."

"But he took you—and kept you—in his truck, and I saw it. He should be put away!"

"Scott, I know you are right, but I just don't want the hassle now. I don't want to be questioned by the police. I don't want to get involved in a criminal prosecution. Suppose they don't charge him? He will be angry at the accusation. He knows my address. He has my phone number. I don't want to move, and I don't want to live in fear. I want to put this behind me. It's over. I'm OK now. Please understand."

Scott did understand. He had seen the hardship that victims of crimes endured in the criminal justice system. Even though the courts, and the victim-witness advocates, try to make the experience as easy as possible, the journey through the system for the victim is usually difficult. Lost time, multiple court appearances, stressful interrogations by attorneys—all with little compensation except the satisfaction of seeing the perpetrator punished. And that was not always a sure thing. Indeed, Scott did understand. Reporting this crime was the right thing to do, and he knew it. But Jennifer had the right to make this decision; she was the victim, not him.

"OK, Jen. I'll call Triple A and find out if and where your car was dropped off."

Scott found the phone and made the call. The operator checked and confirmed that the Toyota had been towed and left at Marvin's Foreign Auto in Garden City. Scott told Jennifer he would call in the morning to make sure the shop was working on it so that they could pick it up Saturday afternoon. He moved toward the door.

"Jen, before I leave, is there anything I can do for you now? Do you need anything?"

"Scott, would you stay? I guess I'm not as brave as I would like to be. I guess I'm still afraid."

"Of course. I'll stay as long as you want."

He joined Jennifer again on the sofa, placed his right arm around her shoulder, and reached for her hand. She closed her eyes, let out a deep breath, and rested her head on his shoulder. Neither spoke. They remained there for a while. Jennifer seemed to be calm now, and he reached over and dimmed the lamp on the table beside the sofa. She was breathing deeply and soon was asleep from the physical and mental exhaustion. Scott did not move until he was sure she was sleeping soundly.

Then he carefully picked her up from the sofa and took her to the bedroom.

As he laid her on her bed and placed the bed covers over her, she briefly opened her eyes and softly said, "Thank you, Scott."

He turned out the lights and returned to the sofa to sleep. Before turning off the lamp, he looked at his watch. It was almost 2 a.m. He removed his shoes and placed a small pillow under his head, but he was not sleepy. His mind was racing with the events of that night. That terrifying ride in the tow truck should never have occurred. He was disappointed in himself for not seeing the danger. There simply was no excuse. It was 3 a.m. before he fell asleep.

CHAPTER 4
Saturday, August 19

Scott awoke about seven. He looked in on Jennifer, and she was still sleeping soundly. He left a note and drove to his apartment. He reflected on the previous evening and wondered if he should take it upon himself to inform the police. But Jennifer wanted to put the episode behind her, and that should be her decision. He must concentrate on his work. The Vandera trial, his first felony trial, was scheduled for Wednesday. He had tried two misdemeanor jury trials and a half-dozen non-jury trials during his summer internship, but this was much bigger. He had a lot of preparation to do in the next three days.

At 10 a.m. he checked the yellow pages and found the number for Marvin's Foreign Auto in Garden City. Yes, they had the car; yes, it was the starter solenoid; and yes, it would be finished by noon. He waited an hour to call Jennifer. She was up and seemed to be in good spirits. She said she had been reading the assignment in Contracts, her first class on Monday morning. Neither mentioned the events of the previous evening.

As planned, Scott picked her up at noon, and they drove to Marvin's Garage. Jennifer insisted that he follow her home and come in for lunch.

"I make great sandwiches."

Scott needed no urging. While Jennifer fixed the sandwiches, Scott carefully viewed his surroundings. Although he had stayed there the night before, he had not noted the uniqueness of the apartment. The house, built in the late 1800s, still contained the original wood floors, elaborate wainscoting, and stone fireplace. In addition to the living room, the apartment had one bedroom, a dining room, and a kitchen. Every room was oversized, with twelve-foot ceilings. Just as impressive was the decor. Scott knew little about interior decorating, but he knew this was a professional job.

"Your apartment is beautiful."

"Thanks. I love it. I found it and moved in during my first year at SCAD. It came with some basic furniture, but my mother did the rest. I told you that I was spoiled."

They had a leisurely lunch and a relaxed conversation about school, family, and friends—anything that came to mind, except the harrowing tow-truck episode. That was never mentioned by either, as if it had never happened.

Jennifer told Scott that Nicole Chapman, a first-year class-mate, was coming in midafternoon and that they were going to re-view the assignments and discuss the cases for their Monday classes. Scott also had an afternoon of studying planned. When he left, he told her he would give her a call that evening.

• • •

When Scott called around seven, Nicole was still there.

"We are just now going over the cases for our Civil Procedure class," Jennifer said. "We finished the Torts assignment. I think I'm going to like that course. *Wrongful death, negligence, fraud*—it could have been a criminal law book the way those terms kept appearing. Nicole's dad is a civil trial attorney. He told her that she had better master civil procedure and torts, and then get a job as a prosecutor for trial experience, if she wants to succeed in his line of work."

"Yeah, I've heard that's a pretty good career path for a plaintiff's attorney. My supervisor at the DA's office told me he had that path in mind when he took the job in the DA's office. He's African-American; he says he doesn't know if that's helped him or hurt him in his career, but he's had several job offers from Savannah law firms, both plaintiff and defense. Right now, however, he says he prefers prosecuting. He's applied to the U.S. Attorney's office in Atlanta. He went for an interview a month or so ago."

"Did he get it?"

"I'm not sure. He says there's more paperwork to submit. He says he doesn't have any political pull, but I think he'll get the job. He's got experience."

Scott and Jennifer continued to talk, mostly about classes and campus events. Again, the Friday night truck ride was not mentioned by either. They just wanted to forget it.

Eventually, Scott said, "I shouldn't be wasting your time. I just called to see how you were doing. Sounds like you are doing fine. You are still planning on meeting me tomorrow, aren't you?"

"Of course. Thomas Courthouse, at four."

They hung up. Neither thought for a moment that the phone call was a waste of time.

CHAPTER 5
Sunday, August 20

When Jennifer arrived at Thomas Courthouse Sunday afternoon, Scott was down front, practicing his opening statement before an imaginary jury. He stopped when he saw Jennifer.

"So, this is where you hang out on the weekends?" Jennifer asked.

"And on many weeknights as well. This is my second home—Thomas Courthouse," Scott said. "Did you know that Justice Thomas was born just a few miles south of Savannah?"

"No, but I assumed there was some Savannah connection."

"Yes, he was born in a very small community with a fitting name, Pin Point—it's down near Skidaway Island. Founded by freed slaves right after the Civil War."

"Interesting. Are you Savannah Law's 'in residence' historian?"

"No, not their historian, but I am one of their PR guys. I'm proud of this courthouse and courtroom. They were completed at the beginning of my first year here. We've got a jury box big enough for twelve jurors, plus two alternates. And we can accommodate three judges on the bench. During my first year, a three-judge panel from the Georgia Court of Appeals came down from Atlanta and heard arguments in three or four actual cases—finally."

"What do you mean, 'finally'?" asked Jennifer.

"I mean the dean had repeatedly invited the court to visit and hold a hearing so the students could observe, but they always found a reason not to come—budget restriction, docket too heavy—always some excuse. The real reason, of course, was that we're the newest law school in Georgia and don't have much alumni influence. Do you know how we finally got them to come?"

"Not a clue."

"Jaak. He overheard some of the senior members of the Moot Court Board complaining about the court not visiting Savannah Law. Turns out Jaak was the roommate of one of the court members. They roomed together for the entire two years Jaak was at the University of Georgia and had kept in touch. One phone call from Jaak, and voila! They set a date during the spring semester to coincide with Savannah's big St. Patrick's Day celebration. Jaak hosted a party at the Library that night and invited all the judges and what must have been half the legal community in South Georgia. It was a blast."

"You were there?"

"Yeah, I was just in my second semester. The faculty and Moot Court Board members were invited, but not the entire student body. So I asked Jaak if I could help by drifting around with drinks and hors d'oeuvres. He said 'sure,' he could use some free help, so Jeff, who was my roommate at that time, and I dressed as waiters and pitched in. Jeff spilled a tray of drinks, some of it on a judge's wife, but she thought he was cute, and they ended the evening laughing and dancing to one of Juri's big-band CDs. The judge wasn't amused. But that's typical Jeff—you saw him in action Friday night."

"I did, and that makes three who think that Jeff is cute."

"Three?"

"Yes. The judge's wife, me, and *Jeff*. But is he as good in the courtroom as he is on the dance floor? And are you ready for that trial Wednesday?"

"I'm getting there. I was practicing my opening statement when you arrived."

"Could you give me an idea what the case is about?"

"Sure. It's a burglary case. Involves a CVS store in Savannah— happened last April. The manager arrived in the morning and found the front door unlocked. Then the chief pharmacist opened the door to the pharmacy area and found all of the drawers pulled out, shelves open, and so forth. He looked up to where the skylight had been, and it wasn't there—just a rope hanging down. Broken glass everywhere. On the floor, they found a metal chisel and a crowbar. Apparently, the burglar knew he would need tools to break into the narcotics storage area but hadn't expected the safe to be so strong. It wasn't a typical metal cabinet but a large commercial safe. The pharmacy crew inventoried all the drugs. Nothing was missing."

"So, if nothing was missing, do you really have a burglary?"

"Sure, breaking into and entering the store to commit theft is enough. The burglar doesn't have to succeed."

"How did they catch the guy?"

"He worked at the store. His name is Charles Vandera—twenty-two years old. On the day they discovered the burglary, he didn't show up and didn't call in. He was away from work for two days. Said he had been ill. No alarms had sounded during the burglary, so the detectives suspected it might be an inside job. Charles was the only employee who was scheduled to come to work that day who didn't show up. So he was already a suspect. And when he did return, an assistant manager noticed two minor cuts on his forearm, three to four inches long. The skin was red around the cuts, and they looked fresh. Once the detectives learned of the cuts on his forearm, they gave him a Miranda warning—maybe a bit early. He took the warning and refused to talk to the detectives."

"But you must have more evidence than that."

"We do. Of course, his refusal to talk isn't evidence. We can't even tell the jury that he refused to talk."

"How about fingerprints? On the tools, or the cabinets, or anywhere else in the pharmacy area?"

"Nope, no fingerprints. The tools were wiped clean. They dusted for prints on the cabinet door handles and counters and found a few, but none matched his. All the usable ones could be traced back to one of the pharmacists. And they found no usable fingerprints on the front door, which he apparently used to exit the store."

"How do you know he left through the front door?"

"I don't. But it was unlocked—and I doubt he climbed back up that rope."

"Did they find the ladder? He must have used a ladder to get up on the roof. Any fingerprints on it?"

"Yes, it was an aluminum ladder, and they did find finger-prints, some good ones. They belonged to a father-and-son painting crew that had just been hired earlier that week to paint the building. They left the ladder behind the building when they got word that the dad's mother had passed away in Mississippi. They were attending her funeral that day. Detectives checked it out—solid alibi. They gave fingerprint samples, and all the identifiable prints on the ladder were theirs."

"Did they find any blood on the broken glass from the skylight?"

"Nope, but a good question. No one saw any, but no one really looked. It was cleaned up pretty fast. The store hired someone to replace the skylight the same day the break-in was discovered. By the time Charles showed up for work with the cuts on his forearm, the glass had been placed in a garbage bin and carted off."

"So, all you have is his not showing up for work and cuts on his arm?"

"No, we have more. They also found a retinoscope—a light that eye doctors use when examining eyes. It's like a small halogen flashlight, but it can focus precisely with a small intense beam."

"So how does this light fit into your evidence, other than another burglar tool?"

"The detectives were really curious. They had never seen one outside a doctor's office. It didn't belong to any of the pharmacists, so it must have been brought there by the guy who came down the rope. Makes a great tool for a burglar of a downtown store because it doesn't light up the room, and the light would be difficult to see by someone passing by on the street. By the end of the third day, they were focusing on Charles. But they were playing it close to the vest. The detectives knew they had a key piece of evidence. It didn't take them long to determine that Charles's mother, Mary Vandera, worked for an optometrist in Savannah, a Doctor Talley."

"Don't tell me his mother was involved in this burglary."

"No, not intentionally. Majewski, the lead detective on the case, stopped by Dr. Talley's office. Majewski showed him the retinoscope and asked him if he had ever seen it. Dr. Talley said it looked like an old one he had once used. He said it had begun to show wear, and he put it in a storage closet until one day when Mrs. Vandera told him she could use that kind of light in her hobby. She's a gem collector. She asked about buying it, but Dr. Talley just gave it to her. But he couldn't be sure that it was the same one. He hadn't seen it in a couple of years. It just looked similar."

"So, he couldn't positively ID it?"

"No, but Majewski wasn't through. That evening, he went to Mrs. Vandera's home. He showed it to her and asked if it was hers. She looked surprised. She examined it and immediately said yes, she was sure it was hers. It had the same markings and wear marks on it, including a small quarter-inch dent just to the right of the on-off switch. All Majewski told her was that they had found it, and they would eventually get it back to her."

"Did she know about the pharmacy break-in?"

"Don't know, but she couldn't have any knowledge of the connection of the retinoscope to the burglary unless her son told her. The police haven't released any info about it. Only the detectives and the pharmacists know about the retinoscope. Even the other clerks don't know about it. And we don't expect Mrs. Vandera to find out until we call her as a witness."

"You're going to call the defendant's mother to testify? Mrs. Vandera is going to have to testify against her own son?"

"Yep. You have a problem with that?"

"Well, I don't know. Never thought about it."

"Personally, I do have a problem with it. But I have a bigger problem with *not* using that evidence. Charles Vandera committed this burglary, of that I have no doubt. It's a serious felony. He can get up to twenty years. This is his first adult arrest. He's young and perhaps he'll learn from this and turn his life around. Maybe not. Who knows? I'm not exactly thrilled at calling a mother to testify against her son. According to Majewski, she lives in a small home in Port Wentworth, and Charles lives with her. From what I've heard, she's a decent, hard-working woman. But I can't let sympathy interfere with presenting the case. The right thing is for the son to plead guilty, accept his punishment, and get on with his life. We offered a reasonable pretrial. Jeff made it clear Friday night that Charles still insists on going to trial."

"Do you think Charles told his mother the truth about the burglary?"

"I have no idea, but if he's like most defendants, he will deny it to his mother. And if she is like most mothers, she will believe him."

"But won't you have to reveal where the retinoscope came from to the defense? You've got to give the defense a list of all witnesses and your evidence, right?"

"Right—in most cases. But here in Georgia, the defendant has to request it in writing. Vandera and his attorneys, for some reason we can only guess, did not 'opt in,' as it's called. So, no reciprocal discovery. He doesn't get our evidence, and we don't get his. We had to furnish a witness list, along with a copy of the indictment, prior to arraignment, but that's about it. We don't know anything about witnesses he may be planning to call. But he doesn't know much about our case either."

"Isn't that strange—that they haven't opted in for discovery?"

"Yes, I think it's very strange. So does my supervising attorney."

"You mentioned him before—what's his name?"

"Grady Wilder. He's been with the DA's office about ten years. He's a graduate of Georgia State Law School—pretty sharp guy. We work well together. Gives me enough rope to hang myself but keeps a strong arm on that rope. So far, he's kept both of us out of trouble. And he's better with the Socratic method than any of my professors. Questions me, gets my answer, sees where I am heading, asks another question to make me think and focus in the right direction, gets my answer, then another question and so forth—*never* gives an answer to any of my questions. He just lets me arrive at it myself. I've learned more in the Prosecution Clinic than any course I've taken in law school."

"Sounds like a cool guy. Why does he think Vandera hasn't entered into reciprocal discovery?"

"Grady says we can only speculate. Usually the defense wants all of our evidence. This is a rare case. Vandera apparently isn't planning strictly an alibi defense. And we don't know if he is aware of our finding the retinoscope and tying it to him through his mother. We don't know if his mother told him about Detective Majewski's visit. But she had to bail him out, so she's well aware that he is charged with burglary. And she'll have lots of questions. Will Charles tell her the truth? We don't even know if Charles told his attorneys the truth.

Defendants often lie to their attorneys and let them get ambushed at trial."

"So you think the defense has really blundered by not opting in?"

"Maybe not. It leaves the prosecution in the dark too. We don't know anything about the defense—who their witnesses may be, or what they may have to say. It's possible that Charles knows about the retinoscope being found and that his mother identified it as being hers. This may lead him to claim that he loaned it to someone or that it was stolen, or lost, or who knows what."

"You said Vandera apparently wasn't planning an alibi defense. Why? Wouldn't you expect that?"

"Yes, we did expect it. So, we filed a written 'demand for alibi defense.' On our demand, they have to provide the specific place he claimed to be and any witnesses who would support his claim. Since they didn't provide it, they can't put on witnesses saying he was at home, at Joe's Bar, or surfing out on Tybee Beach. However, it doesn't prevent his testifying that he was somewhere else. He just can't bring in witnesses to support him."

"So what do you expect he's going to do for a defense?"

"Frankly, we don't know. It's got us guessing. But his defense is *his* problem. My problem is to get this case ready for trial and prepare for whatever defense he brings. So, ready to listen to my opening statement?"

"Sure." Jennifer walked into the jury box and took a seat in the midsection.

Scott stepped behind the lectern, turned on its small light, and placed several note cards across the top. Then he stepped out in front.

He began, "Ladies and gentlemen of the jury . . . ." And for the next six or seven minutes, he explained the offense of burglary and gave a basic outline of the evidence that the state would be presenting. He described the scene in the pharmacy area when the pharmacists arrived. He noted the tools that were left, but he made no mention of the retinoscope. He addressed Vandera's unexplained absence for two days after the burglary and the fresh cuts on his arm that were observed when he returned.

"Ladies and gentlemen of the jury, what I have described is the crime of burglary. I have told you when, where, and how it took place. What I have not yet revealed is the one crucial piece of evidence that ties the defendant surely and inescapably to this crime. When that is presented, you will be convinced, beyond a reasonable doubt, that Charles Vandera is guilty as charged."

Scott walked over to the lectern, scooped up his note cards, and walked to where Jennifer was still seated. "What do you think?" he asked. "Are you ready to vote?"

"Not really. And I surely couldn't vote him guilty right now. You want my critique—someone who hasn't spent the first day in a law school class?"

"Sure, that's why I asked you to come. Of course, I want your critique. The jury hasn't spent a day in a law school class either. Tell me, if you were on the jury, what would you be thinking right now?"

"I would be thinking about what you didn't say and why. Even if I believed all the evidence you told us about, you haven't connected this burglary to Vandera. I would be doubting your case. Right now the jury is going to have to accept on blind faith that you have evidence to tie Vandera to the case, and they just may not do that. They may think, 'Well, if you have that evidence, why aren't you telling us about it now?' I think first impressions are extremely important, and I don't think that was a good first impression—except for your delivery. Now *that* was good. Handsome guy, great voice, great courtroom presence. I just might overlook the fact that your evidence is missing." Jennifer smiled.

Scott managed a smile too. "I'm glad I have thick skin. But I know you're right. I feel the same way. I was just hoping it wouldn't come off that way to a jury. You say it does, and I have to live with that unless I decide to let the jury know up front about the retinoscope. Anything else?"

"Yes, I do have something else, but I'm kind of tentative on this—I may be way off base. You start your opening with 'ladies and gentlemen of the jury.' I read somewhere that it's best for the prosecutor to address the jury with the phrase 'members of the jury,' the theory being that this is an inclusive phrase, while 'ladies and gentlemen of the jury' is a divisive phrase."

"A divisive phrase? Lawyers have been addressing juries in that manner ever since women began to serve on juries. Seems to me to be a very respectful salutation."

"But don't you see you're putting your jury into two groups, 'ladies' in one, 'gentlemen' in the other? The defense may want them separated, but the prosecution wants them as a unit; 'members' does that. You want them to think like a unit. Your verdict has to be unanimous. Just a suggestion. You did ask for suggestions, didn't you?"

"Yes, I did, but I've never, ever, heard anything like that and never thought of it. Sounds like psychobabble to me. Where on this green earth did you hear that, Jen?"

"I'm not sure. Read it somewhere. After I decided to go to law school, I began reading everything I could get my hands on about trials—especially books by trial lawyers like Gerry Spence and F. Lee Bailey."

"F. Lee Bailey's books?"

"Yes, I have a couple."

"He was *some* trial lawyer. Do you know what happened to him?"

"No, what?"

"Disbarred. Got in trouble down in Florida—accused of misappropriating a client's funds and lying to a federal judge. Disbarred in both Florida and Massachusetts. How about that, go from having your face on *Time* as one of the most famous lawyers in the country to being disbarred."

"I didn't know that. Burn the Bailey books?"

"No, of course not. I read one of his books this summer. Lots of practical stuff in it. I also like Jake Ehrlich."

"Jake who?"

"Ehrlich. He was a criminal defense lawyer from the forties and fifties. From San Francisco. He defended Billie Holiday, Errol Flynn, Howard Hughes, and just about every Hollywood star who got into trouble. He wrote over a dozen books, but they are out of print and hard to find. An old lawyer in my home town, a friend of

my mom, gave me a couple of Ehrlich's books from his own collection when he heard that I was going to go to law school. There's a
book about his life titled *Never Plead Guilty*. The school library has
a copy; good book."

"I like the title."

"Yes, clever title—and Charles Vandera is taking his advice.
But now, back to your suggestion, 'members of the jury.' I'm going to
try that, Jen; maybe there's something to it."

Scott and Jennifer heard the front door to the courtroom
open. They looked up to see a man entering. "That's Professor
Nolan," said Scott. "He teaches Property."

"Nolan? I will be in his class," said Jennifer.

The professor walked down the center of the courtroom
towards the jury box where they were seated. He was about the same
height as Scott and appeared to be in his early thirties. His light-
brown hair hung to his shoulders in the back and almost covered
his ears on the side. With pale-grey eyes and soft features, he had
what might best be described as "average guy looks"—reasonably
handsome but not someone who would turn heads on the beach.
Scott and Jennifer stood, and Scott introduced her. Jennifer informed
him that she would be in his class, which was meeting for the first
time on Monday.

"I hope Scott is tutoring you, Jennifer. He was one of my better
students, but, unfortunately, I don't think he's going to be practicing
real property law. I believe he wants to be a prosecutor, right, Scott?"
He was addressing his question to Scott, but his eyes had remained on
Jennifer, shifting and darting across her entire body.

"Well, Professor, at least for a while. I have a trial coming up
Wednesday, and I asked Jennifer to listen and critique my opening
statement."

"Did she give you any pointers?" His eyes remained on
Jennifer.

Scott hesitated a moment before answering and then said
with a forced laugh, "As a matter of fact she did—said I had a lot of
work yet to do."

"So you apparently are interested in trial work also, Jennifer?" asked the professor.

"I am," she replied. "And I just hope I'm cut out for it."

"Well, you'll find out before you graduate. We have a solid trial advocacy program here at Savannah Law. The students compete in a number of trial competitions. Scott, you've been active in these competitions. When are they scheduled?" For the first time since the introduction, he turned to face Scott.

"The first one is the William Daniel Competition in Atlanta in November; at least it was last year," said Scott.

"Jennifer would be eligible to try out for the team, wouldn't she, Scott?"

"Not right away, Professor. The team advocates are selected from second- and third-year students. Evidence and Trial Advocacy are prerequisites for the team."

"Well, I would think those courses would be required for the team advocates but not the witnesses. Witnesses are considered part of the team, aren't they, Scott?"

"Yes, Professor."

"Who selects the witnesses?"

"The coaches," replied Scott.

"Would that be something you would be interested in this semester, Jennifer?" asked Nolan. He supplemented his gaze with a smile.

"I *am* interested," she said as she responded to his smile with one of her own.

"Good. Maybe something can be worked out. Professor Leyton is in charge of the program. I'll speak with him about getting you involved, and I'll give you a call."

And then, for only the second time since entering the courtroom, he turned to look at Scott.

"Now, Scott, I want to ask a favor of you. You are aware that Dean Adams is stepping down at the end of this school year?"

"I have heard that. Sorry to see him leave. I think he's been good for the school."

"I agree," said the professor. "I plan to campaign to replace him. I'll announce this shortly after the faculty meeting Tuesday afternoon. I expect Dean Adams to officially notify the faculty of his retirement at that meeting. But it's no secret. He's already informed the Board of Trustees. I'm not sure who, if anyone else, on the faculty will be vying for the job, but I'm going to aggressively pursue it. And that's where I need your help."

"*My* help?"

"Yes, of course. The Dean Search Committee will be appointed by the Board of Trustees. I don't know who will be on it, but they surely will have student representation; most search committees do. They'll probably have a student group interview each candidate, but more than that, I'm sure that you, as president of the Student Bar Association, will be a voting member of the search committee. So I'm asking for your commitment to support my candidacy."

"You really think they'll have a student representative?"

"I have no doubt; I'm sure they will. Now, can I count on you?"

Scott hesitated a moment before responding. "Professor Nolan, you have been with the school since its opening, and everyone is aware of your excellent reputation. And your father played the major role in establishing Savannah College of Law. How can you miss?"

"Thanks, Scott. I may need to get in touch with you. Do you have a cell phone?"

Scott wrote the number on a piece of paper and handed it to Nolan.

"I will keep you informed as things move along, and *you* keep *me* posted. And Jennifer, I'll get back to you after I speak to Professor Leyton. Do you have a phone where I can reach you?"

"Sure, probably my cell phone would be best. I usually carry it with me. But I'll give you the number at my apartment also." She took the same paper that Scott had just handed the professor and wrote both numbers on it.

"Thanks. Now, in the meantime, make sure you keep getting your beauty sleep—it's working just fine." As he said it, he winked at Jennifer and departed.

Jennifer and Scott stood without speaking as the professor walked up the center aisle and exited through the door he had entered.

"Did he wink at you as he left, Jen?" asked Scott, his annoyance showing.

"I think so. But maybe it was just a tic," said Jennifer with a grin.

"Yeah, I'm sure it was. That was some conversation. *You* get an invitation to join the trial team as a witness without going through the tryout procedures, and *I* get invited to support his so-called aggressive pursuit of becoming the next dean at Savannah Law. And did you hear him say he wants me to keep him posted? Posted about *what?*"

"What I noticed, Scott, was that when he asked for your commitment to support him, you avoided his question."

"You *are* perceptive. But I don't think he even noticed."

"No, I don't think he did. He apparently was pleased with what you said and just missed what you didn't say. But to me it was obvious. You never said you would support him. Why?"

"I have my reasons. But for starters, I didn't like the pressure he was trying to apply by asking for my commitment in front of you. I don't know who else will be in the running. He says we will be interviewing all of the candidates. How can I know which candidate I will support until I see the field? Why should I commit now? Frankly, I don't like what I just saw. He meets you for the first time, has a five-minute chat, can't take his eyes off you then leaves with a wink—and he wants me to support him as dean?"

"Oh, Scott, don't start imagining things. He was just being friendly. But let's suppose he did have what one might call a 'wandering eye.' Am I not a worthy target?" Jennifer asked with hands outstretched and in a mock-hurt voice.

Scott thought for a moment; then he smiled. "That's a great question. You are going to make a super advocate. And of course, the answer is *yes.*"

"You said you had your reasons for not saying you would support him. Then you said, 'for starters,' you didn't like him asking you directly. OK, that's for starters. What else is involved?"

"I think it would be best if we just left it at that."

"Come on, Scott. Level with me. You don't like him—that's obvious. You must have reasons."

Yes, Scott did have his reasons. He thought the professor was either spineless or corrupt, and probably both. It stemmed from a classroom incident during Scott's first year. Two students had been caught cheating during the final exam in his Property course. Not only did the proctor observe them passing notes, but there were two other witnesses to the incident, one being Scott. The notes were confiscated by the proctor, and statements by the two witnesses and the proctor were delivered to Professor Nolan. When grades were posted, all students received passing grades. The two students were never prosecuted by the honor court, and they remained in school. One of the students was related to a member of the Board of Trustees. Still, Scott saw no good purpose in telling Jennifer of this two-year-old incident.

"Yes, I have my reasons. But, as I said, let's let it go at that. Maybe I just need a bite to eat. This is your last free night before your law school classes wrap you in total drudgery, so let's go to dinner—and I'm buying. How about Six Pence Pub on Bull? What do you say?"

"Six Pence Pub it is; that's one of my favorite restaurants," said Jennifer, and they walked from the courtroom to Scott's Camaro parked nearby.

CHAPTER 6

The Six Pence Pub was also one of Scott's favorite restaurants. It was small and casual, served good food, and was reasonably priced—a nice place to take a date.

Service was quick. They both ordered shepherd's pie, a specialty of the house. The conversation was lively and light. However, the earlier meeting of Professor Nolan in the courtroom was still on Scott's mind. He took his beer mug in both hands, mischievously looked over the top at Jennifer, and winked.

"I'm just playing professor," Scott said, smiling.

Jennifer smiled back but otherwise ignored the comment. "Speaking of the professor, you told him that you were aware of the role his father played in establishing Savannah Law. What was his role?"

"I don't know a lot about it; I wasn't here, but I've picked up bits and pieces. Howard Nolan, Professor Nolan's father, was the moving force behind the founding of the law school. He became chairman of the Board of Trustees and all on the board were his friends—all prominent Savannah movers and shakers."

"Which means that Professor Nolan will have a big advantage? All his dad's friends are on the board?"

"Well, not exactly," said Scott. "Howard Nolan died two years ago, during my first semester. There was a big write-up about his civic activities, especially his contribution to the school. And there was something in the article about a scandal—well, an 'alleged scandal' may be more appropriate. I don't recall much about it, but apparently some of the board members were so upset they resigned. So, the board may not be stacked with Howard Nolan's friends now. My aunt worked as a secretary for one of the trustees who resigned."

"You have an aunt here in Savannah?"

"Well, I did. She was instrumental in my coming to Savannah Law. She died quite suddenly a year ago."

"I'm sorry," said Jennifer. "Were you close?"

"We became close. She was my mom's older sister, a widow, who had lived in Savannah for about forty years. When my mom mentioned to her that I was interested in law school, she told her about Savannah Law. She had an apartment over the garage in her back yard and offered it free of charge to me if I would come here. It's less than three miles from the campus. Both of her children had moved out of state, and she was pleased to have a relative nearby."

"You were lucky," said Jennifer. "Nice to have a rich aunt."

"No, she wasn't rich, but she was a very nice aunt. She even suggested that I get a roommate. She said I could have him—she required it be a 'him'—pay rent to me and share expenses. So, I applied to Savannah Law, got accepted, hooked up with Jeff as my roommate, and that's how I ended up here."

"What happened to your living arrangements after your aunt died? Are you still in the apartment?"

"I lucked out. Her two children, my first cousins, sold the property subject to a *free* lease of the garage apartment to me through my senior year at Savannah Law. They didn't have to do that, but they did, and it really helped me out financially. I guess they get free legal advice forever."

The conversation continued, mostly about classes, professors, and school activities. Jennifer had many questions.

"I'm really interested in the possibility of getting involved in that trial competition that Professor Nolan mentioned—the Daniel Competition. Tell me about it."

"I think it's a great idea—for next year. You shouldn't try to get involved your first year. Professor Nolan is doing you no favor."

"OK. Not a good idea. I understand. You've made your point, but tell me about the competition."

He had indeed made his point, and he sensed her annoyance.

"The competition is sponsored by the Georgia Bar. It's always a criminal case. It's set up like most competitions, with two advocates and two witnesses on each team. It starts with opening statements by each side and then the prosecution case, defense case, and closing arguments. Takes three or four hours. Trial lawyers judge the advocacy skills of the students. To win the competition, you have to be good on both sides, prosecution and defense. You may be defending the case in the morning and prosecuting in the afternoon. I wasn't on that team, but I was on our Southeast Regional team last February, in Birmingham."

"How did you do?"

"We got to the final round. Talk about a trial you will never forget, that was one! I think of that trial often and wonder what we could have done differently. It was only my second competition, but my partner, a senior, had been in four or five. She was pretty stoic about it. 'Get used to it,' she said. 'Sometimes you just get served up some home-cooking.'" Scott gave a light chuckle.

"'Home-cooking'? You mean home-court advantage?"

"Well, Marie, my partner, thought so. She was from New Jersey. When she spoke, it was pretty obvious she wasn't from Alabama. We got our butts kicked."

"Tell me about it," said Jennifer.

"We were in a big courtroom in the federal courthouse in Birmingham. We had some really tough matches in the preliminaries but made it unbeaten to the final round. Right after the semi-finals that morning, there was a coin toss to see which side we would represent in the afternoon. We lost the coin toss, and the other team chose the defense. We really didn't care—we thought we were equally good prosecuting or defending. We had lunch, briefed our witnesses one last time, and went to the courtroom to set up our table. That was the first time we got a good look at our opposing counsel—two gorgeous blondes, put together right in all the right places."

"That's important?" asked Jennifer, with a disapproving look.

"Well, it never hurts. But let's just say they were professional looking—dark blue suits and matching shoes, white button-up blouses, and hair styled to perfection. We went over and introduced ourselves. I started a conversation with the one who was going to make the defense opening statement. She couldn't have been friendlier, or seemed more harmless. She had a soft Southern drawl. It was obvious as she stood there in that Birmingham courtroom that she was not too far from home."

Jennifer put her left forearm on the table to get comfortable. She had a tentative smile on her face as she looked directly into Scott's eyes and said, "Go on."

"Right on time, the presiding judge, a superior court judge from Mobile, walked in and took his seat on the bench. He was followed by the jury, trial attorneys who would be scoring us. There were fourteen. And not one—not *one*—was female. And *not one* was under the age of fifty. We found out later that they weren't from just the Birmingham area but from all over Alabama. It was like homecoming! It took them a long time to get settled in the jury box—they were shaking hands and slapping backs.

"We went through the usual preliminary matters and pretrial motions, nothing unusual. Took less than ten minutes. My opening statement was next. As I walked up in front of the jury, I was feeling really good—I was 'in the zone.' I gave the opening statement of my life, best I had ever given. I could hear Marie mentally clapping as I walked to my seat.

"Then the defense counsel gets up. She walks to the lectern and steps out to the side, eight to ten feet in front of the jury. She takes her time, eyes the jury from one side to the other several times, smiling, and making sure she has their complete attention.

"Then she begins—in that beautiful, lilting, honey-filled Alabama voice. 'Ladies and gentlemen of the jury: What you just heard from . . .' —she stops, turns, looks straight at me, and points with an open hand—'this *persecutor* . . . oh, I mean *prosecutor* . . .' —and as she says that, she smiles at her deliberate misstatement and continues, 'is not evidence. The evidence comes from witnesses, not *persecutors* . . . oh, excuse me, I mean *prosecutors*.'

"I turn to Marie, and she's rolling her eyes and turning away, trying not to laugh. We had seen a lot of juvenile cheap shots and made-up facts in trial competitions but never, ever anything as hokey as that. To us it was comical. But we didn't see anyone on the jury laughing. They're looking intently at this young lady, and she's continuing: 'This defendant comes into this courtroom today clothed in what the *law* says . . .'—and she raises her voice on *law*—'is the cloak of innocence. Before these . . .' —she pauses, smiles, and gets it right this time—'*prosecutors* can convince you that this defendant is guilty, they must completely remove the cloak of innocence.'

"Then she slowly opens her coat, exposing the front of her blouse with its four or five buttons. Then she says, 'Each of these buttons has to be removed before the cloak of innocence can be removed. They must undo *every* button.' She pauses, looks down at her ample bosom then back at the jury. As she does, she says in that soft Southern voice, 'Button by button . . .' —and with that, she unbuttons the top button. Twenty-eight eyeballs zero in on that top button. Then her hands move to the next button, and she says, 'by button . . . ,' and to the next button, and she repeats, 'by button.' She does that for every button. She actually only unbuttoned the top one. But after every unbuttoning gesture, she looks down at her breasts and then back up at the jury, all with a smile. And I'm thinking, man, this is so contrived, this is so mawkish, so unprofessional—we're going to breeze through this trial. No way could we lose this one.

"The witness examinations go as planned. We're on a roll, winning every objection. Marie does the closing argument. She nails it. The other member of the defense team, of course, does the defense closing. Her voice is a bit stronger, but every word has the same honey-dipped sweetness. She walks within four or five feet of the jury, surveys them from side to side with a coy smile, pats her left shoulder with her right hand, and says, 'See, the cloak is still on.' Then she opens her coat, pokes her chest forward, and goes from top to bottom, touching each button and repeating, 'And *this one* is still buttoned.' Those same twenty-eight eyeballs follow her at each stop along the way.

"I look over at Marie. She gives another eye roll and turns to keep from laughing out loud.

"Marie does a quick rebuttal, and we depart the courtroom while the jury deliberates. All of our team—coach, advocates, witnesses—gather at the end of a corridor off from the courtroom. After the congratulatory hugs and handshakes, we start making plans for the trip to Texas for the National Finals.

"In less than ten minutes, a bailiff comes to tell us the results are ready to be announced. Marie and I go to our table and wait for the announcement. The presiding judge makes the usual comments about how impressed the judges were with everyone's advocacy skills and how difficult it was to choose a winner . . . blah, blah, blah. Then he says, 'But the jury has spoken, and . . . .' He waits a moment—I guess expecting a drum roll, then says, 'The winner is the *defense*,' and points to the defense table.

"I'm in shock, complete disbelief. So is our coach. He's sitting in the first spectator row. He stands up and says, 'You mean that table, don't you?' pointing to our table. The presiding judge doesn't have time to respond before one of the jury members calls out, 'No! The defense was the winner—and it wasn't even close'!"

Scott stopped. He had finished his story, and he just shook his head from side to side as if he were still in the courtroom, in shock and disbelief.

A smile came over Jennifer's face, followed by a chuckle. "So, you got a good—and *long-lasting*—taste of 'home-cooking.'"

"Yes, and there's a moral to the story somewhere—I just haven't found it," said Scott. He looked at his watch; it was almost eight o'clock. He knew Jennifer had an early class in the morning, and she had already mentioned that she still had work to do on a couple of the cases. He suggested they leave.

On the drive back to the campus where Jennifer had left her car, Scott remembered the conversation he was having with Jennifer before the tow truck arrived. "Friday night you were about to tell me about the courthouse in Springfield. Did you ever go there?"

"Yes. Jaak took me and my team for a visit one Friday. His friend, who was the clerk of court, gave us a tour and a bit of the history. There was a trial going on, and we went in to watch. It was a murder trial, a twenty-year-old woman defendant charged with shooting her twenty-four-year-old husband. They lived in a small mobile home. She shot him right through the heart—one shot and he was dead. Her defense was that she was justified because she suffered from 'battered wife syndrome.' Are you familiar with that?"

"Somewhat. I saw the TV movie *The Burning Bed*, where the wife poured gasoline on her sleeping husband. I believe the jury eventually acquitted her. Apparently the jury believed the husband got what he deserved."

"Same defense in this case. But her lawyers were struggling with their defense. They had some real problems."

"Like what?" asked Scott.

"She didn't have any evidence that she was abused except her own testimony. And he was *inside* their mobile home when she shot him, and she was *outside*, with a scoped rifle. I was fascinated and wanted to stay for the rest of the day, but my teammates were ready to go. At the next recess, we were on our way out, and I spotted a guy with a steno pad in his hand and a pen hooked behind his ear—obviously a reporter."

Scott interrupted. "Don't tell me you bummed a ride back to Savannah with the reporter, and your friends left with Jaak?"

"Right. I didn't get back to Savannah until almost seven that night. The judge was running a tight ship and wanted to wrap up the trial that week. He scheduled the trial to reconvene at eight-thirty Saturday morning. I was so caught up in it that I drove back Saturday to hear the rest of it. And by then, I knew I wanted to go to law school."

"So you credit Jaak for setting it into motion?"

"No question I was hooked; I was surely going to law school. Of course, SCAD doesn't have a prelaw curriculum, or any majors that law schools seem to prefer, and that made me think about transferring. But I liked SCAD. The registrar outlined a proposed schedule of courses for the remainder of my time there, and I took it to the admissions director at Savannah Law. She looked at the courses and said that if my grades and LSAT were competitive, I could be admitted, despite my *quirky* path."

Both Scott and Jennifer smiled. "My bad," said Scott. "I'll never use those words again, I promise."

They were now approaching the parking lot, where Jennifer had parked her Toyota. "It's over there, far side," said Jennifer, pointing.

Scott drove slowly toward her car and parked. The sun was setting behind the big water oaks on the west side of the parking lot. Jennifer stood by the driver's door and fumbled through her purse for the keys.

Scott placed his left hand on her right arm, and with his right hand, gently pulled up her chin and softly kissed her cheek. Then he said, "Good night, Jen. I'll call you tomorrow night and see how your first day went."

Jennifer smiled and said, "Yes, please do. And thanks for the dinner and the afternoon." She then got into her car and drove away, wishing that he had taken a few moments longer and *really* kissed her.

CHAPTER 7

Jaak spent Sunday afternoon in his lounge at the Library, as he usually did on Sundays when his wife visited her sister in Charleston. Part of the time was devoted to examining sales receipts and purchase invoices for the Library. But for most of this afternoon, he was engrossed in *Beach Road,* a thriller by his favorite author, James Patterson. It was a wonderful afternoon of pure reading enjoyment, and he was looking forward to the evening when his poker group would assemble for their weekly game.

As he finished and closed the book, he looked at his watch and noted that "20" appeared in the date window. It was August 20—a date that always brought back strong memories of that date in 1968.

Fresh out of Parris Island boot camp and the Infantry Training Course at Camp Lejeune, he had shipped out to Vietnam as a PFC. Assigned to Charlie Company, First Battalion, Third Marines, near Quang Tri, in the northern part of Vietnam, he barely had time to learn the names of the other members of his squad before he saw his first combat. This was Operation Lancaster II/Jupiter, a search-and-destroy mission into the DMZ. Charlie Company was the first unit in, landing by helicopter. The landing zone immediately came under heavy mortar fire. The battalion suffered seven dead and ninety-nine wounded. Jaak was not one of the wounded in the initial landing, but four days into the operation—August 20, 1968—a mortar round exploded nearby, and a piece of shrapnel tore into his left forearm. The blast left him dazed and with ringing ears for a while, but the shrapnel did not cause serious damage to his arm. After his wound was stitched and treated, he rejoined his squad. He would remain with Charlie Company for the remainder of his thirteen-month tour in Vietnam. By the time he "made his bird"—the Marine Corps term for catching his flight out of the country—he had received another Purple Heart, had been awarded a Bronze Star Medal, and had been promoted to corporal.

All this seemed so far in the past, yet each August at this time, he returned to that first combat operation and that exploding mortar round almost forty years ago. And each August, he gave a silent prayer of thanks that he survived not only Operation Lancaster II/Jupiter but also thirteen months of combat, all in the I Corps Area, near the DMZ.

Despite such strong memories, his Vietnam service was not something open for discussion by either family or friends—not because he had psychological scars, but because he felt such discussion would be boring at best, and at worst, could be conceived as self-adulatory "heroism." He recalled one of his professors at the University of Georgia, after hearing an Army veteran discuss a personal Vietnam experience, respond using the word "rodomontade"—a word unfamiliar to Jaak. He could not tell if the professor was impressed or perhaps incredulous, but he himself had thoroughly enjoyed the story. Leafing through his ever-present dictionary, he found it meant "boastful or bragging talk or behavior." The experience reinforced Jaak's personal belief that only someone who had been there could appreciate such wartime experiences.

The Vietnam war was not a popular war, and Jaak knew it. There was no awe-inspiring photo like the one by Joe Rosenthal of five Marines and a Navy corpsman raising the Stars and Stripes atop Mount Suribachi. But there was the ugly, unforgettable photo of General Nguyen Ngoc Loan using his pistol to execute a captured Viet Cong prisoner on the streets of Saigon during the 1968 Tet Offensive. No, it was not a popular war, and only occasionally, when an old comrade from his Marine Corps days would visit, did he permit himself to recount his combat experience. There would be no whispering of "rodomontade" behind his back.

The law students who visited the Library were not unmindful of Jaak's military service. Marine Corps memorabilia was prominently displayed around the Library. Recruiting posters, such as "We Didn't Promise You a Rose Garden," hung behind the bar. His gold-framed Honorable Discharge certificate hung from the wall in his lounge. To the left of it, in a matching frame, was his promotion certificate to sergeant, awarded a few weeks before his discharge. And on the right, his Bronze Star Medal with Combat "V". And that was it. There was no mention of his two Purple Hearts. Sometimes a friend, aware of those two awards, would comment that they were missing from the display. If pressed for an explanation, he would just chuckle and say that if anyone should receive a medal for his being wounded, it should be the North Vietnamese soldier who fired the round. He had survived both wounds without any disability and considered his two Purple Hearts to be in a different category from those disabled veterans who had made a permanent and precious sacrifice. Nevertheless, he was personally proud of them. He thought of them as his *private* rodomontade; they simply were not for public display.

Jaak's reverie was broken when he heard the roar of a motorcycle pulling into his parking lot. He knew it was Jimmy Exley from Springfield, one of his oldest and closest friends. Jimmy always drove the round trip of fifty miles on his motorcycle and was usually the first to arrive for the Sunday night poker game. He and Jaak grew up together, though Jimmy was a year older and a grade ahead of Jaak in school. He joined the Army the year he graduated from high school. He was shipped out to Vietnam, seriously wounded the second month there, hospitalized for a month, and medically discharged—all during Jaak's senior year in high school. Jimmy entered the University of Georgia the year Jaak joined the Marine Corps. Three years later, when Jaak arrived at Athens to begin his studies, Jimmy was a senior and helped Jaak get acclimated to college life. When Jaak left college to help his ill parents, Jimmy was already established in business in Springfield and helped Jaak through those difficult months.

The front door was unlocked, and Jimmy was soon in the lounge, taking off his well-worn leather.

"That didn't sound like your old Harley Fat Boy. What are you riding tonight, Jimmy?"

"Honda Shadow. Got it for my wife."

"For your wife?"

"Yeah, pretty good trade, don't you think?"

They both laughed. Jimmy's wit was well known and at times predictable, as just demonstrated. But Jaak loved him dearly and always gave his jokes a hearty laugh. Jimmy ran an insurance agency and dabbled in real estate. Besides motorcycles, his true love was the outdoors: fishing in the summer, and any kind of hunting—deer, duck, dove, but especially quail—in the fall and winter. He had the perfect gun for every type of hunt. For Jimmy, recreation was time to be spent in the field. The exception was poker; he rarely missed Jaak's Sunday night games.

The poker group had been meeting Sunday evenings in the lounge at the Library for almost six years. This was the first game after the summer hiatus. There were seven regulars, including Jaak, and three or four alternates who filled in when a regular was unavailable. Juri was one of the alternates, but he only played when Jaak was away.

Malcolm Zitralph, a retired Savannah Police Department Detective, was the next to arrive. Jaak met Malcolm soon after Jaak opened his first bar, Tun Tavern. Tun Tavern was located in a prime spot in the high-rent district on River Street. It was an expensive undertaking, made even more so when it was hit by a burglary during which Jaak lost not only his new safe but also several cases of bar supplies. Malcolm worked the case, solved it, and he and Jaak became close friends. After retiring from the police department, Malcolm went to work for Verizon Wireless, working as a network trouble shooter.

The rest of "the usual suspects," as Juri enjoyed calling Jaak's poker friends, arrived soon afterwards. Professor Denis Nolan was the only player in the group from Savannah Law. He was an early patron at the Library, often stopping by after classes to chat with students and have a beer. And, being a bachelor, he frequently had dinner there. When Denis spied the poker table in the lounge, he asked to be included should a game be organized. When Jaak hosted the first game, he invited Denis to join, and he had been a member of the group since. Another regular was Rench Renshaw, a Savannah banker who worked with Jaak when Jaak purchased some business property on East Bay Street in the early nineties. Pete Hanson, Jaak's accountant, and Bill Northrop, an architect who had been active in the Historic Savannah Preservation projects, were the other regulars. Jaak consulted with Northrop when he was renovating the Library, and it was Northrop who had suggested and designed the custom-made poker table. Bill was the last to arrive. Chips had already been distributed, and Malcolm had won the deal.

Bill was carrying an ice chest as he walked through the door. "Kodiak Brown Ale. Who's ready?"

All hands went up, and he began popping the bottle caps. The beer came in twenty-two-ounce bottles from the Midnight Sun Brewing Company. His brother in Anchorage sent a case of this special brew every summer, and Bill always shared it with his poker friends.

Bill threw his twenty into the box holding the "entry fees," and with these preliminaries completed, Malcolm started to deal. He looked at the ante on the table and declared, "Pot's light—ante up!" A chip was flipped into the pot by Pete.

"You accountants, always hiding the money," said Malcolm, and then, in a monotone sing-song chant, he continued: "*Omaha high-low, double flop, pot luck, rotation betting, cards read, discard one.*" And with that, the Sunday night poker game began.

When the evening ended, the winners were the usual winners and the losers, the usual losers. Top winner this night was Pete, who had an accountant's approach to the game: cautious and patient. His winnings were $55, which was about average for a top winner on any evening. The "big loser"—which in this low-stakes game was a term impacting ego, not finances—was Denis, at $65.

"Glad to help with your daughter's tuition, Pete. And your wife's kitchen renovation," Denis said with a forced laugh as he was leaving. But there was no mistaking the disappointment in his voice.

CHAPTER 8
Monday, August 21

Winston Adams was in a reflective mood. He sat at his desk and gazed out the window onto the courtyard. He had been dean of Savannah College of Law since it opened, but this would be his last year. He would officially announce his retirement plans Tuesday afternoon at the first faculty meeting of the new semester. It would not really be news—almost everyone at the school already knew. Savannah College of Law had grown in enrollment, endowment and, more important, prestige during his administration. It was now fully accredited. The faculty was stronger, and new buildings graced the campus. An accreditation visit by the ABA inspection team was scheduled for the spring semester. Accreditation visits were scheduled every seven years and were heavy administrative burdens on law schools, even well-established ones. But Dean Adams was actually looking forward to this inspection visit. He was confident that the faculty and the trustees would be proud of what they would find in the final report.

Roxanne Kennedy, his secretary, buzzed to tell him that the registrar, Deborah Channing, was on the phone. Deborah was one of his first hires when he was appointed dean. He had previously served as dean at two other law schools and as assistant dean at two more. She was by far the best registrar he had worked with. In fact, he had "stolen" her from the last school where he had served as dean. They shared many school secrets and had tackled many problems as a team. Next to his wife of forty years, she was his closest confidant. She was also serving temporarily as Director of Admissions while the regular director, Kathy DeBarr, was on maternity leave. He picked up the phone on his desk.

"Winston Adams," he answered.

"Dean, this is Deborah. I have the initial statistics for this semester's entering students. Would you like me to bring them over now?"

"Yes, this is a good time," he said. He put down the phone and continued to gaze out the window, reflecting on how fast the time had passed. While Savannah College of Law had not grown into one of the so-called elite law schools, it had grown considerably in peer respect during Winston's deanship. *U.S. News and World Report*, which purports to rate all accredited law schools in the United States, had given it a higher rating each year. Almost seven hundred applications had been received last year, and Savannah College of Law had accepted only 185. Total student enrollment was now 480, and Winston was proud that he knew most students by name, a claim few law deans could make.

The financial scandal that hit Savannah College of Law in its third year was a distant memory to most at the school, although Winston thought of it often. It resulted from the Board of Trustees' eagerness to expand the physical facilities on the campus. Winston vigorously opposed the idea, arguing that the small endowment should be used to attract outstanding new faculty and not for new buildings. Nevertheless, the trustees, led by the board chairman, Howard Nolan, proceeded with their plans, which included a new administration building, a large classroom building, and two large wings to the library.

After Winston realized that they were going ahead with the building program despite his advice, he tried to have them substitute a courtroom for the reading room that was planned for one of the wings to the library. Instead, they *added* a complete new building with one large courtroom. The building was later named "Thomas Courthouse."

Howard Nolan, as chairman of the Board of Trustees, appointed a committee chaired by a close friend to oversee construction of the project, and he instructed the committee to proceed with all due haste. Proceed with haste they did. The job was awarded to one of Howard's own construction companies on a cost-plus contract. With little incentive to keep the cost down, and no independent oversight, the cost skyrocketed, and the school's endowment vanished. Howard, already one of the wealthiest men in town, became wealthier.

Winston spent the next three years in a campaign to complete the buildings and restore the endowment. He was successful with both projects. Because the school had been in existence for such a short time, there were no rich alumni available to replenish the depleted funds. But Savannah business and civic leaders were anxious to have the school succeed, and they assisted with the endowment drive. Buildings and classrooms were named in honor of major contributors, and the necessary funds were raised. Soon Savannah Law's endowment was greater than it had been before the construction project depleted it. But Winston never forgot how the trustees had failed to exercise any fiscal oversight on the building project. He was convinced that others on the board besides Howard had shared in the spoils from the project.

When it became clear that the school had weathered the storm, Winston decided it was the appropriate time to retire. He could now retire with pride in his accomplishments and a feeling of assurance that the school was ready for its future challenges.

There was a gentle knock on his door. Deborah entered, and before either said a word, they went through their private, silent ritual. To any observer it would be unremarkable. But to Winston and Deborah, it was a ceremonial occasion. The ritual dated back to those turbulent years when the trustees overruled Winston's objections and began the new construction project. Winston had a group photo of the Board of Trustees prominently displayed on the wall. One day while Deborah was in his office, he was fuming about the "crooks" involved in the building process—"they're just a bunch of crooked bankers and real estate developers!" Then he walked over to the photo and moved its horizontal axis, leaving it on an odd tilt. "There, now we can see you for what you are—*crooked!*" he shouted. As Deborah left, she walked to the photo, straightened the frame, and silently walked out the door. The next time, however, it was Deborah herself who walked over to the photo and angled it in the same crooked position in which Winston had placed it during her last visit.

And thus the ritual began and continued. Each time Deborah visited, she would turn the photo, and each time upon leaving, she would return it to its original position. The ritual, as silly as it was, never failed to get a chuckle out of Winston. Though he was eventually pleased with what the building project accomplished, he never changed his conviction that they were indeed a bunch of crooks, especially the board chairman, Howard Nolan. Winston was convinced that Howard had personally, substantially, and illegally enriched himself through the building project, backed by loans from Howard's own bank and built by his construction companies.

So, on this Monday morning, the first day of classes for the new semester, Deborah marched in, tilted the photo, and immediately took a seat in a chair beside Winston's desk. She did not wait for Winston to suggest that she be seated. Such formalities had been dropped between them years ago. However, one formality Deborah observed was the use of his title. She always addressed him as "Dean." They quickly got to the business at hand.

"You are going to be pleased with this entering class," she said. She handed Winston a chart that she had prepared that morning. "I've listed the twenty-fifth to seventy-fifth percentile LSAT scores and GPA ranges for the past three years. You can see they get better each year."

Indeed, Winston was pleased. "Kathy has done a wonderful job. She sent me a picture of her new baby and says she will be back in early October. I surely look forward to that."

"Not as much as I do," said Deborah.

"Anything else of interest that I should know? You have toured recently with your divining rod, haven't you?"

In Winston's early days as dean, he made a practice of walking around the campus daily and talking to the students, as well as visiting the staff offices at least two or three times a week. Recently a set of bad knees had cut down on his walking, and he relied heavily on Deborah as his eyes and ears. She was a popular member of his staff and had many friends and confidants. Her job kept her in constant contact not only with students but also with faculty. Should something new or awry occur, she would be one of the first to know.

"Everyone, or most everyone, has heard that you are going to announce your retirement. And, of course, there is much curiosity and speculation about your replacement."

"That's understandable; I kind of wonder about that myself," said Winston. "Any rumors or bets?"

"Not exactly, but I have heard that Professor Nolan is planning to apply."

Deborah noticed a distinct frown on Winston's face. Any decision on a new dean was months away, and even speculation was a bit premature. She knew, however, that politics within this faculty—any college faculty—could be intense, and sometimes cutthroat and devious. She was not one to repeat pure gossip, but Winston should not be caught unaware.

"I don't have personal knowledge of this, but I have heard from a pretty good source that Professor Nolan has approached most of the younger tenure-track professors for support."

That did not surprise Winston. But the prospect of the son of the "crooked banker" taking over was not a pleasant thought. He did not expect Denis's efforts to receive much traction, as he had limited teaching experience and no administrative experience. Nevertheless, he enjoyed a strong camaraderie with the younger members of the faculty, and now there were as many of those as older faculty. And Winston knew a well-orchestrated bid, with the support of the younger faculty, could bring a disrupting influence that would be felt for years.

Winston recalled the events that led to Denis's hiring. His father, Howard, was chairman of the Board of Trustees from the school's inception. During Winston's first few months as the new dean, before the school opened, he kept the trustees apprised of progress, including the hiring of staff and faculty, by weekly reports. For the first semester, they would need only five full-time professors plus two research and writing instructors. In one of their conversations on staffing, Howard informed Winston that his son, Denis, was an attorney in Chicago practicing real property law. He asked Winston to consider Denis for the property slot. Howard knew the position had not been filled, and Winston felt he had little choice but to at least consider Denis. Besides, the new school was not yet offering salaries that would attract prominent or experienced professors, and Howard's son had *some* experience in real property law, limited as it was.

The weekend Denis flew down from Chicago for his interview, Howard hosted a party at his luxurious beach house overlooking the ocean on Tybee Island. He invited all of the members of the Board of Trustees, Winston, Vice Dean Bechtel, and the three faculty members who had previously been hired, along with a number of prominent Savannah business leaders and their spouses. It was quite an affair, with a lavish menu of superb food and wine and a live band playing on the patio. Howard spent the evening introducing or reintroducing his son to the guests.

Winston remembered that he had been quite impressed, not only with the event, but with the number of prominent Savannah civic leaders in attendance. Conspicuously displayed in the large entry foyer of the house was a mock-up of the new Savannah College of Law campus, including models of all the buildings then under construction. Designed by a team of seniors at Savannah College of Art and Design, it was beautifully done. Winston had to give Howard high marks for the promotion of the law school—and his son—that evening.

Winston found Denis to be personable and intelligent. Denis was a magna cum laude graduate of the University of Virginia School of Law with a couple of years of experience in real estate practice, and Winston could envision him as a very valuable addition to the faculty. Winston was a pragmatist; having the son of a major benefactor and chairman of the board on the faculty should be a positive factor in ensuring continued financial support for the school. On the other hand, Winston could see the potential disaster should Denis not prove equal to the task. It would be messy, perhaps ruinous to the school, should it be necessary to terminate him for any reason.

The Faculty Hiring Committee met with Denis for a couple of hours and discussed his application but did not insist on a full law school transcript. Had they done so, they might have noted that he "sat out" the spring semester of his second year. The transcript would not have provided many facts, but perhaps it would have precipitated further probing and uncovered the reason: he was facing a plagiarism investigation.

It was only by chance that Winston learned of the plagiarism accusation. He was at an academic conference the year after Denis was hired when he met a professor from the University of Virginia who was familiar with the incident. The professor merely mentioned to Winston that he had heard that Denis Nolan was teaching at the new law school in Savannah and was happy to know that Denis was able to put the unfortunate matter behind him. When Winston inquired about the "unfortunate matter," the professor became reticent and appeared embarrassed. Upon being pressed by Winston, he eventually told of Denis being accused of plagiarizing a seminar paper. The professor was not involved in the investigation but recalled the incident because he was Denis's faculty advisor. This was an extremely severe accusation at the University of Virginia. Since 1842, under its honor system, expulsion was the required sanction for any student found guilty. The investigation proceeded slowly. Denis decided not to register for classes until the matter was resolved. The trial was scheduled for February. When February arrived, it was discovered that the plagiarized paper was missing and could not be located. Exactly who had it last was never determined. Without the paper, the trial could not be held, and the case was closed. The school agreed to expunge all reference to the charge and the investigation from Denis's official files, but the record of a lost semester on his transcript was unavoidable.

Winston had never mentioned this disclosure to anyone. However, now that Denis was considering applying to succeed him as dean, he could not help but wish that someone at the University of Virginia would suddenly find that missing plagiarized paper and resurrect that canceled student trial.

After a moment of deep thought, Winston responded to Deborah's news. "Professor Nolan is an ambitious young professor. But I wonder if he has given any thought to what is required of a dean. Setting salaries of your close friends is difficult and can have a chilling effect on the relationship. Denis would find that being dean can be a very lonely job."

"And I would no longer be able to twist that photo," Deborah said with a mocked frown.

Winston smiled. "Of course, you would. I'll personally hang that photo on your office wall when I leave."

Then he continued. "At the faculty meeting tomorrow, when I officially announce my retirement, I will also announce the names of those on the Dean Search Committee and discuss the search process. And, Deborah, I want you to give a report on the admission statistics for the incoming class. I'll have you listed early on the agenda. You don't have to stay unless you prefer."

"Dean, the entertainment value of a faculty meeting is unsurpassed, but Tuesday afternoon I'm going to be busy with drop/add. I won't be staying. Now, please excuse me. I'm sure my office is full of anxious students already."

With that, she put the photo upright and left.

CHAPTER 9

Monday evening about seven, Scott called Jennifer. He wanted to know all about her first day. He recalled his first day of law school. He had been well prepared but still anxious and nervous as he entered each classroom. Jennifer assured Scott that all went well.

"Did you and Nicole find anyone to join your study group?"

"Yes, we now have a four-person group. I'll be preparing the outline for Property, and Nicole will take Civil Pro. The two new members will do the outlines for Torts and Contracts."

"Sounds good." Scott paused a moment and added, "Jen, my trial is still set for Wednesday. I doubt if we finish it in one day, but by Friday night it will be behind me. How about we go out and celebrate?"

"I'm for that . . . we'll both be ready to celebrate," said Jennifer.

"I'll pick you up at your place at six. There's a flag football party on the beach—it's always a great time. We have the pavilion at Memorial Park at Tybee reserved. Basketball, volleyball and, of course, the beach. Or we can just sit around and relax. There will be food and music. OK with you?"

"Sure," Jennifer replied. She paused a moment. Then she said, "Scott, something's bothering me a little. I started to call you last night. I'm a bit nervous, maybe paranoid."

"Not unusual for the first week of law school. In my class, three students quit the first week. But I promise you, it will get better."

"No, it's not that. I'm fine with school. But last night when I drove back to my apartment, there was a tow truck parked right in front. It looked like the same tow truck that I had been in, but I couldn't be sure. It drove away as I parked."

Scott was now sure that Jennifer should have followed his advice and called the police and reported her Friday night abduction. But that was her decision, and he did not mention it.

"Jennifer, keep your cell phone with you at all times. And don't get out of your car if you are concerned about your safety. Call 911. Savannah police are very fast."

"Yes, but what would I have told them? 'There's a tow truck parked in front of my apartment'? They would have laughed all the way back to the station."

"No. They may have asked why you were concerned. And maybe you would have told them."

"Maybe. But not likely. Perhaps I'm just a bit paranoid right now. I'll be all right. See you at six, Friday." And she hung up.

CHAPTER 10
Tuesday, August 22

It was Tuesday afternoon and Crawford Classroom was filling slowly. The faculty meeting was scheduled for four o'clock, just a few minutes away. Those already seated were mostly the younger professors, and for some, this was their first faculty meeting.

At precisely four, Dean Adams entered, looked around, and made his usual announcement: "We were scheduled to begin at four, but something must have held up our faculty, so we'll have to wait until we have a quorum." It was the routine and rarely varied. Then he would walk over to one of the faculty members and start a conversation—about anything, as long as it was noncontroversial and could be ended quickly. He kept an eye on the professors as they entered and could usually tell when a quorum was present. When that number was reached, he would call the meeting to order.

When he was younger, serving in his first deanship at a Midwestern law school, he made a determined effort to start faculty meetings precisely at the scheduled time. It made no difference. No matter how much he cajoled, pleaded, or threatened, the faculty filed into the meeting room no faster. After several attempts at starting on time but still having no quorum, he wondered why he should even try. What earthly difference did it make? Faculty meetings were acknowledged by all who attended as useless in the extreme. Little, if anything, worthwhile was ever accomplished. Why not just discontinue the whole practice of having regular faculty meetings? If something really important were to surface, he could call a special meeting. So, on the date that the agenda was usually distributed, he announced that the faculty meeting had been canceled. And the next time, the same announcement. After three canceled meetings, the rumblings began. And after the fourth, he received a petition, signed by two-thirds of the faculty, demanding an accounting for his action and a resumption of the faculty meetings. The only accounting he provided was a quiet chuckle to himself. But he did, once again, schedule the faculty meetings to the satisfaction of most but not all of the faculty. Some of the older professors, who rarely attended, had not even noticed that they had been discontinued. The new faculty meetings, like the old, never started at the scheduled time, but Winston learned to live with the time-challenged professors.

Winston recognized that faculty meetings at Savannah College of Law were no different than at any other law school. The meetings were simultaneously worthless *and* indispensable. They may not accomplish much, but they provided a sense of community by having the professors in the same room at the same time. And they provided camaraderie. The second year into his deanship at Savannah College of Law, Winston started a tradition. Immediately after each meeting, he invited all to the faculty dining room for cheese and crackers with wine—furnished from the "Dean's Supplemental Entertainment Account." What the faculty did not know was that the account was subsidized entirely from his own personal funds. Even after a disagreeable and raucous faculty meeting, the mood was one of congeniality when the wine flowed. Winston considered it money well spent.

Professor Velma VanLandingham settled into her usual seat at her usual time, about ten minutes after the hour. That meant a quorum was surely present, or nearly so. Winston requested that Professor Charles Rose, who had been elected faculty secretary at the last meeting of the spring semester, check numbers for a quorum. He quickly gave Winston a thumbs up, and Winston called the meeting to order.

"I wish to welcome all of you back and give a special welcome to our newest faculty members." He then introduced the four new members of the faculty. "Belinda Chapman, who comes to us from the Foley and Lardner law firm in Washington, will be teaching Wills and Administration of Estates. Bernadine Garcia, who just finished a two-year clerkship with the Fifth Circuit Court of Appeals in New Orleans, will be teaching Research and Writing. Robert Paver, who was with Allan, Schwartz and Powell in Atlanta for three years and who served as general counsel for Irving Electronics for five years, will be teaching Administrative Law. Pamela Bell, who has been at Emory for the past three years teaching Civil Procedure, will be teaching the same course here." Winston asked the new members to stand, and as they did, the assembled faculty burst into a hearty applause. The first faculty meeting of the new semester had begun.

"The minutes of our last faculty meeting were included with the agenda. Each of you should have received a copy. Do we have any corrections or amendments to those minutes?" Winston asked.

Professor VanLandingham stood to be recognized. She was tall and broad and had a strong voice to go with her strong body. "I was in attendance at that meeting. I recall that quite clearly, and I am sure I can find others to attest to my attendance. It was held in the Telfair Classroom. I recall that because this classroom, our usual meeting room, was being used for a final exam. As a matter of personal privilege, I would like my attendance to be noted in the minutes. I move to amend the minutes as distributed to reflect my attendance."

"Velma," responded the Dean, "your name is included in the minutes. The names are in alphabetical order."

"Not my name, Dean Adams; my name is spelled with a capital 'L' after 'Van.'"

Everyone in the room, even those working on their daily Sudoku puzzles, looked at the minutes of the last meeting and the names listed as being in attendance. There it was, "Velma Vanlandingham"; the capital "L" was missing.

Belinda Chapman, who was attending her first faculty meeting and had just been introduced, whispered to the professor sitting on her right, "Is this for real, or is this a joke?"

Belinda had turned to Brian Latimer, a tenure-track associate professor who had been at Savannah Law three years. He whispered back, "For real, for sure. Velma is very protective of that last name. This occurred last year at our first faculty meeting. I believe Professor Rose did it on purpose this year, just to tick her off. Velma has few social graces—correction, no social graces—but she is one hell of a good contracts professor."

After a brief pause, Winston turned to the secretary and said, "Charles, you will correct that spelling, won't you?" Charles smiled and just nodded in agreement. Velma was appeased and sat down.

Winston then called on Deborah Channing to give the report on the fall semester entering class. She did so, giving the faculty most of the data she had given Winston the previous day. She then briefed the faculty on the tentative numbers for the spring entering class that would be arriving in January. The outlook for the spring semester looked good, according to Deborah. "Any questions?" she asked.

Professor Sarah Taff-Rothchild stood. She wanted to know how many, if any, students in the entering class were from her alma mater, Smith College. Deborah said she did not know if any were from Smith but that she did not recall any.

"I am not surprised. I have heard of no special recruiting trips to Smith despite my request last fall. The admission of Smith students to our student body would be a sign of visible progress."

"I agree," said Deborah. "Smith is a wonderful school of superb academic standing. The problem is the distance. Its location in Massachusetts is outside our regular recruiting area. The Admissions Committee directed that the office concentrate on colleges within 750 miles of Savannah. As it was, Kathy and her recruiting assistant could visit only a fraction of the schools in that area. And, of course, Kathy's travel was curtailed somewhat by her pregnancy. I do recall she sent an e-mail to all professors asking if any could assist her by making a recruiting visit to his or her alma mater, regardless of the location. The school would pay travel and hotel expenses. She told me she received only a few responses. Did you perhaps respond?"

"Of course not. Her job is recruiting. My job is to teach those she recruits. All I asked then is what I ask now: make a special effort to recruit at Smith."

Martin Swazey, one of the older tenured professors, who was hired the year after the school opened, raised his hand, and Winston gave him the floor. "I got that e-mail, and I volunteered to recruit at Georgetown. It's 578 miles. I know. I drove it. I recommend it to anyone—volunteering to recruit at your alma mater. Also gave me a chance to spend some time with my good friend Senator Dick Durbin. He and I were classmates at Georgetown, so we go back a long way. I told him I thought he should make a run for president in the next election. We need someone with his vision in the White House. Dick asked me to join him for lunch with Nancy—Nancy Pelosi—but I had to get back to Georgetown for some student interviews."

This was typical Swazey. The new faculty members were getting a good taste of professorial ego. Swazey could not go more than two faculty meetings without reminding the faculty of his good friend and former college classmate, Dick Durbin, and if not Senator Durbin, some other prominent "personal friend." And usually he would throw in some "special work" he had performed for the school, such as driving 578 miles to assist with recruiting. He did not mention that his daughter and two grandchildren lived in nearby Alexandria, and that was his main purpose for visiting Georgetown. This was, however, the first time he had mentioned Nancy Pelosi— and on a first-name basis, no less.

Professor Geraldine Polanski, who taught domestic relations, had her hand raised to speak when Winston broke in to get the meeting back on track. "Methods of recruiting are important, but let's leave that to our Admissions Committee, or ask to have it placed on the agenda for a future faculty meeting. Are there any specific questions for Deborah concerning her report?"

There were none. Committee reports were next. The reports took less than ten minutes. Some in the back row continued reading the mail they had received in their faculty mail boxes that afternoon. Some continued working their crossword puzzles. And some pretended to actually have an interest in the proceedings. No "old business" was on the agenda, and the only "new business" was committee assignments. That went quickly. Winston asked for one or two additional volunteers to serve on the Admissions Committee because of the maternity leave of Kathy DeBarr. Two hands went up, both from junior professors not yet tenured.

"Thanks," said Winston. He then made the announcement that had been anticipated by all. "I will be retiring at the end of the spring semester. I don't think that has been any secret, but it's now official. My letter was submitted to the Board of Trustees at their last meeting."

The entire faculty, including those on the back row, stood and rendered a loud and sustained applause. It was obvious their applause was not from hearing that Winston was leaving but from a deep and heartfelt appreciation for his deanship. Those who had been members of faculties at other law schools *knew* that he was one of the best, and the others sensed it.

Once the applause subsided, he continued. "Harry Ramsey, the board chairman, has appointed a dean search committee to be headed by Ben Sterner, vice chairman of the board. Wilbert Tebeau, another board member, will also serve. From the faculty, Vice Dean Bechtel and Professor Marjory Hoffman have been appointed. Both have informed me that they are not candidates for the position. The president of the Student Bar Association will also be a member, as well as Jacqueline Hinesley, president of our alumni association. I have been appointed a non-voting, ex officio member of the committee. Our registrar, Deborah Channing, will serve as secretary to the committee.

"The board has indicated they would like the committee to complete its search and send three names to the board by the end of January. The board will, of course, make the final selection. This will be a national search, so it's a tall order for such a short time frame. Ads announcing the vacancy have been placed in the next issues of the *Journal of Legal Education* and the *ABA Journal*. The ads will also appear in several major newspapers next Sunday. And, of course, all accredited law schools are being notified. Should any of you wish to apply, please contact Deborah for the details of submitting your application. Do you have any questions about the search or the search committee?"

Denis Nolan raised his hand. "I note you have six members on the search committee. For voting purposes, an odd number would be best. And since you have two faculty members and two board members, it would be appropriate to have two members from the student body. I wish to make a motion that another student be appointed to the committee and that he or she come from the first year class. The new dean will affect that class more than any of the others."

"Denis, the board chairperson is tasked with the composition of the Dean Search Committee. I have no authority to change the composition."

"Dean, I would hope you would at least ask. I am sure there are several first-year students willing—perhaps anxious—to serve. I have met several whom I could recommend. Would you mind inquiring if he would accept another student on the search committee?"

"I would like to hear from others on the faculty. Any comments on Professor Nolan's suggestion?" asked Winston.

The back row did not even look up. However, Chad Kittler, a young, fully-bearded assistant professor dressed in his usual Levi's and black Izod polo shirt, spoke up. "Why not?" he said. "More students would make it more democratic. They have substantial money and time invested in this school. The process would make the dean—whoever he might be—more acceptable."

Velma VanLandingham was listening and without raising her hand or requesting the floor, roared, "Did you say whoever *he* may be? *He* may be! You are assuming that the new dean will be a *he*? This underscores the insidious and pervasive discrimination that the female members of this faculty—and all faculties in all law schools— continue to face. I want to second the motion of Professor Nolan, if that was indeed a motion, and I wish to amend his motion to make sure that any student so appointed is a female student. I think we all know that the other student, the Student Bar Association president, is male! *This makes me fighting mad!*"

Even those on the back row, previously engrossed in their games, suddenly became awake and were focusing on Velma, who was now standing, brow wrinkled and eyes threatening. Winston saw that this was not heading in any direction he wanted to go. He quickly decided to head off any confrontation that may be developing, although he could not imagine anyone on the faculty confronting Velma on this subject. It was one of her favorites—the male domination of law school administration. And certainly no one was going to confront her when she announced that she was "fighting mad," which she frequently did.

"Velma, I am sure Professor Kittler meant only *whoever the new dean may be* and had no intention to infer it would be or should be a male." Winston looked at Professor Kittler, extending his hand in a gesture inviting Kittler to speak.

Kittler had slumped down in his seat during Velma's outburst but quickly spoke up. "Yes, of course, Dean. And Professor

VanLandingham, I apologize for my inappropriate remark—
inappropriate *and* inadvertent."

Velma glared at the young professor but said nothing. She
was a full professor, and tenured. He was an assistant professor
only on a tenure *track*, always subject to derailment by vote of the
tenured faculty. He would be sure to make a private apology the
following day.

Winston was ready for the meeting to end. It had started on
a bad note and appeared to be ending on one. There was another
faculty meeting scheduled for the following Tuesday, and hopefully
things would go more smoothly.

Velma was still standing as Winston faced the faculty and
asked, "Any further announcements?"

This was a time for any member of the faculty to announce
a new program, an award, or perhaps the forthcoming visit of a
distinguished guest to the campus. No one spoke up, and Winston
was about to call for adjournment when Geraldine stood and began
to speak.

"I was in the cafeteria yesterday as well as today, and I
note they are still serving margarine made with hydrogenated oil. I
don't think I have to remind anyone that we must keep not only our
environment but also our food safe and healthy for our students. We
are falling behind. I think a faculty-student committee should be
formed for the purpose . . . ."

Before she could finish her sentence, she was interrupted by a
roar from an unidentified male member on the back row. "Agenda!
Agenda! That's not on the agenda!"

Stunned, Geraldine stood still, with her fingers pressed
against her top lip.

"Yes, Geraldine," Winston said. "You may want to place that
on our agenda for a future meeting."

"Move to adjourn" came from the same voice that had
interrupted Geraldine. It was followed by "second" from a faculty
member who did not even look up from his third Sudoku puzzle of
the afternoon.

Velma was still in her "fighting mad" stance. "As a point of
privilege," she said, "I move the previous question. You haven't taken

a vote on Denis's motion for another student on the Dean Search
Committee. Denis, you do accept my amendment, don't you?" And
without waiting for Denis to respond, she continued, "I call for the
previous question before we vote on the motion to adjourn."

Winston had presided over hundreds of faculty meetings.
Early on he had mastered *Robert's Rules of Order*—something
necessary in governing a room of lawyers, especially law professors
who not infrequently were prone to make obscure, pedantic motions;
amendments to motions; and amendments to amendments, resulting
in an unstructured and ambiguous morass that no one understood
and no one could restate. Few faculty members took the time to
understand the rules, which were specific and prioritized. It was not
unusual for a member to throw out a term such as "point of privilege"
and "call for the question." Winston's mastery of both *Robert's Rules*
and group dynamics equipped him for a solution to this apparent
impasse. He would say a few words to smooth the ruffled feathers of
Velma and shepherd the meeting to a quick adjournment.

"There is a motion on the floor to adjourn and, as we all
know, under *Robert's Rules of Order*, that motion takes a mere
majority vote and is not debatable. However, as Velma has pointed
out, a recommendation was made by Denis that we should have a
first-year student on the Dean Search Committee. And Velma has
suggested that if such an appointment is authorized, it should be
a female student. I will take that up with the board chair, Harry
Ramsey, later this week, and report back to you at our meeting next
Tuesday."

Winston did not take a vote on the motion to adjourn. He
merely said, "Now, do I hear any objection to the motion to adjourn?"
He knew there would be none. Both Velma and Denis appeared
pleased with Winston's intercession; Velma was even managing to
smile. "There being no objection, we stand adjourned until next
Tuesday, same time," he said. "I invite all of you to the faculty dining
room for libations to celebrate the beginning of another semester and
to welcome our new colleagues."

The faculty were already out of their seats and beginning to
walk out by the time Winston had finished his invitation. Belinda
Chapman and Brian Latimer were among the last to leave.

Belinda was still a bit dazed by the afternoon's proceedings. "So, Brian," Belinda said, looking around to make sure no one was listening, "this is what we have to look forward to every week or so?"

"Not exactly . . . sometimes it's much worse. But you will get used to it, or rather *numbed* by it. Frankly, I find it a bit of fun. You see a side of people you otherwise would never see. Faculty meetings just bring it out. I decided early on that I could be miserable, sit on the back row, and ignore the show, or get a front-row seat and enjoy it."

By now, the room was empty except for the two of them.

"Tell me more about Velma. Is she all there? And do you suppose she plans to apply for the deanship?"

"Apply for the deanship? I doubt it," said Brian. "But is she *'all there'*? That depends. Socially, she's as out of place as a penguin on Tybee Beach. Interpersonal relationships? She has none and apparently has no desire to acquire any. She has a reputation for being a real mean witch. And something tells me she enjoys that reputation. The students refer to her as the 'Dragon Lady.' But with regard to her teaching skills, is she *all there*? You bet. Perhaps the best on the faculty. She never attends alumni events, but the alumni always ask about her. She not only gives them a solid grounding in contract law but also teaches them how to study. And she gets them ready for the bar exam."

"How well are we doing on the bar?" asked Belinda. They were now standing next to the exit. "Mind if I take a seat?" Belinda sat down in the nearest chair without waiting for a response.

Brian took the seat next to Belinda. "Bar passage rate? Exceptional. Savannah College of Law grads have finished high on the Georgia Bar Exam every year since our students became eligible to take the exam—usually first or second place. Winston is primarily responsible for that."

"How so?" asked Belinda.

"He knew that as a new law school, all eyes would be on the bar passage rate. We couldn't afford to do less than excel. Our tuition is much higher than the tuition in the state schools, so we couldn't expect to get enough applications to cherry-pick our students. We were an unknown quality, and the quickest way for a new law school to fail is to have a poor bar passage rate. The reverse is also true. The best way to rise above the pack is to have a superior bar passage rate. So, Winston insisted not only that the curriculum include every subject included on the Georgia Bar Exam but also that every subject tested by the exam be a required course. Well, I'm not sure we have them all, but we have most of them."

"Makes sense to me. My law school had only one required course after the first year."

"But that wasn't all. He added more days per semester and more classroom hours than required for accreditation. And he put an emphasis on class attendance. He believed in the old Woody Allen quote that 'eighty percent of success is just showing up.'"

"How about the faculty? They surely have to teach longer. Do they complain?"

"What law faculty doesn't complain? They have the cushiest jobs in the legal community and bitch all the time, and not only about teaching or writing requirements. But, down deep, they are proud of this law school and the bar passage rate."

Then Belinda asked, "What about Professor Nolan—Denis? What do you know about him? Did you find it a bit unusual that he was requesting a first-year student to serve on the Dean Search Committee?"

"Denis was here when I got here three years ago. He's one of the original faculty members. He's a strange bird at times. I don't have a clue to what he had in mind with that request. But he had a purpose; I'm sure of that. Did you know his dad, Howard Nolan, was the school founder?"

"His dad established Savannah Law?"

"That may be an over-statement. Ten years ago, there were no law schools in Georgia south of Macon. A number of business leaders and local politicians got together to push the legislature for a state law school in Savannah. Everyone was on board for it to be established at Armstrong Atlantic State University. They thought they had it locked up with the legislature, but it got sidetracked until the next legislative session. Then the business leaders changed strategies—they decided to establish a private law school. With Howard taking the lead, they found the necessary money, much of it coming from Howard. So I guess he could be called the 'founder.' He certainly was the moving force behind it. He served as chairman of the board until his death about two years ago. Powerful man."

"Denis surely seemed interested in the composition of the Dean Search Committee. Do you think he will be a candidate?"

"Sure, I know he will. He told me so when he came to my office yesterday. Said he wanted me to know that he would be applying, and he told me of some programs he wanted to establish if he became dean."

"Like what?"

"More money for summer writing grants, for one. And more pay for those of us on a tenure track, so we can catch up with tenured professors sooner. Then he asked me if I would support him."

"And you said . . . ?"

Brian did not answer directly. "Belinda, both those programs would involve money in my pocket. Denis believes that everybody will follow the smell of money. Just let me say, he's wrong on that. But we should head for the dining hall. You need to be there. Winston will be looking for you."

CHAPTER 11

Immediately after the faculty meeting, Denis Nolan went to his office to place a phone call. Even though it was now after five o'clock, when most businesses in downtown Savannah switched to "answering machine mode," Denis knew his call would be answered by a human voice.

"Savannah Global Trade."

Denis recognized the voice. It was Carolyn, an executive secretary who never left the office before her boss, and her boss rarely left in the evenings before seven. She had worked for Harry Ramsey, president and CEO of Savannah Global Trade, an international shipping and warehousing company, for as long as Denis could remember. Harry Ramsey was now chairman of the Board of Trustees of Savannah College of Law. He and Howard Nolan had been friends for forty years before Howard's death, and he had known Denis from infancy.

"Carolyn, this is Denis. Is Harry available? I need to speak with him."

"I'll put you right through," said Carolyn, and within seconds, Harry Ramsey was on the line.

"Harry, I just came out of a faculty meeting. Winston informed us of your Dean Search Committee. The faculty was impressed by the people you appointed. Solid choices."

"Glad to hear that, Denis."

"I called to also tell you that the faculty feels it needs another member from the student body, preferably a first-year student," Denis said, as he swiveled his chair and placed his feet up on the window ledge. "Still, that would place only two students on the committee, but it would give the students a better sense of having a voice. Winston said he would call you, but I'm not sure he's convinced we need an additional student. So, I'm giving you a heads up. The faculty feels strongly that a student rep from the entering class should be appointed."

"I'll see what Winston's take is on the issue. He usually has pretty sage advice on such matters."

"I agree, Harry. It's just in this case the whole faculty—and I've spoken with most of them—are in agreement that this would be good for the student body. Getting them involved with the selection would go a long way to ensuring a smooth transition. Sorry to bother you with this . . . I know you are busy. Just want you to be aware of the situation when Winston calls."

"Never too busy to speak with you, Denis. And by the way, are you planning to apply for the job?"

"I haven't given it much thought, Harry. But I wonder if there might still be some bad feelings lingering on the board. There were some who were down on my dad, and I'm afraid that may stand in my way."

"Nonsense. Even if there were some who were upset with your dad, they certainly are not upset with you. That should not deter you. Give it some serious thought."

"I will. We have a great school, and I want to see it continue on the track that Winston has placed it. Maybe I could be of service."

"I'm sure you could, Denis. And thanks for the call."

Denis left his office for the faculty dining room. The party was still in session. Winston and a number of faculty members, including all of the newly hired, were gathered at one end of the room near a table with trays of assorted sandwiches, cheese and crackers, and dishes of nuts. Denis noted Chad Kittler by himself, at the other end, near one of the side doors. He was holding a glass of wine and wearing an unhappy face. Denis poured himself a glass of wine and joined Chad.

"Let's step outside," said Denis.

There was a small patio with three tables outside the faculty dining room. The faculty used the area when the weather allowed, but today was hot and muggy, and all the faculty had remained inside the air-conditioned room.

"Thanks for your support for another student on the Dean Search Committee," said Denis. "Sorry you had to endure the wrath of the 'Dragon Lady.'"

"That porcine bitch," Chad said through clenched jaws. "She gets her kicks rolling her fat, tenured ass over any junior faculty member with the mettle to speak in her holy presence. She probably has her eyes on the Dean's Office. Do you think she . . . ?"

Before Chad could finish his sentence, Denis interrupted him. "No, no, no. She wouldn't want the work that goes with the job, though no doubt she would enjoy the hassling that goes with it. But you don't have to worry about ever calling her 'Dean.' Won't happen. As I told you last week, my hat's going into the ring, and I think I'll have the faculty's support."

"Good," was Chad's quick response. He put his wine glass to his mouth and drained it. "I'm going back in. I'm empty."

"Before you go, Chad, I need your help with that recommendation I made—the additional student on the search committee. I spoke with Harry Ramsey, the board chairman, a few minutes ago. I told him Winston would be calling him and that the faculty was behind my recommendation. That may not be exactly the case, but I didn't hear anyone in opposition, and at least one faculty member supported me." Denis winked and slapped Chad on his chest with the back of his hand. "So, if Harry does authorize another student member, I have the name of a new female student that I want to submit. I would appreciate you also recommending her. It's Jennifer Stone. I've met her, and she's sharp. I doubt if any others on the faculty will submit a recommendation. I think Winston would appoint her if Harry gives him the OK."

"Sure, Denis, OK with me. But remember, when you become dean, who got you there." He laughed, and then said, "How about sending me an e-mail with something about her so I can personalize my recommendation."

"Will do. Now, let's go in for that refill." Denis and Chad walked inside, refilled their glasses and helped themselves to the sandwiches. But Denis did not stay long; he had *another* phone call to make.

• • •

Jennifer Stone was in her apartment, arranging her desk to begin the night's study, when her phone rang.

"Hello," she answered.

"Hello, Jennifer. This is Denis Nolan."

Jennifer was surprised but recognized his voice. She searched for a response, wondering what this call could be about and if she should respond or wait for him to continue. After an awkward pause, she said, "Yes, Professor."

"I wanted to speak to you after class but thought it best to call you tonight. I was delighted to meet you Sunday. And I want to give you a special welcome to our law school. Since you were present during my conversation with Scott, you are aware that I will be actively campaigning to be the new dean. I believe there is a good chance another student will be added to the Dean Search Committee, and I would like to nominate you. Would you be interested?"

Jennifer paused to make sure she understood the question. "*Interested?*" She was flattered. "Of course, Professor."

"Good. It's not final, of course, so keep it on the QT. I'll keep you informed. How are things going so far?"

"Fine, Professor."

"I want you to know that I'm here for you. If you need advice or just someone to talk to, stop by my office."

"Thanks." Her voice was restrained and hardly audible. But she was thrilled. She knew she had made the right career choice.

CHAPTER 12
Wednesday, August 23

S cott Marino was up early Wednesday morning. He was ready for this day. He had packed his briefcase carefully the previous night with everything he would need for the trial, which was scheduled for 9 a.m.

As he drove to the Chatham County Courthouse that morning to prosecute his first felony trial, he reflected on a day, ten years before, when he was at the courthouse in his hometown in Murfreesboro, Tennessee, for a different type of court appearance. On that occasion, he was attending a juvenile detention hearing—his own. He had been picked up two days earlier for joyriding and was being held in juvenile detention. He was in his junior year of high school. The purloined vehicle was owned by his baseball coach, and he knew his coach would be at the courthouse to testify. He was both terrified and embarrassed. This was his second juvenile offense, and he also had several citations for truancy. He wasn't sure what penalty he would face, and he feared the worst. But instead of testifying against him, his coach worked out a deal with the prosecutor. He would personally take on the responsibility of supervising Scott. He knew that Scott's father had died when Scott was quite young and that his mother was a hard-working woman struggling to provide for her family. Scott had more baseball talent than any student he had ever coached, and he believed he was an exceptionally intelligent young man. He was confident that all he needed was another chance, encouragement, and supervision. He would help Scott get a part-time job, and the money would be put aside so that he could eventually purchase his own car. It worked out as planned. Scott finished high school with honors, obtained a scholarship to Alabama, and bought and restored his first car—a well-worn 1984 Camaro Z28, which was still his pride and joy.

Scott cleared the security checkpoint at the courthouse at 8:30 a.m. and took the elevator up to Courtroom D on the second floor. Courtroom D was not as large as some of the other courtrooms in the building, but it was quite ample. The judge's bench was raised several feet from the floor and located in the far right corner. The United States flag hung from a staff on one side, the Georgia state flag on the other, and an enlarged facsimile of the Great Seal of Georgia was displayed on the nearby wall. The judge's bench exuded authority, even in the absence of the judge. The witness box and a table for the clerk were just below the judge's bench. Extending lengthwise on the left side of the courtroom was the tiered jury box with fourteen plum-red arm chairs. In the center, the court arena, were two large tables for counsel, each accompanied by three ruby-red arm chairs.

Richard Evans, the DA investigator assigned to the case, was already in the courtroom when Scott arrived. Richard had worked on the case with Scott since the beginning. He had been with the office for over twenty years and had investigated almost every crime covered by Georgia law and a few that weren't. Richard was a walking warehouse of knowledge about Chatham County's criminal courts. He was friends with the bailiffs in each courtroom and had gathered information about the temperamental peculiarities and eccentric courtroom and trial management styles of every judge on the criminal bench.

He and Scott got along well. When Scott heard that Judge Karen Vesely would be presiding over the Vandera trial, he asked Richard for an assessment of what to expect from the bench.

"She's my favorite—experienced and mature," said Richard.

"*Mature?*" asked Scott. "How old is she?"

"It's not her age," said Richard. "By 'mature,' I mean she doesn't suffer from 'robe-itis.'"

"Robe-itis?"

"Yes, 'robe-itis.' It's the disease that sometimes infects newly appointed judges. They get an overwhelming feeling of self-importance. They pontificate and interrupt rather than listen. Some seriously affected with robe-itis actually strut rather than walk. They enjoy displaying *their* knowledge in front of the jury and making the *attorneys* look stupid. But you will enjoy trying your case before Judge Vesely. If you are prepared and professional, she won't interfere."

If Richard's appraisal of Judge Vesely was correct, Scott knew he would have no problem presenting his case. Yes, he was ready.

Scott had been in Courtroom D several weeks previously for a pretrial conference on the case and had been introduced to Judge Vesely by his supervising attorney. Under rules established by the Georgia Supreme Court, third-year law students may assist at criminal trials as prosecutors or defense counsel to the extent permitted by the presiding judge. The judge must administer an oath similar to the oath taken by members of the bar. Jeff Swenson also had been there with his supervising attorney, Charlie Roberts, an attorney from the public defender's office. Judge Vesely administered the oath to both students and welcomed them to her courtroom. She reminded the two supervising attorneys that they must be physically present throughout the proceedings and asked them to outline the parts of the trial that the students would be undertaking. She appeared surprised when informed that Scott would serve as lead attorney throughout the trial, examining all witnesses and giving the opening statement and closing argument. To Scott's great relief, she placed no restrictions on his participation. And in the ensuing weeks, Scott had worked hard preparing for this trial. Now, it was time to deliver.

Scott and Richard were going over the witness list when Grady Wilder walked in. He took the third seat at the table and listened as Scott and Richard discussed the logistics of the case. He didn't interrupt; this was Scott's case.

Just after Grady arrived, Jeff Swenson walked in with Charlie Roberts and the defendant, Charles Vandera. The three took their seats at the defense table. Jeff had a large briefcase and began to unload it. Papers, law books, and file folders were soon scattered across the table. A few minutes later, a young woman came into the courtroom and handed some papers to Jeff, and soon he and his supervisor became engaged in a lively but secretive conversation. Scott wondered if they were going to try to reopen the plea negotiations. The plea offer by the prosecution had been terminated when Vandera had not accepted it by its Monday noon deadline. Scott was not authorized to make any further offers, and he had no desire to make any. He was ready for trial today.

Promptly at 9 a.m., Judge Vesely entered the courtroom. The bailiff stepped smartly forward, holding a seven-foot oak staff decorated with thin streamers and a gold eagle at the top. With swift vertical movements, he rapped sharply on the floor three times and ordered all persons to their feet with formal language heard only in Chatham County courts. Counsel, as well as the few spectators seated in the courtroom, quickly rose and stood in place. This formal pageantry to call the court to order had been observed in the Chatham County courts since the middle of the eighteenth century when Georgia was a British colony. Although it was abandoned in other courts in Georgia, it remained an important and unvarying tradition in Chatham County. The only change was that the Crown's seal, originally on the top of the staff, had been replaced by the American Eagle, and the thin streamers hanging loosely from the top of the staff no longer represented the colonies subject to the Crown. The decorated wooden staff served as the "mace" of the Chatham County courts. It symbolized the authority of the court, just as the mace of the English Parliament symbolized Parliament's authority. This brief pageantry by the bailiff with the wooden staff never failed to impress—and startle—visitors caught unaware.

The judge took her seat at the bench, and the trial of Charles Vandera was underway. The jury panel was not yet in the courtroom. Judge Vesely called the court to order, folded her arms, and looked directly at the defense table.

"Earlier this morning, I received a notice from the defense requesting a hearing before calling the jury. I believe the defense has a motion to make."

A hearing? A motion? All of this was news to Scott. He felt a mild sense of panic. No lawyer welcomes a surprise—at least not from the other side.

"Has the defense served this motion on the prosecution?" she asked.

Charlie Roberts spoke. "No, we have not, Your Honor. We just had it typed this morning and delivered to this courtroom a few minutes ago. We apologize for the apparent untimeliness of this motion, but we just discovered the error in the indictment late last night. Had we been aware of the error earlier, we would have filed a special demurrer. We believe the error is of such significance that we should be heard on this motion before we continue with the trial."

As Roberts spoke, Jeff walked over to the prosecutor's table and handed a copy of the motion to Scott.

Roberts continued, "May I approach, Your Honor, with your copy?"

"Yes, let me see it."

Roberts delivered a copy to the judge, who then looked at the prosecution table. "So this is the first you have heard of this?"

Scott spoke up. "We had heard nothing, Your Honor, until you spoke of it a minute ago. And, of course, we haven't had time to read the motion."

"Neither have I. Mr. Roberts, why don't you tell us what is contained in your motion."

"Yes, Your Honor. The state has charged the defendant with the crime of burglary, but as we argue in our motion, the indictment is defective. The indictment reads that the defendant, 'on or about April 24, 2006, did unlawfully break and enter, with the intent to commit larceny therein, a CVS Pharmacy Store where business is conducted, said store being owned by CVS Pharmacy, Inc., and located in Savannah, County of Chatham, and State of Georgia, such act being contrary to the laws of the State of Georgia, and the good order, peace and dignity thereof.'"

"And in what way do you maintain that it is defective, Mr. Roberts?" asked Judge Vesely.

"It does not inform the defendant of which Savannah CVS store was entered. There are at least ten CVS stores in Savannah. While the state may have one in mind, the indictment does not. The state could have any one of the ten in mind. We cannot defend against such a vague indictment. The indictment is too general to place the defendant on notice as to the location of the crime. We move to dismiss it."

"And Mr. Marino, your response?" asked Judge Vesely.

Scott's heart was now pounding, and his mind was racing. Did he just hear the words "move to dismiss it"? Those were frightening words. He had prepared for, and been ready for, almost anything but *this*. He had focused on preparation for the trial of the case, not on the technical integrity of the indictment. He had not drafted the indictment nor presented the case to the grand jury. He was assigned the case after all of that was completed. Perhaps Grady would step in and respond. But this was *his* case, his only case, and Grady had dozens of his own to handle. If a mistake had been made—and Scott now was pretty sure there was a mistake—it was his responsibility.

"Yes, Your Honor," Scott began. "Not only is this motion untimely, the defense has known since May that the store involved is the one at 1128 East Grissom Avenue. I have personal knowledge that both defense counsel have visited that store for the purpose of examining the location of the break-in. The defense has not been misled. And by waiting until today, just minutes before jury selection, they have waived any error in the indictment. However, to ensure that the defense is put on notice as to the exact location of the pharmacy, the state moves to amend the indictment by inserting the words, 'at 1128 East Grissom Avenue, Savannah' in place of the words 'in Savannah.'"

Judge Vesely looked at the defense table. "What does the defense say to the motion to amend?"

"We certainly oppose any such motion, Your Honor. We would dispute that the prosecution has authority to amend a faulty indictment in a case such as this. Only the grand jury can breathe life into a faulty indictment. The prosecution cannot replace the grand jury, as they are attempting to do in this case," replied Roberts.

"Does either side have any case law in support of your argument?"

Both the defense and prosecution replied that they did not have any case law available at that time. Scott argued that because the prosecution had just received the motion to dismiss, he needed time to research the issue.

Judge Vesely agreed to give him until 10:30 that morning at which time she would reconvene the court and hear anything additional that either counsel might have, including case law.

Both the defense and prosecution teams rushed out of the courtroom. Scott had his laptop with him. He went to Grady's office, hooked up to the Internet and was soon on Westlaw, a legal research service. As Scott began his research in Grady's office, Grady

went to inform Nick Cox, felony section chief, of the situation. Nick
was in his office when Grady walked in with the news. Nick knew
Scott from his internship during the summer. "What the hell," roared
Nick. "Why the fuck didn't Scott note that deficiency weeks ago?
Savannah detectives busted their balls on that case. The paper did
a special article on it—'Rope for Dope.' Now it goes down the tube
because some damn third-year clinic student can't read."

"You're sure it's lost, Nick?" asked Grady.

"Damn right, it's lost. Vesely's not going to spend time on a
case that's going to be bounced on appeal. I can't believe Scott could
be so damn careless. I thought, of all the clinic students we've had,
he was one of the sharpest."

"He is," said Grady. "He's put this case together as well as
anyone could. He was ready for everything in this trial but the one
thing that several experienced prosecutors also missed. I had it for
a month before I gave it to him. I didn't catch the problem, and our
intake division, which drafted it, didn't catch it either. I don't recall
who took it before the grand jury, but he or she didn't see it either.
And the defense says they didn't note it until last night—but I'm
skeptical of that. The bottom line is that the case was assigned to me
for trial, and I missed it. So let the blame fall where it belongs."

"You bet, I'll do that. And when Vesely grants the motion—
and she will—you rework the language, take it to the grand jury,
and get another indictment. And don't let Scott screw it up. Where
is Scott now?"

"In my office, checking law and cases. We are due back in
court at ten-thirty."

Grady left Nick's office and went to his own office where
Scott was seated behind the computer. "Find anything helpful?"
asked Grady.

"Yes, helpful to the defense."

"Like what?" said Grady.

"*State versus Tommy Green*," Scott replied. "A 1975 case
from the Georgia Court of Appeals. Defendant was charged with
burglary of a building. The indictment alleged it belonged to Darvin
Byrd, located in Columbia County, Georgia, but failed to specify
the location of the building. The court's reasoning is not a model

for clarity, but the holding is. The location of the building must be specific. No question, this indictment requires a street address. I'm prepared to concede it's defective, but I would like to argue that we should be allowed to amend the indictment because the defense has not been misled and has been dilatory in bringing this matter to the court's attention. They knew all along where the pharmacy was located. That never was in doubt. What do you think?"

"Scott, I know you are anxious to get this trial underway today, but I think we have a loser. Nick Cox thinks we have a loser. And I'm convinced Judge Vesely will tell you that you have a loser. Now, here's my advice. Let's go back in that courtroom and concede our error. No motion to amend, no waiver argument, no excuses. We take our lumps and then get this case back on track. Nick says if the judge grants the motion to dismiss, we are to redraft the indictment, take the case to the grand jury again, and then take it to trial. Let's go."

That was not what Scott wanted to hear. In his view, this motion was a sham—a typical low-ball defense trick. So far the morning had been a stressful eighty minutes. He now wondered if he would ever get another shot at trying a felony case after screwing up this one.

"The judge is not going to be happy," said Grady. "Wasted day. She has felony cases backed up, and it will take a lot of her time to get back on track. I'll tell her we concede the defense motion, and she can take it out on me."

"No, this was my case. I'm the one who fucked it up, so let me handle it," said Scott. "I'll just tell the judge that we found nothing to support our argument. And I'll also advise her of the *Green* decision."

They walked out of Grady's office on the sixth floor, took the elevator down to the second, and walked toward the courtroom. Scott was surprised to see Jennifer standing in the corridor.

"Security told me the Vandera trial was in Courtroom D, but I found it empty," said Jennifer. "Have you started?"

"Started, and about to end," replied Scott. He was trying to manage a smile, but what appeared was a smile occasioned by pain rather than pleasure. He was still reeling from the unexpected setback in the case and was embarrassed. "I'm about to tell Judge Vesely to dismiss the indictment."

Jennifer observed the stress in his voice and decided not to ask why. "OK, in that case, I'll just take a seat in the back row."

Scott and Grady sat down next to Richard. At the same time, Jeff, Roberts, and the defendant entered and took seats at the defense table. The bailiff, clerk, and court reporter were already in the courtroom, and within a few minutes, Judge Vesely entered from the door near her bench.

"All rise!" ordered the bailiff.

Judge Vesely took her seat and motioned for all to be seated. She then asked if either had anything further to present on the motion. Scott was the first to rise.

"Your Honor, I have researched the issue involved in the motion to dismiss the indictment. I found a case on point: *State of Georgia versus Tommy Green*, at 218 S. E. 2d 456, a 1975 case. It supports the argument made by the defense that this indictment is fatally defective. I'm unable to distinguish the defect in this case from the defect in the *Green* case, so we do not oppose the motion by the defense to dismiss the indictment. I would add, however, that the state does intend to seek a superseding indictment of this crime, with an amendment that will include the specific location."

"Anything from the defense?" inquired Judge Vesely.

Roberts rose to speak. "In view of the state's concession, Your Honor, we have nothing further. However, we believe the state should be prevented from bringing a second indictment. The dismissal should be with prejudice."

"No, Mr. Roberts. I am dismissing the indictment without prejudice. I cannot predict how the state will proceed from here, but nothing in my ruling prohibits the state from proceeding before the grand jury with a properly worded indictment. Court is adjourned."

"All rise!" commanded the bailiff, and Judge Vesely departed the courtroom.

Scott turned to Grady and asked, "How soon before the next grand jury convenes?"

"There is a session scheduled sometime this week. I'm not sure of the day. How soon can you have the witnesses ready?"

"I have all the necessary witnesses on standby right now," said Scott. "I can have them here on a couple hours notice."

"I think we can do it. Go to my office; I'll meet you there as soon as I can clear it with Nick." Grady and Scott gathered their notes and briefcases and began to walk out. When Scott reached the back of the courtroom, Jennifer was standing by the door.

"Scott, think we could meet at the Library later today? I'd like to hear all about this when you have a chance. I have a meeting with my study group at four but should be through by six. See you there at six or so?"

"Sure, six," said Scott, and he hurried down the corridor and took the elevator to Grady's office.

CHAPTER 13

Jennifer was already at the Library when Scott arrived. She was examining the books on the shelves that surrounded the large room. The shelves were organized by law subject area in alphabetical order, clockwise around the room: Administrative Law, Advocacy, Appellate Practice, Bankruptcy, Business Law—dozens of different subject areas. The vast majority of the books were donated by students—many from graduating students who never wanted to see a law school book again. Professors donated their extra copies, and sales representatives from law book publishers frequently stopped by with recent editions when visiting the school. Jaak always treated the bearer to some special hospitality at the bar.

"I see you're admiring Jaak's law book collection," Scott said.

"Yes, I've seen these shelves every time I've been here but never looked to see just what was on them. This is impressive. Most of the books recommended by my professors are right here. Who maintains the Library's library?"

"Willard Gentry. He runs the acquisition section of the school's library. This is his hobby—I guess it's his only outside activity. He has a severe speech impediment and some other physical problems, but he's one super librarian. See that small desk over by the bar? That's his catalog desk."

"You mean all these books are cataloged?"

"Every one."

Scott saw Juri across the room, standing behind the bar waving at Scott to come over. "I see Juri is calling, and I could use a beer. How about you, what will you have?"

"I'll have a glass of iced tea." They walked over to the bar and arrived just as Juri pushed a mug of beer toward Scott.

"On the house?" joked Scott.

"No, on *Scott*. But I put sixteen ounces in that twelve-ounce mug because you're special. And because you always bring beautiful girls to brighten this place up. Jennifer, you're Scott's third this week, but by far the best looking. Right, Scott?"

"Juri, that's a loaded, unfair question, and you know it. But, if an answer is required, the answer is 'yes.'"

"Right answer," said Juri. "Now, you two sit down; I've got a good one."

"Do we have a choice?" Scott asked. He motioned for Jennifer to take a seat at one of the bar stools.

"This lady enters the drug store," Juri began. "Steps up to the pharmacy counter and rings the bell. Pharmacist comes out and asks, 'What can I do for you?' Lady says, 'I want some arsenic. I'm going to poison my husband.'" Juri took a quick step backward and brought a frown to his face. His jokes were always animated.

"Pharmacist says, 'Lady, I can't help you with that, and you shouldn't be talking like that.' She says, 'Well, I've got a photo of him in bed with your wife.'" And with that, Juri stepped forward with a smile on his face. "Pharmacist says, 'You didn't tell me you had a prescription.'"

They all laughed, none heartier than Juri. Scott ordered iced tea for Jennifer. When the tea was delivered, they picked up their drinks and moved to a nearby table.

Scott told Jennifer all about the problem with the indictment. "We're going to take it to another grand jury later this week; maybe I can redeem myself for screwing up."

"You think it was your fault?"

"Sure. I should have caught the error. But I was so wrapped up in the process of proving the case, I missed it. I guess the tree was hidden by the forest. It was my case to prosecute, so, yes, my responsibility. I'm just glad they're going to give me another chance."

Scott and Jennifer sat and quietly talked. The album *Blue Is Green* was playing in the background. When the vocalist, Tierney Sutton, began to sing "Autumn Leaves," they quit talking and just listened.

"Juri has good taste in music. That's one sensational voice," Jennifer said when the song was over. She turned and surveyed the room. "I wonder where Jaak is; I haven't seen him tonight."

"He has some civic club meeting on Wednesdays. Something going on about every night with Jaak," said Scott.

Jennifer looked at her watch; it was a little after seven. "Nicole's bringing over some sandwiches at seven-thirty. I've got to run. Keep me posted on your trial."

Jennifer got into her car as the sun was beginning to set. The rain that had soaked Savannah for the past few days had departed. The air was still humid but felt fresh and clean. She rolled her windows down and enjoyed the cool breeze. She was home in about fifteen minutes. Most of the spaces on the street were filled; she felt lucky to find a parking space not far from her apartment.

A car, two spaces down from where she was parked, caught Jennifer's eye, perhaps because it was a Camry like hers, or because it was the only one that was occupied. There was a man inside, sitting in the driver's seat, facing forward and away from her so that she could only see the back of his head. She grabbed her backpack and went inside. She looked out a window, and there was the man pulling out of his parking space. As he was driving off, he turned and briefly looked at her apartment. He looked familiar . . . she wondered if she had seen him before. And then she recalled: "I've got a Camry just like yours, except it's black and two years older." "Oh, no . . . no," she said quietly to herself. Even the possibility that the man could have been Craig filled her with fear. Then she saw Nicole pulling into the space just vacated. The sight was a relief.

Nicole brought in a covered plate of sandwiches, and Jennifer turned on the coffee maker. They sat down at the kitchen table and began comparing class notes and briefs. Jennifer did not mention to Nicole what she had just seen. It would be such a long and involved story, and they had a lot of studying planned for the evening. Besides, she thought, this was her problem, not Nicole's. But the disturbing view of the black Camry remained in her mind.

CHAPTER 14
Thursday, August 24

Professor Fred Leyton was seated in his office Thursday morning, going over some class assignments. Leyton had been at Savannah Law for four years and was head of the Trial Advocacy Department. It was an assignment for which he was well qualified. He had a law degree from the University of Florida, five years of experience in the litigation department of Holland and Knight, and a master's degree in trial advocacy from Temple Law School.

There was a knock on his door. He looked up and saw Denis Nolan entering.

"Hi, Denis. Ready for the new semester?"

"Not quite. Still grading last spring's exams," Denis said with a grin. "You know how Channing is—wants to get grades in before the students graduate. We need to straighten out her priorities."

"Drop those long essay questions, Denis. What you need is a good multiple-choice exam."

"Tried that. Takes too long to write the questions. I think this semester I'll mark the steps out my back door with A through F, throw the papers, and see where they land. Law school teaching would be a great job if it weren't for students and exams." Both Denis and Fred laughed at his joke, and then Denis added, "But I didn't come in to complain. I came in about your student trial competition program. I'm wondering if I can be of any assistance. I'm interested in what you've been doing. And I now have a special interest."

"Special interest?" asked Fred.

"Yes, a very special interest. I want Savannah Law to have one of the premier trial advocacy programs in the country, and I want to be dean here when it happens. If you haven't heard, I'm putting my name in for the deanship. I believe this school can vault into the national scene in trial advocacy under your leadership. And I'm hoping you agree."

Fred was taken by surprise and hesitated before replying. He had known Denis for four years and had never heard him express any interest in trial advocacy.

"That's my goal, too. And the only way that can really be done is by our students competing in—and winning—trial competitions. That's how Stetson keeps its first-place position for trial advocacy in the *U.S. News and World Report* ratings year after year—they keep winning."

Fred paused. He realized Denis seemed to be more focused on two trophies in the bookcase than on what Fred was saying.

"The trophy on the left is from the Southeast Regional last winter. We were in the finals," said Fred. "The semi-finalist one on the right is from last fall's William Daniel competition in Atlanta."

"That Daniel competition . . . it's scheduled again in a couple of months, isn't it?" asked Denis.

"Yes, first weekend in November. Nate Grant from the U.S. Attorney's Office will be coaching. He coached one of our teams last year, and he's very good."

"Fred, I wonder if I could help with that competition. As I said, I'm going to make a serious run for the deanship here, and I want to get up to speed on all the activities at the school. I'm sure you already have the advocates picked for that competition, but maybe I could help with selecting some good witnesses. I know at least half the students here. Perhaps Grant could use some help in making sure that the witnesses are prepped and available for practice."

Fred remained puzzled at Denis's new interest in the trial competition teams. He knew that Denis had many friends among the faculty, and he also knew of the family connection to the Board of Trustees. Although he had not given it much thought, perhaps Denis had a good shot at the deanship. It would be good to have his support. A large budget was required each year for competition travel. That was a good reason to take Denis up on his offer.

"Of course, Denis. Any support you feel you can give. I'll call Grant and tell him of your offer. I'm sure he will be pleased. But I must warn you—Nate Grant is driven. He will be on campus almost every night getting that team ready, and he will expect the witnesses to be ready and on time. It's a big commitment of your time, Denis. Do you really want to get involved in this?"

"I wouldn't be here otherwise. I'm serious about the deanship, and I have high aspirations for Savannah Law. Fred, you can count on me backing your program. And I hope you will be backing me. Can I count on your support?"

Fred was uncomfortable with this conversation. He had nothing against Denis; he considered him to be a friend. But law school "dean politics" was something new to him. Is this the way it works—faculty members lining up support and getting commitments from colleagues? Fred had no experience with this process. But something simply did not seem right. Denis's eyes were now focused on Fred, and time was up. He needed to respond *now*.

The phone rang. Fred reached for it. "Hello." He was silent as he listened to the caller. "I'm in a conference with a colleague right now. Could I return your call in a few minutes?" Fred was silent again. Then he turned to Denis and put his hand over the phone. "It's one of our student interns. She's in trial downtown, and she has a problem. The judge has given her a ten-minute recess. She needs my advice. Denis, please excuse me, but I must take this call . . . in private. I'm sorry."

"I understand," said Denis. As he walked to the door, he turned to Fred and said, "Please, let Grant know I'll be there to help with the witnesses, and I'll call him tomorrow. OK?"

Fred lifted his left hand, which was covering the phone receiver and gave Denis a thumbs up as he walked away. Fred was relieved their conversation was over.

CHAPTER 15
Friday, August 25

Scott arrived at Jennifer's apartment Friday afternoon at six sharp. He pressed the door bell, and a few moments later, Jennifer was standing in the doorway wearing black spandex shorts and a black pullover top. Her blonde hair was pulled back in a ponytail. Her eyes sparkled as she welcomed Scott with a broad smile. Scott took a step back from the door.

"Wow, you look great!" he said.

Jennifer had a silk, yellow-gold jacket in her hand and began to put it on. As she did, Scott noticed an embroidered bee on the jacket. And just below the bee was the word, "Bees."

"Is that a team outfit?"

"It was—volleyball, but it's mine now. You did say there would be volleyball, didn't you?"

"Yes. You don't have to play." Then he stepped forward, put both hands on the sides of her shoulders and looked her up and down. "But you are obviously ready to play!"

"I am. That's my sport. I wasn't a star, but I was pretty good. I made the varsity. This is our gear; they let us keep it."

"Varsity? They have *varsity* sports at SCAD?"

Jennifer curled her lips, expressing mock hurt. "Of course. We're in the Florida Sun Conference of the NAIA. No football, but we have baseball, basketball, cross-country, golf, soccer, tennis, swimming, and volleyball. And we have an equestrian team. Did your school—football-crazed Alabama—have an equestrian team?"

Jennifer knew that Scott played baseball at Alabama. She knew he would take her jabbing remarks about his alma mater in jest, but at the same time, she was serious and perhaps a bit indignant. Savannah College of Art and Design had an excellent athletic program. Not big time nationally, but the Bees did well in the Florida Sun Conference.

"Well, I guess you're right—I don't know much about SCAD athletics." This evening was not getting off the way he had hoped.

"We should be able to get in a couple volleyball games before dark. If you are ready, let's go."

"Let me get my cap," said Jennifer, as she left the doorway and went to a hat rack where several baseball caps were displayed. She picked one, purple with gold lettering.

Scott read the lettering on the cap out loud. There were two embroidered lines. The top line read, "One half haughty." The bottom line read, "One half naughty." Then, sort of as an afterthought, Scott merely added, "Cute." But he realized that he had just experienced the top half.

They walked out to the street where Scott's Camaro was parked. The sky was overcast, and a light mist had dampened his windshield. He hoped the rain held off. There were still a couple of hours left before sunset, and he wanted to see this haughty girl's athletic skills.

As Scott pulled away from the curb, he asked about her classes. He was especially interested in her Property class. The scene of their meeting Sunday with Professor Nolan was still floating around in his mind. He wondered if Professor Nolan was eyeing her in class as he did in Thomas Courthouse. He would not ask, but maybe Jennifer would give him a clue.

"I like my classes. All except Research and Writing. No matter how hard we work, we can never complete all they put on us. I spend more time on R & W than any other class and for less credit hours. Explain that, Scott."

"Can't. It was the same when I took it. I have a friend at Emory, and he says the same thing. It just goes with the course, apparently at every school."

They discussed a few of her courses, but Jennifer never mentioned Professor Nolan. Scott turned left on Whitaker Street and drove south. Whitaker would take them to Victory Drive, a split highway with a wide median embraced by a canopy of moss-draped oaks. It was not the shortest route but one Scott often took to Tybee Island. The median was lined with tall Sabal palms towering over eye-high azaleas. The beautiful old homes that graced both sides of the street were surrounded by colorful shrubs and flowers and perfectly manicured lawns. It was spectacular each March when the azaleas were in full bloom, but even on a misty afternoon in August, it presented a vista of unsurpassed natural beauty.

Jennifer gazed out the window, fascinated by the sight of the oaks, palms, and azaleas that seemed to be sliding backwards as the Camaro continued east on Victory Drive. She turned to Scott and said, "Victory Drive is gorgeous, even in the fall. Lady Astor obviously never made this drive."

"Lady Astor? I've heard the name, but who was she?"

"She was a woman from Virginia who became the first female member of the British Parliament."

"And you say she obviously never made this drive?"

"Right. She visited Savannah right after World War II and is remembered for remarking that 'Savannah is a beautiful lady with a dirty face.' If she had seen the beauty of Victory Drive, she would have overlooked the part about the dirty face."

"I expect that comment upset quite a few people."

"She was famous for upsetting people. She was quite a socialite in England but also quite a politician. She and Winston Churchill had a number of verbal battles. There's a story that she once said to Churchill, 'If you were my husband, I'd put arsenic in your coffee,' to which Churchill responded, 'And if I were your husband, I'd drink it!'"

Scott laughed. "You know, I've heard that story somewhere but didn't know it involved Lady Astor and Churchill. Both obviously had sharp wits. The British would like that, but I bet the people of Savannah didn't appreciate her wit."

"They didn't," said Jennifer. "But some give her statement credit for starting serious thoughts about the city and its future. Some say it played an important role in the Savannah historic preservation movement. The movement got underway shortly after her visit, but it may be just speculation to say her comment played a part."

"Your school played a big role in the preservation movement, didn't it?" asked Scott.

"We've restored a lot of buildings downtown. They are scattered all over the Historic District, and many of them now serve as classrooms."

"And equestrian facilities . . . and volleyball courts. But I'd rather hear about you. Did you play in high school? Was volleyball a new sport for you?"

They drove on toward the beach, through the town of Thunderbolt and over the bridge spanning the Wilmington River. Great expanses of saltwater marshes appeared on both sides of the highway. Scott listened attentively as Jennifer recounted some of her high school and college activities. Yes, she played high school volleyball, beginning in her sophomore year. Scott interrupted occasionally to get more details. He loved the sound of her voice, and the sparkle in her eyes, as she spoke. He had a difficult time keeping his eyes on the road. This was turning out to be a perfect evening.

They arrived at the pavilion at Memorial Park at a quarter to seven. A small crowd was already there. Two volleyball games were in action. Scott introduced Jennifer to a couple of friends at the pavilion who were presiding over food and drink preparations. Then they walked over to one of the courts and sat on a nearby bench. Jennifer was curious as she viewed the various colors, designs, and pictures on the players' T-shirts. All had the same logo on front—a blue football on a red background and the words "Savannah College of Law" in white lettering. But the backs were different, all with some strange animal picture. Jennifer turned to Scott and said, "What's with the T-shirts?"

"I'm surprised you haven't asked what's with the party. This is the biggest, or one of the biggest, of the semester. Flag football is the major sport at Savannah Law—usually eight to ten teams competing each semester. The different T-shirts are for the different teams, and the teams are named for the nastiest, meanest, most lethal animals in the universe."

"Yes," said Jennifer, pointing to a young man dressed in Levi's and a white T-shirt, standing in the back court ready to serve. "There's a 'Strawberry Frog.'" The shirt photo was of a poison dart frog, in bright strawberry color. Over the photo were the words "STRAWBERRY FROG." Underneath were the words, "LEAN, MEAN, HOPPING MACHINE."

"The Frogs were spring semester's first-place team," Scott said. "They party free today. They also get to plan the menu. The rest of the teams pick up the tab. And the last-place team prepares and serves the food. That was the 'Cnidarians.' There's one." Scott was pointing.

Jennifer looked over at the man, who was carrying a box of food. He was wearing a T-shirt with a picture of an orange-colored sea urchin shaped something like a jellyfish. It had long, sharp, green tentacles protruding in a menacing fashion. Underneath were the words, "SIMPLE ANIMALS WITH A STING!" Then she noticed another player with a deadly looking spider on his back. Above the spider was written "FUNNEL-WEB SPIDERS" and below, "SPECIALISTS IN MUSCLE PAIN & CEREBRAL EDEMA."

"Must be a pre-med student that didn't get into med school," said Jennifer.

"We should be able to get in a game soon," said Scott. "Here, the volleyball games are played to fifteen points. The winning team stays on the court for the next six challengers—guys or gals. Ready to see if your game is still there?"

"I'm ready to see how *rusty* I've really gotten since last fall."

The crowd was getting larger, and other "dangerous animals" were appearing. A "Porcupine" walked by with the words, "WE ARE JUST A BUNCH OF PRICKS."

As Jennifer was observing the crowd, she spotted a friend she knew from SCAD, Kira Courtman. Kira was one year behind Jennifer at SCAD, and they had taken a couple of classes together. Jennifer got up from the bench, turned to Scott, and said, "Come on, I want you to meet a friend." Scott followed, and Jennifer made the introductions. Bill Anderson, one of Scott's friends, was Kira's date. Bill held his hands out, palms up, and pointed them at Scott.

The three looked at Scott, and for the first time it dawned on Jennifer—Scott was the only guy at the picnic not wearing a T-shirt with one of those weird animals.

"Yes, Scott, where's your T-shirt?" said Jennifer. "Aren't you on a team?"

"I am," replied Scott. And with that he removed his top shirt and tossed it to a nearby bench. Standing erect and playfully flexing his biceps, he proclaimed, "I'm a proud 'Pigdog'!" He then turned around to reveal the back of his T-shirt. A strange two-headed animal, featuring a pig's head and a dog's head attached to the body of an animal bearing little resemblance to either. Above the weird animal appeared four words:

RUDE
CLASSLESS
BOORISH
SLOBS

Scott recited the words out loud, and then added, "Which means 'Pigdogs' will make great lawyers." They all laughed. Then Scott heard a familiar voice behind him. "We'll test that soon, if you can get that sorry case together. Vandera wants a speedy trial."

It was Jeff Swenson. Jeff turned to face Jennifer.

"Jen, didn't I warn you about this rude, classless, boorish, slob? You really shouldn't be seen with him. It will quickly ruin your reputation on campus. He's bad."

Jennifer recognized Jeff, who was dressed in his team's dark-green T-shirt. He was facing her, so she could not see his team's "terrifying animal."

"Hi, Jeff. But this is the best I could do—no one else asked." She laughed and gave Scott a tight hug around the waist. Then she whispered in his ear, out of the hearing of anyone: "Are you *bad*? I hope so."

Scott was caught by surprise, but quickly recovered. "Test me," he whispered back.

Scott looked over at one of the volleyball courts and saw a game had just finished. The losers were walking off, and the winners were raising their arms in victory and yelling, "Who's next?"

"Come on, Jen, let's get in the game. Jeff, I'll see you in court."

As Jeff turned to walk away, Jennifer saw the picture on the back of his T-shirt. It was a large gray whale. Over the picture, in large black letters was "SPERM WHALES." Under the picture was "SIZE DOES MATTER."

Scott saw Jennifer staring at the back of Jeff's T-shirt. "Yep, typical Jeff," said Scott. "He designs his team's shirts. The league banned the one he designed last year, so that's the best he could do this year. Or, more accurately, the worst he could do and still field a team."

Jennifer had a blast on the court. Scott saw that she really was good. They stayed on the court until someone came to inform them that the kitchen would be shutting down soon. The sun was setting, and no one seemed to be able to find the switch to turn on the court lights. Both teams walked to the pavilion.

Scott and Jennifer sat down at a table with some of Scott's teammates to enjoy good food and conversation. There were funny stories of law professors and former students, high school and college foibles, and disastrous adventures in foreign countries, mixed occasionally with career plans and aspirations. The evening was passing quickly.

About nine o'clock, Scott took Jennifer by the hand and stood. "Excuse us," he said, to the others at the table. And that's all he said. He picked up his long-sleeved shirt and motioned for Jennifer to pick up her jacket. Jennifer followed his lead, and hand-in-hand they walked to the beach.

The sun was now completely down, and a quarter moon was rising over the Atlantic, partly obscured by some scattered clouds. It was a beautiful evening. The heavy rain that had appeared earlier in the day had passed through, and even the slight mist that had fallen a few hours earlier had disappeared. They walked for several minutes on the sand, just a few feet from the water that was quietly washing ashore in thin ripples.

Jennifer was the first to speak. She stopped, looked up at Scott, and said, "I'm so glad to be with you. This has been a perfect evening."

Scott placed his right hand on her chin and pulled her lips up to his. They held their kiss as Scott placed both arms around her and pulled her close. They lingered in this embrace until Jennifer pulled back and said, "Let's go back to my place. This uniform is sweaty and sandy. Do you mind?"

Scott made no verbal response. He kissed her again, took her hand, and they walked back to Scott's car. Scott could see dark clouds approaching, and by the time they reached the car, the quarter moon was no longer visible.

A slight drizzle began to fall before they left Tybee Island. It was a dark, half-hour drive back to Savannah, and by the time they arrived at Jennifer's apartment, it was raining heavily again. Scott found a parking spot on the street close to her apartment. He did not have an umbrella, but the rain was of no concern to either. Jennifer put her cap on, and Scott said, "One, two, three, go!" They made a mad dash for Jennifer's front door, which was protected from the rain by the wide stairway that led to the second floor.

Once safely there, Jennifer reached into a pocket of her jacket, found the key, and handed it to Scott. He was about to turn the key when he noticed the lettering on her cap: "One half haughty, One half naughty."

"Well, Jen, which half is it now?"

"Let's go in and find out."

Even in the darkness, Jennifer's eyes sparkled as she smiled. She waited for Scott's reaction. He brought his lips down to hers, and with his hands under her shoulders and his palms firmly on her back, he pulled her toward him. They stood in this embrace, protected from the rain and unmindful of the headlights from the traffic passing nearby.

Scott kept her firmly against him, their lips meeting and their tongues touching eagerly. Scott lowered his palms from her back, slowly moving them downward and pulling her into him.

She did not resist. She pushed her breasts against his chest and sighed. "I think I already know," she said.

The passion in her voice made Scott weak. His heart was pounding as he fumbled with the keys to open the door. Jennifer took his hand and led him into her living room. She found a small table lamp and turned it on.

Next to the lamp was a phone, and the phone's answering machine was flashing and beeping. Her urge was to ignore it. It could not be important—certainly nothing as urgent as the need she now felt. She thought it was probably Nicole. Nicole had promised to call about getting together on Saturday for a study session. But if she didn't answer, the message machine would continue to send out its annoying signal every few seconds.

She pushed the "play" button. It was her mother's voice, and it was stressed. "Jennifer, it's Mom. I'm at the Hilton Head Medical Center. It's 8:30 Friday night. I drove your father here—to the emergency room—about an hour ago. He was in extreme pain in his stomach and chest area. They are running a number of tests on him now. I'll call you again when I know more." That was all, and there had been no second call.

Jennifer stood by the phone, stunned for the moment, but she did not hesitate. "Scott, I have to go. You do understand?"

"Of course. I'm so sorry," said Scott. He wanted to say a number of things: that she should wait until the morning; that her father was being taken care of; that her mother would not want her to be driving home at night, and certainly not in the rain. All of this was good advice, but he knew—unquestionably *knew*—she would ignore it, so he just said, "I'll help you pack. You get your things from the bedroom; I'll put your books and laptop in your car." Scott knew the classes she was taking and the books that went with each class. He placed them in her backpack. He knew that there was a good chance Jennifer would not be returning the following week, but, hopefully, it would not be as serious as her mother's call suggested.

Jennifer quickly emerged from her bedroom with a small suitcase. "I'm ready," she said. Her car keys were in her hand.

Scott opened the front door, grabbed the laptop and backpack in one hand and a large umbrella in the other, and waited for her under the stoop. Jennifer followed, carrying her suitcase. She locked her door, and Scott opened the umbrella to protect her from the now steady rain. Scott placed everything on the back seat, and Jennifer quickly settled behind the wheel. He folded the umbrella and handed it to Jennifer through the open window. Tears appeared in her eyes, but she smiled. Scott bent down, gave her a quick kiss on her lips, and began to withdraw his head from the window.

"No, Scott," she said, as she reached out and pulled his head toward her with her left hand. She gave him a passionate kiss, released her hand from his head, and, still smiling, said, "I'll call you."

Before Scott could respond, she was pulling out of the parking space.

As Scott drove back to his apartment, he kept wondering about the advice he should have given. Was there something else he could have done to help? He had the same sinking feeling he had when he saw her riding off in the tow truck the previous Friday night.

CHAPTER 16

Jennifer had driven to Hilton Head many times. She knew the shortcut from her apartment to Talmadge Memorial Bridge, which would take her across the Savannah River into South Carolina. But she had driven only a few blocks when her car sputtered. The engine seemed to die for just a moment and then ran smoothly again. The engine hesitated a couple of more times, and she knew she needed to see a mechanic. The car had to get her to Hilton Head.

Then it occurred to her: as much as she had tried to forget the events of the previous Friday night, she remembered Marvin's Foreign Auto in Garden City. It was only a few miles away, and it was open at night. The tow-truck driver had said it was open until ten, sometimes later. It was just a little after ten now. She bypassed the entry to Talmadge Bridge and drove to Garden City.

In about ten minutes, she was at Marvin's Garage. It was a well-lit, modern, three-bay facility. Two of the bays were occupied, but the one closest to the office was open. It was still raining, so Jennifer drove her car into the empty bay. The engine was running smoothly now, and she wished she had just taken the bridge and gotten on her way. But she was here, and she felt she should at least have the problem checked by one of the mechanics. And she hoped she would not have to wait long.

A white-haired gentleman in mechanics clothes met her as she opened her door. "Don" and "Marvin's Garage" were written on the front of his shirt above one of the pockets. "Can I help you?" he asked.

"I had a problem a little while ago. My engine was skipping. It cut off suddenly a couple of times and then started up again. It seems to be running OK now, but I've got to get to Hilton Head tonight—my dad's in the hospital there. I want to make sure there's nothing really wrong with my car. Could you check it out for me?"

Don got into the driver's seat, raced the engine, and listened. He got out and walked over to Jennifer, who was standing in front of the car. She had been listening carefully also. Her ears were not trained like a mechanic's, but she heard nothing unusual.

"It sounds OK now," he said. "Maybe you just got some water on the spark-plug harness or one of its contacts. I don't think it's serious. Of course, it could be any number of things—PCV valve, oxygen sensor, or even the catalytic converter could be clogged. If it gives you any more trouble, bring it in, and we'll run some tests."

"So you think I'm safe to drive to Hilton Head tonight?"

"Do you really have to drive over there tonight? You could run into some heavy rain."

"Yes, I've got to go. My dad was taken to the hospital a couple of hours ago."

"I'm real sorry to hear that," said Don. "Make sure you try to avoid deep puddles."

"I will," Jennifer said. "What do I owe you for your time tonight?"

"Oh, nothing. Nothing at all. I just hope you have a safe trip and find your dad's OK."

"Thanks," Jennifer said, as she got into her car and cranked it up. The engine sounded fine.

She buckled her seat belt and began to back out of the bay. As she backed, she had a clear view of all the bays to her front. In the farthest bay from the office, she saw a man standing and looking her way. He was wearing a dark cap or bandana. In the rain, she could not make out his features clearly, but he looked vaguely familiar. And he was standing next to what appeared to be a black Camry. Apparently, he had been working on the vehicle, as its hood was up. When she turned her car to get back on the street, her headlights revealed a clearer view. No . . . no, it couldn't be, she thought. I'm just still upset, maybe even paranoid. She was relieved that the vehicle stayed in the bay and did not follow her as she headed for Talmadge Memorial Bridge.

She was about halfway across the bridge when the rain began to slacken. It had not stopped completely, but visibility was much better. She hoped it would stop. She did not like driving in the rain or the swishing sound of the windshield wipers. Her thoughts were now constantly on her dad. Her mother was not an alarmist; she would not have called unless she had great concern. Jennifer turned on her radio. It was tuned to 97.3 KISS FM, featuring mostly top-forty songs. Perhaps the music would help ease her mind.

Her car seemed to be running smoothly, but it seemed that the acceleration was not fully responsive. She pressed the gas pedal firmly, and the car seemed to hesitate before accelerating. Then it sputtered momentarily, like it had earlier. She pressed it firmly again and got the same response and another sputter or skip. This time it was slightly more severe. She decided not to test it again, as it seemed to aggravate the problem.

She crossed over into South Carolina on US 17. She passed SCAD's Equestrian and Athletic Center on the right. This was an often traveled and familiar route for Jennifer. It would take her to SC 170 and then to a shortcut to US 278, the main highway into Hilton Head.

As she turned onto SC 170, she noticed that the vehicle immediately behind her also turned. The rain had now stopped, but the roads were still wet. Because of the earlier acceleration problem and the wet roads, she was traveling only about forty-five miles per hour. She expected the car behind her to pass, but it did not; it continued to tailgate her. She hoped the car would stay on SC 170 when she turned onto the shortcut. However, when she turned, it continued to stay right behind her.

The short cut was a narrow two-lane asphalt highway that went through a rural area. On both sides of the highway were pastures, palmetto trees, small creeks, and swamp land. It was a lonely, desolate road but an easy one to travel—no stop lights or stop signs and very lightly traveled this time of night. A few farm houses could be seen, well off the road.

No other cars were on the highway going in either direction, so Jennifer slowed a bit to give the car an opportunity to pass. It did, but as soon as it passed and moved in front of her, it cut its speed, and she had to slow down also. It slowed to about forty miles an hour. Strange, she thought.

Jennifer was annoyed; she needed to get to the hospital. Despite her earlier problem with her gas pedal, she decided to press down hard and pass, but when she did, the vehicle ahead increased its speed, and she was not able to pass. Then, for the first time, she noticed: it was a Toyota, a black Camry. Fear now displaced her worry. Could it be him? Was that him back at Marvin's Garage . . . in the far stall, listening to her conversation with the mechanic? She recalled that she told Don she had to get to Hilton Head. In fact, she recalled saying it twice. He was a tow-truck operator. He would know the area well and the exact route she would take.

It *was* him. She now knew that for sure. But as long as she could keep traveling, she was safe. At the same time, she thought it best to get her cell phone ready. She already had it programmed to dial 911 with the push of a single button. Her handbag was beside her on the passenger side, and she opened it to get her phone. Then she remembered: it was on her bedside table being charged. She never went anywhere in her car without her cell phone, but in her rush to leave, she simply forgot it.

The black Camry was now traveling only thirty miles per hour, and Jennifer was staying a safe distance back. She wondered just what he was planning—just how much danger was she in? What sort of evil was he contemplating as he drove? But as long as she kept driving, she was safe. It was now almost eleven o'clock, and few cars had passed—none going in her direction. She wanted to see lights approaching from the rear, but she saw none.

Jennifer had traveled this road many times but never late at night. She knew there was a small "quick stop" food and gas station on the road, but she could not remember exactly where or how far. If she could just get to that station. But would it be open this late? Her engine had skipped twice as they drove at the slower speed, but it quickly recovered. She maintained her distance of five or six car lengths, and the vehicle ahead continued at the same thirty miles an hour.

Then she saw it: the lights of the "quick stop" station just ahead at a cross road. She had made it!

Jennifer was greatly relieved to see the black Camry proceed past the station. She turned in and stopped in front of the last gas pump. She could feel her hands shaking as she turned off the engine. Through a large glass window in the storefront, she could see a man and woman inside. They looked to be in their sixties or early seventies. One was sweeping, and the other was behind the cash register, apparently counting cash and making notes.

Jennifer wasn't sure what she would do next or who she should call. The sheriff? The South Carolina Highway Patrol? Who covered this rural area? She was opening her car door to go into the store when she saw the lights of another vehicle pull up and stop at the gas pump behind her. It was the black Camry. And yes, *it was him.*

She ran from her car to the store, opened the door, and shouted, "Please, help me!" Her eyes were darting from the man to the woman and back again.

"What is it, child?" asked the woman, looking up from behind the cash register.

The man put down his broom, and walked over to where Jennifer was standing. "Yes, what is it?" he repeated.

"That man there! That man out there! He once took me . . . kidnapped me . . . in Savannah . . . in his tow truck, and I'm sure . . . I'm sure he will do it again. Please, the sheriff, the highway patrol, someone. Please. Please." Jennifer knew her outburst sounded like the confused rambling of a crazed person, and she wished she could have been more in control and coherent. She was on the verge of tears, but she was trying hard to compose herself.

"I'm sorry," she said, in a much calmer voice. In the store, she now felt safe. "It is a complicated story, but this man knows me and has followed me from Savannah. I'm on my way to Hilton Head. He tailgated me for a while and then passed in front of me and would not let me pass. He works for a tow-truck company in Savannah. He has been stalking me. Tonight he saw me and followed me. I'm afraid. Could you please use your phone, or let me use your phone, to call someone?"

The man went to the door and opened it. Only Jennifer's car was parked at the pumps. He then turned to face Jennifer.

"There's no man out there—just one car. Is that your car?"

Jennifer looked. Only her car was visible. "Yes, that's my car, but he must be close by. Maybe he moved to the parking area behind the store."

Without further conversation, the man walked out of the store and disappeared. He was back soon. "There is no car anywhere around, except your car and my car, so I don't know what the sheriff could do. My wife and I have to close up now. We were closing as you drove up. Do you need gas? We can wait for that, I suppose. I really don't know how long it would take one of the sheriff's cars to get here. We've had to call them a couple of times. They usually arrive in fifteen or twenty minutes, maybe a bit longer at night. I have the number if you want to call. You are free to wait there by the pump until they get here, but we have to close up and go. My boss says our insurance policy requires us to close up at eleven every night."

"I understand," Jennifer said. But she needed some time to think about her options. "And, yes, I would like to get some gas."

"We'll wait 'til you finish," the man said.

However, he immediately began turning off some of the lights inside and the big outside sign with the gas prices. Outside, only the lights on the pumps were now on.

Jennifer walked to her car, began filling her tank, and considered the situation. Her options were quite limited. She could either proceed to Hilton Head, hoping she had seen the last of him, or call the sheriff and wait in the dark. Assuming a deputy eventually arrived, what could he do? Her stalker was nowhere around.

It took less than ten dollars to fill her gas tank. She removed twelve dollars from her wallet, walked back to the now darkened store, and handed the money to the lady, who was standing by the counter, waiting. "Thank you for your trouble, ma'am."

"You be careful, young lady," said the man.

And with that, he turned off the last light, and all three walked out of the store together. Jennifer got into her car, fastened her seat belt, and started the engine. The engine sounded good, and there were no warning lights. She saw the man and woman get into their car and drive away.

The rain had completely stopped, and the sky was clearing. A few low clouds were moving swiftly across the quarter moon. Except for her recent experience, and the relentless worry and fear that it was now causing, it was a perfect night for driving. If all went as expected, she would be at the emergency room at the hospital in less than an hour. Finding one's way around Hilton Head Island was not easy for an outsider, but Jennifer had lived there during most of her recent summers, and she knew the area well. Just last June, she had her ankle x-rayed at the hospital after twisting it in a ladder accident. She would have no trouble finding her way to the emergency room. Even though it would be after midnight, she knew her mother would still be there. She started her car and drove onto the narrow blacktop road.

She had driven only a few miles when she got a wake-up call to remind her that she was a long way from a safe haven at Hilton Head. Her car sputtered. She pressed the gas pedal. It hesitated, then quickly caught up to run smoothly, then hesitated again. She pressed hard. But the engine stopped completely. She was now coasting and losing speed rapidly. No matter how hard she pumped, the engine refused to cooperate. She pulled onto the small confining shoulder of the narrow asphalt road. There was not enough room to completely pull off the road without going into a grassy ditch. The car came to a complete stop.

The cloud cover had receded, and from the light of the quarter moon and her headlights, she could see scrub palmetto, fetterbush, and pond pines lining both sides of the highway, extending as far as the car lights carried. There were no houses, no open fields—not even a sign or a fence—anywhere in her sight. And there was no traffic. She had not passed a single vehicle since leaving the store.

Jennifer was at once frustrated, frightened, and angry. Except for the recent problem with the starter, her Camry had never given her a single problem. It was still under warranty, and she had carefully attended to its maintenance. And now, in the middle of a desolate stretch of the South Carolina low country in the middle of the night, it stops. Completely. In her frustration, she pounded the steering wheel with both hands. Her mind was completely void of anything she could do to end what was turning into a nightmare. She had no cell phone. She had no knowledge of automobile mechanics or what could be wrong with her car. And even if she did, she had no tools, no spare parts. She did not even have a flashlight. She needed a tow truck but had no means to call for one. And the very thought of a tow truck rekindled the fear that really had never left.

Jennifer's fear and frustration were mixed with worry and concern for her father. She needed to be there with her mother. She tried to start her car again. She heard the starter grind, but the engine would not catch. Never had she experienced such a complete state of helplessness. She turned off her radio; it was a distraction, and she needed to think. She turned on her emergency flashers and checked to see that her doors were locked. Her mind was engulfed in fear, both from what she knew and from what she did not know.

With her car lights off, the outside view revealed only a vague outline of the dark road. The pine trees and palmettos were no longer visible, but every now and then, she could see a faint flash from a firefly. She rolled down her window, and the eerie, lifeless silence outside increased her fright. She rolled up the window and checked again to ensure that the doors were locked. Then, with a sigh of complete frustration, she sat back forcibly in her seat and placed her hands against her cheeks. "Think," she said to herself. She tried but nothing changed.

She glanced up and into her rear-view mirror. What first seemed to be only a few flashes from distant fireflies was quickly morphing into car headlights. With luck, it could be a sheriff's deputy or highway patrolman. Perhaps a trucker. More likely a motorist returning from a night in Savannah. And, hopefully, sober. But would the vehicle stop? Her emergency lights were blinking. It should be clear that assistance was needed. But, again she wondered, would it stop?

As the vehicle got closer, she could see that it was not a truck. It was a car. A small car, obviously not a patrol car. It pulled up slowly behind Jennifer's Camry and stopped about fifteen feet back. Jennifer turned her head toward the stopped car. Its bright lights made it difficult to see clearly, but someone was getting out. As the person moved toward the front and into the headlights, she could finally see who it was: it was *him*!

The lights from his car illuminated his features. He was wearing a head scarf, similar in shape to the one he was wearing when she first saw him, but this one was black with multiple white Iron Cross images. She noted the dark blue T-shirt, perhaps the same one he was wearing the previous Friday night, and the multicolored armbands of Xs tattooed into his skin in the midportion of his biceps. He was just as she remembered him.

He walked up to the driver's door and looked in. The headlights from his car clearly outlined Jennifer's features.

"I've been looking for you," he said, loud enough to be heard through the closed windows.

Jennifer did not respond. She did not even look at him. She looked straight into the darkness ahead, every muscle in her body tightening with fear.

"I said, I've been looking for you," he repeated.

Jennifer maintained her view and again disregarded him.

"Look, I come to help. I'm trying to be your friend. Are you afraid of me?"

The only sound inside the car was the pounding of Jennifer's heart. She could actually hear it. She wasn't sure of her next move, but she knew she would not respond to anything he said. Not now, not ever.

"OK, I understand. I did scare you last week. But I would never hurt you. I want to help you. I think I know the problem. It's a wire under your dashboard. I know these Camrys inside out. Mine had the same problem a few months ago. Open up. I'll fix it and you can be on your way."

Again, there was no response. But Jennifer, in her heightened state of pure panic, for just a fleeting moment thought that maybe the only safe way out of this was to cooperate.

"I said, I come to help!" He was now shouting. "Open the damn door! I'll drive you to Hilton Head." There was no response.

"Better yet, let's just drive off to a motel in Ridgeland. You would like that. Sure you would. I know you would." He was now slapping the glass of the door. "Are you hearing me? Are you hearing me?" he shouted.

Still the only sound Jennifer made was her heart pounding.

"Do I need to break this window to knock some sense into your fucking head? Do you hear me? Do you hear me? I want to help. You need help. You got no lawyer-boy now to help. You think he's going to drive up and rescue you again? Hell, no! You got me! And I'm gonna break this fucking window if you don't open up!" He continued to slap the window and rattle the door handle.

Jennifer's terror had reached its apogee, and her thoughts, which so far had been paralyzed by fear, were gradually returning. She knew he meant what he said. He would break the window, and he would eventually open the door. But she was determined that she would not be carried off or assaulted without a fight. She reached for the only defensive weapon available, the umbrella that Scott had used in helping her load for her trip. It was resting against the passenger door. It had a steel tip and she would use it. She would stab for the face. She knew she would likely lose in the end, but she would make him pay.

"I'm going to get a hammer. And when I get back, you better have this door open." He slapped the glass once and turned back to his car.

Jennifer turned to watch him go, and as she did, she noticed a car coming toward her from the rear. It was a few hundred yards away. Her mind was now working again, in self-preservation mode. She realized that her tormentor would now have to wait to let the car pass before returning to her car, which was parked with its left tires a foot or two onto the road. The approaching vehicle would surely see her car and veer to the left to avoid a collision. And this would give her a chance. She would open her door just before the car reached her and lean her body out, facing the approaching vehicle. Anyone seeing her face would know this was an emergency—indeed, a desperate plea for help.

As the moment for action approached, she opened the door. Holding on with one hand and waving frantically with the other, she faced the car and yelled with an exaggerated facial expression: "Help meeeee!"

She watched for the car to slow. It did not. And there were no brake lights. It quickly disappeared into the darkness.

She then saw him approaching. He was almost at her open door. She reached with both hands to close the door, and with all the strength she could muster, she slammed it.

She heard an anguished cry. His left hand had been caught between the closing door and the door jam. From the light still coming from his car's headlights, she could see his wide eyes and the pain on his face. As he held his left hand limp, at shoulder level, she saw the blood oozing from the tips of his fingers. With his right fist, he pounded the window.

"You bitch! You bitch! You fucking bitch! You gonna pay!"

He shook his left hand at the window, and the blood splattered across it. He moved to the front of her car and shook his hand at the windshield. Blood splattered again over the glass. He shook it again, and more blood splashed on the windshield. He was bleeding profusely from the tips of his fingers, and he obviously wanted her to see the blood he was spilling. She did, and it had the effect he wanted: total, unmitigated terror.

She watched as he removed the black scarf from his head and carefully wrapped his bleeding hand. Then he walked back towards his car. The blinding headlights kept her from seeing him open his door or enter his car, but she knew without a doubt that he would return. And he would have a tool to break her window. She clutched the umbrella in both hands, the steel end pointing at her door.

He walked slowly from his car toward hers with a long, heavy metal object in his right hand, his wrapped left hand hanging limply at his side. Instead of stopping at her door as she expected, he moved to the front of her car and menacingly held up the object for her to see.

"I'm going to count to three, and you better by damn have that door open," he yelled.

With that, Jennifer dropped the umbrella, turned the ignition key, which had remained inserted, and the engine came alive immediately. She pressed the gas pedal, and the engine responded as if it knew its role in this drama. Jennifer heard the thud as the front left side of her car hit him. She saw him fall to the asphalt, and she heard a series of expletives hurled at her as she drove away. She knew, from the incessant roar of his voice, that he was not gravely injured and, undoubtedly, would follow. But as long as her engine continued to respond, she would be safe.

Jennifer looked frequently into the rear-view mirror for car lights but saw none. She was familiar with the highway and its fifty-five and, at times, forty-five miles-per-hour speed limit, and at any other time, she would have obeyed it to avoid a speeding ticket. Tonight she was traveling seventy or more, hoping she would receive one. She would have welcomed the sight of flashing blue lights behind her, but she traveled without interruption. Only when she turned onto US 298 did she slow. There were cars and trucks traveling in both directions on the four-lane highway and houses, communities, and gas stations along the way. Her car was running fine; she was going to make it.

It wasn't until she pulled into the parking lot at the hospital that she gave any thought to why she decided to make that final, successful attempt to start her car. And, in fact, she could not recall actually making the decision. Surely, it was survival instinct.

She found a parking spot close to the emergency entrance to the hospital. It was well after midnight. She walked into the emergency waiting room and found it almost empty. The admissions clerk told her that her mother was with her father and she would inform her that Jennifer had arrived.

It was difficult to tell who was the happiest as they embraced. Her mother had come into the waiting room with a worried look but was now smiling. She explained to Jennifer that so far doctors had not determined if it was her father's heart, but that was likely to be the diagnosis. However, the EKG had not revealed any heart-muscle damage. He had severe pain in his chest for several hours after arriving at the emergency room, but the pain had ebbed somewhat. The ER physician had arranged for the hospital's cardiologist to see him first thing in the morning. He would be moved to a hospital room shortly, and then she and Jennifer would go home for some rest.

Jennifer did not mention the terrifying events of her trip. Her mother had enough worries for now. Maybe she would tell her tomorrow, maybe later, maybe never. She must try to put this evening behind her. Her only plans now were to get a good night's rest—and find a garden hose to wash the blood from her car.

CHAPTER 17
Saturday, August 26

Scott was up early Saturday morning. He wanted to call Jennifer right away, but decided to wait. If she stayed late at the hospital, she would be still sleeping.

His mind raced back to the previous evening at the party and what Jeffrey Swenson had said: "Vandera wants a speedy trial." Maybe the trial of Charles Vandera would be sooner than he expected. He would like that. He had a couple of new cases to prepare, which meant a full day's work ahead of him every day for the foreseeable future.

Scott felt lucky to be assigned to the Chatham County Superior Court where he could prosecute felonies. Most students were assigned to the State Court and were trusted only with simple misdemeanor cases and traffic violations. Some students spent their entire internship in traffic court. Even worse was to get municipal ordinance or fish and game violations.

During his first week in the clinic, Scott was given his first trial assignment: examine one of the primary witnesses in a felony case that Grady was prosecuting. Later in the same trial, Grady had Scott cross-examine one of the defense witnesses. Grady was pleased with his performance and that same week gave him his first case, one of auto theft. It was not a complicated case, but it did have a lineup identification issue. Scott was disappointed when the defendant entered a guilty plea. The following day, he was given another case—the Charles Vandera case.

As soon as he made a pot of coffee and had his usual breakfast of cold cereal, he began work on the two new cases. He called Jennifer's cell phone several times but there was no answer. Shortly after 11 a.m., the phone rang. He hoped it was Jennifer, but it wasn't. It was Grady.

"Scott, I need to brief you on some important matters. Do you have some time today that we can get together?"

"Sure, where are you now?"

"Downtown at the office."

"I'll be there in about twenty minutes."

Saturday's traffic was light, and parking was no problem. He showed his DA intern pass to the courthouse security officer and took the elevator up to Grady's office on the sixth floor. Grady was at his desk, a stack of case files in front of him.

"Hi, Scott, thanks for coming. I wanted to tell you that I've accepted a position with the U.S. Attorney's Office in Atlanta. I'll be leaving in two weeks."

"Grady, I'm sure sorry to hear that news, but I know it's where you wanted to go from here. But two weeks—that's pretty short notice, isn't it?"

"Not really. I told the boss two months ago that I had been offered the job, pending a background check. He was supportive and has been making some in-house adjustments anticipating the move. He just asked that I give him two weeks' notice when it was final. I did that yesterday. I'm to be at work in Atlanta on September 10. Now that's where you come in."

"Where I come in? How?"

"You see these case files?" Grady pointed to a stack well over a foot high. "I've got at least a dozen more, and I have to arrange for someone to take the ones I can't close within two weeks. A bunch of them will plead. Nick says he will reassign the two murder cases, but he wants me to see if anyone wants to volunteer for the other cases. No, I'm not asking you to volunteer for any—you have enough on your plate right now. However, I do want to bring you in on the Harrison case."

"That convenience store robbery?" asked Scott.

"Yes, that's the case."

Scott was somewhat familiar with the Harrison case. Grady brought him along in July when John Harrison was arraigned for armed robbery at a Fast Eddie's convenience store on Waters Avenue. The defendant made an impression on Scott, mainly because of the perpetual smirk on his face throughout the arraignment. He was a handsome guy with a roguish sort of demeanor. *Butch Cassidy and the Sundance Kid* came to mind when Scott saw him that first day in court. His body language was saying, "No problem; I'll be gone soon."

Harrison had good reason to feel that way. He had been on a twelve-month crime spree throughout north Florida and south Georgia. Authorities believed he committed at least seventeen armed robberies, all at night and all involving convenience stores. He had already been arrested and tried in three different counties on robbery charges and had been acquitted each time. This would be his fourth trial and the last one that was pending—it would be the final opportunity authorities would have to put away this one-man crime machine. Harrison always worked alone, late at night, and had a simple MO. He cased the stores thoroughly, making sure that only one or two employees were on duty and that there were no customers. Then he struck quickly by putting a shiny snub-nose .38 caliber revolver right in the face of the clerk. He presented himself as anxious to use the gun. In all his robberies, not a single clerk had fought or physically opposed him, and he left no physical evidence. He always hid his car away from the store, so there was never a make, year, color, or license number to give to responding officers.

In many of the robberies, no identification was made by any witness. In the three cases that had gone to trial, an identification had been made in a pretrial lineup. However, the lineup was always months after the robbery, and the witnesses did not exhibit much confidence at trial. Harrison never left a physical clue, and the juries apparently were reluctant to rely on identification from a single eyewitness, especially one with a snub-nose revolver thrust in his or her face. Harrison always took the stand in his defense and always had a good story of where he was at the time of the robbery. He never used an alibi witness; his alibi defense usually consisted of watching a movie or TV in some distant town—alone. He frustrated prosecutors by never calling alibi witnesses. Prosecutors find it easy to ferret out the truth from a lying alibi witness, but it is difficult to cross-examine a defendant who claims to have been alone, especially one as well-spoken, well-dressed and physically appealing as John Harrison always appeared on the witness stand.

"He's put in a demand for speedy trial," said Grady. "We have only two witnesses who saw Harrison there, and we have no other evidence—no gun, no fingerprints, no forensics of any kind. And the robbery is over two years old. One witness, the guy working the cash register, picked him out of a photo lineup. But the results of the lineup were suppressed at a hearing last week because the officer conducting the lineup lost some of the photos that were used. We can't even mention the photo lineup at trial. I haven't spoken to the second witness, a guy named Josh Johnson. He was a soldier stationed at Ft. Stewart at the time, but he's been discharged. Richard Evans has been trying to track him down since the arraignment in July. We thought for a while he was dead or had disappeared from the face of the earth, but a couple days ago, Richard located him in Breckenridge, Colorado, working at a fishing lodge on the Blue River."

"Will you be able to get him here in time for trial?" asked Scott.

"Don't know. Richard wants to personally serve a subpoena on him."

"Richard is going to Colorado?"

"Not a chance! Richard wants to get to the Blue River for some fly fishing. He's a good guy, and I would like to send him. He deserves a boondoggle as much as anybody, but that's just a big waste of money. We can get this witness served by one of the Colorado sheriff's deputies. The subpoena would be just as effective—which is not at all."

"Not at all?" said Scott. "You mean not good, even if he's personally served?"

"Well, here's how it works. We prepare the subpoena and start the paperwork so that we can get him a plane ticket, and he can get reimbursed for his expenses if he's willing to come. But, no, we can't force him to come just by serving him with a Georgia subpoena. We have to get a Colorado court order. If a witness wants to fight it, he can delay for weeks, and we just don't have time for that. So, since we don't have a stick to use, we have to use a carrot—make it easy on him, get the tickets to him, transportation to and from the airport, hotel reservations, and so forth. We appeal to his sense of justice and service and wave the flag. After all, he did serve in the Army and was honorably discharged, so we're not working with a scumbag. That's where you come in."

"Me? How?"

"Meg Flanders, who just came up from misdemeanors, was going to second chair this case with me, but she had some emergency surgery earlier this week. She's OK but won't be back in time. I want you to second chair the case if you can afford the time from your classes."

"Sure, I can do it. Besides clinic, I only have two classes, both night seminars."

"Good, you're on. I expect this to be a three-day trial, maybe four. We'll be selecting the jury Tuesday, the day after Labor Day, and there are some defense motions to be heard Tuesday, too. Here's a duplicate file for you—copies of everything I have on the case."

Grady handed Scott a thick manila folder and continued. "Johnson will be flying in on Wednesday—if he's willing. We sent the subpoena and the tickets to Colorado to be served by a deputy there. Richard tells me the tickets are from Denver via Atlanta, arriving in Savannah at 1:15 p.m. I want you to meet him at the airport, prep him for trial, and bring him to the courthouse. You'll do the direct exam of Johnson. While you get him ready, I'll be busy presenting the case with the other witnesses."

"Other witnesses? You said you had only those two witnesses."

"Well, those are the only bona fide witnesses, but we'll have more. I don't ever go to trial with just one or two. Juries won't convict with one or two witnesses. We'll call at least five or six more—first responders, photographers, investigators, fingerprint dusters, auditor, store owner. They won't add a thing to the evidence except faces and numbers. Jury trials require it, Scott. Politicians stuff ballots; prosecutors stuff witnesses. These extra witnesses add a dimension to the trial that juries expect. The jury wants to know how well the case was investigated. Were there any other leads, any other suspects? And they want photos and diagrams. But the only evidence that will place Harrison at the scene is coming from the eyewitnesses. And I don't know if I'll have one or two. I'll be depending on your help for that second one. Think you can handle it?"

"Of course," said Scott.

"Good. Now let's go have lunch. I'm buying."

Scott and Grady left the courthouse, taking Grady's car to a small restaurant by the river. They discussed the Harrison case and the witnesses Grady would be calling. They also discussed the Vandera case, which had gone to the grand jury for a second time on Thursday. This time, Scott was confident it was a good indictment because he drafted it himself. He told Grady about Jeff's statement at the beach party that Vandera would be demanding a speedy trial.

"How soon can you get the Vandera case ready?" asked Grady.

"Give me a day to notify my witnesses, and I'll be ready."

"Then we'll give him a speedy trial if that's really what he wants. I'm clear for Thursday and Friday. The case I had scheduled for those two days in front of Judge Vesely is going to plead. You check Monday, and if the defense really wants to go that soon, we'll do it. If I don't clear it before I leave, that's another I'll have to hand off."

They drove back to the courthouse where Scott had parked his car. They made plans to visit Fast Eddie's to observe the conditions of the crime scene as it would appear at night. They agreed to meet there at 10 p.m.

It was 2 p.m. when he opened the door to his apartment and saw that his answering machine was blinking. It was a message from Jennifer.

"Sorry to have missed you. I'm at home but I'll be leaving for the hospital shortly and will probably be there for the rest of the day. They have some tests to run, and we still don't know much about what's causing his pain. I don't have my cell phone so you can't call me. I just wish I had your cell phone number, but this is the only number I have. I'll call later."

•   •   •

At 10 p.m., Scott drove into the parking lot at Fast Eddie's, and Grady pulled in just behind him. They told the clerk on duty why they were there and walked through the store, observing its layout and lighting. They went outside, sat in Grady's vehicle, which was parked in the same space where Johnson had parked, and observed the cash register through the large glass windows. They observed with the car headlights on and with them off. They could see that Johnson would have had a clear view of the robbery from his car. He would be a good witness. They walked behind the store and along the streets, looking for the places Harrison could have parked his getaway car.

When Scott returned to his apartment almost an hour later, there was another message from Jennifer. He hit the play button.

"Hi, Scott. Sorry to miss you again. Just want to give an update. The doctors now say it's not Dad's heart but his gallbladder. They plan to operate Monday. So I'll be staying through Monday, returning Tuesday if all goes well. I'll miss two days of classes, but at least I have the books you put in the car. Thanks. I've had lots of study time in the hospital waiting room. If you can, call me between one and four tomorrow afternoon. 843-811-9690. I'll be home."

CHAPTER 18
Sunday, August 27

Scott called Jennifer Sunday afternoon. She answered on the first ring.

"Hi, Jen, how's your dad?"

"No change. They still plan to operate tomorrow. The doctor says he doesn't expect any problems."

"Good. And you?"

"I'm fine. But my Camry isn't. It's got a problem. My mom's going to take it to the dealer this week. I'm going to be driving my dad's car back to Savannah. You won't laugh, will you?"

"Why should I laugh?"

"It's a 2004 Pontiac Aztek."

"So?"

"One of the design classes at SCAD voted it 'the ugliest car of 2004.' You must have seen one."

"In fact, I have. And I agree. But I would rather have a mechanically sound Aztek than a sick Camry. You didn't tell your dad about the design class vote, did you?"

"Of course, I did. But he had already bought it. It was sitting in our driveway. He got a big kick out of the honor."

They talked for half an hour. Scott told her he had been assigned second chair in another felony case. She wanted to know all about this new case and about the Vandera case. Did Jeff still want a speedy trial? Was the trial on for this week? Had he been on the campus? Anything going on there? Finally, the call ended, with Scott promising to call again Monday evening. Scott sat back in his chair and smiled. No special reason; he just felt like smiling.

And once again, Jennifer did not mention the events of her drive home Friday night. Not even a hint.

CHAPTER 19

Jaak left church before the service was over, as he always did on the third Sunday of each month. He had a busy afternoon ahead of him. It was a two-hour drive on Interstate 16 to the Carl Vinson VA Hospital in Dublin. He had to pick up his van and his "crew" and get on the way no later than noon. The hospitalized veterans would be gathering for the show in the auditorium at three o'clock, and he did not want to disappoint—something he had never done in the ten-plus years of planning these Sunday afternoon outings. Arranging for two hours of entertainment each month was challenging, but Jaak enjoyed the challenge and the satisfaction that went along with it.

Today his entertainers were a five-piece, country-western band and a ventriloquist-comedian. He was familiar with the band; they were good. He had invited the comedian on the recommendation of Juri. This was an unpaid gig, and there were not many individuals anxious to give up a Sunday afternoon to put on a free show. But there were enough, and somehow Jaak had always been able to put together a decent entertainment package. Some performers would ask to be invited again after receiving the always warm reception from the veterans.

When Jaak first began his monthly visitations, the veterans were older. Now, there was a younger group, mostly veterans of the Iraq War. And while the popularity of country music had not diminished, the younger veterans enjoyed a more diverse range of music. But, regardless, when the afternoon entertainment ended, there was always a standing ovation and celebration that would remind Jaak of the USO shows he saw in Vietnam. He had vivid memories of the Bob Hope Christmas Tour in 1968, with Rosie Grier, Miss World, and Les Brown and His Band of Renown, as well as the many other lesser-known entertainers who visited the troops in that far-away place long ago. The cheering that followed any rendition of Ferlin Husky's "Detroit City" was fresh in his mind, like it was yesterday. Every touring USO show played their own version, but the refrain remained the same: *I wanna go home, I wanna go home, oh Lord, I wanna go home.*

Jaak gave an advance warning to the bands that they would likely get a request for that song, as well as "We Gotta Get Out of This Place," by the Animals. The vets would go wild, and Jaak would find himself with moist eyes.

The band and the comedian were both well received. And, yes, there was a request for "Detroit City," with many of the vets and Jaak joining in with the lyrics that ended with the usual stomping, clapping, and cheering.

After the show, Jaak took his group to dinner at a popular restaurant near the hospital—the only "payment" the entertainers would receive. Jaak always picked up the tab, except when the Bank Notes entertained. On those occasions, once or twice a year, the bank executives insisted that they treat.

After dropping off his passengers, Jaak returned to the Library. He was tired, but he was looking forward to the poker game with his old friends.

CHAPTER 20

It was almost nine when Jaak arrived back at the Library, and the poker game was in full swing. All the "usual suspects" were there—Jimmy, Malcolm, Denis, Rench, Pete, and Bill. Juri was sitting in for Jaak. The game was briefly suspended while Jaak reported on the show that afternoon, and Juri counted his chips to check out and make room for his brother.

"Who's the big winner tonight?" asked Jaak, eyeing the table and seeing the big stack of chips in front of Denis.

All the heads turned to Denis, and Denis smiled. "About time. I've been supporting you guys for a long time. Sent your kids through college and built additions on your houses. Lady Luck finally smiled on me."

Jaak gave Denis a thumbs up. He was glad to see that Denis was finally getting a break.

Before sitting down to play, Jaak walked to the refrigerator and brought out a beer. Looking at the strange label, Jaak asked, "Fine-looking beer. Who brought it?"

"I brought it from Asheville," replied Pete. "Was up there for a convention last week. They have some neat breweries using that mountain water. I could use one myself. How about handing me one, Jaak. Anyone else?"

A couple of hands went up, and Jaak complied. He sat down, and after slowly pouring his beer into a glass, he held it up in a salute.

"Here's to Denis. May his luck *remain*, except when I'm in the *game*. Deal!"

The game continued, as did Denis's winning streak. When the evening was over, he cashed in $95 worth of chips, the clear winner for the evening. It came mostly at the expense of Jimmy and Bill, who did not seem to mind, for over the years, most of their winnings had come at the expense of Denis.

Juri remained at the Library, occasionally returning to the lounge to kibitz. After the game was over and all had departed, he came in and sat down near Jaak.

"I was glad to see Denis finally have a big night," said Jaak.

"I guess it was OK, but can't say it really thrilled me," said Juri. "He changed his favorite game from five-card stud to Texas Hold 'Em and Omaha. Maybe that helped. Or maybe it was the cards—he brought a fresh deck. Do you suppose he took that deck out to Bonaventure for Minerva to put her voodoo on it?" Juri stood up. "Been a long day for you . . . and me," he said. "I'm out of here. See you tomorrow."

"Yeah, good night. I'll lock up," Jaak replied.

He was tired and did not immediately get up. Instead, he sat at the poker table. His short conversation with Juri remained in his thoughts, and a comment that Juri had made as he was leaving began to trouble him. "He brought a fresh deck." That was puzzling. The gang often brought something to share, such as the beer Pete brought from Asheville, but no one had ever brought a fresh deck of cards.

Jaak was curious. The long metal case that held the chips and cards was still on the poker table. He opened it. Where there had been one deck, now there were two. Both were Rider Back decks— the classic, double-ended design with the winged cherub astride a bicycle. One deck was obviously quite new; someone had indeed brought a new deck.

Jaak removed the cards from the box. He did not want to admit to his suspicion, not even to himself. He shuffled them and dealt them several times, carefully observing their appearance on the table. He felt for uneven edges, ridges, and different thicknesses. Nothing unusual. There were no apparent markings anywhere that he could find. The cards had the customary numbers and royalty figures on one side and, on the other, the winged cherubs riding bicycles within large circles, surrounded by an elaborate filigree design. Also, within the circles were a dozen or so small wing-shaped objects resembling sea gulls as they appear in a seascape, soaring at a distance. Jaak spread the cards face down on the table and looked at them from various angles and saw nothing unusual.

Relieved and a bit chagrined that his suspicion appeared unfounded, he was about to put them away when he recalled something else that Juri had said: "He changed his favorite game from five-card stud to Texas Hold 'Em and Omaha."

The comment rekindled Jaak's curiosity. He had not given Denis's choice of games any special thought when he was playing, but now, as he reflected on the evening, Juri was correct: Denis had indeed abandoned his five-card stud game for Texas Hold 'Em and Omaha. In the years that Denis had played at the Library, Jaak could not recall a single game in which Denis had dealt Omaha or Texas Hold 'Em.

In casinos, the community cards stay in the deck until dealt, concealing the backs of the cards and any special markings they may have. But the way the Library gang played Omaha, as well as Texas Hold 'Em, the flop (first three community cards), the "river" and the "fifth street" cards were dealt down immediately, in a five-card row. Thus, the backs of these five cards were visible throughout the betting, and when Omaha double-flop was played, the backs of ten cards were displayed across the table.

He separated the cards by suit and placed them face down in separate piles, four horizontal rows of thirteen cards each. He looked carefully for a few moments—very carefully—and it hit him. The rows *were* different, almost indiscernibly different, but indeed different. At first he could see no specific color, mark, or figure that made them different. He then took one card from the "club row" and one from the "hearts row," placed them side by side, and examined them closely. He went over each part of the intricate design. After several minutes, he saw it, *the difference*.

It was so simple, so imperceptible. It was the cherub's arms and legs. On the club card, on the cherub's *right* arm at the elbow, there was a dark gray line, about an eighth of an inch long, where the elbow would bend. It looked quite natural, perhaps a shadow. Had the mark been anywhere else on the card than at the bent elbow, it might have been noticed. But its placement made it undetectable— just a shadow. On the heart card, on the cherub's *left* leg at the knee, there was an identical dark gray shadow line. He compared the other suits and found similar marks. On the diamond cards, the mark was on the cherub's *left* arm at the elbow. On the spade cards, it was on the cherub's *right* leg at the knee.

Jaak was sure that the numerical value of each card also was hidden in the design. He separated the cards by their numerical value, then took a 4 and compared it with a 10. Then a 6 with a 2. It took almost half an hour, but he found what he was looking for—at least he found a clue. It was the varying number of "sea gulls" surrounding the cherubs. In the upper portion of the circle containing the cherub, each card always contained ten winged objects, four on the right of the cherub and six on the left. In the lower part of the circle, there were more winged objects, but the number varied, some cards having none and some as many as four.

He studied the cards carefully. He noted that the 3 contained exactly three winged objects in the lower portion, which initially seemed to be the key. Then he noted that the 8 also had three winged objects. Additionally, all kings had three. Solving the code was not going to be so simple. For the next two hours, he arranged and rearranged the cards in various stacks and positions according to the number of winged objects, the value of each card, its suit, and any other way that came to mind, but he could not unlock the riddle.

It was now 3 a.m., and he was extremely tired. It had been a long day. His mind was darting between puzzlement and confusion, indignation and anger, but all of these emotions were trumped by the sick feeling in his stomach. Apparently, he and his friends had been cheated by someone whom they knew and respected. Jaak wanted very much not to believe it. Perhaps Denis was unaware of the markings. Surely, it was merely a mistake. Maybe someone had sold this deck of cards to Denis without Denis being aware of these markings. After all, he had known Denis for many years, and he was a good judge of character. And could Juri be sure that it was Denis who brought the cards? He must be careful not to jump to conclusions.

But Jaak was no fool. The evidence was overwhelming. Someone had brought marked cards to the Library. Such conduct among long-time friends . . . . Jaak could not come up with the appropriate word. He left the cards on the table, locked up, and drove home. He went to bed but slept little.

The next morning, Jaak was still pondering the riddle when he arrived at the Library. Juri had arrived first, as he usually did, and was consulting with the chef. They seemed to be in a serious discussion, so Jaak decided to wait before showing the cards to Juri. But he was anxious to solve the mystery. What did the varying number of winged objects mean? He was sure that the value of each card could be determined by anyone with the key.

When Juri entered the room, Jaak was hovering over the poker table, resting heavily on his elbows and peering intently at the cards. He had again separated the cards by suit and spread them out in four rows, face down. Juri joined him at the table. He looked at the rows of cards and tried to determine what was so fascinating to Jaak.

"See anything unusual about these cards?" asked Jaak.

"Rider Backs all look alike, except some are red and these are blue. Am I supposed to see something unusual?"

"No, the idea behind these cards is that you see nothing unusual. Pigeons have poor eyesight."

"This looks like the deck we played with last night. What's up, Jaak?"

"Yes, this is the deck. You told me Denis brought it—right?" asked Jaak, as he removed his elbows from the table and stood upright.

"Yes," replied Juri. He bent down to take a closer look at the four rows of cards that Jaak had laid on the table.

"Still see nothing unusual?" asked Jaak.

Juri continued to look intensely at the four rows. "Just four rows of Rider Backs, Jaak."

Jaak then scooped up all of the cards, shuffled them, and placed the deck on the table in front of Juri. "Take one card of each suit, and don't let me see what you select. Then place them in a row, face down on the table." Jaak pulled up one of the chairs and took a seat at the table.

Juri did as Jaak requested.

When he was finished, Jaak looked at the row of cards, and then quietly said, "The one on the left end is a diamond; next to it is a spade, then a club, and on the right end is a heart."

Juri turned to Jaak with a frown and a seriously puzzled look. Then he turned over the cards. They were exactly as Jaak had called them. "We played with marked cards last night, Jaak?"

"I'm afraid so, Juri."

Then Jaak explained the marking that allowed him to identify the suits. He showed Juri the small sea gulls in each circle. "I know these birds are the key to each card's value," said Jaak, "but I still can't unlock the puzzle. The 3s have three birds on them, but so do the 8s and the kings. There's something else needed and I can't find it. I spent hours last night looking. It has me beat. How about you taking a shot at it?"

"Sure, Jaak. But what about Denis? We . . . you . . . what's to be done, you know, about Denis?"

"I think I know, but I want to sleep on it for a day or so. I don't want to act while I'm angry. And right now I'm pretty pissed off, as well as feeling some deep-down hurt. Denis was my friend— our friend, friend of everyone in the poker group. I've got the same feeling now that I get when a close friend dies. Sure, he was the usual loser, but his losses were a pittance. What—twenty, thirty, maybe fifty dollars—for five hours of entertainment? It couldn't have been the money. He's got plenty and makes plenty. It had to be something else. Pride, I guess. But we've all lost at times." Jaak paused, and seemed to be thinking. Then a smile came to his face, and he continued. "Denis is the dumbest damn poker player I've ever seen. He never got it. The gang's going to miss his money." Jaak's smile developed into a chuckle.

"You are going to ban him from the poker game?" asked Juri.

"Do you think I have a choice?"

"I guess not. What will you tell the others?"

"Nothing. And I will simply tell Denis he is no longer welcome, and why. That's it. As much as I would like to tell the gang that they've been playing with a duplicitous bastard, I won't. We have a friendly poker game—I don't want it to develop into a gossip table. They only see him on Sunday nights. They will no longer see him. End of story. I trust you will not bring this up."

"Of course not, Jaak. But they'll ask about Denis's absence."

"And they'll simply be told that, for personal reasons, Denis is no longer playing. And I assure you that after I confront Denis, he will indeed have personal reasons for not playing. I'll see him sometime before Sunday. He usually comes in at least once during the week. And if I don't see him before Sunday, I'll call him."

"You going to ban him from the Library bar also?" asked Juri.

"No, but I have a feeling that after I speak with him, we won't see him around. You are sure it was Denis who brought the cards?"

"That's how I recall it—I'm ninety-nine percent certain. A couple others came in about the same time, so I can't be absolutely certain, but I'm pretty sure it was Denis."

That was not certain enough for Jaak. If he was going to accuse Denis of planting marked cards, he wanted more than "pretty sure." Jaak had some detective work in front of him. First and most important, was it Denis? Could he be certain, one hundred percent? Second, he wondered where Denis, or anyone else, could have found such shrewdly and expertly marked cards. And, third, he wanted to know the key to the part of the puzzle he was missing—the value of each card.

"I've got to make some phone calls," Jaak said and promptly departed for his office.

The most likely place to start was with the shops in the area that sold magician supplies. He called an old friend, George Jones, Savannah's "Mr. Magic." Jones was an expert magician, as well as an illusionist and mentalist, who had joined Jaak on two trips to the VA Hospital to entertain. Jones told Jaak that he knew of only one place in Savannah that might have such cards: the Magic Castle. Jaak put the deck of cards in his pocket and drove to Savannah Mall.

• • •

The Magic Castle was a small shop in one of the lightly traveled mall corridors. Boxes of inexpensive magic tricks, puzzles, and games lined the shelves along the wall. Advertisements for Harry Houdini straightjackets, unicycles, magic supplies, and magic shows were displayed throughout the store. In the rear was a long glass showcase with accessories of all types: linking rings, knotted ropes, small coins, half coins, folding coins, fake bills, silk handkerchiefs—almost anything the aspiring amateur magician would want.

No other customers were in the store. A tall, thin, middle-aged man wearing black, horn-rimmed glasses—the only clerk in the store, perhaps the shop owner—was seated behind the glass counter. He stood up to welcome Jaak. Jaak gave him a friendly "good morning," pulled the cards from his pocket, and placed them on the counter.

"Do you sell cards like these?" Jaak asked.

"Bicycle Rider Backs? Sure," the man responded.

"These are not standard Rider Backs. They are marked," said Jaak.

The clerk picked up one card and said, "Marked? Where?"

Jaak pointed to the marks.

The clerk examined the card carefully and said, "Yes, we sell this type, but not often. I can recall only one order in the last year or so. Most of our customers are amateur magicians, not card sharks. They usually use cards they can read by touch—shaved edges or raised dots. We keep those in stock. But these cards have to be ordered from a broker in Hong Kong. May take a month or so, and they are quite expensive."

"How expensive?" asked Jaak.

"I don't recall. Let me see if I can find the invoice for that last order." The clerk walked a few feet to a metal filing cabinet and returned with a file folder filled with pink invoices. He flipped through the pages. "Here it is," he said, as he placed the invoice on the counter top.

Even upside down, Jaak could read the top part of the invoice: "Purchaser: Denis Nolan." A telephone number was also listed, but Jaak couldn't quite make it out, and he didn't really try.

Juri's recollection—"pretty sure it was Denis"—was now confirmed. Jaak had the most important information he came for. But he still wanted the key to solving the numerical value of each card.

The clerk ran his finger down the pink invoice and then looked up at Jaak. "The price is $149.99 plus tax. I see from the invoice it takes about three weeks for delivery. There isn't much demand for them, so we require payment in advance, and they are not returnable."

"So there are no cards like these in stock," said Jaak. It was more of a statement than a question. Then he asked, "Would you know how to read these cards? I don't have the key. I'll pay for the information."

"Sorry, I can't help you. The answer—the key, as you call it—comes packed with the deck. I've never even seen one."

"So the only way I can find out how to read this deck is to order another deck for 150 bucks or so?"

"Yes. But even then, I'm not sure the new deck would have the same marks. These are custom cards, produced in China. I wish I could tell you more, but I can't. You pay; I order. When they get here, I'll call you; you pick up the cards—and the cards and the key are yours. That's about it."

"Thanks," said Jaak, and he turned and walked out. He realized he had all the information that he was going to get from this visit to the Magic Castle, but it was enough.

Jaak was now sure of what he must do with regard to Denis, and he would do it this week. He still had not solved the mystery of the "sea gulls"; it really bothered him that he found the birds but not what they represented. When he got back to the Library, he tossed the deck of cards on the poker table. He would take another crack at the puzzle when he had time.

CHAPTER 22

S cott practiced with his flag football team Monday afternoon. It was the first practice of the semester, and he left the field tired and a bit bruised. After a hot shower, he called Jennifer.

"Hi, Jen. How did it go today?"

"The operation went well, but they want to keep him in the hospital for a couple more days. If he's still doing OK in the morning, I'm planning on returning to school tomorrow afternoon."

"Good. I know your dad will do just fine."

"How are things there?" asked Jennifer.

"I ran into Professor Nolan this afternoon," Scott said. "He asked if I knew why you had missed his class, and I told him. He said he had the case file for the Atlanta trial competition and was holding a witness role open for you."

"I wonder if I'm taking on more than I should," said Jennifer. "Missing these two days of classes is going to put me behind, and I'm afraid this witness business is going to take more time than I can afford."

"I wish I could convince you of that. You really have no business getting involved in this during your first semester."

Jennifer's response was quick and curt. "Don't go there, Scott. You know that I'm entitled to make my own mistakes."

"Yes, as you say, you are entitled to make your own mistakes. But you should know something that I doubt Professor Nolan will tell you. And that is, once practice gets underway, it's going to be almost every night. Just give it serious thought."

"I've already given it serious thought. I'm going to do it."

"OK. I just hope I have more luck convincing a jury than I have convincing you."

"Scott, I appreciate your advice, and I know you are right. My mind tells me you are, but my heart says 'go for it.' I'm just going to make the time."

Scott knew now that he was going to be seeing much less of Jennifer this semester than he had hoped. Between his trials and trial preparation and her classes and trial competition practice, joint leisure time for them would be rare. Professor Denis Nolan would be seeing a lot more of Jennifer than he would. Nolan and Jennifer would be traveling together to Atlanta in midsemester, and they would be gone for several days—and nights. What had prompted Nolan to make this offer to a first-semester student? Scott was sure that he knew, and he was also sure that Jennifer did not have a clue. Scott recalled the meeting in the courtroom when Nolan did not—and perhaps could not—take his eyes off Jennifer. He also recalled Nolan asking Scott to support him in his campaign to become the new dean. It made Scott smile. *Sure* he would.

CHAPTER 23
Tuesday, August 29

Dean Adams had been at his desk for two hours when Roxanne buzzed him on the intercom. The registrar had the final fall enrollment figures ready, and she would like to bring them by at his convenience.

"Tell her this would be a good time, to come right over."

Deborah's office was only a few doors down, and she was knocking on Winston's door within minutes. As soon as she was invited in, she walked briskly to the framed photo of the Board of Trustees and moved it into the usual crooked tilt, laid the fall enrollment report on Winston's desk, and took a seat.

The enrollment figures were good. As usual, there were a few transfers to state law schools by students who received late acceptance letters. If tuition cost was the primary concern in school choice, it was easy to understand why someone, given the chance, would leave Savannah Law for a state school. Nevertheless, there had been only a half-dozen transfers, and he knew the faculty would be pleased with the latest enrollment report.

"Deborah, I'd like you to be there this afternoon to present the report to the faculty. There may be questions, and you are the expert. Would you mind?"

"That will be fine, Dean. I'll be there." In fact, she did mind. She had a stack of reports to complete, and drop/add was still in progress. Besides, she would prefer dental surgery over a faculty meeting. But Winston was right; the registrar should be there to present the report.

"Anything you think I should know before the meeting this afternoon?" asked Winston.

"Yes, you should know Denis is actively seeking your job. Of course, you know that, but you probably don't know how much progress he's making."

"No, of course not. How much progress *is* he making?"

"I believe investors call it 'due diligence.' He's doing a lot of that—talking one-on-one with all the faculty members, laying out his plans as dean."

"Apparently he's gone beyond due diligence," said Winston. "That's the step *before* you make a decision. He's already made his decision; that's pretty clear. But you say he's 'laying out his plans as dean.' Let me guess. Everyone, at least everyone on the voting faculty, gets a pay raise, right?"

"Everyone on the voting faculty, yes. No promises to the staff yet, but I'm sure that's just an oversight."

"Sure, just a minor oversight. Have you heard of anyone else on the faculty who is considering applying?"

"Haven't heard a word about anyone other than Denis," said Deborah. "But I've received inquires from a number of faculty members and administrators from other law schools. I've mailed application forms to them. Ben Sterner phoned me this morning. He's calling the first meeting of the committee for the afternoon of September 15. That's a Friday. I'll be mailing notices this afternoon. We should know soon if we need to increase our advertising for the job. Personally, I expect we'll have plenty of applicants."

"Well, we know we have one. Let's hope we have more. Anything else, Deborah?"

"Nothing except I've been burning with curiosity about the faculty meeting last week."

"Burning with curiosity? About what?"

"About Denis. I left after I gave my report, but I've heard about it."

"Now you've piqued *my* curiosity, Deborah. What have you heard?"

"About his so-called motion, if that's what it was, to have a first-year student on the Dean Search Committee."

"If the saying is true, about curiosity killing the cat, I guess you have a dead cat on your hands, Deborah. That pitch for a first-year student on the committee was rather strange, even for Denis. I'm not sure what he has in mind, but I'm sure he's given it much thought. I think he has a Machiavellian gene. And your curiosity won't be quenched when I tell you what Harry Ramsey said when I called him."

"You called him about it?"

"Of course. I promised I would, so I had to. Frankly, afterwards, I found myself wishing I had not made that promise, but at the time, I was trying to prevent a rather unpleasant situation from developing further. Velma was in her 'fighting mad' stance." Winston chuckled lightly.

Deborah grinned. "Yes, I also heard about that. I've seen that stance—not a pretty sight."

"I thought it was time to end the meeting. After all, it was our first faculty meeting of the year, and we had several new faculty members and had planned a nice little reception for them. So, when I said I would contact Harry Ramsey about adding a first-year student, I thought I was merely expediting a quick and peaceful end to the meeting. It wasn't until I spoke with Harry that I realized how determined Denis was to have that first-year student added to the committee."

"What did Mr. Ramsey say?" asked Deborah.

"As soon as I mentioned the 'Dean Search Committee,' he said Denis had already contacted him about it. That surprised me. But I was even more surprised when he said he had given it some thought and liked the idea. 'So do it,' he said. That ended the discussion."

"So Denis had greased the way. What do you think he has in mind?"

"At the faculty meeting, he said he had 'a few' he could recommend. But I have no doubt he has a particular student in mind—someone he believes will look favorably on his candidacy. How can he be so sure and so fast? But that's Denis. It's going to be an interesting semester. I will inform the faculty this afternoon and request nominations. Now, Deborah, we have not only failed to resolve your curiosity but have replenished it. Anything else on your mind?"

"No, Dean, I think that's enough. I'll just go bury my dead cat. I'll see you at the meeting this afternoon."

After Deborah left, Winston looked at the center of the righted photo and saw the smiling face of Denis's father. Indeed, he thought, the apples don't fall far from the tree.

CHAPTER 24

It was 4 p.m. The second faculty meeting of the new school year was about to begin, and, as usual, it would begin late. Dean Adams had just entered and made his customary announcement: "We were scheduled to begin at four, but something must have held up our faculty."

Then he walked over to where Bernadine Garcia, the newest Research and Writing hire, was seated and wished her a happy birthday. She smiled and looked surprised. She should not have been. Winston never failed to remember each faculty member's birthday with a personal office visit or a phone call. He asked Bernadine how her first week went, asked if she had found suitable housing, and told her how pleased the school was to have her there.

Brian Latimer was already seated in his usual spot on the far right in the first row when Belinda Chapman arrived. "Mind if I take this seat? I may need an interpreter," she said. Smiling, she took the seat beside him without waiting for a reply.

Professor VanLandingham arrived and settled into her seat, signaling that a quorum was likely. This was soon confirmed by Professor Rose, and the meeting was called to order. The minutes were not read, as they were attached to the agenda. This time, Professor VanLandingham's name was correctly spelled, and the minutes were approved on voice vote without objection.

Deborah Channing presented the final fall enrollment report. She answered a few questions, after which Winston said she was free to leave or to stay. She quickly accepted the offer and left.

He then gave what was always listed in the agenda as the "Dean Scene"—changes and additions to committee assignments, new programs and staff appointments, commendations, report on Board of Trustees meetings—anything that should be of interest to the full faculty.

His final announcement was that he had contacted board chairman Harry Ramsey, and he had agreed to have an additional student—a first-year student—placed on the Dean Search Committee. Immediately Denis Nolan's hand was in the air.

Rather than recognizing Denis, Winston merely said, "I'll be pleased to receive recommendations. Please include the reason for your recommendation. I want to make the appointment soon. The first meeting of the committee is scheduled for September 15."

Denis's hand went down; apparently, the dean had answered his question.

Several committee chairpersons gave their reports. There was no "old business," so Winston turned to "new business." The first item of new business had been placed on the agenda by Professor Polanski. The topic was "Savannah College of Law's Challenge to Global Warming." Winston invited her to the lectern.

"I attempted to speak at the last faculty meeting but was ruled out of order. Rudely, I might add. I was attempting to address a serious health issue here at our law school—trans fat and partially hydrogenated vegetable oils used in our school cafeteria. But after that meeting, I began to realize that there were more serious problems here. Not only are we paying little attention to our students' health, but, more important, we're paying *no* attention to the health of our planet. It's time we awoke to the major problem facing us today—*global warming*!"

The words "global warming" came from her lips almost at a shout. She was obviously warming to her subject; her voice now had the fury and vehemence of a war protester and the shrilling pitch of fingernail-scraping across a blackboard.

"And, of course, you ask," she continued, "'What does this have to do with Savannah Law?' And I answer, 'Everything!' And then you ask, 'But what can one little law school do?' So here is my answer—my challenge—to this faculty. I have a motion to make."

Professor Polanski produced a legal-size yellow pad and began to read. "Assignment of parking spaces in our student parking lots shall be based on the carbon footprint of the student's vehicle. Vehicles with the lowest carbon emissions shall be given a decal for parking in the closest student parking lot, which shall be named 'Gandhi Parking Lot,' in honor of Mahatma Gandhi, who once said, 'One must care about a world one will not see.'

"Those students who choose to drive to school in lumbering, gas-guzzling, demons—the Escalades, the Tahoes, the . . . the . . .

you know, the SUVs and such—their vehicles will be assigned to the farthest parking lot, which shall be named the 'George W. Bush Parking Lot' to remind students of the absence of leadership on global warming by the president and his administration.

"I further move that a committee composed of faculty, staff, and students be appointed by the dean to administer and supervise this policy, assigning each vehicle a parking decal utilizing fuel efficiency data from the U.S. Department of Energy."

She lowered her yellow pad. "That ends my motion. I ask that you join with me in this important, though small, step. In the words of Neil Armstrong after he first walked on the moon: 'One small step for a man, one giant leap for mankind.'" She smiled and walked slowly from the lectern to her seat.

Dean Adams moved to the lectern to preside. "There is a motion before the faculty. Do I hear a second?"

"Second" came a voice from the Sudoku section on the back tier.

"Any discussion?" asked Winston.

There was an awkward silence for a few moments as the faculty members turned to each other with puzzled looks. Belinda Chapman looked at Brian Latimer with a whimsical smile, hoping for his usual discerning advice.

"You are on your own on this one, Belinda."

Professor Smithfield, who rarely had anything substantial or worthwhile to say, held up his hand. When Winston gave him the floor, he did not disappoint.

He was seated on the left side of the rear row, and despite all of his personality faults, of which he had many, he did have a commanding voice. "Geraldine was wrong. Armstrong did not say 'a man.' He flubbed his lines; left out the 'a' before man, making it contradictory. 'Man' and 'mankind' mean the same. So what he really said was his small step for mankind was a giant leap for mankind. He blew it."

Another voice from the opposite side of the back row was heard. "Wrong! Armstrong did put in the 'a'—static drowned out the 'a' in the transmission—they analyzed the transmission and found the 'a'."

"*They* analyzed it? They 'who'?"

"NASA! They had it on tape."

"Yes, and the *New York Times* got those same tapes and came to the opposite conclusion."

While the argument about the first communication from the surface of the moon continued, Belinda Chapman turned to Brian Latimer, and whispered, "You can't just abandon me—what's going on?"

Brian smiled and answered quietly, "This happens every time Geraldine puts one of her proposals before the faculty. Bless her soul, she's the faculty's foremost activist. She means well, and most of what she presents has merit, but it's always a half-key off. And it seems to always bring out some of the worst in our faculty. Smithfield couldn't sleep tonight if he didn't prove again that he's smart, well read, and the faculty's trivia expert. He may be right about Armstrong—I think I read the same thing somewhere. But who cares? He's really insufferable. Are you ready for this to end? I am, and I hope Winston is."

Professor Matthew Bruce, who taught Civil Procedure, entered the debate by raising his hand high to catch Winston's eye. "Matt, you have the floor," Winston said. Bruce, a tenured professor with an abundance of common sense, stood and moved to the end of the row where he could view the entire faculty as he spoke.

"Geraldine, you bring up a very timely issue, and I'm sure I speak for many on the faculty when I say I share your concern about global warming. None of us is unmindful that leading earth scientists have warned that this is one of the most pervasive threats to our environment. But some of us have questions concerning the appropriateness of the policies and action that your motion will require. Let me address a few of them.

"First, fairness. The motion addresses the problem only by policing the students. Nothing in the motion restricts or limits faculty or staff. There are quite a few SUVs and large trucks in our faculty and staff parking lot. I don't think students begrudge the fact that our parking lot is the closest to the school—and frequently filled with empty spaces—but I am sure we would be courting substantial discontent if we were to implement this proposal.

"Second. Implementation of the proposal would be an administrative nightmare. The registration and monitoring process for our students' vehicles is difficult enough, involving so many vehicles. Now you are proposing that these vehicles be registered and monitored for fuel efficiency and carbon emissions. This proposal diverts not only time but resources from our primary mission of education.

"Third. The tools to implement the proposed policy are illusive. Gas mileage does not always correlate with carbon emission. Some vehicles rated at twenty-seven miles per gallon produce more carbon emissions than vehicles rated at twenty-four miles per gallon.

"Now, Geraldine, while I oppose your motion, I support your purpose. We can and should do more. We all need to look around the campus and at home for other places to conserve. But, Geraldine, and fellow faculty members, let's vote this down but do what we can to support the purpose." Bruce then took his seat in the midsection once again, and the room quickly erupted into fifteen to twenty individual conversations.

Winston rapped sharply on the lectern to bring the meeting back to order. "Any further discussion *on the motion?*" he asked.

Professor Nathan Bedford Forrest Lee raised his hand. Lee was one of the original faculty members, having come to Savannah Law in the twilight of a notable career at Yale where he was Nicholas Debevoise Distinguished Professor of Constitutional Law. He left the cold confines of New Haven for health reasons, agreeing to teach at Savannah Law for a couple more years. In Savannah, his health greatly improved and he remained. As at Yale, he was genuinely and universally admired by both students and faculty. Lee was one of the few conservative faculty members at Savannah Law, as he had been at Yale. And he was one of only three registered Republicans on the faculty.

Lee did not often speak at faculty meetings. When he did, it was something profound and important that had been missed by other faculty members, or something wry or ironic. Winston recognized Lee to speak, and he rose with an impish grin.

"I urge a vote in favor of this motion," he said. "Although I must admit it would be a bad policy and present an arduous task to implement, it has one salient, positive feature that cries out for a favorable vote. And that is a pitiful, distant, sandspur-filled field will become the 'George W. Bush Parking Lot.' This is historic—the first and, likely, only time that any member of our faculty has ever proposed any building or place on our campus to be named in honor of a Republican president."

There was good-natured laughter as Lee took his seat, and Winston called for a voice vote. Only one voice was heard in favor, and that was from Professor Lee, who shouted his "yes" vote with a broad smile on his face. Geraldine looked apprehensively around the room for signs of support and, finding none, remained silent. The "no" vote followed, and it easily carried. After a quick motion to adjourn, the faculty members retired to the Faculty Dining Room for their weekly libations. Savannah Law had survived another meeting of the faculty.

CHAPTER 25

Jennifer arrived back in Savannah Tuesday afternoon. She had missed two whole days of classes but had made arrangements for a catch-up session at her apartment with Nicole. Scott and Jennifer played telephone tag Tuesday, and the sun had set before Scott finally heard her live voice. She was at her apartment. He wanted to tell her that he really wanted to see her now and spend some time together, but he knew that Nicole was already there. Thus, he merely asked, "When can I see you?"

Without hesitation, Jennifer answered, "Now! Can you come right now? Say 'yes'!"

"Yes, but isn't Nicole there now?"

"She is," answered Jennifer. "And we're just getting started, but Scott, please come. I've missed you. You don't have to come in. Park outside and I'll come out. I won't take much of your time."

Take all the time you want, thought Scott. All night would be just about right. But he just said, "I'm on the way."

Jennifer saw his car pull up and park. Turning to Nicole, she said, "I'll be back shortly," and rushed out the door.

She saw Scott getting out of his car and rushed to him. In the darkness, Scott could not see the tears that were welling in her eyes. He put his arms out to welcome her in a firm embrace. Scott held her until he felt tears slowly rolling down her face.

Scott stepped back but still held his hands around her waist. "What's the matter, Jennifer? You're upset."

How right he was. The roadside terror of Friday night was replaying in her mind. It had been bottled inside for almost four days. She had told no one. She had planned to tell Scott about the ordeal when she saw him in person. Now she was conflicted by the joy of seeing him and being held in his arms and the image of the monster that she faced on that darkened South Carolina highway on Friday night.

The tears continued, but she managed to say, "Scott, I'm just so glad to see you. It's been a long four days. I've got . . . we've got a lot of catching up to do. Nicole was kind enough to help me tonight.

Can I see you tomorrow night? I'm out of my last class at five. Can we meet at the Library then? Say 'yes'!"

Jennifer's demand to say "yes" was easy for Scott. He hoped it really was that she wanted to see him, to spend some time together. But he was not at all sure that the tears were because she was so glad to see him. He wondered if they were caused by the pressure of school or her father's illness, or perhaps both.

As he said "yes," he leaned over and gave her a kiss. Jennifer responded with the same intense passion as the last time: Friday night under the outdoor stairway at her apartment—which now seemed months ago to both of them.

For a moment, Scott thought of telling her that their meeting the next day would have to be brief because he had much work to do on the Vandera trial set for Thursday. But he knew it would not be brief. He would stay with her Wednesday night as long as she would let him.

CHAPTER 26
Wednesday, August 30

When Jaak arrived at work Wednesday morning, Juri was already there, as usual. "Got something for you, Jaak," he said, motioning Jaak over to a table where he had the marked Rider Back cards displayed. "I think I found another clue."

Jaak gazed down at the deck of cards. Juri had them arraigned in three stacks, face down.

"It took me a while because I was concentrating on the fancy design around the edges, and the circles within circles, and the big wheel in the middle. But I found it where I least expected it, and I guess that's the trick of designing marked cards. It's not easy to see unless you know what you are looking for. Look where the hands of the cherub, or whatever is riding that bicycle, are placed on the handlebars. Look at those handlebars. What do you see?" asked Juri.

Jaak peered closely at the back of the cards. After a minute or two, he stood and said, "Juri, I looked at those cards Sunday night and Monday morning until my eyes hurt. I saw nothing then, and I see nothing now."

"Look at the left end of the handlebar—the small oblong white mark—apparently the handlebar grip," Juri said, pointing to a card on the stack on the right side of the table. "Now look at the left end of the handlebar in the center stack. The small white grip is missing."

Jaak took another look, and after a moment, he just stood there nodding his head. He saw it clearly. It was so cleverly done— just a short white oblong mark on the end of the handlebar. It blended so well. Jaak could not help but admire the simple, but elusive, design. "I see it, Juri. What's in the third stack?" asked Jaak.

"The same mark, but on the *right* handlebar. There are three different designs in the scheme. Mark on right handlebar, mark on left handle bar, and no mark on either. That's the key."

"The key? How?"

"Look at the top row—the stack with all aces, 2s, 3s, and 4s. Those cards have no marks on the handlebar grip. And the middle row—5s, 6s, 7s, 8s, and 9s. That row has the mark on the right side. And the bottom row—the row with 10s, jacks, queens, and kings—the mark is on the left grip." Juri turned to Jaak with a grin, inviting a comment from Jaak.

Jaak didn't speak. He picked up a 3 from the top row. He recalled from his examination on Monday morning that all the 3s had three of the small sea gulls in the lower part of the circle. Then he picked up an 8, which he recalled also had three gulls in the lower part of the circle. Next, he picked up a king—also with three gulls.

And it came to him. It was so uncomplicated yet so shrewd. Just add five if the mark is on the right grip. Add ten if the mark is on the left grip. And add nothing if there is no mark on either side. He picked up a card, with the mark on the right grip from the second row. It had three gulls. The math is easy. Add five. Jaak turned the card over. An 8.

Jaak was pleased to know the entire code, but it really made no difference, for the cards would never be placed in action again. He would just keep them somewhere as a visible reminder. But a reminder of what? Man's greed, deceit, guile, double-dealing, duplicity? Or perhaps it was none of these but, instead, a man's excessive pride and the embarrassment from being the sheep that was sheared every Sunday night. Jaak would neither guess at nor judge the motive behind Denis's deception. He would just confront him with the evidence and terminate his welcome at the Sunday-night poker table.

CHAPTER 27

It was a few minutes before five when Scott arrived at the Library to meet Jennifer. The evening crowd had not begun to arrive, and the Numark system was playing some of Juri's favorite jazz. Scott took a seat at the bar, and he and Juri began a lively conversation about their favorite subject and team—specifically, baseball and the Atlanta Braves. And, as usual, it involved the Braves' dismal play in recent weeks. Their chances of making the playoffs looked dim.

"Slim to none," Juri complained. "Philadelphia and the Mets look strong and are getting stronger. The Braves can't hit, and they can't pitch. Stick a fork in 'em, they're done."

Juri enjoyed discussing baseball with Scott. Scott had been involved in the Braves' organization for two years after graduating from Alabama. As a third baseman, he had been selected "All SEC" in his senior year. He had applied for admission to the law school at the University of Alabama, but he also had major league aspirations, and his college coach encouraged him to "go for it." His tryout with the Braves organization in the spring of his senior year was successful, and upon graduation he was sent to the Danville Braves of the Appalachian League. After a year, he was promoted to the Rome Braves in the Class A South Atlantic League. And that was as far as he went. Eventually, he recognized that although he was an exceptional fielder, he wasn't exceptional at the plate. After two years in the minors, he knew that baseball wasn't going to be his career. He applied to several law schools, but with his aunt promising a free apartment and Savannah Law offering a partial scholarship, his choice was clear.

Scott looked at his watch. It was ten after five. Jennifer said she got out of class at five, so he knew that she would be there soon.

"Who's the jazz singer?" asked Scott.

"You don't recognize that voice? That's Amy Winehouse. 'October Song' from her 2003 album, *Frank*. Do you like it?" asked Juri.

"Not especially, but an interesting name for an album, *Frank*. Is that some guy she's singing to?" asked Scott.

"Nope. 'Frank' is Frank Sinatra—her idol when he was singing jazz. So maybe she is singing to him. Some people think that the name came from her lyrics being so 'frank,' but that's not true, although some of them are pretty raw. I don't play them when the family dinner crowd is here—but on a slow, late afternoon like today, I put her on. She's got *some* voice. Too bad she needs constant and perpetual rehab." Juri paused a few moments and then added, "Scott, speaking of 'constant and perpetual,' you keep looking at your watch. What's up?"

"Jennifer's meeting me here after her last class. She'll be here soon," said Scott.

"Well, you've got time for a couple stories," said Juri.

He always used 'story' instead of 'joke,' but Scott knew what was coming and began to smile.

"Guy walks into a lawyer's office, says, 'If I give you five hundred dollars, will you answer two questions?' The lawyer says, 'Sure, what's the second question?'"

Scott laughed, and Juri continued.

"I guess you heard about that band of terrorists who took a busload of lawyers as hostages. They called a radio station with a list of demands and added that they were going to *release* one lawyer every hour if their demands weren't met." As usual, Juri laughed heartily at his own joke.

Scott laughed along with him but added, "Juri, you know you're not supposed to tell lawyer jokes. I heard Jaak tell you that."

"Right. And speaking of Jaak, I better get that Winehouse CD off the player. The next couple of songs are a bit raunchy."

Juri replaced the CD with another jazz singer. When he returned, he said, "That's Billie Holiday's 'Body and Soul'—she was another tragedy. Seems like the great jazz and blues singers carry the same curse. And if Amy Winehouse doesn't get her life together, she'll end up like Holiday and Janis Joplin."

"And how's that? I know about Winehouse, but Holiday and Joplin? I'm not a jazz historian."

"Early death from drugs and alcohol—must be part of the profession. Holiday had a history of drugs and died of cirrhosis of the liver. She was forty-four. Janis Joplin—a hell of a blues and jazz singer—died of a heroin overdose in a Hollywood hotel room. She was a member of the Twenty-Seven Club."

"Twenty-Seven Club? Come on, Juri, quit talking in code. I told you I don't know jazz history."

"Oh, it's just for famous musicians who died at age twenty-seven. Joplin was twenty-seven. Jimi Hendrix, Jim Morrison, Brian James, and Kurt Cobain are also members of the club, and there are a dozen or so more. Most, but not all, drug connected. And Amy Winehouse is headed that way if she doesn't get some serious rehab. And she's just twenty-three."

Another customer came in, took a seat at the bar, and Juri went over to take his order.

Scott checked his watch again. It was almost five-thirty. Maybe he misunderstood the time. He stepped down from the bar stool and headed for the alcove to give Jennifer a call. As he did, Jennifer came hurriedly through the doorway. She had a backpack filled with books and a large envelope in her hand.

"Sorry I'm late, Scott. Professor Nolan left a voice message on my cell to check with him after my last class. He gave me the case file for the Daniels Trial Competition. He wants to meet with the witnesses tonight at seven in his office. Also wants us to have read through the file by then, especially the witness statements. That's what's in this envelope."

Scott took the envelope in one hand and Jennifer's hand in the other and led her to a nearby table in the Study Hall. Jennifer removed her backpack, and they sat side by side.

"Not much notice," said Scott. "He wants you to have read this by tonight, and you pick it up at five?" Scott opened the envelope and flipped through the file. "Ninety-six pages—that's two hours or more." He was irritated, and it was showing. And he knew it was showing.

"Sorry, Jen, if I seem miffed. But I was really looking forward to seeing you tonight. I hadn't expected to share that time with some professor, especially Nolan."

"Neither did I," said Jennifer. She noted the "especially Nolan" comment but ignored it. She was as disappointed as Scott.

This was to be a special night, and she had a lot to tell Scott. But it wasn't shaping up to be very special.

Scott was about to ask her how Professor Nolan knew her cell phone number when he recalled that she had supplied it the first time they met in Thomas Courthouse. And that irritated him even more.

"Looks like our night is planned *for* us, not *by* us," said Scott. "I think we should get a quick bite to eat right here so you can have a few minutes to look at that case file before your meeting."

Jennifer had hoped to tell Scott about her Friday night trip. She was still seeing that hand shaking and splattering blood on her windshield. She needed to get it off of her mind. But again, it wasn't the time or place.

They ordered sandwiches and talked. She had spoken with her mother earlier in the day. Her dad was continuing to improve. She and Scott made small talk about school, her classes, and Scott's case scheduled for the next morning. They made a date for Thursday, same place, at six.

Scott walked with her to the Savannah Law library where she would have about an hour to read the case file before the team meeting with Professor Nolan.

As she entered, she asked herself, "Just what are you getting into?"

Scott was in a somber mood as he drove back to his apartment. It had been a disappointing evening, and he still had work to do on the Vandera case, scheduled for nine the next morning. And he was concerned about the work piling on Jennifer. Professor Nolan was doing her no favor, but he had been unable to convince her of that. Now that she had started, he knew she would not back out. The good part, if there was one, was that the competition would be over in early November, and she would have the rest of the semester to concentrate on her classes, and maybe some time to spend with him. Now, though, he had a long night of trial preparation.

•   •   •

At seven sharp, Jennifer knocked on Professor Nolan's office door and was quickly invited in. Nolan was seated at his desk. As she entered, he immediately got up and walked to greet her.

"Hi, Jennifer. Please be seated." He pointed toward a light-tan leather sofa.

Jennifer looked around at the large office and its impressive furniture. An L-shaped wooden desk and credenza occupied the space in front of the picture window overlooking the courtyard. Floor-to-ceiling wooden bookcases were on both side walls, perfectly matching the color and wood of the desk and credenza. Jennifer could not be sure, but it all appeared to be Brazilian rosewood. What she was sure of was that she had never seen such expensive office furnishings in any faculty office at Savannah College of Art and Design. In addition to the leather sofa and its matching club chair, there were two intricately carved Chippendale-style arm chairs. A large Persian rug, with a distinct Tabriz geometric pattern and multicolored silk highlights, extended from the entryway to the desk. On the wall near the doorway were framed diplomas and certificates of admission to the Illinois and Georgia Bars. The credenza held two 8×10 photo frames. An LCD monitor sat on the desk. Other than that, the desk, credenza, and walls were bare: no other pictures, books, papers, or clutter. A *very* neat office, Jennifer thought, as she took her seat on the sofa.

Nolan took a seat in the leather chair next to the sofa. "We'll be working together for the next few weeks, so I thought this would be a good time to get to know you a little better. Today I called Nate Grant, the coach, to ask about the practice schedule, but he was in court and hasn't returned my call. I'm really looking forward to working with you on this. I'll also be going to Atlanta with you and the team. It will be a lot of work, but maybe we can have some sightseeing time, too. Atlanta's an exciting town—we should have some fun."

Nolan paused, apparently searching for something additional to say. His extended silence gave Jennifer time to wonder why the other witnesses were not present. Nolan had said he would be meeting with the *witnesses*—plural—at seven.

To remedy the awkward silence, she said, "The other witnesses . . . who will be coming?"

"There was a mix-up. But I'm pleased you are here. I'll meet with the others later. How do you like the office?"

"It's beautiful," Jennifer responded. But she was wondering about the "mix-up." It had been clear to *her* that the meeting was at seven.

"Don't worry; it's not from tuition money." Nolan gave a light chuckle. "I decided that this would be my home for a while. I had a little extra money and brought in a professional decorator. I'm glad you like it."

Again, an uncomfortable silence. Maybe, Jennifer thought, he expected *her* to take charge of the conversation.

"How long have you been at Savannah Law, Professor?" She already knew the answer, but it was a safe question.

"I was one of the original faculty members. Came down from Chicago, where I was practicing. Interviewed for the real property slot, accepted it, and have been here since. But how about you, Jennifer? Tell me about yourself."

Jennifer proceeded with a brief sketch of her family and undergraduate studies and threw in the story of her trip to Springfield that led to her interest in the law. The professor leaned forward in his chair to listen. When she had finished, he had more questions: Was she enjoying law school? Was she in a study group? What was her "lifestyle" like now? How did she spend her leisure time?

She still held in her lap the envelope with the case file he had given her. Surely he had noticed it, she thought. But she had been there a half-hour or more, and he had said nothing about the case file, her witness role, or the purpose of the visit. Perhaps *she* should broach the topic.

"I brought the file, but I'm not sure of my witness assignment," she finally said.

"Have you had time to read through it?"

"I did, but I'm afraid my reading was not very thorough. There are a lot of details in that first statement that were not clear. I kept flipping back to the deposition."

"You are ahead of me. I really haven't read any of it yet. I will this weekend."

Again there was a long pause, but Jennifer decided to let Nolan take charge of the conversation. He was still leaning forward in his chair, gazing straight at her, but perhaps he was preoccupied with something else. He appeared to be struggling to find something to keep the conversation moving but couldn't.

Nolan put his left hand to his temple and began to rub it vigorously. "I'm sorry, Jennifer, but I feel a headache coming on. I can usually ward it off with an aspirin. Excuse me, I have some over at my desk."

Nolan went to his desk. He opened a drawer and removed a small tin box. He quickly opened it, removed a large, white tablet and placed it in his mouth. He then opened a bottle of Aquafina, took a few sips, and returned to his seat in the leather chair.

"I think that will work," Nolan said and smiled at Jennifer.

It was obvious to Jennifer that it was not aspirin that he took from the tin box.

The phone rang. Nolan jumped as if startled and went back to his desk to answer it. There was a short conversation, and Nolan returned to his chair.

"That was Nate. Said he will be in court all week but will try to have a complete schedule by Friday. He's working with the student advocates on case analysis this weekend. He doesn't expect to need witnesses until sometime next week."

Jennifer was relieved not to have to dive immediately into practice. She needed some time to catch up with her missed classes.

"Then I'll be going, Professor." She stood. "Time to hit the books. But I do want to compliment you again on your beautiful office."

"Thanks, Jennifer, but, please, you don't have to leave. I'm really not busy tonight."

"I really must be going, Professor. Thursday is another busy day for me, and another R & W paper is due. Thanks for your help." Jennifer walked to the door, opened it herself, and walked out.

In the hallway, she laughed to herself at her parting words, "Thanks for your help." What help? Just what was that "meeting" about anyway? Strange, very strange, she thought.

CHAPTER 28
Thursday, August 31

Jennifer was up early Thursday morning. She had quite a bit of reading to do, plus a couple of cases to brief before her first class. She reflected on the meeting the previous evening. It was uneventful yet a bit unsettling. Maybe it was, as he said, just to get to know the students who would be helping as witnesses. *Students*, plural. But she was the only student. And she thought about his questions concerning her "lifestyle" and "leisure time." She had never thought about her "lifestyle." That seemed to be an odd question for a professor to ask a new student. She was glad she had simply ignored the question. And leisure time? So far, she had found very little.

Jennifer made a pot of coffee and some toast. Then she sat down at her dining table with her case book and began to read. She had a couple of hours to study before her first class.

At 8:30 a.m., she put her books and papers into her backpack and walked to the front door to leave. There, placed just inside the screen door, was a large sealed manila envelope. Apparently, Nicole or one of the other study-group members had left some material for her. She had not heard the door bell. Perhaps they were in a hurry and knew she would find it when she left for school. She put her backpack down and opened the envelope. There were no papers in the envelope, only a piece of cloth.

As Jennifer looked more closely at the contents, she saw that it was a black head scarf with white crosses, and it was covered with dark red stains. She knew immediately who had left it there.

• • •

Scott was in Judge Vesely's courtroom by 8:15 a.m. on Thursday. He did not get much sleep Wednesday night. Yes, he was nervous, but he took some comfort in Grady's advice that this was actually *good*. Even experienced attorneys are nervous before the start of a jury trial. It means that the adrenaline is pumping; the mind is in a heightened state of alertness.

Richard Evans, the DA investigator, arrived at 8:30 a.m. He brought with him the photos, diagrams, and charts that Scott would use as exhibits. Just a few minutes later, Grady arrived. The three were reviewing the prosecution plan one last time when the defense team of Jeff Swenson and Charlie Roberts, along with the defendant, entered and took seats at the defense table.

At 9 a.m., Judge Vesely entered from a side door. The bailiff delivered three sharp raps with the tall wooden staff and called, "All rise!"

Counsel and spectators were quickly on their feet. The judge took her seat, motioned for those now standing to be seated, and called the court to order. Scott stood and announced that the prosecution was ready; Jeff did the same for the defense. The trial of Charles Vandera for burglary of the CVS store was officially underway.

Scott was surprised that the defense had no additional pretrial motions. He had anticipated motions attacking the second indictment process and the pretrial discovery. He also expected a motion—he wasn't sure what form it would take—regarding Mary Vandera, who was listed as a prosecution witness. But there were none, other than a request that she be exempted from the sequestration motion and allowed to remain in the courtroom during the trial. The trial quickly moved to jury selection.

Jury selection was the part of the trial that Scott knew was his weakest. His trial competition experience had given him practice in all phases of a criminal trial except jury selection. Just how do you peer into the mind of a juror to really determine fairness and impartiality? And did he really want a "fair and impartial" jury? The defense surely did not. They wanted every juror to be slanted toward the defense. Should the prosecution team seek a jury favorable to the prosecution?

Scott wasn't going to debate with himself whether he ethically could seek a jury skewed to the prosecution side of this case. Even if he were so inclined, the defense had plenty of tools to ensure his failure. This was an adversarial process. The defense could ask almost any questions to explore the mind of every juror. Afterwards, they would have unlimited challenges to strike from the panel anyone shown to be unfair or partial. And on top of that, they had nine peremptory challenges—challenges to exercise as they chose against any juror, no reason needed. Scott's job was just to ensure that the jury did not end up as a "defense jury." He may not have a "law and order" jury, but he would do his best not to end up with a jury that would convict only if they had fingerprint or DNA evidence, or a sworn confession. He knew that television programs such as *CSI* had accustomed the public to expect forensic evidence at a criminal trial, and he had none to present.

Scott had prepared a jury profile of the *good* and the *bad* jurors from the prosecution perspective. It was subjective and unscientific, and Grady had warned him not to put much faith in categorizing jurors by demographics. But he had to start somewhere. Good jurors would be business owners; professionals such as dentists, insurance brokers, and accountants; former military and law enforcement personnel; single mothers; mainstream Protestants; northern Europeans; government employees; handicapped persons; and anyone over sixty. Bad jurors would be mothers of teenage boys and young men; musicians—especially rock musicians; artists—especially tattoo artists; anyone with multiple tattoos; motorcyclists—especially tattooed motorcyclists; dancers—especially exotic dancers; anyone with a prior criminal record; and any recent college graduate with a degree in sociology. This last "bad juror" resulted from a warning he had heard from an experienced prosecutor: "Never accept a college grad with a sociology major. Don't ask why. Just don't do it."

Scott looked at his jury profile of the good and bad jurors one last time. He wanted to remind himself of various elements in the profile. But just what was he to do with the musician who was also ex-military? The former policeman with multiple tattoos? Or perhaps the handicapped insurance broker with a degree in sociology?

He did not have an answer for these questions, and when the voir dire was over, he discarded his list of good and bad jurors and exercised his challenges the same way most experienced attorneys do: by a simple subjective appraisal. Do I like this juror? Am I comfortable with this juror? And does this juror appear comfortable with me? In the final analysis, occupation, marital state, or handicap status did not enter the equation at all. Scott exercised six challenges, the defense eight, and then the jury panel to hear the case of *State of Georgia versus Charles Vandera* was sworn.

Judge Vesely gave the newly sworn jurors preliminary instructions and looked toward the prosecution table. "You may make your opening statement."

Scott walked to the lectern and placed his notes on top. Then he moved directly in front of the lectern. He would not need notes.

"Members of the jury," he began, "the state has charged this defendant with the offense of burglary. Judge Vesely will instruct you later that burglary is an unlawful entry into a building with intent to commit a felony or theft. In this case, it is a burglary that took place at the CVS Pharmacy, 1128 East Grissom Avenue, right here in the city of Savannah. It occurred in the early morning hours of April twenty-fourth of this year, when most of the workers at that pharmacy were safely sleeping in their homes. There was one employee who was not at home asleep but, instead, was out prowling the city." Scott paused, turned to look at the defense table, and pointed directly at the defendant. "That employee is seated at that table. His name is Charles Vandera. Let me outline for you just how the defendant prepared for and committed this crime.

"It is after midnight. The pharmacy is quiet inside—not a sound—and it's been that way since the night manager locked up and departed shortly after 11 p.m. But had you been nearby, outside, you might have heard the slight scraping sound made as Charles Vandera placed an aluminum ladder against the building. But maybe not; this was a quiet, stealthy crime, carefully planned.

"It is a strong and tall ladder. It has to be, because Charles Vandera plans to get to the very top and onto the roof of the building. As he climbs that ladder, he has a lightweight but strong rope with him. It is a solid braided polyester rope, thirty feet in length, with knots tied at intervals along the way. He has a chisel, a small crowbar, and a small flashlight. And he has something else: a pair of latex gloves on his hands.

"He completes his climb, and once on the roof, he walks over to the area where there is an air-conditioning unit. This unit is near a glass skylight with an acrylic covering—a safety measure to protect the glass beneath it. He must remove, or at least breach, that outer cover and then break the glass beneath. He chisels. He stops, and he listens. He's careful to make as little noise as possible. At this time of night, traffic is light, and there is no other noise to muffle his crime. He breaks through the acrylic cover. So far, so good. Now, the skylight glass is all that is left.

"The glass is not thick; it's no match for his crowbar. It shatters, and most of the glass crashes to the floor below. But not all. There are still a few jagged edges along the sides. With the entry hole now made, it's time to secure the rope. The air-conditioner unit is only five feet away. He ties one end of the rope securely around the unit. He then drops the other end through the hole, and then the crowbar and the chisel. Now he has to drop his five-foot, nine-inch frame through the hole while holding onto the rope. Not a difficult job for a young man, but there is danger—the jagged edges of glass around the sides. It is dark, and although he has a flashlight, he must be careful. A light on top of a roof well after midnight would be suspicious. Into the hole he goes. It's not far to the bottom, and the knots on the rope give him support for both his feet and his hands. All is going as planned, except he cuts his forearm on the jagged glass.

"Charles Vandera is now in the pharmacy. Shelves upon shelves and cabinets and drawers surround him. Wooden shelves with small hinges and small locks. He pulls on the cabinet doors, grasping the bottoms or the tops, wherever he can get leverage. Some pop off immediately. Some require the crowbar. Before him now are all sorts of medicines and drugs in all types of containers. But as he looks through the piles of drugs he has uncovered, he is puzzled."

Scott held out his hands, palms up, and looked slowly from one side of the jury to the other before continuing.

"Where is the good stuff—the stuff he came for? The stuff that would cause him to crash through a skylight and burglarize a pharmacy in the middle of the night? Then he saw it: the big safe— the seven hundred-pound, solid-steel safe with the electronic lock— the size of a small bank vault. Attack it with a chisel and crowbar? No way. For Charles Vandera, the evening is over. He has no use for the beta blockers, diuretics, asthma inhalers, and antibiotics that he found. What he wanted—the *real* drugs—are safely locked in that big seven hundred-pound vault. With no chance of breaking into that safe, he turns to his escape route, which he had planned as carefully as his entry. As an employee, he knows the security system, and it takes only a moment to disarm it. That done, he's out the front door.

"What has he accomplished? Substantial damage to a pharmacy. Cuts on his forearm. And the loss of his burglary tools— the thirty-foot rope, an eight-inch chisel, and a crowbar. But there was something else he lost, something much more valuable. Something he left on the pharmacy counter . . . a tool that silently says, 'This crime was committed by Charles Vandera.'"

Scott stopped. He wanted to see the reaction from the defense table. Glancing ever so slightly to his left, he got it: a *puzzled* look from both defense counsel—a look of "what the hell is he talking about?" Scott knew then that Charles Vandera had made the same mistake that had damned so many criminal defendants over the years: he had lied to his counsel. Scott continued with his opening statement.

"That, members of the jury, is how Charles Vandera committed the crime of burglary of the CVS Pharmacy at 1128 East Grissom Avenue, here in Savannah, on April twenty-fourth of this year. Now let's turn to the investigation of this crime and the evidence."

Scott began to describe the discovery of the break-in, the arrival of the detectives and the forensic team, and the taking of statements. He then turned his attention to the day the defendant first reported back to work, two days after the burglary with visible cuts on his arm.

"Charles Vandera was not arrested that day. The detectives had other evidence to examine and other leads to follow. It was not fingerprints that led to his arrest. There were none. Latex gloves don't leave finger prints. You will learn that Charles Vandera left behind on the pharmacy counter something more revealing, more incriminating, than fingerprints. And you will be convinced beyond any reasonable doubt that Charles Vandera is guilty of this crime as charged."

Scott took his seat, and as he did so, he received a thumbs up from Grady discretely out of the jury's view. Whatever the state of Scott's nerves when the trial started, they were now settled and calm. He was going to enjoy this trial.

Judge Vesely looked at the defense table and asked if the defense wished to make an opening statement. "We would like to reserve our opening until the prosecution has presented its evidence," responded Jeff.

"The state may call its first witness," said Judge Vesely.

Scott's first witness was the night manager, who testified to setting the alarm system and locking the store for the evening. The store manager and the morning pharmacist were next. Their testimony concerned their observations upon arrival at the store in the morning and the absence of the defendant from work for two days. There was little cross-examination. It was now past noon. Judge Vesely recessed the court for lunch and ordered the trial to reconvene at 2 p.m.

Over the noon hour, Grady and Scott discussed the witnesses to be called in the afternoon. They still had the two detectives, the forensic investigation team, and the assistant manager who first saw the cuts on the defendant's forearm. And, of course, the defendant's mother, Mary Vandera. It was obvious that the prosecution case would not be finished that day. So far, the cross-examination of the state's witnesses had been limited. But Scott knew he would soon be facing an all-out attack on the quality of the investigation. The defense would surely put the detectives and their investigation on trial.

"The claim of a sloppy, negligent, ineffective investigation is a common defense tactic," Grady had warned. "Where are the fingerprints on the crowbar—on the ladder—on the chisel—on the cabinet doors—on the counter tops—on the front door—on the alarm system? Where are the print matches to the defendant? What did the detectives do to trace the origin of the crowbar—the chisel—the rope? If Charles Vandera cut himself entering through the skylight, why was no blood found anywhere in the store? Why did they let the glass get hauled away, and why didn't they try to recover it? What about the painters and their ladder? Why didn't they interview the painters' friends and relatives?"

And so on it would go. So far, the state's evidence had not connected Charles Vandera to the burglary in any meaningful way. That would come when Mary Vandera identified the retinoscope. And he needed Mary Vandera to testify truthfully without realizing the significance of her testimony. If she realized that she was *the* witness who would assure her son's conviction, would she lie? Only a fool, Scott thought, would expect a mother to knowingly incriminate her son in a felony.

The retinoscope would have to be identified by the forensic team as having been found at the crime scene. And normally the forensic team and the detectives would testify before Mary Vandera; they would be necessary to establish the "chain of possession" before the retinoscope could be admitted into evidence. But this was not a *normal* case. A defense team totally in the dark about the prosecutor's case is not normal, and certainly a mother offering critical testimony against her son is not normal. Scott decided to call Mary Vandera as his first witness of the afternoon. He did not want to give the defense a full evening to ponder the mystery evidence he had alluded to in his opening statement.

• • •

Judge Vesely gaveled the court to order promptly at 2 p.m.

"Call your next witness."

"The state calls Mary Vandera."

Mary Vandera was seated in the rear of the courtroom, alone. Although she had been attentive to the proceedings, she did not get up when her name was called. Her eyes were opened wide, but otherwise she had an expressionless face and remained seated. Scott was certain she had not been informed by the defense counsel of why she was there. How could they? They had no clue why she was on the state's witness list.

Seeing that she made no movement to come forward, Scott told a bailiff that Mary Vandera was the lady in the blue dress in the back of the courtroom. The bailiff walked to where she was seated and escorted her to the front of the courtroom. She was sworn and took her seat in the witness chair.

"Would you please state your name, and spell your last name for the court reporter," said Scott.

"Mary Vandera. V-A-N-D-E-R-A."

"Do you know the defendant in this case, Charles Vandera?"

"Yes, he is my son."

Scott pointed in the direction of the defense table and said, "And that is your son seated on the far side of that table?"

"Yes."

Scott picked up a large envelope from the clerk's table, one of several that had been marked for identification at the beginning of the trial. Because the defense had "opted out" of reciprocal discovery, the defense would be seeing the evidence for the first time. Scott walked to the defense table and offered the envelope to the defense counsel for examination. Both Jeff and Roberts opened the flap of the envelope and peered in. Jeff held the flap open and placed it in front of Charles Vandera to view. He peered inside briefly and then turned his head to look directly at his mother.

Scott retrieved the envelope, turned to the judge, and said, "Your Honor, may I approach the witness with an exhibit?"

"No!"

The shout came from the defendant. Before Judge Vesely could respond, Charles Vandera stood and again shouted, "No!"

Immediately his defense counsel stood and forcefully pushed him back into his seat. A bailiff moved swiftly toward the defense table and stood between the jury and the defendant. From the small courtroom crowd, there was a hushed silence. The eyes of the jury shifted rapidly between the defense table and the judge's bench.

With the defendant once again seated and quiet, Charlie Roberts looked at Judge Vesely and said, "May we have a moment, Your Honor?"

An emotional and lively whispered conversation took place at the defense table. Charles Vandera continued to shake his head negatively. Scott returned to his seat and conferred with Grady.

Judge Vesely looked at the ongoing conference between defense counsel and their client for several minutes and then stated, "Mr. Swenson, the court is ready to proceed. Are you and your client now ready?"

"Your Honor, may we approach the bench?"

The judge gave her approval, and the two defense counsel, along with Scott and Grady, walked to the bench for a whispered conversation.

Jeff was the first to speak. "Your Honor, we would request a brief recess. We would like to discuss a possible plea with the prosecution."

Without hearing from Scott or Grady, Judge Vesely announced the court would be in recess, and the bailiff escorted the jury from the courtroom.

"Mrs. Vandera, you may step down from the witness stand. Please remain in the courtroom," said the judge. "Counsel, I'll give you ten minutes to discuss a possible plea. If you can't reach an agreement in that time, we'll reconvene and continue. I have a full schedule of cases next week, and we need to complete this case by Friday evening."

The four counsel huddled at the prosecution table to begin their discussion. "The defendant will take the pretrial agreement as previously offered," said Jeff.

"That pretrial offer expired Monday," said Scott. "We've subpoenaed our witnesses, and we have a sworn jury. That pretrial offer was made to save money and the time of the court, as well as witness time, jury time, and counsel time. He pleads straight up if he's going to enter a plea. There is no plea agreement for him to accept."

"You may think there is no advantage to the state to accept the old pretrial, but, in fact, there is. Your evidence is not as strong as you may think. Not to be trite, but take a clue from Yogi Berra: 'It ain't over 'til it's over.' You have a long way to go. There is a chance—a good chance—of acquittal," said Jeff.

"We'll take that chance," said Scott. "He pleads straight up and no pretrial, or we call his mother back to the stand and continue. His call."

Jeff did not respond but walked back to the defense table for a conversation with the defendant. This time there was no animated or emotional conversation. Jeff was explaining the situation, and the defendant was merely nodding. Whatever the decision, it was finally settled.

Jeff did not return to give Scott the defendant's response. He looked at Judge Vesely, who was still at the bench examining some papers, and said, "Your Honor, the defendant wishes to enter a plea to the charge."

Scott was disappointed to hear that. He had prepared hard and wanted the experience this trial would give him. At the same time, he knew it was the best outcome; a jury conviction still has to survive an appeal while a guilty plea is rarely overturned.

The defendant entered his plea of guilty, and Judge Vesely remanded him to the sheriff for custody until a sentencing hearing could be held.

After Vandera was led from the courtroom by the bailiff, Jeff walked over to shake Scott's hand. "Congratulations, Scott—you win. I'm just sorry it ended this way."

"You mean by a plea? Even without the pretrial, it's best for your defendant. The judge may cut him some slack. A conviction was coming sooner or later, so what's the difference?"

"No difference now, but there could have been a big difference, Scott. You were going to be in for a surprise or two," replied Jeff.

"I was going to be in for a surprise? Bigger than the one you got when I brought out that little flashlight for his mother to identify?"

"That was no surprise, Scott. How about meeting me at the Library so we can discuss it and hoist one to our first felony case?"

"I'll see you there."

After a short conversation with Grady, Scott gathered his papers and briefcase and left for the Library.

CHAPTER 29

Scott arrived at the Library a little after four and took a seat at the bar, alone. A few customers, mostly students with books propped in front of them, were seated at tables in the Study Hall. Jeff arrived in a few minutes and joined Scott at the bar.

Juri was not immediately behind the bar, but as soon as he saw Scott and Jeff, he came over. He knew about the scheduled trial and that Scott and Jeff were on opposing sides. Several of their friends, other clinic students, had been in at lunch time and were discussing it. It was always big news among clinic students when a fellow student actually got to try a felony case.

"Ah, the two of you, together again! Did you kiss and make up?" asked Juri.

"My mouth is much too dry to kiss. I need something wet and cold. Set us up with your coldest draft," replied Jeff.

Juri turned to fill the order, at the same time proclaiming, "It's half-price trivia time!" This was an offer he frequently made—answer the trivia question and the beer was half price. He placed two cold mugs of beer on the bar in front of them.

"And for you, Jeff," he said, "who was the only president to be married in the White House?"

Scott quickly said, "Juri, that's way too tough for Jeff; he couldn't tell you who occupies the White House today."

"Of course, I can," said Jeff. "That's Ralph Nader. And to answer *your* question, Juri, that has to be Theodore Roosevelt. I know his first wife died."

"Wrong. And for you, Scott, whose picture is on the $100,000 bill?"

"There's a $100,000 bill?" asked Scott.

"Was at one time, but no longer. I'll even give you a clue. He was a president of the United States—and not Ralph Nader."

"Thanks—that was going to be my first guess. So, how about John Adams. I'm doubling my chances. There were two of them, so with either one, I win."

"Wrong, and since you doubled up, I'm doubling your tab."

"So give us the answers. You can't just say we're wrong," said Jeff.

"I can, and I did. Like your professors would tell you, look it up; that way you won't forget."

"But I *want* to forget. My mind can only retain so much," said Jeff.

"You sure leave yourself open," Juri said with a laugh as he moved over to wait on a customer.

"Let's get a table," said Scott.

They left enough cash on the bar to pay their tab and brought their beers with them.

"I'm curious about your defense strategy," said Scott. "And your comment about a 'surprise or two' for the prosecution. Weren't you caught totally by surprise when the defendant decided to change his plea? We certainly were. I guess he didn't want to sit there while his mother identified the retinoscope as one she owned."

"Wrong," said Jeff.

"Wrong? He knew he was about to be put away by his own mother, didn't he?"

"No; Charles didn't plead guilty because he was afraid his mother was going to tell the truth. He was afraid she would lie. He was concerned that his action had caused his mother to be placed in a position to commit perjury. And she was about to do that."

"How? Wasn't she going to identify the retinoscope as hers?"

"No way, Scott. She was going to collapse your case. She knew from the beginning that she was the link to putting her son in prison, and she sure wasn't going to let that happen with her testimony."

"You're telling me she knew all along why she was on the prosecution list? I can't believe her son would tell her he committed that crime. I actually felt sorry for her, poor soul."

"Yeah, 'poor soul.' She was way ahead of you guys from the get-go. Do you think she would forget about that visit from the detectives and her ID of that retinoscope?"

"But the defense opted out of discovery. What did you know about our case? We thought it really strange . . . why would you do that?"

"Didn't need your discovery. Just think, Scott, if a defendant tells you everything—when, where, and how, what he left behind and what he didn't leave behind—what do we learn from discovery?"

"You could have learned if we had forensic evidence—fingerprints, blood."

"Yes, the blood part bothered us initially. If the forensic team found blood, you had him cold. But they never tried to get a DNA or blood sample, so eventually we were pretty sure you didn't find any blood. And as far as fingerprints were concerned, we weren't worried. I can't tell you what Charles told us—privileged, you know. But just suppose he was wearing thin latex gloves throughout as you said in your opening statement. We don't worry about fingerprints, do we?"

"No, but you and I both know clients don't tell you everything. You were taking a chance."

"No, *we* weren't taking a chance; *Charles* was. We warned him that it was his ass that would sit in jail, not ours. He's smart enough to know he had to level with us. And when we discovered he had leveled with his mother, we knew we could rely on him."

"So his mother was going to commit perjury—and you were going to let her lie through her teeth to the jury?"

"Not our witness who would be lying; it was *your* witness," said Jeff.

Scott held his beer in both hands and studied Jeff's response. After a moment's pause, he said, "True, our witness. Our witness would be lying, but you and Charlie Roberts would be the only ones aware of it. Don't you think that the Rules of Professional Conduct require that you inform the court that perjury is taking place?"

"Scott, the Rules of Professional Conduct require us to represent the accused zealously, not foolishly. Do you really think the defense has the responsibility to tell the court that the prosecution witness is lying?"

"Yes. The rules require that a lawyer make disclosure to avoid a criminal or fraudulent act being perpetrated on the court by his or her client. Charles's mother was acting in concert with your client. He obviously solicited her false testimony."

"Wrong, Scott; on the contrary, he obviously had no desire for her to testify falsely. Once he saw his mother was going to perjure herself, he made his decision to plead guilty. Have you already forgotten that?"

"That's a bunch of BS, and you know it. You've already said you didn't opt in to discovery because you didn't need it. You knew we had no fingerprints, and you knew the mother was going to deny ever seeing or possessing the retinoscope. So you and Roberts both were content for the false testimony to come from that woman. You were a two-man welcoming committee for the testimony. As you said, she was going to 'collapse' our case. What happened was as unexpected by you as by us—none of us expected that little night-creeping criminal to have a conscience, if that's what you want to call it. He got cold feet just as his mother was going to commit perjury."

"Scott, you're a good prosecutor. Have I complimented you on your opening statement? Should have, damn good. I was envious. And now you make another good argument. But face it, the situation you are complaining about is not covered by the Rules of Professional Conduct. Our client wasn't going to commit perjury. Your witness was. The rules don't require us to do anything in that event. OK, we could *request* that Charles speak with his mother and tell her to *please tell the truth*. Yes, Mrs. Vandera, make sure you tell the truth so Scott Marino can send your son to the Georgia Penitentiary for the next five years. But how real is that? We'll just have to agree to disagree on this."

Jeff stood. "I've got to go—got to find a couple witnesses to bribe for a trial scheduled for next week. By the way, how are you and Jen getting on? That's a cute gal. I sure don't understand what she sees in you. Give her my love when you see her, and tell her I miss her terribly."

CHAPTER 30

As soon as Jeff left, Scott walked over to the shelves holding the donated law books and found a copy of the Georgia Bar Handbook. He sat at his table, leafing through the Rules of Professional Conduct, determined to find the provision covering the situation. He found a rule that seemed to be on point, but it was qualified by a "however." The "however" emphasized that the "ethical" duty may be qualified by the constitutional provisions of "due process" and "right to counsel" in criminal cases. How ethics and the Constitution could conflict made no sense to Scott. He was thumbing through the rules again when he felt a pair of soft, warm hands reach around his head and cover his eyes.

"Let me guess," said Scott.

"OK, but if you guess wrong, you are in big trouble," replied Jennifer.

She took a seat next to Scott. "How's the trial going?"

"It's over," said Scott. "He pleaded guilty. How's your dad doing?"

"I spoke with my mom at noon. He was discharged from the hospital this morning. He's doing OK. Still some pain, but overall, good. He'll have to take it easy for a while. They're supposed to leave for a cruise in two weeks, and he's determined to make it. I'm going home after my last class tomorrow. But your trial—he pleaded? That was unexpected, wasn't it?"

"You bet. I'll tell you all about it later. How was the meeting with Professor Nolan? And how are your classes going?"

"Classes are going . . . well, that's about all I can say—they are going. Everyone feels overworked and behind. Misery loves company, so there's plenty of company. My study group keeps plodding along. Never enough time. Every professor seems to think his or hers is the only class we have. And the Research and Writing course is ridiculous with its time commitment. I have a big research paper due . . . ."

Jennifer stopped in midsentence. She saw Professor Denis Nolan entering from the alcove and walking in their direction.

Denis had apparently spotted them as he entered. As he approached, he gave a broad smile and said, "The Dean Search Committee at work. Hello, Scott, and hello, Jennifer. Mind if I join you?"

Without waiting for a reply, he sat down at their table. "Scott, you must be tutoring her. She's doing so well in my class that I'm going to offer her a job as my research assistant. And speaking of doing a good job, she's going to make a great witness for the trial team. I'm really looking forward to watching her performance in Atlanta."

The broad smile continued, and he had not taken his eyes off Jennifer since he sat down. "And Jennifer," Denis continued, "has Dean Adams called you about joining the Dean Search Committee?"

"No, I haven't spoken with him."

"Well, expect a call. I'm counting on you two."

"Denis, could I see you for a moment, over in the lounge?"

The voice came from about twenty feet away. The three of them recognized Jaak's voice. and they turned at the same time.

"Sure, Jaak." Denis got up, turned to Jennifer, and said, "I'll be back shortly; don't go away. I have something special to tell you."

Scott and Jennifer remained seated and watched as Denis followed Jaak toward the private lounge. Scott was the first to speak.

"Research assistant . . . Dean Search Committee . . . looking forward to watching you perform in Atlanta. If he was saying that to rattle my cage, he succeeded. I should give him an old-fashioned Tennessee knuckle sandwich, but that would be too messy on his soft, miserable face. Maybe I'll just knife the tires on his new Lexus."

Jennifer turned her head to keep Scott from seeing her failed attempt at suppressing a smile at his outburst. But she didn't say anything. She didn't blame Scott for being annoyed; she thought Nolan's comments were a bit much also.

•　•　•

Jaak quickly closed the lounge door and waved Denis to take a seat at the poker table. On the table, face down, was a deck of playing cards. Jaak picked up the deck.

"Denis, recognize these?" He held the deck in front of Denis.

Denis cocked his head to the left and seemed to squint with his left eye when he answered. "Do I recognize them? Should I recognize them?"

"That's two questions—and neither is an answer," said Jaak. He then spread the deck face down on the table.

"Jaak, what is this about? Why the quiz?"

"These are the cards we played with last Sunday. Look closely. Now do you recognize them?"

"No, I don't recognize them. What's going on with you, Jaak?"

Jaak picked up a card from the pile, flipped it in front of Denis, face down, and said, "Jack of hearts, right Denis?"

There was no smile on Denis's face now. His breathing became shallow and rapid. He did not respond.

Once again, Jaak repeated, "Jack of hearts, Denis. Right?"

When again there was no response, Jaak took another card and flipped it face down on top of the first card. "Nine of spades."

Still no response from Denis. Then another card.

"King of clubs," said Jaak.

Denis merely stared at the cards; he said nothing. Jaak quit flipping after the fifth card. Finally, Denis spoke. "I don't know what you're up to or where you are coming from, Jaak, but apparently you think these cards are marked, and I'm responsible."

"Right," said Jaak.

"Well, you're wrong. This conversation is offensive. I'm surprised you would dishonor our friendship with such an insinuation."

"It's not an insinuation, Denis. It's an accusation. And I'm surprised you would dishonor our friendship—and the friendship of our group—by bringing marked cards to the table."

"That's a lie, Jaak. If those cards are marked, they didn't come from me."

"Enough of your crap, Denis. You purchased those cards at the Magic Castle. You paid $149.99 plus tax. They were not in stock.

You had to place a special order and wait. And when they arrived, you brought them to the Sunday game."

Denis had been seated, but he hurriedly got up from his chair and stood, facing Jaak. Jaak stood also; he was expecting a physical confrontation. It did not come.

"OK, Jaak. So you know," Denis said through tightened lips. "But you've got to know also that it was all in fun. It was just a lark. I thought someone would catch on to it Sunday night. It was going to be a joke. But no one caught it, so I decided to just play along and wait to tell everyone about it at our next game. I plan to return all the money the gang lost. It was just a joke."

Jaak, who stood a couple inches taller than Denis, looked straight into his eyes and said, "You won't be returning any money here, Denis. I'm sorry it came to this, but you are no longer welcome. If you want me to return the money for you, I will do it, assuming you know how much each lost. I would be pleased to deliver it to each player and tell them what you say happened—and that you say it was just a joke. But if you prefer not to, I understand. In fact that may be advisable."

"What do you plan to tell them, Jaak, on Sunday night? I warn you, slander me and my name and you . . . ."

Jaak interrupted. "Hold on, Denis. Be careful about issuing warnings to me. You are smarter than that. I'm not out to do you harm. I'll simply tell them that for personal reasons you will no longer be playing. And that will be the truth, because I'm telling you *personally* that you are not playing. End of discussion. Now, I have some work to do."

With that, Jaak walked to the door and held it open for Denis to leave. Denis needed no prodding. He walked out and immediately departed the Library.

• • •

Scott and Jennifer saw him leave. "That's strange," said Scott. "Didn't Denis ask you not to go away, he had something to tell you?"

"He did say he would be back. I think he was addressing both of us," said Jennifer.

"He was looking only at you—as he did in Thomas Courthouse. I didn't like it then, and don't like it now. He eyes you like you are the only one in the room . . . and I'm just a potted plant."

"Would you like him to *eye* you and make *me* the potted plant?" Jennifer asked, laughing.

"Nope. And I wouldn't want him winking at me either." Scott smiled as he looked at Jennifer. "Jen, I'm sure glad to see you laughing. Tuesday night, you were in tears. You said they were 'happy tears,' but I'm not so sure. And last night you seemed a bit down. Tonight you are your old sparkling self—you must be getting a handle on the law school time squeeze."

"You are very perceptive, Scott." She hesitated a moment before continuing. "But it's nothing to do with law school. I've been walking around frightened since my trip home last Friday night. It was like carrying a heavy weight on my back, but this morning it was lifted . . . by what you might call the last straw. I decided I would not run, hide, whine, or whimper. I would not be afraid. I would fight it."

Jennifer then began to tell Scott the whole story, beginning with her trip to Marvin's Foreign Auto, the tailgating by the black Camry, the man and woman at the "quick-stop" store, and her car stalling on the darkened highway. She recalled every detail of Craig's futile attempt to get her to open the car door and the door slamming on his hand. When she got to the part about the blood spurting from his fingertips and being deliberately spattered against her windshield, she paused for a moment. The vivid memory of that ghastly sight stirred the same intense emotion that she experienced the first time she saw it. With a deep breath, she finally returned her focus to Scott and continued her story.

As she described Craig's head scarf being used as a bandage and the car mysteriously starting and hitting him as she accelerated, it was obvious to Scott that she was still shaken. But the relating of the events of that night was serving as a valuable catharsis for her. He continued to listen intently as Jennifer described finding the envelope with the bloody head scarf inside.

"That's when I decided this guy could beat me emotionally and physically if I let him. My choice. I said to myself, 'Self, I'm mad as hell and I'm not going to take it anymore.' I would never be in my apartment, in my car—or anywhere—without some protection. As soon as I got out of my first class this morning, I looked up local gun dealers. Gun City, near Savannah Mall, looked like a good place to start." Jennifer paused, and her lips tightened into a determined look before she continued.

"I told the clerk I was looking for a hand gun, one I could keep in my purse for self-defense. He showed me three or four small pistols. The one I liked was a Beretta 21, but it was four hundred dollars. That was more than I could pay, and I told him so. He asked me a bunch of questions about my experience with guns, and when it became apparent that I had none, he suggested I put a deposit on the gun, take a gun-safety course, and get a concealed-weapon permit. He told me to go to the County Probate Court to apply for the concealed-weapon permit. He then told me he would let me have it for $250."

"You bought the gun?" asked Scott.

"Not yet. But I plan to get it after I take the gun-safety course and get the permit. I'll probably have to put the safety course off until the end of the semester. The clerk showed me another weapon called a Dragonfire Mace Gun. It shoots mace up to twenty feet, even in the wind, from a cartridge that resembles a shotgun shell. Shoots through eyeglasses, masks, and clothing. It came with a one-shot water cartridge for testing and training. I bought it and tested it at the gun shop. It was easy. I've got it loaded now with a mace cartridge. Want to see it?"

Jennifer opened her purse, and Scott peered in.

"Looks lethal. Are you sure you can legally carry that in your purse?"

"I don't know, but with what I've been through, in the immortal words of Rhett Butler, 'Frankly, my dear, I don't give a damn.' I've been frightened, abducted, chased, cursed, and intimidated for too long. Like I said, I'm mad as hell and I'm not going to take it anymore."

Scott sat back in his chair with a bemused look on his face. He was proud of this girl. She had spunk. She had come through a series of terrifying events, and she was now ready to take on her tormentor.

This on top of one of the most difficult academic challenges anyone ever faces—the first two weeks of law school. Scott visualized how frightened and upset Jennifer appeared after the terrifying tow-truck ride through the streets of Savannah and compared it with the confident, assured Jennifer now sitting next to him, displaying her lethal-looking mace gun. She was going to do well in law school. And she was going to make one super trial lawyer.

Scott also thought of the man who had terrorized Jennifer. He was still freely moving around Savannah, and he obviously had not given up his obsession with her. Scott was glad that she had taken these self-protective steps.

"You have every right to be mad as hell," said Scott. "And I hope it's helped to work up an appetite. How about let's go some-place to eat—a special place. I want to celebrate our finally getting to spend some time together tonight."

"Scott, you're not going to like what I'm about to say."

"Then don't say it; let's just go find a place to celebrate."

"But I have to say it. We're going to have to hold that celebration later. You know this is Labor Day weekend—no classes Monday. Half our study group is leaving town. We met for lunch today, and they all voted to have a group study session tonight. I voted for Monday night, but two of them won't be back until late Monday. They say they need to go over the outline for the Property class. That's the one I'm responsible for. They complain that Professor Nolan skips around too much, and they are depending on me to pull it together. I don't know that I can do that, but I feel I really need to be there. I'm torn. I really wanted this to be our night."

She looked at Scott as if she had asked a question and was waiting for his response. But Scott did not have an answer for her dilemma. True, he had a reply—to hell with the study group! Let the study group work it out without Jennifer. Professor Nolan had spoiled the previous evening with that case file. And now Professor Nolan's "skipping around" is confusing Jennifer's study group. Professor Nolan was getting to be a real pain in the ass. Jennifer had already said that she would be going home Friday, so when did she expect their celebration to begin? He just sat there, slowly shaking his head. The smile had left his face.

After a few moments' pause, Jennifer spoke again. "Why don't you come home with me this weekend? We have plenty of room. Meet my folks. They would love to meet you. I've already told them about you. Say 'yes'!"

Scott had never resisted Jennifer's "Say yes!" command. Certainly not this time. But he would have to modify it. He had promised Grady to meet with him Friday afternoon on the Harrison case. He had additional work of his own, and he knew Jennifer also needed time during the long weekend to study.

"Yes. But I'll drive over Saturday morning and stay until Sunday afternoon. OK?"

"Sure. We'll celebrate at Hilton Head."

• • •

Juri usually closed up on Thursday nights. Thursdays were not busy nights at the Library, but tonight was unusually quiet. He had spent most of the evening behind the bar talking with a couple of regulars. At ten, he released the one cook still on duty and walked to the storage room to check on needed supplies. He came back by the lounge and was surprised to see Jaak still there, seated at the poker table, with the Rider Back deck of cards spread in front of him.

"Jaak, I thought you had gone home. I just told Millie to start closing up. Something on your mind?"

"I suppose so," said Jaak. "Just a disappointing week. You think you know people, and then you realize you only know their shadow. And it's a dark shadow."

"You must be talking about Nolan. Have you seen him since Sunday night?"

"Saw him earlier this evening."

"How did it go?"

"About as expected. At first he denied any knowledge of the cards. Then he admitted he brought them, but it was all part of a joke. Says he was planning to pay them back this Sunday."

"And you don't believe him?"

"Juri, get real. I already knew he was a cheat. Now I know he's a liar, too. If he said Monday followed Sunday, I'd have to check a calendar. Of course, he got angry when I told him he was no longer welcome. It's just disappointing. And I liked the guy. Our Sunday-night gang liked him, too."

Juri stood silently for a few moments. He could see that his older brother was troubled by the affair, but he could think of nothing to say.

Jaak broke the silence. Smiling for the first time, he picked up the marked deck of cards and said, "Hey, Juri, want to see a card trick?"

Juri laughed, and they quickly locked up the Library and went home.

CHAPTER 31
Sunday, September 3

All the regulars except Denis arrived for the Sunday-night game by seven. The chips were counted and distributed by Rench Renshaw, the self-appointed banker for the games. Rench had served as banker since the first game and rarely missed.

As he was counting out the chips, he turned to Jaak and asked, "Is Denis coming?"

"Denis won't be coming. He's giving up on our poker game. Personal reasons."

"Giving up—you mean for good?"

"Yes, for good," replied Jaak.

"Sorry to hear that," said Jimmy. "I'll miss him."

"You'll miss the money that he showered on us like Old Faithful," said Pete.

"Yeah, that too, but he seemed to be an OK guy. I met his dad once," said Jimmy.

"Howard Nolan? He *owned* Effingham County, didn't he?" asked Pete.

"Just the timber and good farmland; he let us own the swamps and pin oaks. I met him while deer hunting with a buddy one day in December about twenty years ago."

"He was a deer hunter?"

"No, but I was," said Jimmy. "I was on the Savannah River, on a big high bluff near where Ebenezer Creek empties into the river. My buddy took a deer stand a couple hundred yards down from me. It was cold, and, I guess he just got tired of waiting and not seeing anything, so he built a fire. I saw the smoke and pretty soon heard some loud talking, so I went to see. The man identified himself as Howard Nolan. I knew who he was because I had seen a photo of him a couple times in the Savannah newspaper. Pretty well-known guy, even then. He let us know in no uncertain terms that it was his property, and we were trespassing. Of course, we knew that. We had walked right past his house. I guess it's Denis's house now. Big block and stucco house surrounded by a tall chain-link fence. We gave him the old, 'Yes, sir; sorry, sir; lost our way, sir; we were just leaving, sir; won't happen again, sir.' That always works when you get caught hunting on someone's property. Got to give them at least five 'sirs.' He didn't call the sheriff, and we appreciated that. I'm really sorry to hear Denis is leaving the table."

Bill Northorp, the architect, entered the conversation. "Maybe he's just up to his ass with that cemetery monument business. I hear it's not going well."

"What 'cemetery monument' business?" asked Pete.

"The one over in Bonaventure. His architect has been hassling with—maybe hassled *by*—the city for over a year."

"Never heard about it," said Pete.

"Me, neither," said Jaak. "What's going on?"

"Both his father and mother are buried in Bonaventure," said Bill. "Denis's dad had great expectations for Denis. Denis would have a large family, and all would be buried in the family plot with a big memorial. Shortly after his wife died, he bought two big lots from the city."

"Wait a minute," said Jimmy. "Savannah owns the cemetery? In Effingham, cemeteries are owned by churches. Bonaventure is owned by Savannah?"

"Not only Bonaventure but Colonial Park, Greenwich, and a couple of others—all owned and maintained by the city," said Bill. "Those lots that Howard Nolan bought were each twelve-space lots that cost almost ten grand each."

"I could buy a whole cemetery for that, maybe two," said Jimmy.

"I shouldn't say 'bought,' because the city doesn't actually sell the real estate," continued Bill. "What the city sells is interment rights, along with perpetual care. I've seen the Nolan space. It's beautiful. Big live oak trees and a spectacular view of Wilmington River. Not many spaces that big left in Bonaventure, and none with such a view. His dad wanted a family monument to match the beauty of the site. And with his money, he could hire the best architect available."

"Hire an architect to put up a tombstone?" asked Jimmy.

"Not a tombstone . . . a memorial. His dad brought in a big architectural firm from Chicago, one of the biggest in the country—

specializes in museums and art galleries. I was involved with them a couple years back. They hired me as their local architect on a big downtown project. They wouldn't listen to anything I told them about local codes and Savannah's historical preservation agenda. They got bogged down in permits, and eventually the project faded away. Now that same firm is back in Savannah on Denis's nickel, thrashing it out with the city's cemetery department. I haven't seen the design, but a friend of mine who works there told me they've never seen anything like it."

"Meaning what?" asked Pete.

"Meaning big—huge—colossal. It's even bigger than the one originally planned by Howard. Seems Denis gave the architect instructions that his family memorial was to be a walk-in, visitor-friendly mausoleum. And it must be topped by a marble tower higher than any others, including the Rauers monument."

"You mean that tall, white obelisk?" asked Jaak. "It's over fifty feet high."

"But that's what Denis wants. Something tall and modern and technological—a walk-in building *under* the tallest obelisk in Bonaventure Cemetery. The technology in the building is to be videos on plasma screens, highlighting all of the enterprises that Howard was involved in. There would be a list of his activities, which could be called up by voice activation. Say the word 'bank,' and the history of Savannah First Savings Bank and every other bank that Howard had been involved with would appear on the screen. Say 'law school,' and the history of Savannah College of Law would appear."

"Say the word 'crook,' and a big picture of Howard would appear," said Malcolm, the retired detective.

They all laughed.

"Could be," said Bill. "The whole project is on hold. There aren't a lot of rules on the type of monument that can be erected on a family lot, only a vague regulation that the structure can't be offensive or detract from the appearance and dignity of the cemetery. The written permission of the Director of Cemeteries is required, and he has refused to approve the design. Denis hired a big-name trial lawyer from Chicago to get the approval—Max Gordon."

"*The* Max Gordon? Man, that could cost some money," said Pete. "I saw him gloating on CNN after he got an acquittal in LA—some Hollywood actor charged with killing his wife. He and the prosecutor were walking out of the courthouse, and cameras were everywhere. He had a big grin spread across his face, and the prosecutor looked like he had just come up for air and there wasn't any."

"I saw Max Gordon being interviewed by Geraldo Rivera a couple of months ago," said Malcolm. "Geraldo was giving one of his suck-up interviews, and toward the end, he asked Gordon if it was true that he was the highest-paid criminal defense lawyer in the country. Gordon said it was true and that he was worth every dollar. He bragged that one of his clients called him on the phone the day before a trial to ask if the trial was to start at nine, or at nine-thirty. Gordon claims he sent him a bill for a thousand dollars. 'That's my minimum for a phone conference,' he said. What an asshole."

"Who, Gordon or Geraldo?" asked Rench.

"Both," said Malcolm. "But Geraldo's mustache makes him look the part."

They all laughed. Rench had finished counting out the chips and placed them in stacks in front of each player.

"Fighting Savannah City Hall is usually a losing cause, and fighting City Hall to put a memorial like that in Bonaventure has as much chance as finding Malcolm sober on St. Patrick's Day. Maybe Denis's dad, when he was alive, could have pulled it off. He had the power to catch lightening in a jar. But not Denis. Not gonna happen," said Rench. "Now, let's play poker."

And the Sunday-night poker game was underway—without Denis and his marked cards.

CHAPTER 32
Monday, September 4
Labor Day

It had been a terrific two days. Jennifer and her family were wonderful hosts, and Scott's plan to return early Sunday afternoon failed under the weight of their hospitality. Jennifer's dad was making a rapid recovery. He insisted on taking all of them to dinner Saturday night at Boathouse II, overlooking the salt marsh on Skull Creek. A talented, female, blues vocalist with a guitar provided live music, and the skilled chefs provided fresh-off-the-boat seafood cooked to perfection. It was an absolutely delightful evening, made even better when Jennifer's parents retired early and left Jennifer and Scott to entertain themselves.

That, of course, called for a ride out to the beach and a walk along the edge of the surf. The beach was mostly deserted. The only sound was the steady, soft lapping of the incoming waves. The ocean breeze was gentle and steady. Scott had learned to savor the smell of salt-filled air since arriving in Savannah, something he had not experienced while growing up in Tennessee or attending college in Tuscaloosa. He and Jennifer made their way slowly down the beach, illuminated only by a crescent moon and a few distant stars. There was an effervescent sparkle in the churning waves a few yards offshore. They spread a thick, cotton blanket on the soft sand between two large dunes. The passion they had felt for each other the previous weekend was quickly ignited. Finally—a few hours together and alone.

It was a perfect evening and well after midnight when they returned home. Sunday started with a late brunch then another beach trip, some sightseeing, and a late-afternoon cookout for Jennifer's dad to demonstrate his "skill with a grill." Good conversation mixed with frequent laughter filled the patio.

As night fell, Scott and Jennifer drove off to find whatever nightlife was available on Sunday night in Hilton Head. The evening passed too quickly. It was after eleven o'clock when they returned to Jennifer's home, and Scott began his drive back to Savannah.

Now, Monday, he was going to have to buckle down. He had a presentation to prepare for his Tuesday-night seminar and lots of preparation still to be done on the two additional cases he had been assigned. A major task, however, would be to clear Jennifer Stone from his mind. He had often heard the famous quote by Professor Story, "The law is a jealous mistress and requires a long and constant courtship." He knew that was good advice. He wanted to focus "long and constant" on his law school projects, but his mind kept wandering back to the past two days.

By noon he had completed his preparation for his Tuesday-night seminar, and the rest of the afternoon he worked on trial preparation for his two cases. Grady called in midafternoon to discuss some last-minute preparation for the Harrison case, which was scheduled to begin the next day. In late afternoon, he met some friends for a pick-up basketball game at Savannah Law. When he returned to his apartment, there was a text message on his cell phone. "I'll be back late. Catch you tomorrow. Jen."

After a quick shower and a meal of frozen pizza, Scott settled in for an evening of study, surrounded by his trusty laptop and stacks of law books. He was back in his routine. The "jealous mistress" would be pleased.

CHAPTER 33
Tuesday, September 5

S cott arrived at the Chatham County Courthouse shortly after eight and went directly to Courtroom K on the fourth floor where the Harrison case was scheduled for trial. Grady was already in the courtroom. Scott noticed the nameplate on the judge's bench: "LAWRENCE J. DESANO."

"Have you tried any cases before Judge Desano?" asked Scott.

"Quite a few," said Grady.

"Good judge?"

"Damn good judge," replied Grady. "He was a prosecutor for ten or twelve years before becoming a judge, and he's been on the bench for over fifteen years. Runs a tight courtroom and brooks no nonsense. I've found him to be completely fair, but criminal defense lawyers complain he's still a prosecutor at heart. He begins court proceedings in criminal trials by looking over at the defense table and asking, 'Is the defense ready to proceed?' After the defense counsel responds, he looks over at the prosecutor and asks, 'Are we ready?' emphasizing the *we*."

"You're kidding!" said Scott.

"Yeah, kidding. But some of the older attorneys say it happened frequently during his first years as a judge. I've never witnessed it. I like to see him on the bench when I'm trying a case, but most defense counsel aren't too thrilled at the sight."

Richard Evans entered the courtroom and walked over to speak to Grady. "I've got some bad news about Josh Johnson," said Richard. "No chance of his getting here for the trial. I just got a call from Jim Thayler, the Colorado deputy who's been trying to track him down. Johnson doesn't have a phone line to his house, but Thayler drove out to his home just outside Breckenridge and talked to his wife. She said he was the guide on a three-day, fly-fishing trip on the Blue River. She gave Thayler his cell phone number, and Thayler gave it to me, but so far my calls have gone unanswered. Pretty remote country, not good cell phone service. I called every hour, no luck. Bottom line, you can scratch him as a witness."

"That really *is* bad news, Richard. It leaves a single eyewitness, the clerk on duty," said Grady. "But he's a good one. Clean record, mature guy about fifty. He made a good ID from the photo lineup."

Sidney Ellis entered the courtroom and approached them. Sidney was the assistant public defender assigned to defend Harrison. Normally friendly and cordial, even during trials, he had a grave look on his face. "I think I'm going to be relieved—or, as the media will say, 'fired.'"

"You, Sidney, fired? You been sleeping with your boss's wife?" asked Grady.

Sidney's grave look was replaced by a smile and a quiet laugh. "No, no. Not that kind of firing. My client is firing me. Harrison claims he has money for a private attorney now. I just informed Judge Desano. He wants to see us in his chambers right away."

Grady, Sidney, and Scott left immediately for the judge's chambers. The defendant was not present; he was still in lockup at the jail. Once all were seated, Grady introduced Scott to Judge Desano, explaining that he was a certified clinic student, and that with the judge's permission, he would be assisting on the case.

"I always welcome clinic students in my courtroom," said Judge Desano, "but I rarely see them, even for a visit. And it's even rarer for one to actually assist with a trial. I'm pleased to give my permission for you to participate in this case, Mr. Marino." Then he looked sternly at Sidney and said, "You have some sort of motion, Mr. Ellis?"

"I don't have anything in writing, Judge. I got a call from the jail this morning that my client, Mr. Harrison, wanted to see me ASAP, that it was very important. I just got back from visiting him. He says he has money, and he's hiring a private attorney. I was surprised at what he told me. I can't get into details, but I made a couple of quick calls and verified that he does have money for a private attorney and one is on the way to Savannah now. He's flying in on Delta, arriving at 12:35 p.m. This was a total surprise to me, and I believe it was to Mr. Harrison, too."

"How could it have been a 'total surprise' to the defendant? He either knew he had the money or he didn't. Explain that, Mr. Ellis."

"I wish I could, Judge, and I hope you understand that what was told to me this morning was not only news to me but also was a conversation subject to attorney-client privilege. The money to hire the attorney is available, so he's not entitled to a public defender. I will be preparing a written request to withdraw. Could we postpone any further proceedings until tomorrow? By then, I am confident, it will be clear why this matter came up so late and why it is so important that we don't proceed with the trial today. We aren't stalling, Judge. I'm ready to go to trial, and I'm sure Mr. Wilder is also. But this is an unexpected turn of events that could not be anticipated by anyone. As soon as the new attorney arrives, it will be clear that it was unavoidable."

"You better make sure of that, Mr. Ellis. We have a large jury pool already assembling for this case. We have witnesses . . . well, the DA has witnesses . . . who have been subpoenaed. Delays are costly. And, frankly, it's beyond me how this sudden availability of money could not have been foreseen. Apparently, you want me to believe he just won the lottery?"

"Of course not, Judge. But I do want you to believe that as an officer of the court, I'm not trying to mislead you. This was sudden and unexpected. I had no knowledge of it until this morning."

"I'll give you until 3 p.m. You and that new attorney be in my courtroom then. You can try to convince me you should be off the case. You put in a request for a speedy trial. Are you withdrawing that request?"

"I need to speak with my client about that, Judge."

"Don't bother. I'm going to give him a speedy trial whether he wants one or not. You say you are ready. The DA says they are ready. And I'm ready. This case has been on my docket long enough. I will see you at 3 p.m. Sharp." Judge Desano stood, the signal for counsel to depart.

Once outside, Grady asked Sidney if he could shed any more light on the matter. Sidney said he could not, but he was sure it would all be cleared up at the three o'clock hearing. Then Grady asked, "Sidney, do you know the name of the new attorney?"

"I do," said Sidney. "But that is also information that I learned from my conversation with my client. This privileged stuff sometimes is difficult to sort out, and I prefer to play it safe. You obviously are going to find out this afternoon, but still, I prefer not to say right now. I can tell you, he is someone you have heard of and he's from out of state. I've got to get back to the office and prepare my motion to withdraw. I'll see you at three." Sidney headed for the elevator.

•   •   •

Scott and Grady returned to Courtroom K at 2:45 p.m. Sidney, his client, and his client's new attorney, were seated at the defense table. Grady recognized the new attorney immediately. Indeed, the defendant must have won the lottery, thought Grady. Grady and Scott walked over to introduce themselves. The new defense attorney stood and gave Grady and Scott each a vigorous handshake.

"Max Gordon," he said. "Better known as 'Sneak' Gordon. That's what my friends—both of them—call me." He grinned and gave a chuckle at his joke.

Gordon was a rotund man in his fifties, about five feet, seven inches tall with sharp features accentuated by his small, pointed nose. His thin, brown hair was balding in the back, and what remained in front was parted evenly in the middle and held in place with the help of a heavy hair spray. He was dressed in a dark, pinstriped suit with the pretentious wide, peaked lapels fostered on style-conscious yuppies by fashion ads in some men's magazines. It made no difference to Gordon that he was no longer—and perhaps, never was—a yuppie. He wore the trial-mandated gold Rolex on his left wrist and gold and jeweled rings on two fingers of his right hand. As if that were not enough to set him apart from the local attorneys, he was wearing his signature pink handkerchief, hanging loosely from his front breast pocket, and profoundly clashing with his yellow power tie. He appeared completely out of place in Courtroom K of the Chatham County Courthouse on this hot September afternoon. Had he been carrying an umbrella, anyone seeing him would have been sure that the Penguin had come to Gotham City.

Of course, Scott had heard of Max Gordon, one of the most successful trial lawyers in the country. In fact, he had one of his books, *Max Gordon's Secrets of Cross-Examination*, a book light on secrets but heavy on self-laudatory stories of his trials. But Scott had never heard the name "Sneak" Gordon.

When they returned to the prosecution table to await Judge Desano, Scott asked, "Did he introduce himself as *Sneak* Gordon?"

"Yes," said Grady. "He's proud of that nickname. And I assure you, it is appropriate. I'll tell you about it later."

Judge Desano entered the courtroom promptly at three. After three quick raps on the floor with the wooden staff by the bailiff, the court was called to order. Judge Desano turned to Sidney.

"Do you have a motion, Mr. Ellis?"

"Yes, Your Honor, a motion to withdraw as counsel." Sidney walked to the bench and handed Judge Desano his motion and added, "I have only briefly outlined the reasons for this motion, but I have discussed it in detail with both my client and his new counsel and would like to explain in more detail, if I may, Your Honor."

"Please do, Mr. Ellis. I'm all ears."

"Judge, the accused in this case, John Harrison, is the estranged son of former U.S. Senator David J. Harrison. The two have not seen each other in . . . ."

Sidney was interrupted by Judge Desano. "Are you referring to David Harrison, ex-senator and now candidate for governor?" As he spoke, Judge Desano wrinkled his brow into a surprised and concerned look.

"I am, Your Honor. And Senator Harrison is providing the funds for the defense of his son. I am not at liberty to go into the details or cause of the estrangement, but they have not seen each other or even spoken since a few months after John Harrison graduated from Princeton three years ago. The son took up residence in Panama City Beach, Florida, working variously as a clerk in a convenience store and as a waiter in a beach restaurant. Senator Harrison sought the whereabouts of his son for over three years without success. Over the Labor Day weekend, Senator Harrison learned that his son may be the 'John Harrison' who was awaiting trial in Savannah on armed robbery charges. Senator Harrison wanted to assist him, but he didn't know if his son would accept his assistance. Working through an intermediary, he learned that the 'John Harrison' awaiting trial was, in fact, his son and, further, that his son would be grateful for his help. Senator Harrison engaged Mr. Max Gordon of Chicago, Illinois, and Mr. Gordon has filed his Notice of Appearance with the clerk. I would like to introduce Mr. Gordon. Mr. Gordon, perhaps you would like to state your bar membership and qualifications."

Gordon stood, but before he could speak, Judge Desano said, "That won't be necessary. I am quite aware of Mr. Gordon. In fact, Mr. Gordon, you have been in my court before, haven't you?"

"Correct, Judge, but I'm willing to forget that appearance if you are," Gordon said, cocking his head sideways with a forced grin on his face.

Judge Desano ignored the remark. "Mr. Ellis, have you turned over all your files relating to the defense in this case?" he asked.

"I have, Your Honor. We met for over an hour in my office. Of course, if I find anything else that is pertinent to the defense, I will see that Mr. Gordon receives it. And I have filed my request to withdraw as attorney in this case with the clerk of court."

The judge turned to the defendant. "Mr. Harrison, are you satisfied with Mr. Gordon now taking over your defense in this case?"

"Yes, sir," said the defendant.

"Based on representation of counsel and with the stated concurrence of the accused, I am relieving Mr. Ellis of his duties as counsel. The Office of the Public Defender will have no further responsibility in this case. As of now, Mr. Wilder, you will serve all pleadings in this case on Mr. Gordon or his local counsel. This case is scheduled to resume at 9 a.m. tomorrow. Does either counsel have anything further before we adjourn?"

Mr. Gordon was rising from his seat before the judge completed his sentence. He had a severe frown on his face. "Judge, we can't possibly be ready for this case tomorrow. My team will not even be in place until the end of the week."

"Your *team*? Apparently your PR team is already in place. My bailiff informs me that WTOC-TV called at one-thirty to see what time the hearing in the Harrison case would start, and they are already setting up outside. What can you tell me about that, Mr. Gordon? Did you already issue a news release?"

"Your Honor, I did. But I gave strict orders to the press and the news channels that it was not for release until tomorrow, after this hearing. And all the release said was the name of the defendant and that I would be handling the case. I did not reveal that the defendant was the son of Senator Harrison. It was WTOC that picked up on the high-profile nature of this case. Apparently, WTOC jumped the gun."

"No, Mr. Gordon, *you* jumped the gun. This case is not going to be tried in the media. Don't make me issue a gag order. I don't like to police gag orders, and you wouldn't like the way I police them. I expect you to control your so-called *team*. Now, are you asking for additional time to prepare this case?"

"Of course, Judge. No way we can be ready tomorrow. I will be filing papers as soon as I can have them prepared, requesting that the trial be postponed until December, or later."

"What will be the state's position on this request, Mr. Wilder?"

"We absolutely oppose any delay in this trial, Your Honor. The defense asked for a speedy trial, and we busted our . . . well, we have worked very hard to get this case ready for trial today. We oppose any further delay."

"Let me save you some work on preparing papers requesting further delay, Mr. Gordon," said Judge Desano. "This case goes to trial either tomorrow morning or this coming Monday. Your choice. We are on the record, and the court reporter will record your choice. What will it be?"

"Monday, and since we are on the record," said Gordon, "let the record reflect my objection to having to make this choice. No attorney should have to prepare an armed robbery trial in six days. That is unconscionable, and I will renew my objection in any appeal that may result from this case."

"Well, you just do that, Mr. Gordon. And you make sure you have your *team* in place and ready for trial Monday. Speaking of your team, who have you engaged as your local attorney—who's sponsoring your appearance?"

"I haven't engaged any local counsel, Your Honor. Since Mr. Ellis was on this case already, I assumed no additional local counsel would be necessary. That's the way we do it in Chicago and most other jurisdictions where I've tried cases. And that includes about twenty different states."

"Well, you assumed wrong. Mr. Ellis is no longer on this case, and you are not a member of the Georgia Bar, are you, Mr. Gordon?"

"No, Your Honor, but I have tried cases in Georgia courts—several in Atlanta and one here in Savannah. I'm quite familiar with Georgia criminal court procedure."

"You are not saying that case you had here three years ago demonstrated your knowledge of Georgia procedure, are you, Mr. Gordon?"

"I prefer not to comment on that, Judge. I just request that I be allowed to bring in my team to try this case without local counsel, if you will permit that."

"Have you filed the appropriate papers to appear pro hac vice, both with this court and the General Counsel of the Georgia Bar?"

"The General Counsel of the Georgia Bar?"

"Yes, the General Counsel. Are you familiar with Superior Court Rule 4.4, Mr. Gordon?"

"I believe I have a copy, Your Honor."

"That wasn't my question. Are you having a problem understanding the question?"

"No, Your Honor. I'm vaguely familiar with the rule; my team is working on it."

"You—and not, as you say, your team—should have already complied with the rule. You need to get a corrected Notice of Appearance filed ASAP—one that complies with Rule 4.4. And let me be clear on one thing: I'm not about to let you try this case without local counsel. In fact, unless you align yourself with local counsel in the next twenty-four hours, you're off this case and Mr. Ellis is going to try it. This case is going to trial Monday, with or without you. Do both of you understand that?"

"I do," replied Sidney.

"And I do also, Judge," said Gordon. "I apologize for the mix-up. I'll obtain local counsel today."

"You make sure your local counsel can be in my courtroom to begin trial at 9 a.m. Monday. There will be no delays to accommodate the attorney's schedule. And have the attorney provide a copy of his or her Notice of Appearance with Mr. Wilder just as soon as it's filed with the clerk. Now, do you have any other matters for the court?"

"Yes, Your Honor. Bail. The defendant is still in jail, awaiting this trial. His bail was set at $100,000. We request he be released on his own recognizance, without having to post bail. This young man's father is running for governor of Georgia, after a distinguished career as a United States senator. The defendant will be in the limelight of the press every waking minute of every day. He poses no risk of fleeing. He poses no threat or danger to any person, the community, or to property. And if you can't release him without bail, then we request his bail be substantially reduced. For someone who poses no significant risk of flight and no threat to the community, bail of $100,000 is excessive and unconstitutional."

Gordon took his seat and Judge Desano looked at Grady for a response.

"Your Honor," replied Grady, "Mr. Gordon suggests that this defendant does not pose a flight risk. Perhaps we should call his father to testify about that. Mr. Ellis has told us David Harrison had sought the whereabouts of his son for *three years*. In three years, with all the resources he could muster, he could not find his son. We have been given no reason for his disappearance for three years. But we know why he would go into hiding now, should he be released. Upon conviction for armed robbery, he faces a minimum of ten years in prison. Let me emphasize, that is a *minimum* of ten years' imprisonment, and under Georgia penal statutes, no chance of early release. Common sense and logic says this three-year truant from his family is a serious risk to flee. He has proved he can hide. We emphatically oppose any bail reduction."

"Motion for bail reduction denied. Anything further, Mr. Gordon?"

"We ask that you reconsider your denial of our request for more time to prepare for trial."

"Denied. Court is adjourned until Monday, 9 a.m." Judge Desano stood, gathered his papers, and departed from the courtroom.

A bailiff walked over to the defendant and escorted him out. Max Gordon and Sidney Ellis followed. Once outside in the courtroom corridor, Gordon requested that the bailiff stop for a moment so that he could have a brief conference with his client. The bailiff stopped just long enough to tell Gordon that he could not authorize such a conference. However, the stop was long enough for Gordon to snap a photo of his client with a small digital camera. The bailiff looked annoyed but said nothing and quickly moved his prisoner along.

Ellis reacted with surprise. "What's with the photo shoot?" he asked Gordon.

"My standard procedure," replied Gordon. "You never know when you may need a current photo of a client."

Scott observed the photo session at a distance. He thought it a bit strange, but the trial had taken a curious twist from the start: Sidney Ellis is "fired," Max Gordon is "Sneak" Gordon, and the indigent defendant turns out to be the son of a prominent—and very wealthy—politician.

In the courtroom, Grady remained standing but was silent for several minutes. Then he slowly began gathering his books and papers from the table. It was obvious to Scott that he was concerned, even stunned, by the sudden change of events. Scott and Richard waited for Grady to speak.

When he did, he merely said, to no one in particular, "Houston, we have a problem."

"Meaning what?" asked Scott.

"Meaning the office has a problem. I won't be here to try this case, and someone is going to have to step in and step in fast. My first day at the U.S. Attorney's office in Atlanta is Monday. This was to be my last case here."

"Could you delay the Atlanta job for a week? You've got this one prepared, and it promises to be in the media spotlight," said Scott.

"Media spotlight? You've got that right. Gordon will attempt to try this in the media, for sure. But you know, Scott, in most cases, it doesn't really help the defense. In fact, I think it hurts most cases, but some criminal defense lawyers try all their cases in the media. Gordon is one of them, and he will keep it there. I doubt that this case will get underway Monday. If I could be sure, I might request a few more days here. But I'm not going to. I know Desano says it's going Monday, but I expect something to come up to delay it. Nick's going to have to reassign it . . . probably to Meg Flanders. I hope you can help her. Are you available next week?"

"Of course. One good thing about this delay is that maybe we can get Josh Johnson back."

Richard Evans had been listening and spoke up. "I'll call Thayler. We've already sent a check for witness fees and made airline reservations. We can update the reservations and maybe get him here Monday or Tuesday."

"Good," said Grady. "Now, let's get back to the office. I need to let Nick know that his friend 'Sneak' is back in town."

"You seem to know 'Sneak.' What's the story?" asked Scott, as they began to slowly walk from the courtroom to the elevator.

"I know *of* him. I've never had a case against him, but he defended a case here a few years ago. Nick was the prosecutor, but I followed the case pretty closely. The name 'Sneak' is his calling card. He earned it at Notre Dame, and he's proud of it."

"Proud of it?"

"You bet. Do you follow Notre Dame football, Scott?"

"Somewhat. I'm more into the Southeastern Conference, but I have a subscription to *Sports Illustrated*, so, yes, I guess I follow Notre Dame football."

"So you're aware of the Michigan–Notre Dame rivalry?"

"Sure, one of the oldest."

"Well, that little plum-shaped defense counsel, with the pink handkerchief hanging from his coat pocket, played in one of those games."

"He played football—for Notre Dame? You're putting me on."

"No, he was on the Notre Dame football team in the late 1960s or early 70s. Small running back, third team or so. He rarely got in the game, but he had one great play in his college career—against Michigan. Gordon got the ball and somehow squeezed through the defensive line to score, and Notre Dame went on to win the game. The announcer raved about it being a great sneak through the Michigan line, and that's where the 'Sneak' nickname came from. The nickname should have been forgotten as soon a he graduated, but he wouldn't let it. He made sure everyone remembered 'Sneak' Gordon."

"OK," said Scott. "He likes the name, but now, over thirty years later, no one remembers his football days, and the name 'Sneak' is hardly one to be proud of. I would think he would be embarrassed to call himself 'Sneak.' But that's how he introduced himself: 'Sneak' Gordon. That's weird."

"Not when you hear him in court. He gets into his name during jury selection. 'My name is Max Gordon,' he says, 'but everyone calls me *Sneak*.' Of course, that's not true. Very few people remember his nickname, and fewer call him by it. But he continues, 'I want to make sure none of you will hold that name against me, so I want to explain where that name came from.' Then he goes on to tell about his sneak through the Michigan line and how the name stuck."

"Prosecutors and judges let him get away with that hokum?" asked Scott.

They were now at the elevators, but they stopped to continue the conversation. Several elevators arrived, opened their doors, and departed as they stood talking.

"I don't know. As far as I know, he's only tried that one case here in Savannah. Multimillion-dollar drug bust. Nick Cox was the prosecutor. It was at least three years ago. Defendant was from Colombia, South America. The feds wanted him, but the locals arrested him and wanted first crack at him, so we took him to trial here first. Want to guess who the judge was?"

"Desano?"

"Good guess. And do you know how the trial ended?"

"No clue. But I gathered from the repartee between Desano and Gordon that Desano was not pleased with something."

"Pleased? Desano went into a rage at Gordon when the trial ended, and he showed today that he's still pissed."

"Why?" asked Scott.

"Desano doesn't forgive or forget. Escobar, the defendant, was in jail custody for trial, but his defense counsel, Gordon, made sure he appeared at trial dressed in the standard defendant attire: blue polyester suit and red tie. On the first day of trial, during a break in jury selection, the defendant just disappeared. Gone—without a trace. The newspaper carried a story on it every day for two weeks. Desano was embarrassed. And apparently he thought Gordon had some part in the disappearance. A big investigation followed. Other than finding fault with two deputies—who blamed each other—no one was really held accountable. But the newspaper criticized everyone: the judge, the prosecutor, the defense counsel, even the clerk of court. Everybody connected with the case."

"They ever catch him?"

"Not that I know of. But I haven't followed it since then. In fact, until Gordon appeared in court today I haven't thought much about it. But I can guarantee he will pull that football crap on the jury again. He always does."

"Always does? You said he's only tried that one case here in Savannah."

"True, but *USA Today* did a feature series on him—'Max Gordon, America's Most Successful Trial Lawyer,' or something like that. You can probably find it in the newspaper's archives on the Internet. He always tries to get that football story before the jury. Juries love that kind of talk. They are usually laughing by the time he finishes his story. The articles detail how he talks to the jury about his great sneak through the Michigan line. A self-deprecating story with great gusto—body language and all. Of course, he ends up being the hero, but it's funny. Anytime the defense can get a jury laughing, it's ahead of the game. Damn few really amused juries convict, and defense attorneys know it. Max Gordon has perfected it."

When the next elevator arrived, they got in for the ride to the sixth floor. Grady asked Scott to come with him to Nick Cox's office to brief him on the afternoon hearing.

"You want the good news or the bad news first?" asked Grady.

"Bad news. I always want the bad news first," replied Nick.

"The Harrison case has been continued. Defendant has a new lawyer."

"And the good news?"

"Sorry, I don't have any good news. The new lawyer is Max Gordon, hired by the defendant's father, Senator David Harrison. Gordon's bringing his team to town and already has the attention of the press and TV."

"Son of Senator Harrison on trial and fucking Max Gordon defending! No, that doesn't make me happy. And it's not going to make the boss happy."

"Desano's not too happy, either."

"Desano's case?" asked Nick.

"Yes, and he's going to start the trial Monday. Gordon asked for a delay, but Desano was adamant: Monday at nine."

"Damn, I'd like to have another crack at Gordon," said Nick. "I still believe his team orchestrated that escape by Escobar. But I've got a murder trial starting Monday. What are the chances we could get the case postponed? Apparently, this is what the defense wants. We could both submit written motions to Desano for a continuance until sometime in October or November, or even December."

"There are very few things in this world that I am certain of, Nick, but one of them is that Desano is going to try this case Monday, come hell or high water. That motion would just waste time and piss off Desano. You just need to get this case reassigned this afternoon. I can help until Friday, but I'm leaving for Atlanta Saturday morning.

"The problem, Grady, is finding someone to take this case on such short notice. Every other prosecutor has a full plate this coming week."

"How about Meg? She was to second chair it until she had the surgery. I know she's new to felonies, but she was well thought of in misdemeanors. Is she back?"

"Got back this morning. But I hate to saddle her with this case, especially on such short notice."

"Scott has been working with me on the case. He could help her. Right, Scott?"

"Sure. I'm familiar with the evidence. I don't have any trials scheduled for two more weeks. I could devote full time to it."

"OK, Meg it is. Go brief her."

Scott and Grady went to Meg's office with the news. She listened carefully as Scott and Grady relayed the day's events.

"Can we get to work on it tonight?" asked Meg. "I've got a medical appointment in the morning. Routine, but I'll be gone most of the morning. Monday will be here too soon."

"Sure," said Grady. "OK with you, Scott?"

"OK with me," replied Scott. It was not really OK. He had a seminar class at seven, but this involved a real trial, and maybe he could get an active part in it. The seminar could proceed without him.

"Then let's meet in my office in an hour," said Grady. "I have all the exhibits and investigative reports. Meg, I'll give you my trial notebook, and we can discuss the whole prosecution plan. I'll send out for pizza, and we'll work as long as it takes."

CHAPTER 34

At the same time Sidney Ellis was in Judge Desano's office informing him that John Harrison had hired another attorney, Winston Adams was in his office preparing for the third week of the new semester. Deborah Channing arrived promptly at ten for an appointment, and after the zany photo ritual, she took her seat.

"No substantial change to the fall enrollment, and I'm not ready to report on the spring entering class. I didn't see anything on the agenda for the faculty meeting this afternoon that affects my office, so, unless you want me there, I'm going to skip it."

"Sure, skip it. It should be short. A few committee reports and one agenda item submitted by Denis Nolan."

"I saw that," said Deborah. "But I didn't quite understand it. 'The relationship of Savannah College of Law to the Library Bar and Grill.' What does he mean by that?"

"Beats me," said Winston. "I guess I'll find out this afternoon. He's never mentioned anything about the Library to me, good or bad. I know he visits there quite frequently. Maybe he wants to annex it. He has the money to do it."

They both laughed.

"Did you receive my memo adding a first-year student to the Search Committee?" asked Winston.

"Yes, and I personally notified the student of her selection. Jennifer Stone. A bright young lady. I think you made a good selection."

"Not my selection; she was the only nominee. Several professors submitted her name, including Denis."

"Dean, I think there is something you should know. Professor Nolan contacted me about the possibility of academic credit for students on the trial team. He apparently is involved somehow with the coaching of one of the competitions. He had a list of students, and Jennifer Stone was listed as a witness."

"I know you think this is coming as a surprise," said Winston, "but, Deborah, I'm well acquainted with Denis. Nothing surprises me. Let's hear it." His usual smile faded into a frown.

"I explained that giving academic credit for their work on the trial team was not a decision I could make. It would have to be submitted to the Curriculum Committee and finally approved by the faculty before any academic credit could be granted. Jennifer is also a student in his Property class. And this morning, I received a call from Carol in the business office wanting to know her academic status. Carol said Professor Nolan had submitted Jennifer's name to be his student research assistant. Carol wanted to know her class status, as it had been omitted from the application. When I told her Jennifer was in her first semester, Carol was surprised. And a bit annoyed. She said she thought everyone on the faculty knew that first-year students were ineligible to be research assistants, and she would have to disapprove the application. Dean, he seems to have a close involvement with this student. I'm not suggesting anything, but I thought you should be aware of it."

"Are you sure you aren't suggesting something, Deborah?" asked Winston, a smile replacing the frown.

Deborah paused briefly before responding. "Perhaps I am, but I just think you should have a heads up on the matter."

"You are right. And I appreciate it. I depend on you to keep me informed—like Velma's latest caper."

"Have you spoken to Velma about it?"

"Not yet. But I need to see her before she meets that class again."

"It's pretty much the gossip of the day on campus. I know it was inappropriate conduct. But coming from Velma, I think it's kind of funny," said Deborah.

"It might have been funny except for the Duke affair. I thought Velma would have avoided that kind of humor—assuming she thought it was humorous—after her last attempt. Frankly, I didn't know Velma had a humorous streak. For that I'm pleased. But I'm going to have a serious talk with her."

Now, how about an update on the Dean Search Committee—how many applications have you received?"

"Sixteen as of this morning. Some very impressive. Professor Nolan is still the lone applicant from our faculty. I've received confirmation from all the Search Committee members for the meeting on the fifteenth. You will be there, won't you?"

"I'll be there. But I will be taking a low profile. The old dean serving on the committee searching for the new dean must not be too visible. This may be a time for the school to bend in a new direction. My job here was to get the school up and running. The new dean will have to provide his or her own vision for the school. With Denis being the sole applicant from our faculty, I suspect you may be worried that Denis may be your next dean. I believe that worry is misplaced. Institutional inbreeding doesn't usually result in the new ideas and creativity needed to move the school forward. And that's why search committees often find that the best applicant is from an outside source, not from the law school's own faculty. Don't worry about Denis. This is a very capable committee."

Deborah smiled. "With that optimistic note, I trust you will excuse me. I have some work to do."

CHAPTER 35

It was a little after four Tuesday afternoon, and the third faculty meeting of the fall semester was about to begin. The seats were filling slowly, and Dean Adams made his customary announcement of waiting "until we have a quorum."

Brian Latimer and Belinda Chapman were already seated and engaged in quiet conversation. "I guess we are waiting on VanLandingham—again," said Belinda. "She seems to carry a lot of weight at these meetings."

It was an unintended pun, but both laughed.

"Yes, she carries a lot of weight, but Winston may be fed up with her latest antic. I just hope he doesn't fire her."

"Fire her? For what?"

"You haven't heard? This campus must not be the gossip mill it once was. Velma is like a bull dog on the students about class attendance. She doesn't believe in the eighty percent rule—she requires one hundred percent attendance in her first-year classes. This semester on the first day of classes, she sent a class roll around for the students to sign. At the top of the sheet, she had written, 'I expect you here for every class unless you are dead.'"

"Unless you're *dead*?" asked Belinda. "That's pretty weird."

"Yes, but it's Velma being Velma. And some semesters she does more than just send that warning—she follows up. That got her fired at Duke, and now, maybe here."

"Bizarre, weird—and in my opinion, *wacky*. But that's not an act that would get a professor fired, is it?"

"No, but as I said, she sometimes follows up, and her prank at Duke did get her fired. Well, not exactly fired, but Duke refused to renew her contract."

"What happened?" asked Belinda.

"During the second week of classes, a female student was absent from class, and Velma fired off a sympathy card—mailed it to the student's parents. Something like, 'Your loss is shared by those of us here at Duke. Please know you are in our prayers.' Unfortunately, the student had not written or called home in a week. The parents panicked. Immediately, they tried to contact their daughter but couldn't. The mother was frantic—wondering if their daughter could possibly be dead. The father called the dean of the law school. Of course, the dean had no knowledge of what was going on. It took more than an hour to find the student and get the parents calmed down. The parents were emotional wrecks by the time they determined that their daughter was OK. And they were very angry—threatened a lawsuit against the school and against Velma. I don't think anything came of it, but Velma was history there."

"That's awful. And she did it again? Here?"

"Not quite. This time, she did it a bit differently. Last Friday was the first day one of her students was absent. Toward the end of the class, when she was sure the student would not show, she told the class she had a sad announcement to make. Gretchen, their classmate who was absent, had died. She had a sympathy card similar to the one she sent to the Duke parents. She passed it around for all the class to sign. Students were shocked to hear of the 'death' of their classmate. Some were visibly upset, tears in their eyes. Right before the class ended, she told the students she really wasn't aware of where the student was, or why she was absent, that she was merely trying to remind them of the importance of class attendance. Some students apparently thought it was funny, and some thought it was appalling. Velma, of course, didn't care what they thought. In her mind, she had simply made her point. I don't think it will get her fired, but there's no way Winston is going to just let it go."

Approximately a quarter after the hour, Professor Rose signaled Winston that a quorum was present, and the meeting was called to order. The minutes were approved, and Winston presented the "Dean Scene." The appointment of Jennifer Stone as a member of the Dean Search Committee was included, as was an announcement that the first meeting of that committee would be a week from Friday.

Winston's announcements prompted no questions or comments, and he quickly moved to committee reports. The iPod gamers, crossword workers, and Sudoku solvers continued to enjoy the quiet oblivion of the rear row.

The final committee report for the day was from the Student Life and Welfare Committee, chaired by Professor Aaron Wingate.

"I have a small issue to bring before the faculty," he began. "One of the student organizations has petitioned our committee to have condom machines—that is, pay machines—installed on the campus. The majority of our committee is in favor of this for obvious reasons—combating AIDS and other sexually transmitted diseases. However, one member of the committee is very opposed and asked that I bring it before the full faculty. Two machines would be installed in restrooms and serviced by a local vending machine company at no cost to the school. We would welcome your comments."

Aaron looked into the audience and saw one hand go up. He turned to face Professor Robert Mitchell. "I'm glad Rob wants to be heard. He is the committee member opposed to the machines on campus. Rob, you have the floor."

About half the back-row gamers raised their heads. Rob rose from his seat on the front row and turned to face the faculty.

"I oppose this for a number of reasons, and not merely because my religion is opposed to the use of condoms. These machines will be like banners hanging from an overpass saying 'Welcome to Savannah College of Law, where sexual promiscuity is officially approved and accepted.' I don't want our restrooms to take on the appearance of an interstate truck stop, and I see no reason for our law school to go into competition with every drugstore and supermarket in Savannah by selling condoms from self-serve machines. I don't want fathers of students walking into a men's room and being hit in the face with the sight of a condom machine. I see no reason that Savannah Law . . . ."

"Wait one moment!" A strong female voice interrupted Rob. It was Velma VanLandingham. She was now standing. "Did I hear you say, 'Fathers going into men's rooms?' Is that what I heard? Aaron, just where does your committee propose placing those condom machines?" She was looking past Rob as if he were not even present.

"Velma, there would be two machines. One in the men's room just outside the student cafeteria, the other in the men's room on the first floor of the main academic building."

"Then I'm fighting mad! Fighting mad!"

With those words, all on the back row abandoned their games to look at Velma.

"It's the same old entrenched sexual bias. Two condom machines. And where do they go? Both of them? In *men's rooms!*" Velma was speaking in her fighting-mad voice and had assumed her fighting-mad stance: veins and muscles taut, eyes blazing.

"Velma, just where would you expect the condom machines to be placed? We are open to suggestions." Aaron remained calm but was obviously exasperated by the sudden and combative intrusion into the discussion.

"Then place one in a women's restroom. I don't care which women's restroom. But if you place a condom machine in a men's restroom, then one must go into a women's restroom. And make sure it is stocked with female condoms." Velma took her seat.

"Female condoms?" Aaron mumbled, to no one in particular. He looked perplexed.

Velma quickly rose again. "Yes, female condoms. They do exist, you know. Or is it possible your committee was unaware of that? They have been in use in Europe for years, and even here in the prudish USA, they have FDA approval. And they also prevent the spread of AIDS and other sexually transmitted diseases—as well as children, which is what most use them for. They can be dispensed through machines just like male condoms. I think your committee's proposal needs a lot more work." Velma sat down.

Winston stood and walked to where Rob was standing. He was inclined to agree with Velma, that the proposal needed a lot more work.

"Yes," Winston said, apparently addressing Velma's suggestion for more committee work. "Aaron, would you and your committee take another look at this? And I want to thank you for bringing it before the faculty. We can take it up later, if your committee wishes, after everyone has had time to give it some serious personal thought." Winston quickly moved to the next item on the agenda.

Brian leaned over and whispered to Belinda, "So, do we or do we not need those machines in the women's restrooms at Savannah College of Law?"

"I don't know, Brian. I guess it's a 'classic college campus condom conundrum.'"

They both laughed.

Winston was still at the lectern, looking over the agenda. He read the next item just as it appeared: "Proximity of the Library Bar and Grill to Savannah College of Law."

As he read, only the tops of the heads of the gamers were visible. It was business as usual on the back row.

"Professor Nolan, I believe this is your item."

Winston took a nearby seat, and Denis walked to the lectern to address the faculty.

"I want to alert you to a critical problem that needs our immediate attention, and that's the business establishment known as the Library Bar and Grill and its effect on our students. Our administration should have identified this problem long ago. A bar so close to impressionable young men and women cannot help but have a corrupting influence. What we are doing is encouraging and advancing the alcoholism rate among our students. For three years, students attend our school with a bar within spitting distance of their classrooms. On any given night, and especially on Friday and Saturday nights, there are more students in the Library Bar and Grill than in our own library."

"Come on, Denis, what's got your hackles up?" A voice from a midrow interrupted Denis. It was Professor Barron Whitaker, "We are a law school, not a licensing board."

"I am quite aware it has a license to operate, but it should not have our approval."

"What approval? Winston, are you giving out those phony licenses again?" responded Barron. A few members laughed, as if an inside joke was involved.

"By doing nothing in response to student complaints, we are indeed giving approval."

Winston spoke up. "What student complaints, Denis?"

"Student Bar Association. Some members, who wish to remain unidentified, came to me last week. Their complaint is that a bar so close to the campus has a corrosive effect on the school, yet the school continues to support it."

"And how do we *support* it?" asked Winston.

"In a number of ways," replied Denis. "Our housing office sends housing information, our registrar sends course schedules, and all of this gets posted on the Library's bulletin board. Every time a professor cancels or changes a class date, it gets posted on that bulletin board in the Library. And our faculty continues to send their extra course books over there. Now the Library's library is more complete and accessible than Savannah Law's library!"

"So what, Denis? Get over it. That's nothing to bitch about," said Barron.

"Hear me out, Barron. It brings me to my main point, and that is that the Library Bar and Grill should never have been located there in the first place. It's in violation of Section 6-1210 of the Savannah Alcoholic Beverages Licensing Regulations. I've researched it. The regulations prohibit the sale of beer and wine within one hundred yards of any school building or college campus. Our failure to oppose its location exposes Savannah Law to liability for accidents and injuries resulting from the sale of alcoholic beverages there."

"Come on, Denis. That's a stretch, and you know it. Besides, the Library is more than one hundred yards from the campus," said Barron.

"Not from my calculations. The east parking lot, the one Geraldine would name the 'George Bush' lot, is within a hundred yards of the Library's small parking lot on its west side. But you don't have to take my word for it. If you agree with me that this would be a serious violation, then vote with me on my motion. Let me read it: 'That Savannah College of Law hire a licensed surveyor to measure the nearest distance from our campus property to the Library Bar and Grill, and if said distance shall be within the distance proscribed by the Savannah Alcoholic Beverages Licensing Regulations, the school shall take such legal action as necessary to have the Alcohol Beverage License of the Library revoked.' That ends my motion."

Winston stood and moved to the lectern. He was trying, unsuccessfully, to suppress a frown. "Is there a second?" he asked.

"Second!" It was Geraldine Polanski. "I've never thought that business should be there in the first place. It's quite wasteful—two large waste bins in the alley behind it, and it seems trucks are hauling them away full every day. Just think of the environmental problems it brings to our community. And now when I think of our possible liability—the lawsuits that Denis mentioned—we should move fast on this."

"There is a motion on the floor, and a second," said Winston. Slowly head tops were being replaced with faces as the back-row crowd abandoned their puzzles. "Any discussion?"

"Could you repeat the motion?" came a voice from the back row.

Winston asked Denis to repeat his motion. Denis complied.

"What a bunch of bull crap! Excuse me, Dean." It was Barron again. "That Library and its bar have been *there* as long as we've been *here* without a problem. That so-called distance problem would have been taken care of by the city years ago. We have no business meddling in this. And as far as *our* liability for injuries resulting from the Library's beer sales—that's bogus. No court has ever stretched any dram shop law that far. And I don't want to sit here and hear a lot of BS argument on it. I move the previous question."

Winston was not surprised at the argument against the motion, but the "motion for the previous question" was unexpected. That motion closes debate, and there had been little debate. There was a quick second.

Off to one side, Denis was still standing. He appeared more surprised than Winston, with his hands outstretched, palms up, as if to plead. "Wait, Dean, there's been very little discussion on my motion."

"And there won't be any more if this motion carries," said Winston. "All in favor, please raise your hand."

"But what are we voting on? My motion is still before the faculty."

"We aren't voting on your motion. If this motion passes with a two-thirds vote, we will vote immediately on your motion. Now, all in favor, raise your hand."

All hands went up except those of Denis, Geraldine, and a few on the back row who had returned to their puzzles.

"Since the motion carried, we will now vote on the motion on the floor—the motion by Denis. No further discussion is permitted at this point. All in favor, say 'aye.'"

Only two voices were heard.

"All opposed say 'no.'"

A cacophony of "noes" and "nays" and plain howls filled the room. Then a lone but clear voice from the back row: "Motion to adjourn."

The third faculty meeting of the semester was quickly ended, and the faculty departed to the dining room for their weekly treat of cheese, crackers, and wine. Except for Denis. He remained seated, staring at a wall. This was certainly no vote of confidence for a deanship.

Denis waited until all had departed and then slowly walked to his office. As he opened the door, he heard his phone ringing. He tried to ignore it, but it kept ringing. The persistent ringing was annoying, so after a dozen rings, he picked up. "Hello, *who is this?*" An emphasis underscored his irritation.

"It's Max! I've been trying to reach you for half an hour."

"I've been in a stupid faculty meeting. I hope you have some good news from the Cemetery Board."

"No. The Cemetery Board is holding firm in their opposition. I'm through with phone calls, letter writing, and threatening lawsuits. My team plans some Chicago-style persuasion. But that's not why I'm calling. I need your help."

"My help? That's a twist. What's up?"

"I'm involved in a criminal case here in Savannah. It's going to be a big case. You'll hear about it on the news tonight. I need you for local counsel. You are a member of the Georgia Bar, aren't you?"

"Illinois and Georgia. But I haven't really practiced in Georgia. Took the bar right after graduation. My dad expected me to join a local firm, but . . . I think you know about that."

"But you have an active Georgia license, right?"

"Sure, but all my litigation experience was in Chicago, and none of it actually went to trial. You know I'm not a trial lawyer. Why would you want me to assist with a big criminal case? I don't know anything about criminal law. The most I could do is find the courtroom."

"That's all I want you to do. Just be local counsel of record. File your Notice of Appearance and show up in court. And stay out of the way. I'll take care of trying the case. My team is flying in tonight. I'll even have them prepare the Notice of Appearance—all you have to do is sign it. The trial starts next Monday."

"You have a team flying in tonight? Aren't any of them a member of the Georgia Bar?"

"Hell, Denis, they aren't members of *any* bar! At least not anymore. I've got three who were disbarred years ago and one who was never admitted, although he graduated from law school at the top of his class. Had a felony conviction he 'forgot' to list on his bar application. But they are all super-smart and experienced. I pay them well, and I depend on them. I do all the trial work, and they prepare my witnesses. It's expensive, but it works, if you know what I mean."

"Of course. Who's your client?"

"Senator David Harrison."

"What trouble is he in? I've heard nothing about it."

"He's not in any trouble. It's his son, John Harrison, who is charged with armed robbery at a convenience store here in Savannah."

"Haven't heard about that either."

"Neither had Senator Harrison until this weekend. He hadn't seen his son in years. They had a falling out. The son took off and disappeared. Now he's here in Savannah and going to trial Monday, and I'm going to defend him. But I need a local attorney. It will pay well. I can bill you out at $500 an hour."

"Trial lawyers get that kind of money?"

"No, I get more. You are not a trial lawyer; you get less. Besides, Denis, you've got more money than my ex-wives."

They both laughed. Gordon's marital failures were legend. His alimony payments rivaled Johnny Carson's.

"How about it. Let's say $500 an hour for pretrial work and $700 an hour at trial. The senator will pay whatever I bill."

Denis responded with a slow whistle and added, "Sounds good. But why stop there?"

"Denis, you are one greedy bastard; that's why I love you. Now, how about it? I need this favor. Desano is going to boot me tomorrow if I don't have local counsel. This is big, easy money, and I want you to have a slice."

Gordon's jovial voice had turned into a plea. He needed a local attorney ASAP—hopefully, a lazy, trial neophyte, incurious and content to remain out of the way. Gordon knew Denis was not lazy, but he hoped the other qualities would apply.

"It's not money I need, Max. It's action on the Bonaventure project. The architects are finished, and I've lined up a construction team for the monument. This has been dragging on for months."

"I understand, Denis. Join me on this case, and when it's over, we—my team—all of us, will devote full time to it. We have a sure way of dealing with bureaucrats. It may be a bit expensive, but it never fails."

"OK, it's a deal," said Denis. "By the way, Gordon, I'm having a function out at my beach house this Friday. If you are still in town, you're invited."

"I've got a hearing in Pittsburgh Friday, but if I can get back in time, I'll be there. Send me an e-mail with time and place."

Jennifer sent a text message to Scott's cell phone Wednesday morning: "Witness practice tonight at 7. But let's grab a bite at the Library early—5:30?"

Texting was now their usual means of communication: convenient, silent, quick. Jennifer was much better at it than Scott; she could text on her cell phone as fast as Scott could type on his computer. Scott's reply was a simple "OK." She knew texting was not his strong suit, but she had hoped for a bit more enthusiastic response.

They arrived at the Library at the same time. There was a small crowd gathered at the tables in the Study Hall, but the seats around the bar were almost empty. Juri saw them enter and waved them over.

"Jaak was just asking about you two guys. Said he hadn't seen you lately. What have you been doing?"

Scott was about to tell Juri about their weekend at Hilton Head when he noticed the TV on the wall behind the bar. There, in living color, was Max Gordon holding a news conference and detailing his involvement as defense counsel in the upcoming Harrison case.

"Listen," said Scott, pointing to the TV. "That's a case I'm helping with."

The three of them listened as Gordon spoke of his role as defense counsel for Senator Harrison's son, "the great system of justice where the defendant is presumed innocent," and how the citizens of "the great state of Georgia" would "come to know the real truth next week." Scott recalled Judge Desano's warning about not trying the case in the media. But what would one expect from someone who enjoyed the nickname "Sneak"?

Juri turned to Scott and asked, "That's your case?"

"No, I'm just a small player in it. Meg Flanders, my new supervising attorney, will be the prosecutor. But I'll be there. Should be pretty exciting with that guy on the defense."

"I'm sure of that," said Juri. "I saw him being interviewed a couple of weeks ago by Greta 'what's-her-name.' It was about the trial of that Hollywood actor who killed his wife. I don't recall the details, but there was a not-guilty verdict—a big surprise because the guy had confessed."

A couple took a seat at the bar, and Juri turned to wait on them.

"We'll talk later, Juri. Jen and I are going to a quiet table," Scott said.

He and Jennifer walked to a table in the back area.

"We better get a menu and get our order in fast," said Scott. He motioned for a waitress, and they placed their order.

"You have practice at seven?" asked Scott.

"Yes. Thomas Courthouse. This will be our first time for the direct exams. I'm looking forward to it."

"Well, I'm glad you are, but it's going to get more time consuming as the competition gets closer. And you'll miss two, maybe three days of classes while in Atlanta."

"Don't start that, Scott. I thought you agreed to let me make my own mistakes and pursue my own opportunities. How many first-year students get this opportunity?"

"None, and for good reasons. You are the first, as far as I know. I still think Professor Nolan should know better. I don't think he's doing you any favor."

"And I think your problem is with Professor Nolan. You really don't like him, do you?"

"Not especially. I have my reasons, but that's a separate matter. And you are correct—you do have the right to make your own mistakes. So, let's change the subject. How's your study group going?"

"Great. We met last night for a couple of hours. Now you tell me about the case coming up Monday. Do you think it will be on TV?"

"No way. The judge on the case—Desano—is not going to let it turn into a media circus. And he's going to be really angry if he hears about tonight's interview."

"*If* he hears? You aren't going to tell him?"

"I don't think so. It was mostly about Gordon, not about the facts of the case. So, no big thing. But I'll let Meg know what I saw. She's in charge of the case."

"You said you were just a small player. But you *are* a player. What will you be doing?"

"Meg's going to let me make the opening statement and examine one of the investigators. We are trying to get a witness in from Colorado—one of two eyewitnesses. Not sure we can get him here in time for the trial, but if he shows, I'll be examining him, too. He was sitting in his car in the parking lot outside the store when it was robbed. We're hoping he can ID the defendant."

Jennifer smiled at Scott. "Doesn't sound like you are a small player to me. Maybe I can get to the courthouse for some of the trial."

"Good. Expect a crowd. I hear Max Gordon usually draws a full courtroom."

The food arrived, and they continued their conversation until Jennifer had to leave for her witness practice. They left the Library and walked together to the fountain in front of Thomas Courthouse.

Jennifer took both his hands in hers, and said, "I'm going to Hilton Head Saturday to check on my dad. I'd really like you to come along. I'm coming back Sunday morning."

"I'm sorry, Jen. You know I would love to, but I'll be pretty much occupied until this trial is over."

It wasn't what she wanted to hear. He gave her a soft kiss on her cheek. They looked into each other's eyes, smiled, and lingered silently for just a moment before Jennifer walked into the courthouse.

CHAPTER 37
Friday, September 8

Jennifer drove to the party alone. She got the invitation on Tuesday. It read simply:

Denis Nolan invites you to a
"September Evening on the Beach"
Friends, food, good conversation, and music
Seven p.m., Friday, September 8th
Informal

There was a slip enclosed with directions to the house on Tybee Beach, but there was no RSVP request and no phone number to call. She was curious as to why she had been invited to her professor's party on the beach, but she quickly decided to go. She discretely checked with her friends to see if anyone else would be going, so that they could share a ride, but no one else had received an invitation. She had planned to tell Scott about the invitation when she saw him Wednesday, but after he expressed such a negative feeling about Professor Nolan, she decided not to mention it.

Jennifer was a bit miffed that she had not heard from Scott since Wednesday night. She still recalled his last words: "I'll be pretty much occupied until this trial is over." That seemed such strange language: *occupied.* She thought back to the previous Saturday night at Hilton Head—that beautiful, romantic evening they spent on the beach. She remembered his fingers gently wandering through her hair and the sensation of his lips across her body. And she remembered every whispered word in her ear. She hadn't heard any words then like "occupied." Was he so occupied that he could not give her a phone call? Or a text message?

It took her longer to drive to the party than she had anticipated, and it was a bit after eight when she arrived. Her main concern was that she was appropriately dressed. She wasn't sure of the meaning of "informal" at a "September Evening on the Beach," but she was wearing the most formal of her informal dresses: a silk, ankle-length, floral sheath. She would rather be overdressed than underdressed. An attendant opened the door and invited her in. Jennifer immediately saw that it wasn't a beach *house;* it was a beach *mansion.* It wasn't simply a living room, dining room, and kitchen but rather a ballroom, banquet hall, and banquet preparation room. The tables in the banquet hall were filled with food, and there was a large built-in bar tended by two red-vested bartenders and surrounded by several guests. Soft jazz could be heard from a small band on the patio.

Denis Nolan spotted her as soon as she entered and came immediately to greet her. "I'm so glad you could come, Jennifer." He stepped back two steps and looked at her intensely. "My, you look beautiful."

There was a pause as Jennifer tried to think of a response. "Well, thank you, Professor" was all that came to her.

"Not *Professor.* Off campus, Jennifer, it's just *Denis.* Let me show you around." He placed his hand on her shoulder, gently steering her toward a group of guests at the far end of the room. "This way. I want to introduce you to some special friends."

The members of the group turned their attention to Denis and Jennifer as they arrived.

"Jennifer, I want you to meet Ben Sterner, vice chairman of the Board of Trustees. And Wilbert Tebeau, another board member. This is Jennifer Stone."

Each extended a hand to Jennifer as they were introduced.

"And Bruce Bechtel, our vice dean and Professor Marjory Hoffman. You probably have already met them."

She had not, but she smiled broadly, and they also extended their hands.

"Jennifer is in her first semester at Savannah Law," said Dennis, "but is not new to Savannah. She's a graduate of Savannah College of Art and Design, architectural history major."

Jennifer was surprised that Denis knew her major. She had never mentioned it in any of their previous conversations.

"Wonderful school. Wonderful school," said Ben Sterner.

"I agree," said Wilbert Tebeau. "My granddaughter graduated from there last May with a fine arts degree. Majored in photography. Whitney Tebeau. Perhaps you knew her."

"Yes, I did, but not well. Wasn't she chosen to represent SCAD at a show in New York last spring? It was quite an honor."

"Yes, that was Whitney," beamed Wilbert.

He and Jennifer then engaged in small talk about SCAD as Denis stood and listened.

At the first break in their conversation, Denis touched Jennifer's elbow and said, "I'm sorry. I haven't gotten you a drink or a bite to eat. Let's see what is still available."

Of course, everything was still available: hot crab canapés, she-crab soup, lumpfin crab cakes, barbequed shrimp, roasted peppers and sherry-glazed sweet potatoes, oysters on the half-shell, and salads of all kinds. And, of course, there at the end of the line was the ubiquitous standing rib roast of beef. It was Savannah cuisine at its finest.

Jennifer took a plate, added a few shrimp and some spinach salad, and quickly moved to the rib roast, which was presided over by a smiling black chef with a sharp carving knife. Denis was just behind her with his plate.

"Give her your most special cut, Hughie," said Denis.

"Is that because she's *your* most special, Mr. Nolan?" teased the chef with a grin.

"Of course, Hughie."

Jennifer hoped she was not blushing. She was appreciative of the attention, since she knew no one else at the party, but it made her uncomfortable. She looked around. There must have been fifty to sixty guests, and not one appeared to be a student. She recognized only a few faces—young faculty members that she had seen on the campus but had never met.

"Would you like to eat on the patio?" asked Denis.

Jennifer nodded and followed Denis outside. There was a phenomenal view of the ocean, a hundred yards or so away. The sun had already set, but there were still streaks of light reflecting on the incoming waves. It was a beautiful, balmy evening. They found a vacant table, and Denis pulled out a chair for Jennifer. Most of the guests were eating at tables inside or were enjoying conversation and drinks in the large ballroom. The patio dance floor was vacant; the band had taken a break.

"I'll get us a drink from the bar," said Denis. "What would you like?"

"Just water, thank you."

"No, I mean from the bar. I'll have someone bring us a drink. Anything—the bar is well stocked."

"Thanks, but water is fine."

"I ordered a case of Cullen's 2002 Chardonnay especially for tonight. I think you would like it."

"Sound's wonderful, but no thanks."

Denis got up and went inside. He was back quickly. And almost as soon, a waiter appeared with a glass of water, two wine glasses, and a bottle of Cullen's 2002 Chardonnay.

"In case you change your mind," said Denis, as he moved one of the wine glasses directly in front of Jennifer.

Jennifer was mildly annoyed. She had not had any problem making up her mind. But it was a beautiful evening, and she wanted to enjoy it. She still wondered why she had been invited to this "September Evening on the Beach." She was the only student there. And he was her professor. He was the host, with dozens of guests, but he was devoting all of his time to her. She was slowly realizing that this was an unannounced "date." The realization was both disquieting and exciting. She knew that most colleges had rules prohibiting a professor from dating a student, but whatever the rule, it was Denis's problem, not hers. It must be OK, or he would not have been so open in front of Vice Dean Bechtel and Professor Hoffman. While she did not find him physically attractive, he was charming and lavish in his attention. She would just enjoy the evening.

Denis steered the conversation to her undergrad years. He asked about her studies, interests, hobbies, and family. There was no mention of her law classes or her witness role in the upcoming trial competition. It was an easy conversation. It was all about her. But occasionally, her thoughts returned to Scott. She wondered if he was still *occupied.*

Jennifer's glass of wine went untouched. They finished their meal, and Denis suggested they go inside. There, Denis introduced her to more of the guests. Many were his father's business associates and their wives. One guest she met was Jacqueline Hinesley, a Savannah Law graduate. Jennifer thought she had heard the name before but could not recall where. They had a short conversation about her practice in Brunswick, Georgia.

It was nearing ten o'clock, and a couple approached Denis to say goodnight. Denis walked with them to the front door, and as they departed, Denis saw a man just starting up the steps.

"Come on in, Max. I had about given up on you."

"I had about given up on me, too. Fly through Atlanta and no telling when or where you arrive. Damn planes are late, coming and going. Wouldn't serve my second martini—air disturbance, they claimed. Hell, what did they expect, we're in an airplane! Lost my luggage. Supposed to deliver it to the Hilton tonight, but who knows about those clowns. If I knew a good lawyer, I'd sue their asses off."

He laughed, stepped inside and gave Denis a firm handshake. He surveyed the twelve-foot ceilings and the large rooms. "Nice hut," he said.

"I want you to meet someone," said Denis.

He and Gordon walked over to where Jennifer was standing alone.

"Max, this is Jennifer Stone, law student at Savannah Law. Jennifer, Mr. Gordon is an attorney helping me with a matter I have before the city."

Jennifer was startled to see Max Gordon standing before her. He looked larger, more imposing, than the short man she had watched on TV Wednesday night. It took her a moment to recover. "Yes, of course, I've heard a lot about Mr. Gordon. But I did not know he was your attorney."

"That's only half of it, Jennifer. Young Denis here is *my* attorney."

Denis could see the confusion in Jennifer's eyes. "Mr. Gordon—Max—is helping me with a problem I have with the city. He's not only the best trial lawyer in the country, he's the best in dealing with bureaucracy. Agree, Max?"

"Of course, I agree. And the most successful, intelligent, richest, *and* modest." Gordon turned directly to Jennifer. "How well do you know this guy?"

"He's one of my professors."

"What subject?"

"Property."

"Too bad. He doesn't know a damn thing about property law. I had to save his ass from going to the slammer for a botched real estate deal in Chicago. Should have let him go to jail. The world would be a better place." Gordon gave Denis a slap on the chest with the back of his hand and let out a loud laugh.

"Now Max, you know that wasn't me. But you did save my partner."

"Yeah, and your partner was a crook—dipping into the trust account. The world would indeed be a better place without his type. But that's the kind of guys I deal with. I get an acquittal and I'm immediately sorry. But right now, I'm hungry. Haven't eaten since this morning. Anything left, Denis?"

"We'll find something, Max. Follow me."

After Gordon filled two plates, Denis escorted him and Jennifer to a table and waved one of the red-vested bartenders over. Gordon ordered a vodka martini on the rocks.

"How about you, Jennifer?" said Denis.

"I'm fine," replied Jennifer.

"Bring a bottle of Pinot Noir—Jayson Sonoma Coast—and three glasses," said Denis, despite the fact that the bottle of Chardonnay had not been touched.

Some of the guests had departed, and many were now on the patio listening to the small band. The martini and wine arrived promptly. Denis poured wine from the bottle of Pinot Noir into Jennifer's glass without comment. She watched as he poured. She said nothing to Denis but turned to look at Gordon.

"I'm curious. You said that Professor Nolan . . . ." She corrected herself. "Denis is your attorney. What do you mean?"

Denis spoke first. "I've agreed to be local counsel on a criminal case that Max is defending beginning Monday. Maybe you saw the case involving Senator Harrison's son in the newspaper?"

"Yes, I did. I also saw Mr. Gordon discussing it on TV Wednesday night. You'll be assisting Mr. Gordon in trying that case?"

"No, Max won't let me get my hands on any part of the case, will you, Max?"

"Hell, no. I'm not going to let a paper-shuffling, real estate lawyer screw up my case. I'm going to pay you . . . no, Senator Harrison is going to pay you, to just sit there. You've got only one thing I need—a Georgia license. I'm going to rent it for a week. You don't even have to take notes. Just stay awake and out of the way. But you, Jennifer, if you can cut a few classes, you might want to come down and see the show. You'll see some things they don't teach you in law school."

"You won't have to cut my Property class. This afternoon, I posted a 'Class Canceled Notice' for all my classes next week."

"I'll try to make it. It sounds exciting," said Jennifer. She did not mention that she had another reason for wanting to attend the trial.

"You better get there early," said Gordon. "There's going to be a crowd. My cases always bring out a crowd—and the media. They all want a show, and they'll get one."

"Like the Patty Hearst case," said Denis. "That was Max's first case—the California trial of the century, until the O. J. Simpson spectacle. Now, I should go see how my guests and my band are doing. Max, take care of my date. And tell her about the Hearst trial." Denis walked out to the patio.

"How long have you and Denis been dating?" Gordon asked as soon as Denis left.

Jennifer had been taken by surprise by Denis's statement, "Take care of my date." So he *did* consider this a date. How strange. When she received the invitation, she had no reason to consider it a date. She carefully considered how to respond to the question. It would surely embarrass Denis if she said this was *not* a date.

"This is our first date." She hoped that would end the matter. It didn't.

"I'm glad to see Denis dating. I knew him for almost two years in Chicago, and I don't recall him dating anyone there. And

I've seen him off and on since he moved back to Savannah and never heard him mention any lady friends. I know his dad would be happy. He bought a big part of Bonaventure Cemetery for his wife and himself—and what he also hoped would be the final resting place for Denis's family. He told me . . . ."

Jennifer broke in. This conversation was making her uncomfortable. "So you knew his dad? I understand he was quite a successful business man."

"Yes, got to know him quite well. After his wife died, he planned a big monument on the Bonaventure plot."

Her interruption did not work. She hoped the conversation would shift away from dating and cemeteries, but Gordon proceeded undeterred.

"It was going to be a memorial to her and the whole family. Had a big-name architectural firm design it but couldn't get approval from the cemetery authorities to start construction. On Denis's recommendation, Howard hired me to take it to court, if necessary. I spent a lot of time with Howard, and we had a lot of discussions about Denis. He was concerned that Denis would never have a family. Denis was their only child. Really disturbed him and his wife that Denis never brought any lady friends home."

Jennifer could not believe this conversation. Were there not ethical rules about a lawyer revealing client conversations—personal and family secrets? And even if not unethical in a legal sense, where was his common decency and propriety? Discussing Denis's dating habits in Chicago was downright tactless and crude. She wondered how someone so lacking in social graces could be so successful in the courtroom. Her life was now focused on becoming a trial lawyer, but if this is the character of a successful trial lawyer, maybe she should reconsider. She attempted once again to change the focus of the conversation.

"Tell me about the Patty Hearst case. Denis said that was your first case."

"Denis is obsessed with the Patty Hearst case. But that's another story."

"Well, I'm not obsessed with it, but I am interested in it. I visited Hearst Castle one summer with my mom and dad. I learned quiet a bit about William Randolph Hearst and his family but not much about his granddaughter, Patty. I knew she had been kidnapped and later tried and convicted for joining in with the kidnappers in a bank robbery, but I didn't know any of the details. I thought I might learn something when I visited Hearst Castle, but there was nothing written about it in the tour literature, and nothing was said about it by the tour guides. I always wondered about her trial. So tell me about it."

"Denis is correct that the Patty Hearst trial was my first case. But I was only on the periphery. F. Lee Bailey was the lead trial attorney, and he had his own permanent team. I was involved with him, if you can call it that, only for that one trial as a research assistant. That was in 1976. I had just graduated from law school. I didn't sit at counsel table, but I had a reserved seat in a row just behind it. When they needed quick research on an issue, they would hand me, or some other research flunky, a note, and off we would go."

"How did you get that job, research assistant for F. Lee Bailey?"

"Personally asked for it . . . a couple weeks before the trial. Just walked up and told him I was a recent law school graduate, a hell of a good researcher, and would work on the case for free, and full time. All I asked was to be in the courtroom to observe when the court was in session."

"You just walked up to F. Lee Bailey and said that? And the job was yours?"

"Actually, I said it to Albert Johnson, his associate. I rarely saw Bailey except in the courtroom. He was spending a lot of time flying off in his plane to Reno when he wasn't in trial. I got my research assignments from Johnson. And he got me on the payroll after he saw some of my research. And why not? I was damn good, and it was not money from his pocket. Patty's dad gave them a healthy budget."

"And they lost. Why do you think the defense lost the case?" Jennifer was pleased that the conversation had left Denis's personal life and Bonaventure cemetery behind. She was beginning to enjoy the conversation.

"Several reasons, starting with the defense strategy."

"Defense *strategy?* What was it?"

"Bailey's theory was that Patty had been 'brainwashed' after she was abducted by the SLA—the Symbionese Liberation Army. He set out to prove she was suffering from 'Stockholm syndrome' . . . that she was so utterly dependent on her captors, she became emotionally attached to them. Kind of like a helpless newborn baby becoming attached to its mother. Under this theory, Bailey would have to convince the jury that Patty was never a free agent, not even when she held that assault rifle while robbing a bank some two and a half months after she was kidnapped. Did you ever see that photo—Patty with that assault rifle slung over her shoulder inside the bank?"

"Yes. I recall a photo like that."

"The prosecution had dozens of similar photos and videos to support their argument that she wasn't brainwashed, including a video of her action during the bank robbery. And there was that message she sent describing one of her captors as 'the gentlest, most beautiful man I've ever known.' Hell, I didn't see how those photos and videos proved anything. They cut both ways. But to prove his theory, Bailey had to put her on the witness stand and have her describe the abuse she suffered. That included sexual abuse. It was a humiliating experience, and the cross-exam made it worse. It was blistering. She took the fifth forty-two times. When a defendant gets on the stand and takes the fifth—bye-bye defendant."

"What could the defense have done differently?"

"Plead guilty to some minor offense and get it over with. Patty Hearst had a lot of sympathy going for her before trial. After all, there was no question that she was forcefully kidnapped from her apartment. No question about that. She probably could have struck a deal without jail time. That would have been my advice, had they asked . . . but, of course, they didn't. I was a lowly researcher, fresh out of law school. But if you go to trial, then you fight like a hungry bear and stay on it twenty-four seven."

"But that didn't happen?"

"It did happen, but the hungry bear was the prosecutor, Browning. He left the courthouse each day to prepare for the next day's trial. Bailey left each day for who knows where. Flying to Reno was a good bet. He gave a short, rambling closing argument to end it, and Patty didn't have a chance. She always believed that his closing argument sealed her doom. When he got up to argue, his hands were shaking, and she suspected he had been drinking. Then, he spilled a glass of water on his crotch, and as he stood there facing the jury, it looked like he had peed in his pants. You think the jury could listen to anything he was saying with that view? She got seven years, commuted to twenty-two months by Jimmy Carter."

"Did you work on her appeal?"

"Hell, no, and I didn't ask. I just got out of town as fast as I could. That was a sorry-ass defense and a sorry-ass result, and I didn't want to be associated with it any longer. Besides, I had a nice job offer waiting in Chicago. I needed to get there fast so I could start studying for the Illinois bar exam. I passed that one, first shot. Took Ohio next and, a year later, New York. Passed them on first try, too. Never took Georgia—that's why I need Denis. I try cases all over the United States, mostly criminal cases. Last year the *New York Times* referred to me as 'the most peripatetic trial lawyer in the country.' Had to look it up. Thought they might be libeling me."

Gordon stopped just long enough to laugh at his own joke.

"But they were right. Look at me . . . here I am in Savannah, getting ready for a trial on Monday that I had never heard of until last weekend when I was home in Chicago. Week after next, I'll be in Miami for a weeklong cocaine trafficking case, and following that, I'll be in Albany trying a . . . hell, I'm not sure what I've got in Albany. I think it's some politician caught with kiddy-porn on his computer. It doesn't matter—I try 'em all. I do all the work in the courtroom, but I've got a gaggle of assistants that get them ready. Got a team already on site in Miami. Flew another team down to Savannah on Wednesday for this one, which I'm going to enjoy. These small-town prosecutors don't know what to expect when they hear I'm coming, and when they find out, it's too late."

Gordon was now in a rapid-fire monologue. This nationally known trial lawyer was proving to be a self-absorbed jerk, totally lacking in social skills. The one-person conversation was all about him.

Jennifer wondered why Denis had been gone so long. As awkward as it may seem, he was her date, wasn't he? The thought that Professor Denis Nolan, her Property professor, was her date amused her, although she didn't know why. She tried to suppress a smile and did so by asking another question. "You said Denis was obsessed with the Patty Hearst case. In what way?"

"The complete experience—her abduction, how she was brainwashed, and just what caused her to become so supportive of her kidnappers."

"But that was in the seventies. That was long before you met Denis, right?"

"Yes, of course. I met Denis many years later in Chicago. Two of the senior partners of his law firm were indicted. White-collar crimes, tax evasion and money laundering—lots of money involved. The feds got an indictment based on the testimony of several clients who each had paid the firm hundreds of thousands of dollars and were dissatisfied with the results. Denis called his father and told him about it. Denis wasn't a target, but his dad was afraid Denis would end up somehow as a fall guy. He was young and inexperienced in the way Chicago operates. That was a wise move. No question, Denis would have been eaten alive if I hadn't gotten in early on. There was a lot of finger pointing—and senior partners, junior partners, and associates like Denis taking sides. The firm had multiple bank accounts, some not on the books, and these clients had been paying directly into them. Big cash payments over several years—right into the pockets of a couple of senior partners, and not a penny paid in taxes."

"Was Denis a witness to any of this or involved in any way?"

"No, but that makes no difference when millions of dollars are involved and the firm needs someone to hang out to dry. Denis had worked on one of the cases involved, and he would have been in it over his head if his dad had not gotten to me so soon. But I took care of it."

"How?"

"You don't want to know. This is Chicago, understand? I spent a lot of time with Denis. I got to know him pretty well. His dad, Howard, came up for a couple of visits, and I got to know him, too. Classy guy, his dad. Really doted on his son. Wasn't too happy Denis was doing real estate closings in Chicago, especially with that firm and some of the people he was beginning to hang out with. Didn't look promising to Howard."

Jennifer did not want the conversation to drift into Denis's personal life again, so she tried to change the subject. "Whatever happened to Patty Hearst?"

"I don't know, but I bet Denis can tell you. While he was living in Chicago, he became very interested in the brainwashing defense that Bailey had used. He started researching the Stockholm syndrome. Same research I had done. He found an old copy of Patty's autobiography, *Every Secret Thing*, and quizzed me to see if her account matched what I had heard at trial. When I came to Savannah last year to discuss the Bonaventure cemetery matter, the movie *Guerrilla*—about the abduction—had just been released. He already had a copy, and we watched it. It was an astonishingly accurate movie. In fact, I didn't really appreciate how bizarre all of it was until I saw that film. I could see he was still obsessed with the Patty Hearst case and the Stockholm syndrome. I suppose everyone has to have a hobby. Mine is causing turmoil in the courtroom. What's yours, Jennifer?"

Jennifer was relieved to hear the question. She had heard enough, in fact, too much, about Denis and Patty Hearst. "Criminal trials," she said. "That's what I hope to do some day. I really enjoy watching the drama in a courtroom."

"Drama? You won't see drama in any courtroom in Savannah. Attorneys here think a criminal trial is a debutante ball. 'Yes, Your Honor. No, Your Honor. May I approach the bench, Your Honor?' They think some almighty judge is in charge of the courtroom. But the judge doesn't run the courtroom. I run the courtroom—not the judge, not the prosecutor. *I'm* in charge. Most trial lawyers are scared, clueless cretins who shouldn't even be allowed in a courtroom. You know how a case has to be tried, Jennifer?"

"As a first-semester law student, I'm sure you know I don't."

"Well, I try them like a knife fight in a phone booth. There's going to be only one person standing when it's over, and I want to make sure it's me. There's no silver medal given after a criminal trial."

Suddenly, Denis appeared. He had yet another bottle of wine in his hand. "I thought by now you could use a refill. What have you two been discussing?" Seeing the glasses were still full, he put the bottle down.

"Your Property class," responded Gordon. "Jennifer was just telling me about the class and how disappointed she was to find it so lacking in challenge. She was hoping you could assign more cases and outside reading."

Gordon and Denis laughed and Jennifer forced a smile.

"I'm out-of-my-mind tired, Denis. I need to head for my hotel," said Gordon. He pushed his chair back and stood.

Denis followed his lead and also stood.

"I'll call you in the morning," said Gordon. "We need to talk about Monday's trial. Not about the case but about looking the part of a successful criminal defense attorney—rich. You gotta flash the gold, Denis. Bring your finest leather briefcase—empty. And get your designer suits out. If you don't have any, go buy some—a different one for every day, and none of that casual law-professor stuff. I want you to look smart, even though I know you aren't. Remember, you're part of the Max Gordon team. When this trial is over, you will be the talk of the town." As he said that, he gave Jennifer an exaggerated wink and Denis, a firm handshake. "I enjoyed talking with you, Jennifer. Now you two enjoy the evening."

Gordon headed for the front door and disappeared.

Jennifer stood. "I should be going, too," she said. "It was a wonderful party, Professor. Thanks for inviting me."

"No, not *professor*, not tonight, Jennifer. Remember, it's *Denis*. The night is quite young, and we really haven't had time to talk. Let's walk out on the patio and listen to the band. They're from Charleston and my dad's favorite group. They've played here many times."

He held her arm and led her out on the patio. But they didn't stop. Denis continued to walk with Jennifer, without further conversation, down the curved steps to the private wooden boardwalk that led to the beach.

Jennifer was caught off guard. She had not anticipated that she would be walking out on the beach with her professor. Maybe she should turn back. But it was a beautiful night and still early. So why not enjoy what remains of this "September Evening on the Beach"? As they walked toward the beach, the soft music from the band followed. About halfway to the beach there was a concrete bench and an outdoor shower area.

"You don't want to get sand in those shoes. Let's take our shoes off and walk down the beach. The party can get along without us."

Even without shoes, Jennifer was not dressed for a beach walk, but she did not protest. They sat down on the bench, removed their shoes, and placed them under the bench. Denis reached for her hand, and they continued down the wooden walkway to the sand dunes at the end, the start of the beach.

The wet sand made walking easy. As they got closer to the water, the music became lost in the gentle, undulating sound of the ocean. The phosphorescent waves were the most colorful Jennifer could recall. She was enjoying the feel of the sand beneath her feet. If someone had told her last week that she would soon be strolling at night on Tybee Beach, hand in hand with her Professor, she would have laughed. She was fascinated and, at the same time, uncomfortable with the situation she found herself in. Neither spoke as they walked slowly along the newly wet sand.

Eventually, Denis stopped and turned to Jennifer. After a deep breath, he said, "Jennifer, from the time I saw you in the courtroom that Sunday, you have been on my mind. I didn't know how to tell you my feelings. It was sudden and powerful, as if a bolt of lightening had struck. I'm sure you have a hard time believing this, but I have never had a relationship with a woman. None. That worried my dad." He paused. "And it worried me. I just felt so awkward and inept around women." Denis took another deep breath before continuing.

"All through high school, I never had a girlfriend. I was homeschooled, and I thought that was the cause of my problem. But it didn't change in college or in law school. Can you believe I have never even held the hand of a girl or a woman until tonight? There has always been a barrier, like a wall I could not break through. I could never take that first step. I can't explain it. I know I disappointed my dad. He would get angry when I refused to discuss it with him. But how could I? I didn't understand it myself. Then I met you—the day before you were to attend your first class. You were about to start a new phase of your life, and suddenly I wanted to start a new phase in my life, too—with you. Can you understand this, Jennifer?"

She could not. But here was a man pouring out his innermost secrets to her. She fought for an appropriate response. None came. She looked away and bit down on her lower lip. It would have been easier if she had some feelings for this man. Some spark, some expectation that this could lead to something more. But there was none. There never would be. She was sure of that. She hoped something would come to her for a response, but she found no words with which to respond.

The silence was broken by Denis. "I was determined that you would be part of my life. Every waking moment since I saw you, you have been part of it. You did not know it, and I did not know how to tell you. So I planned this evening. It was for you. I wanted you to know how I felt, and I was determined to tell you. I simply had to find the courage." He paused, and this time it was a very long pause.

Jennifer remained silent and motionless.

"I have only two goals in life now, Jennifer. One, to be dean at Savannah Law. And . . . and the other . . . the most important goal in my life . . . ." Denis was struggling for words. "Do you think we have a chance . . . together?"

Jennifer was not prepared for this. The simple answer was "no." But on a darkened beach late at night, alone, she felt perplexed and intensely anxious about the question. She was a student; he, her professor. It seemed ethically wrong and inappropriate. The whole situation was unreal and in a very troubling way. And so unexpected. How could she possibly have expected this when she received her invitation Tuesday? But now it was clear. The "September Evening on the Beach" was to be his first date. With her. Could it really be that this man, now in his thirties, had never been with a woman? High school, college, law school, attorney in a Chicago law firm, law professor—had never been with a woman, alone? Not even a date or held the hand of a woman, until tonight? She was not trained in psychology. She had not even taken a course in psychology, but something had to be seriously wrong. His question was now echoing in her mind, demanding an answer. She must choose her answer carefully.

Jennifer turned and looked directly at Denis. "Let me think about it. And perhaps we should start heading back. This wind is a bit chilly now."

Denis reached for her hand again, and Jennifer did not decline. They walked back to the boardwalk silently. They stopped at the concrete bench and put on their shoes. It was after eleven, but the band was still playing.

When they reached the patio, Denis spoke for the first time. "Let's go inside to the bar. It's still open."

Jennifer followed him in. She was glad to be inside, surrounded by others, even if she did not know them. She did not see any of the faculty or board members that she had met when she arrived. The crowd had thinned, and the food had been removed from the tables.

"I'm going to have a Scotch and soda. What will you have?"

"Nothing, I'm fine. And I must be going. It was a wonderful party. Thank you for asking me. I enjoyed the music, the food, and the conversation. And, of course, meeting your friends."

She wasn't sure if she should extend her hand or just proceed to the front door. She decided on the latter. Denis followed. At the door, she turned to look at Denis for the last time.

"Thanks . . . ." She was about to say "Denis," but it would not come. "For a wonderful evening" was substituted.

She began to walk down the steps to the lighted parking lot where her car was parked when she heard Denis speak.

"You promised to think about it, Jennifer. Don't disappoint me."

Jennifer kept walking and did not look back. But she believed she should acknowledge that she had heard him, at least. When she got to the last step, she turned and smiled for just a second and walked briskly to her car.

It was after midnight when Jennifer arrived at her apartment. The light on her answering machine was blinking. Her mind immediately flashed back to the Friday night two weeks before, when the blinking machine brought news that her dad was in the hospital. She pushed the play button and was relieved to hear Scott's voice.

"Where are you? I called your cell; no answer. It's about 7:30. I'm going to the Library. Can you meet me there? Call my cell."

It was too late to call now. She would call in the morning. She lay in bed a long time—pondering the events of the evening—before finally falling asleep.

CHAPTER 38
Saturday, September 9

Jennifer woke late. She called Scott about ten, and they made plans to meet at the Library for lunch before Jennifer left for Hilton Head. The events of the previous evening were swirling in her head, and she was not sure how much, if any, she should tell Scott. Denis's disturbing conduct toward her was not really Scott's concern. But Denis's participation in the trial beginning Monday was. She wondered if Scott knew. She felt no compulsion to tell Scott about "A September Night on the Beach," but she knew she would eventually. And why not? She had done nothing she should hide. She smiled as she recalled the evening; it was one hell of a party.

Scott was sitting at the bar talking to Juri when she arrived. Juri smiled as he saw her walking into the bar.

"There comes that beautiful blonde. Hi, Jennifer. Scott was just telling me a blonde joke. Want to hear it?"

Scott looked disapprovingly at Juri. Their discussion had been about baseball.

"Do I have a choice?"

"No."

"Then let's hear it."

"What goes **VROOM, SCREECH, VROOM, SCREECH, VROOM, SCREECH?**"

"Not a clue," said Jennifer.

"A blonde going through a flashing red light," said Juri, laughing.

"That's not funny, Juri," said Jennifer, faking a frown.

"Then how about this one? A policeman pulls a brunette over after she'd been driving the wrong way on a one-way street. Cop says, 'Do you know where you're going?' Brunette says, 'No, but wherever it is, it must be bad 'cause all the people are leaving.'"

"A *brunette*. Now that was funny," Jennifer said, smiling.

"Where were you last night, Jennifer? Scott sat right here for an hour—looking at his watch every three minutes. Said he was waiting on you. Nursed his one beer; finally gave up and left. So where were you?"

"Out."

"Juri, anyone ever tell you that you talk too much?" asked Scott.

"All the time."

"Jennifer and I are going someplace quiet—and friendly—for lunch. You'll have to find someone else to annoy. By the way, do you know how many bartenders it takes to screw in a light bulb?"

Juri made a "thinking" gesture by putting his right forefinger to his temple, paused for a moment, and said, "No, but if you'll hum a few bars, I can probably fake it."

"Now you guys planned that didn't you—that was a setup," said Jennifer. "Admit it!"

Juri and Scott just laughed.

Scott and Jennifer then left the bar and went into the restaurant area and ordered lunch. Jennifer decided to tell Scott about her "September Evening on the Beach." Not the walk on the beach with Professor Nolan but the beach house, the food, the music, and, of course, meeting Gordon.

"Were there many students there?" asked Scott.

"I was the only student, as far as I know. Several faculty members were there—Vice Dean Bechtel and Professor Hoffman. I thought I recognized a couple of the young faculty, but I didn't speak to them, and I don't know their names. I've seen them on campus. And some members of the Board of Trustees. I was introduced to Mr. Sterner, who I think is the board vice-chairman. Also, a Mr. Tebeau. And I met a lady who was a Savannah Law graduate, Jacqueline Hinesley. We had an interesting conversation. She's in private practice in Brunswick."

Scott interrupted. "What a suck-up!"

"You know her?"

"I'm talking about Nolan. Do you see the connection?"

"What connection?"

"The frickin' guest list, Jennifer! All the folks you've named are on the Dean Search Committee. He plans this colossal beach shindig one week before the first meeting of the committee and invites the entire committee . . . well, almost the entire committee. What a transparent, obsequious, fawning SOB!"

Jennifer was a bit amused at Scott's outburst. But she was also surprised at the connection he made. He was right. She had received the letter notifying her of her appointment to the committee, read it, and put it aside. She now recalled that it listed the names of all the committee appointees. All the voting members of the committee were at the party. All except Scott. She wondered why she had not made the connection herself.

"Did you get an invitation?" asked Jennifer, although she already knew the answer.

"No, but I'm *sure* it was just an oversight. Just an oversight."

Jennifer was now quite aware that it was not an oversight. The evening was planned to specifically include her and exclude Scott. It was now so obvious to her and to Scott.

"There was one particular guest who surely will interest you."

"And who would that be—George Bush?"

"No, but close. Max Gordon, Harrison's attorney."

"*Sneak* Gordon?"

"I don't know about the 'Sneak' part, but he's Harrison's attorney, the guy we saw on TV. And I guess you know that Professor Nolan is on the case as local counsel."

"You aren't serious, are you?"

"I am serious. Apparently, you didn't know."

"I knew Judge Desano demanded that he associate with a member of the Georgia Bar. A copy of the Notice of Appearance was to be delivered to Grady Wilder. Grady may have told Meg Flanders, but this is the first I've heard that Nolan will be assisting with the case."

"I'm not sure you would call it assisting. Gordon said he was just renting his Georgia Bar license for a week. All he's to do is sit there and stay awake. I thought it was pretty insulting, but Professor Nolan just laughed. How is the case coming for you prosecutors?"

"Good. *Very* good. Meg hasn't fully recovered from some recent surgery, so she has given me all of the witnesses—direct and cross. Plus, the opening. She's going to do the jury selection and closing argument. I've been working full time on it. Yesterday, we learned that our second eyewitness has agreed to fly in from Colorado. So things are looking up. If we had gone to trial on schedule, we would have had only one ID witness. Now we have two."

They lingered in the restaurant about an hour, discussing the latest news and gossip around the law school. Scott wasn't sure how long the trial would last, but he thought it would be over by Thursday, or Friday at the latest. They made plans for Friday night.

"Are you sure I can't talk you into coming with me to Hilton Head?"

"There is nothing I would rather do. You know that. But I still have a lot of work to do. I can't let a sneaky Chicago lawyer come to town and show me up."

Scott walked Jennifer to her car. "Call me as soon as you get there," he said.

He could not help but be a bit apprehensive as he watched her drive away alone. But on this trip, she would not be driving at night, and the engine of the "ugly Aztek" sounded smooth and strong. However, he would anxiously await her phone call telling him that she had arrived safely.

Jennifer drove across Talmadge Bridge and on to Hilton Head. She had not breathed a word about her walk on the beach with Professor Nolan. And she had given no further thought to the question that he had posed.

CHAPTER 39
Monday, September 11

It was 8:30 a.m. on Monday, and Scott was in Judge Desano's courtroom, seated at the prosecution table, awaiting the arrival of Meg Flanders. He was up early that morning. He had practiced his opening statement twice and was at the courthouse by eight. He had organized his table in the courtroom in perfect order: his trial notebook immediately in front of him, a yellow pad at its side, and four #2 pencils, newly sharpened and carefully aligned to point in the same direction. He would look organized, even if his mind was a jumbled maze of witness questions, opening statement, evidentiary objections, and complicated legal arguments.

He had promised Meg that he would bring all of the exhibits. He had at least a dozen photos and diagrams of the crime scene. Each was tagged and organized to be readily accessible during the examination of the appropriate witness. He had prepared for and offered—actually he had *asked*—to make the closing argument, but Meg had decided to reserve that for herself. Except for jury selection and the closing, the rest of the trial was his. And it seemed to be falling into place quite well. Last week, he had interviewed Mr. Patel and gone over the questions he would be asking. Patel would be a good witness, Scott thought. And Saturday afternoon, he made phone contact with Josh Johnson, the other eyewitness. Josh had his airline tickets in hand and said he was looking forward to revisiting Savannah, where he had spent many weekends while stationed at Fort Stewart. Josh assured Scott he could identify the man holding the gun on the clerk. He said it was a clear mental picture "still indelible in my mind."

Meg had not arrived when Max Gordon and Professor Nolan walked in. Even though Scott knew both would be in court, he was momentarily startled. Nolan took a seat at the defense table, but Gordon walked over and shook Scott's hand. Gordon was wearing the same ostentatious clothing and jewelry that he was wearing the first time Scott met him, except the yellow power-tie had been replaced with a purple one. The pink handkerchief hanging from his front breast pocket gave him a clownish appearance. At least Scott thought so, and he hoped Savannah jurors would agree.

"Where's the DA?" Gordon asked.

"She will be here shortly," said Scott.

"She? Where's the black guy?"

"If you mean Grady Wilder, he's in Atlanta. He's now with the U.S. Attorney's office there."

"So she's had the case only since last week?"

Scott didn't like the inquisition so decided to give as little information as possible. And he felt no need to answer that specific question. "She's been with the office for several years."

Gordon responded with a frown, but he had no further questions and walked back to the defense table.

Shortly afterwards, the defendant entered. He was dressed as he was the previous week: blue, polyester suit, white dress shirt, and red tie. He obviously had not made bail, as he had an armed bailiff by his side. Apparently, Scott thought, even his dad wasn't sure he would show up for trial. There appeared to be something different about him, though Scott couldn't tell exactly what, as his view was hindered by Gordon's wide body.

Scott had been so busy reviewing his notes at the prosecutor's table that he had not noticed the courtroom filling rapidly. Richard Evans arrived with an enlarged photo of the crime scene mounted on foam board, and for the first time, Scott turned to face the spectator area. He noted that most of the seats had been taken, except for several rows on the left side of the courtroom, which had been roped off to accommodate the jury panel when called from its assembly room. Then, on the other side, he noted a large tripod holding a TV camera. Lettering on the camera read "WSAV/TV." Two men were laying electrical and video cabling down the far wall. Scott recognized a newspaper reporter who was already seated in the front row. And there was a young lady with a steno pad, and a digital camera hung from her neck. He did not recognize her, but she was obviously from some news service. He wondered why the cameras were present. He had never seen cameras in any Chatham County courtroom. He was sure they were not going to be allowed in Desano's courtroom.

He looked at his watch. It was a few minutes before nine. Judge Desano would be entering promptly at nine and would expect counsel to be ready to begin. He was concerned that Meg had not arrived. Being only a few minutes late can put a judge in a very bad humor—or worse. From what Scott had heard, with Judge Desano, it was always worse. He was about to ask Richard to go locate Meg when he saw a young man rushing into the courtroom, heading directly for Scott and Richard. Scott recognized him from the DA's office but had not met him and did not know his name.

"Who is that, Richard? He's heading our way."

"That's Daniel Mackay."

Daniel arrived with a serious look on his face. He was a tall, young redhead, soft-spoken and not much older than Scott. He had been with the DA's Office for almost three years. His present assignment was with felony intake, while finishing his misdemeanor cases. Scott stood and faced him.

"You are Scott Marino, helping Meg on this case?"

"That's right."

"Meg had to go to the emergency room at Candler. Hemorrhaging. She's been admitted, but I don't know anything else about her condition. Nick Cox sent me to request a postponement."

It was now 9 a.m., and as expected, the judge's door, which leads directly to the bench, opened, and Judge Desano walked into the courtroom. A bailiff took his long wooden staff and pounded it three times on the floor.

"All rise," he commanded.

The first-time visitors were startled as usual by the loud raps of the heavy staff, but all in the courtroom were quickly on their feet. The trial of *State of Georgia versus John Harrison* was called to order, and the spectators were instructed to be seated.

Daniel Mackay remained standing, prepared to make his motion for a continuance. But Judge Desano spoke first, and Daniel sat down.

"There is a matter to take up before we begin this trial. Thursday, I was presented with written requests from several parties, among them WSAV-TV, the *South Georgia Times,* and Savannah radio station WTKS. I mention these in particular because they were the first of their particular media to make a written request. Subsequently, I had similar requests from other news media. Specifically, these parties wish to broadcast live or take photos of this trial. I ordered counsel for these parties to be present this morning for a hearing on this issue. Are counsel for these parties present?"

Several attorneys in the spectator section stood and announced their names and the party or parties each represented. Judge Desano invited them to come within the bar and be seated in the jury box. Ten of the fourteen seats in the jury box were quickly occupied.

"Personally, I am opposed to cameras and other recording devices in a courtroom, and I could enumerate my objections. But my personal opinion is unimportant because the State of Georgia has a policy favoring open judicial proceedings. Last year the Georgia Supreme Court addressed this issue in *Morris Communications versus Griffin*. The trial court had denied permission for cameras in the courtroom, after finding specifically that the defendant objected. However, the Supreme Court reversed. And just a few months ago, in our neighboring jurisdiction, Effingham County, Judge Turner denied a request from the *Savannah Morning News* to place a camera in the courtroom during a criminal trial. That decision was also reversed. Now, despite the outcome in those cases, the Supreme Court says I still have discretion, so I want to hear the position of the defense. Mr. Gordon, does the defense have any objection?"

"Absolutely not, Your Honor. The public has an absolute right to be invited into any and every courtroom in America, and because no courtroom can hold all the public, it is essential that the press, TV, and radio be permitted to be present. We emphatically support opening the court to not only still cameras but radio and TV broadcasts."

"How about the district attorney? I don't see Mr. Wilder. Who is representing the state?" asked Judge Desano.

Scott and Daniel eyed each other. "I think I should take this, Scott," Daniel said, as he rose from his chair to address the judge.

"Your Honor. I am Daniel Mackay, an assistant district attorney. The assigned assistant DA to this case, Meg Flanders, became acutely ill this morning and has been hospitalized. I was sent here to request a continuance in this case."

"I'm sorry to hear about Ms. Flanders. We'll take up that continuance request after we finish this hearing. What is the state's position on cameras and TV and radio broadcasts in this trial?"

"We are opposed. This trial already has the earmark of a media frenzy. I personally noted a half-dozen vehicles in front of the courthouse this morning with satellite equipment and cables running everywhere. This case, involving a member of a prominent family being defended by a nationally known trial attorney, is quickly turning into a high-profile spectacle instead of a calm search for truth and justice. From the prosecution's perspective, we don't need any further trial exposure."

Judge Desano turned to the attorneys seated in the jury box. "I've carefully read the briefs that were submitted. All of them. I've also read the Memorandum of Agreement signed by the parties concerning pooling and sharing the photos and broadcasts. Does anyone have any additional argument to present before I rule?"

One attorney rose to address the court. "Just this, Your Honor, and I'm sure I speak for others here in apologizing for the lateness in submitting our requests. However, most of us were not aware of the name of the defendant and his relationship to Senator Harrison until the Channel 11 interview of Mr. Gordon last Wednesday night. We know that you would have desired more time to consider these requests, but we were simply unaware until then."

"You were on TV regarding this case last Wednesday, Mr. Gordon?"

"Eh . . . yes, Your Honor, but only briefly. No real facts were discussed."

"You heard me warn you last Tuesday about my distaste for issuing gag orders, didn't you, Mr. Gordon?"

"Yes, I recall that, Your Honor."

"Well, consider the gag rule now in place. As much as I dislike policing them, I will. I'll be signing a written order, but in the meantime, use your better judgment. I know it will be difficult for you, Mr. Gordon, but I suggest you be neither seen nor heard by the media outside this courtroom."

The judge then turned to the jury box and continued: "Now, with regard to the request for still cameras and TV and radio broadcasts of this trial. Each request is granted. The pooling of the photos and broadcasts as set forth in the memorandum is also approved. There will be only one TV camera, one radio microphone, and one photographer with a still camera. If any of the equipment makes a sound, out it goes. I expect you attorneys to ensure that everyone involved is familiar with Superior Court Rule 22. That rule will be enforced. This hearing is terminated. We will take a fifteen-minute recess before calling the jury, to allow the media to set up their equipment and implement their pooling plan."

At the command "All rise," as the judge departed the courtroom, Daniel and Scott scrambled to their feet, looking puzzled at each other. There had been no resolution to Daniel's request for a continuance. Daniel was confident he could get a continuance at least long enough to determine when—or if—Meg could return. Scott wasn't so sure and didn't particularly care. He was ready for trial and his witnesses were ready. He expected the defense to agree to a continuance, since they had made the same request last Tuesday.

Fifteen minutes later, the court reconvened. As soon as the opening ritual was complete, Judge Desano looked over at Daniel and asked if he still had a motion for continuance.

"I do, Your Honor. I ask for a continuance of two weeks. Our office is quite swamped now with active cases set for trial, but that should provide sufficient time for another prosecutor to be assigned and get ready for this trial, or, hopefully, Ms. Flanders will be sufficiently healthy to continue."

"And you, Mr. Gordon, what is your position on this request?"

"Absolutely opposed. My trial calendar is booked solid through January."

"Last week you urged the court to grant you a continuance until December. What has changed?"

"My calendar has been restructured with additional cases set for trial in at least four different states between now and January. Besides, John Harrison has been incarcerated on exceedingly weak evidence for many months. He has previously demanded a speedy trial and is entitled to one. We are ready for trial now. Today. This courtroom. Just as you ordered last week. We renew our demand for speedy trial."

"I agree," said Judge Desano, and then he turned to the prosecution table. "There can't be one sauce for the goose and another for the gander when setting trial dates. This trial was set in stone last Tuesday. I was the stonemason. Your motion for a continuance is denied."

"But, Your Honor, there is simply no one available from the DA's office to represent the state."

"You are here. Aren't you a sworn assistant district attorney?"

"I am, Your Honor, but, frankly, all I know is the name of the defendant and that he is charged with robbery. I don't know who the witnesses are. I haven't read a single page of the investigative file."

"Have you ever supervised a student intern at a trial?"

"Yes, sir, I have. In misdemeanor trials."

"I believe that under the Georgia Practice Rules, before a student may participate in any trial, the student must be certified by the dean of the law school, take the required oath, and have permission of the trial judge. Any other requirements, Mr. Mackay?"

"No, sir, except a supervising attorney must be present at all times."

"Mr. Marino, how long have you been working on the case and what parts?"

"A couple of weeks, sir. I've been preparing for most all of it, except jury selection."

"So, there you have it, Mr. Mackay. You do the jury selection, and Mr. Marino can handle the rest of the trial. Problem solved." The judge then turned to a nearby bailiff. "Send for the jurors. We are ready to start jury selection."

Scott and Daniel, who had been standing during the judge's questioning, now sat down at the prosecution table.

"Scott, my good friend, I hope you are as prepared as the judge thinks you are," said Daniel. "I still can't believe this situation. There's not a damn thing we can do about it. And cases don't get reversed when the prosecutors get squeezed. When that jury's sworn, jeopardy attaches, and if we fuck it up—well, that's it. Too bad."

Daniel turned to Richard Evans, who was sitting in a chair on the right edge of the prosecution table. Richard, who had been observing criminal trials for over twenty years, was grinning like Lewis Carroll's Cheshire Cat. In fact, the whole scene reminded him of something out of *Alice's Adventures in Wonderland*.

"Down the rabbit hole," he said, just loud enough to be heard by Scott and Daniel.

"Richard, we need to tell the DA what's going on, in case he hasn't been watching TV. So, if you have a clue, go tell him. And if, like me, you don't have a clue, still go tell him. Say something clever, like, 'Surrender hell, we've just begun to fight.' And Richard, tomorrow wear a blue dress shirt—it shows up better on TV."

Scott appreciated the humor Daniel displayed in the face of Judge Desano's ruling, but he thought the situation was not so dire. No doubt it was a shock to Daniel to suddenly have responsibility for prosecuting a felony trial that he had not prepared for. And especially so when the defense counsel was one of the best known in the country and the trial was being broadcast across the state and perhaps across the nation. But Scott was not at all disappointed by the ruling. Yes, he was nervous, but he felt as prepared for this trial as anyone was likely to be.

As soon as Richard departed, the prospective jury panel of local citizens of various shapes, sizes, and colors filed into the courtroom and took their seats in the reserved rows. And it was then that Scott got a better look at John Harrison. He looked different from the way he appeared the previous Tuesday. Scott pulled out a file that contained his mug shot when he was booked into the Chatham County jail. The different look was striking. Could he really have changed that much?

Judge Desano began his preliminary instructions to the prospective jurors, which were brief. As soon as he finished, Scott tapped Daniel lightly on the side to get his attention.

"Daniel, there's a problem," Scott whispered. "We need to speak with the judge."

"About what?"

"I'm not sure," Scott said. "But let's find out." Scott then rose and faced Judge Desano.

"Your Honor, may we approach the bench?"

The judge motioned them forward, and Scott and Daniel began to walk to the bench. Gordon followed. Nolan remained seated. Soon the three were standing directly in front of Judge Desano. Gordon turned and saw that Nolan had not followed and motioned him to join them. He appeared surprised—after all, he was only to "be present in the courtroom and stay out of the way."

"Your Honor," Scott began, just loud enough to be heard by the judge and the other counsel, "I have reason to believe that since our session last Tuesday, the defendant has taken action to change his appearance. I believe there has been evidence tampering. The evidence the prosecution will be presenting is eyewitness identification. The defendant's appearance is the evidence, and any deliberate modification of the evidence would be a criminal act and should not be sanctioned by this court." Scott wasn't entirely sure of his facts or the law, and he wasn't sure what would or should be done if he was correct, but he said it with authority. He paused and waited, not knowing what else he should say on the subject. He thought Gordon would speak, but he didn't. Judge Desano rose slightly out of his chair and looked carefully at the defendant, who was still seated at the defense table alone.

"Yes, I agree, Mr. Marino. There has been a change of appearance of the defendant. What explanation can you give the court, Mr. Gordon?"

Gordon turned and looked at the defendant. He cocked his head to one side. He appeared to be studying his client's appearance, trying to see just what Scott and the judge had seen.

"Well, Your Honor, I can assure you that the gentleman seated there is the same one who was seated there last week, my client, John Harrison."

"I don't want any BS, Mr. Gordon. Your client has been in custody of the sheriff, so I'm not concerned that you brought in a ringer. Did you really think that was my question? My question is what do you know of your client's change of appearance, and don't even try to suggest that you don't see any change of appearance."

Gordon shifted his weight from side to side a couple times and then opened a file he was carrying and flipped through a few pages as if he were searching for the answer. But he didn't immediately respond.

"Do you need a pacemaker for your brain, Mr. Gordon? My question is not difficult. I expect an answer."

"Your Honor, I have a sensitive client, who has lost a bit of hair. Early balding apparently runs in his family. Being aware that he would constantly be in the public eye for this trial, he requested that we provide him with a hair piece to cover his baldness. That's all it is. It certainly is not a deliberate tampering with the evidence, as Mr. Marino suggested."

"So you went out, bought, and delivered a hairpiece to your client in jail. Is that what you are saying?"

"Not me, but a member of my team."

"I see. *Your team*. The district attorney can deal with *your team* and the issue of evidence tampering when this trial is over. But for now the trial will continue, *sans* hair piece."

Judge Desano motioned one of the bailiffs to the bench. "Now listen up, all of you. This bailiff, and the custodial bailiff, are going to escort the defendant out of this courtroom to the nearest holding room and ensure that the hair piece presently on his head is removed, tagged, and returned to the custody of the clerk of this court. If the district attorney wants it, Mr. Marino or Mr. Mackay can come get it. If not, I'll make sure it's eventually returned to you, Mr. Gordon." The judge fixed his eyes on Gordon's partially bald head. "It appears you may find some *legitimate* use for it."

He then turned to counsel. "As soon as you return to your tables, we are going to select our jury. But while you are up here, I might as well brief you on my plans for this trial. I want to finish jury selection today. Do you think you can do it, Mr. Gordon?"

"I'm not sure, Your Honor. I'll surely try."

"You do that. And you, Mr. Mackay?"

"I would hope so. I haven't had time to prepare any questions. I don't even know the jury profile that I should be looking for, so I expect my voir dire to be quite limited."

"That's fine, Mr. Mackay. I expect Mr. Gordon's questions to be quite limited also, because when I get finished with *my* voir dire, there's unlikely to be anything left to ask. I want you to be aware of my voir dire procedure. I will voir dire the entire panel and will follow up with questions to individual jurors based on responses. Counsel will only be permitted to ask appropriate questions that I have omitted. There rarely are any, and if I covered it, don't you try to add to it. I will cut you off, and it can be embarrassing. Understand?"

There was a simultaneous "Yes, Your Honor," and Judge Desano continued. "All we'll be doing today is selecting the jury, and I want it finished early, so those who are selected can go home and make preparation for being sequestered for the rest of the week at an undisclosed downtown hotel. They will be instructed to bring clothes, medicine, and personal items for four days. I have rarely sequestered a jury in a non-capital case, but this one, because of the extensive media coverage, requires it. We will start voir dire as soon as the defendant returns from his 'haircut.'"

The bailiffs brought the defendant back into the courtroom, and immediately Judge Desano began his voir dire: occupation, family, education, prior jury service, ever a defendant, ever a witness—the list of questions was extensive. He was still at it when the court recessed for lunch.

Daniel and Scott made a quick trip to the courthouse snack bar, picked up sandwiches, and took the elevator up to Daniel's office. Daniel was anxious to compare notes with Scott about the jury.

"I think the judge is about finished with his voir dire—at least I hope so," Daniel said. "I don't know how long Gordon plans to be up there, but I don't have any additional questioning. Who do you have on your strike list?"

"Well, there's number seven, that guy with the tattoos up his arms and around his neck. Creepy. And number fourteen—I don't like his laughing and whispering to jurors on both sides. Number twenty-two is dumber than a rock. Did you hear what she said when the judge asked her if she had ever been sued? She said, 'I don't think so. I would have probably heard about it.' She's gotta go."

"Maybe she was just trying to be funny," said Daniel.

"Then that's another reason she has to go."

"Those are all peremptory challenges. Any 'for cause'?"

"None left that I see," said Scott. "Desano has already excused all those that I think deserved a challenge for cause. I'm pretty satisfied with the jury. No college sociology majors—that's a relief. But if you still have a peremptory left, get rid of number twenty-three. He parts his hair down the middle like Gordon. They may be soul brothers."

Richard Evans entered the room. "I just spoke with Josh Johnson. He's still a 'go.' I'll meet him at the airport tomorrow and bring him straight to the courthouse."

"Good," said Scott. "I want to use him as the last witness in the afternoon, after the investigating officers and forensic witnesses. Until he testifies, we won't have Harrison connected to the robbery. We need to do that before the jury leaves the courtroom for the hotel."

Scott reached into his briefcase, took out some papers, and handed them to Richard. "Here are the questions I'll be asking Josh when he testifies. Go over these with him. Write down his answers. I don't want any surprises."

"Richard, we were just going over the jury strike possibilities," said Daniel. "This panel is overloaded with females. We are probably going to have a majority. You've been involved in as many trials as anyone in the office. Women on the jury—good or bad?"

"It usually makes no difference, but in this case, bad. Very bad."

Daniel looked surprised. "Why?"

"Well, he's a handsome guy. Young, bright-eyed, intelligent looking, and the judge is going to instruct a couple of times about him being innocent until proven guilty. The young females will want to marry him, and the old ones will want to mother him. You think they are going to convict him?"

"Well, I don't have enough strikes to get rid of all the women. Besides, I think there's a Supreme Court case that says I can't strike them just because they are female. Right, Scott?"

"Right. Unless they are female sociology majors—they're all fair game."

•　•　•

Judge Desano finished questioning the jury shortly after three. Then he turned to the prosecutors for follow-up questions. Daniel said he had none. The judge then turned to the defense.

Gordon stood and said, "Thank you, Your Honor. I believe you have covered quite well most of the questions I had. If you will give me about ten minutes, I believe I can finish my questioning."

"Ten minutes? Of course, Mr. Gordon. And I intend to hold you to it."

"Thank you, Your Honor. Now ladies and gentlemen, you will recall that early on, Judge Desano introduced me as *Max* Gordon. That is my name, but many people know me by my nickname. I'm about to ask you if you have heard of my nickname, and I ask this because if you have, you may believe there is something sinister or evil about me. I want to explain how I got the nickname so you won't hold it against me or my client." Gordon was smiling as he was speaking and looking intensely from one juror to the next.

"That nickname is 'Sneak.' I'm known by many around this country as 'Sneak' Gordon. It grew out of my college days at Notre Dame, where I played football. Halfback. I was small, but I was fast."

Scott knew what was coming and wanted to object, but Daniel was in charge of the jury selection, and any objections should be made by Daniel. Besides, Scott expected Judge Desano to cut off this charade in a hurry. But Judge Desano seemed to be busy on the bench writing something and said nothing. Scott scribbled, "OBJECT!!!—BS Story" on his yellow pad and passed it to Daniel.

Daniel looked at it, and nodded his head as if in agreement but said nothing. In the meantime, Gordon was proceeding with his tale.

"You've probably heard of our coach at the time, Ara Parseghian. A great coach. And you probably know about our long-standing rivalry with Michigan. Lose to Michigan, but win every game thereafter, and it's still a bad year. That was about to happen in the game where I earned my nickname."

Scott passed the pad once more to Daniel. "OBJECT!!!—BS Story." Again, Daniel looked at it and nodded.

"We were behind by two points. Third and long on the twenty yard line. Tough Michigan line. Been beating up on us all afternoon. Two halfbacks already knocked out of the game, one with a broken leg. Coach sends me in with the play. It's going to be a handoff to me, and I'm to run towards the center of the field to get a good position for a field goal. I look at that Michigan line. That line weighed over a ton. I weighed a hundred and fifty pounds and that's with pads, shoes and helmet—after a slow walk in a heavy rain. Quarterback pops the ball so hard in my stomach, I almost double up. Ouch! I see stars. I'm hurting, but I'm still on my feet, running."

Gordon pantomimed the ball hitting his stomach. He moved laterally in front of the panel, faking a stumble, smiling all the while, and keeping eye contact with the jurors. They were smiling back. Scott felt helpless; he had been warned of this. He was getting a lesson in trial lawyering *and* showmanship. He could understand why Gordon was such a successful trial lawyer. He had a pleasant, easy-to-listen-to Midwestern voice. But more important, he was a hell of a good storyteller.

"And I keep running. Somehow I get through that mighty Michigan line and score. I don't remember a thing until I'm in the end zone. The game was on ABC television, and Keith Jackson was calling the game. He roars into the mike, 'Look at that little sneak! Look at that sneak! Touchdown! Touchdown! What a little sneak!'"

Gordon continued to pantomime the whole event as he described it: running in place, using his fist as the imaginary microphone, and changing his voice to imitate the announcer. The jurors continued to smile, and eventually they were all laughing. Scott recalled Grady's warning, that a laughing jury is not a convicting jury, and he sunk down in his seat until the show was over. He found nothing that Gordon was saying to be funny, but he would concede that the way this balding, rotund ex-jock illustrated the story as he told it was indeed hilarious.

"And that, members of the jury, is when *Max* Gordon became *Sneak* Gordon. If any of you now believe that something evil is associated with my nickname, would you raise your hand?" He paused, smiling and looking from one juror to another, before continuing. "Let the record show no hands are raised. Do any of you, because of my nickname, 'Sneak,' or anything I've said about it, think you might hold it against . . . ."

Judge Desano looked up, for the first time during Gordon's sideshow, and came to life. "That's enough of that, Mr. Gordon. In fact, it's too much. Do you have any more questions, that is, legitimate questions?"

"No, Your Honor. I just wanted to clear that up."

"Mr. Gordon, I think you have clearly demonstrated there was nothing to clear up. We will take a fifteen-minute recess and finish our jury selection."

The bailiff called, "All rise," and the judge and the jurors departed the courtroom. Scott and Daniel remained standing at their table.

"Sorry, Daniel. Grady warned me he would try that football crap and that we should cut him off as soon as he starts. I should have given you a heads up. But why didn't you object when I sent you that yellow pad?"

"Scott, I couldn't think of the correct grounds for objecting, and I didn't think Desano would go for 'Objection, Your Honor, that's bullshit.' What do you think?"

"I think you're right." They both laughed.

• • •

Jury selection was completed by four, and the jury was sworn. Judge Desano gave the jury the standard instructions on avoiding the media and told them to come prepared to stay sequestered in a downtown hotel for three or four nights.

As Scott departed the courthouse, Daniel reached out to shake his hand. "OK, Scott, the rest of the trial is yours. Desano's orders. Let me know how I can help."

"Thanks. I'll let you know, but right now I'm comfortable with the rest. It's really not a complicated trial—a few investigators who have very little to present and two eyewitnesses. Let's go up and see what we can find out about Meg."

They went upstairs to the DA's office suite and were informed that Meg was still hospitalized. No one knew much about her condition, other than she would be there for a day or two.

Scott decided to go straight home. He felt enervated, and the trial had hardly gotten underway. He had heard many times that trials were as exhausting as manual labor. It was true. And tomorrow would be even more demanding. He would go through his trial notebook one more time and get to bed early.

At six, he turned on the evening news. Every channel had highlights of the Harrison case. There was a video clip of the defendant leaving the courtroom to remove his hairpiece, which was called the "Hair Affair." There was no video or audio of the jury selection, not only because Judge Desano's order prohibited any identification of a juror, but also because it had been a boring four hours. Scott watched carefully, expecting to see Gordon mugging for the cameras, but he did not appear. What he did see was an interview of a jury consultant who had been hired by the defense. Standing near the "Eternal Flame" in front of the courthouse and surrounded by TV cameras and microphones, she was explaining her role in advising the defense during jury selection. She was smiling as she talked and looking from camera to camera.

"The selection of the jury is by far the most critical and important part of a criminal trial," she said. "Jurors sometimes come to court with the idea that prosecutors only charge guilty individuals. My job here in Savannah was to make sure that no one with such a preconceived opinion made it to the final twelve to try the case. I was pleased to play a role in the process of seeking justice for John Harrison. We are quite satisfied with this jury. It is an intelligent jury. I have no question that this jury will see that this young man is innocent and will send him home to be with his family."

"To be with his family?" Scott mused. John Harrison had been running from his family for three years. This TV interview was the first knowledge Scott had of the defense hiring a jury consultant. He had seen this attractive lady sitting on the first row behind the defense table passing notes to Gordon. But he had assumed she was a paralegal member of his team. It had not occurred to him that she was his jury consultant, and it would have made no difference had he known. She was a legitimate adjunct to the defense team. But she also should have been subject to Judge Desano's gag order. Scott wondered, but only briefly, if Gordon had arranged for the interview. Of course, he had.

CHAPTER 40
Tuesday, September 12

The news of the trial traveled quickly around the Savannah Law campus, spurred on by the front-page article in Tuesday's morning newspaper. The article read as follows:

Harrison Trial Opening Statements Scheduled for Today

The trial of John Harrison, son of former Georgia senator and now gubernatorial candidate David Harrison, began Monday morning in the Chatham County Courthouse teeming with news media.

Harrison is charged with an armed robbery two years ago at a convenience store on Waters Avenue in Savannah. Nationally prominent criminal defense attorney Max Gordon, of Chicago, assisted by Savannah College of Law Professor Denis Nolan, is in charge of the defense.

A surprise development in the trial occurred Monday when the assigned prosecutor, Assistant District Attorney Meg Flanders, was hospitalized just an hour before the trial was to begin.

Assistant District Attorney Daniel Mackay, who was appointed Monday morning to replace Flanders, immediately asked for a continuance to prepare for trial. After determining that a Savannah College of Law clinic student, Scott Marino, had been working with Flanders on the case and was prepared to proceed with the prosecution, the presiding judge, Lawrence J. Desano, denied the request.

This is the second time Max Gordon has been to Savannah for a criminal trial. On the previous occasion, he was defense counsel for alleged Colombian drug dealer Alberto Escobar who was on trial in Superior Court before the same judge. That trial ended when Escobar escaped from the courthouse during a break in the proceedings. Escobar is believed to be back in Colombia.

During Monday's session, five men and seven women were chosen for the jury to hear the case against Harrison. The trial is scheduled to continue this morning at 9 a.m. with opening statements. The trial is expected to take three or four days.

By the time the first class had started, the Harrison trial was the main buzz on the campus. Scott Marino, the Student Bar president, was going to do battle against not only one of the most famous trial attorneys in the country but also against one of their professors. Some students had already left to get a seat when WSAV-TV, Savannah's CBS affiliate, announced it would be carrying the trial live, beginning at 9 a.m. Soon a paper banner was hanging over the entrance to the Student Center:

HARRISON TRIAL ON OUR BIG SCREEN ALL DAY!

A little after nine that morning, Deborah Channing knocked on Dean Adams's door. Deborah always dropped by on Tuesday morning when a faculty meeting was scheduled, but none was scheduled for this Tuesday. Today her visit would be brief, so she remained standing after she closed the door.

"I guess you are aware of the big trial going on downtown?"

"I am. I read the article in the paper. It took a moment for it to sink in. What do you know about it?"

"Not much. I know Professor Nolan has canceled all of his classes for the week. And I know many of the students in the school have canceled *their* classes to watch the trial. I spoke to two professors who had eight o'clock classes, and they both said over half the seats were empty. Most of the absentees are at the Student Center watching the trial on TV."

"Denis assisting Max Gordon. That's rich. I'm not sure what the educational value of this trial will be, but the PR value to the school hopefully will be richer. But to cancel all his classes? That is quite disruptive for first-year students in their third week. Are you sure, Deborah? Perhaps he arranged for someone to cover? That's a lot of time to make up."

"If he has someone covering for him, the students haven't been told. He sent me an e-mail last Friday, and it read simply, 'Please post that all my classes for next week have been canceled.' I did that. Now, I hope you will excuse me. I have a couple of appointments."

Deborah opened the door to leave and then added, "This is going to be a very interesting week. Why don't you go to the Student

Center and watch the show on TV with the students? It should be good—I've heard about Max Gordon for years. Seeing him in trial in Savannah is special enough, but having one of our clinic students facing him—that tops it all. I wouldn't miss it for anything; I plan to watch as much as I can."

Winston liked Deborah's suggestion. He walked to the Student Center and joined the students who were gathering to watch the show.

CHAPTER 41

"May it please the court, and members of the jury . . . ." Scott Marino began his opening statement to a courtroom overflowing with representatives of the news media and spectators. They had come to see Max Gordon in action but would have to wait until the young prosecutor completed his opening statement.

"Just over two years ago, a well-dressed and well-spoken young man walked into Fast Eddie's at 1443 Waters Avenue, here in Savannah. This is a small convenience store. It has no gas pumps, but because it's the only store in this residential area, it is a busy place. Except late on a Monday night, especially this Monday night.

"The man who walked into the store that night was alone. So was the clerk behind the counter, Vijay Patel. Mr. Patel is the owner of Fast Eddie's. He had been operating this family business, at this location, for over twenty years. This night, because business was slow, he sent his only assistant home early. It was late, and he would be closing soon.

"The man who walked into the store that night was the defendant, John Harrison, seated right there." Scott turned and pointed directly at the defendant. "John Harrison walked to the beverage cooler, opened a door, then shut it without removing anything. He turned around and could see that no one else was in the store except Mr. Patel. He then proceeded along the glass windows that face the parking lot. As he reached the checkout counter at the front of the store, he pulled a short, shiny revolver from his coat pocket. With the pistol pointed at Mr. Patel's head, he demanded money from the cash register, and Mr. Patel gave it to him.

"He then ordered Mr. Patel to disconnect the handset from the phone behind the counter and place it in the bag with the money. As soon as this was accomplished, he quickly departed, leaving through the back door into an alley, and disappeared."

Scott then described the 911 call, the investigation, and the eventual arrest. He concluded his opening statement by walking over to the defense table and standing next to the defendant.

"When all the evidence is in, you will be convinced beyond any reasonable doubt that *this* man, John Harrison, is guilty of robbery as charged in the indictment." Scott took his seat.

Judge Desano looked over at Gordon. "Would you like to make your opening now, or reserve it?"

"Now, Your Honor." Gordon got up from his chair, walked to the side of the lectern, and smiled broadly at the jury.

"May it please the court, and ladies and gentlemen of the jury. Your selection to be members of this jury makes you a part of the most admired and envied criminal justice system in the world. You will have a chance—no, not a *chance*—but rather a duty, to correct an injustice that occurred right here in your home county, when the district attorney decided to prosecute this young man for a crime that he did not commit."

"Objection!" Scott was rising from his seat. "Pure argument, Your Honor."

"Not sure how pure it is Mr. Marino, but it is argument," said Judge Desano. "Mr. Gordon, no argument during the opening, please."

"Yes, Your Honor, of course not," replied Gordon. Then he walked over to the prosecutors' table and slapped it smartly with an open hand. "Members of the jury, the burden of proof in this case rests right here. It's their obligation to convince you beyond every reasonable doubt, that not only was there a robbery, and that the robbery was an *armed* robbery, but they must prove it occurred at 1443 Waters Avenue, here in Savannah, on the date alleged in the indictment."

For a moment, Scott had a sinking feeling. Had he missed something again? Did he have the right date and the right address? The shocked surprise that he had felt two weeks earlier during his first felony trial momentarily returned. Was *this* indictment also defective? Could not be, he thought. He had carefully reviewed every part of the indictment.

Gordon continued. "But there is something else, something more important, that the prosecutors must prove. They must prove that the man who they claim entered that store was Mr. John Harrison, seated right there. And you know what, members of the jury?" Gordon paused and looked slowly from one juror to the other. "They can't do it!" Gordon was getting louder.

Scott thought to himself, more argument, but he would let it go. It wasn't prudent to object to every small matter.

"The prosecutors have only one witness to this robbery," said Gordon. "A witness who had a pistol pointed right in his face."

That's a strange statement, thought Scott. One witness? The names, addresses, and phone numbers of both Mr. Patel and Josh Johnson were given to the defense, as required by reciprocal discovery. Not only that, but Josh had confirmed to Scott in their phone conversation that one of Gordon's team members had contacted Josh at his home in Colorado and had questioned him about his expected testimony. Josh told Scott that he had spoken freely with the caller, telling the caller he would be flying in for the trial on Tuesday. Had Gordon forgotten about this second eyewitness? If so, he was in for an unpleasant surprise.

"I have been trying cases for over a quarter of a century, and during those years, I've defended about every crime there is in the books and faced every kind of prosecutor you will find in this country—good ones, bad ones, and crooked ones. And then there are those who use their office as a political stepping stone. Now, what I think we have here is a case . . . ."

"Objection!" said Scott. "Counsel is continuing to argue, and now he's adding his opinion."

"Sustained. Counsel—all of you, come up to the bench," said Judge Desano. Scott, Daniel, Gordon, and Nolan walked quickly forward.

Once they were assembled in front of Judge Desano, he waved them to a side position, farther from the jury box. A bailiff moved over in front of the jury, a deliberate but mostly ineffective attempt to block the view and sound that he knew would be coming from the bench. Judge Desano had a stern look on his face, and his voice grew louder as he spoke. "Mr. Gordon, you're trying my patience. I have no doubt you know how to make a proper opening statement. But in case you have forgotten, let me explain: it is the time you have to relate the facts to be presented so the jury can understand what is to follow. It is not a time for argument, nor a time for your personal opinion. Do you understand?"

"I do, Your Honor. I apologize."

Judge Desano motioned them back to their seats, and Gordon once again took a position front and center of the jury. "What you are going to learn from the evidence in this case is that the defendant, John Harrison, is the son of Senator David Harrison, presently campaigning for governor of Georgia. Politicians have many friends, and they have many enemies. There is an old rule for politicians: 'Keep your friends close and your enemies closer.' Unfortunately for John Harrison, his father did not keep his enemies close enough."

"Objection, Your Honor. Counsel continues to argue," Scott said, rising from his chair.

"Sustained!" said Judge Desano. "Bailiff, take the jury to the jury room, please. This court will be in recess for fifteen minutes. Counsel, I want to see you in my chambers."

When the four counsel arrived in Judge Desano's chambers, they found the court reporter seated next to a visibly angry judge. Desano asked the attorneys to be seated and looked sternly at Gordon. "Mr. Gordon, perhaps you take me for a tolerant old fool. You may be partially right, but not the *tolerant* part. I am not going to put up with your contemptuous and unprofessional conduct. I am confident you know the appropriate content and the limits of an opening statement. There is to be no personal opinion, no argument or explanation of what the evidence means. Do you understand that?"

"Yes, Your Honor. But may I just say that in Chicago, Dallas, Houston, and other jurisdictions where I try criminal cases, we are given more leeway in the opening."

"Unfortunately for you, Mr. Gordon, this case will continue to be tried in Savannah, Georgia. Now I have given you the rules you must follow. Do you understand those rules?"

"I do."

"Good. Let me explain something else. If you again argue your case or state your personal opinion during the opening, I promise you that I will throw you off the case, or hold you in contempt, or both. Now understanding that, do you want to continue with the opening statement, or just forget it and let the prosecution proceed with its case?"

"Of course I want to finish my opening, Your Honor."

"Fine. This conference is ended."

Scott and Daniel were soon back in the courtroom waiting for the court to reconvene. "What do you think Gordon is up to?" asked Scott.

"I think he's baiting Desano," said Daniel. "Wants to get him angry so that he will make some big mistake on the record for an appeal. He'll also argue that the judge was prejudiced against him. Gordon knows Desano won't throw him off the case. But he might hold him in contempt, because he's pretty pissed off right now. He knows Gordon's deliberately testing him. But Desano's smart. He's pretty much got Gordon cornered on the record. He can't say he didn't understand the limitations."

"I agree," said Scott. "He claimed he knew the rules before we started. He's tried cases in Georgia, one here in Savannah. He may be right about some states allowing argument in openings, but Desano has a right to hold him to his rules. I think Gordon's making a big mistake by continuing to test Desano. We'll see."

The court was called to order, and Gordon began once again. "Members of the jury, as I was saying before I was interrupted, the evidence in this case will show that Mr. John Harrison was not in Savannah, Georgia, when the store on Waters Avenue was robbed."

That's not at all what he was saying when he was interrupted, thought Scott. But Scott was pleased to hear some clue as to what the defense will be claiming, and maybe Desano's warnings were now going to be heeded.

Gordon continued: "As you may imagine, it would be impossible for Mr. Harrison to know precisely where he was two years ago when this crime occurred, but he is sure of one thing, and that is that he was not in Savannah, Georgia, and was not, and never has been, in Fast Eddie's on Waters Avenue of this fair city. Mr. Harrison is not required to prove anything at this trial. Proof is required of the prosecution—proof beyond any reasonable doubt. And where can you find that reasonable doubt? From the evidence, of course. But just as important, from the *lack* of evidence. During this trial I ask you to look carefully in both places, and when you do, you will find no credible evidence linking Mr. Harrison to this robbery. What you will find is a corrupt link to Georgia politics. Now you may wonder how politics . . . ."

Scott was quickly on his feet. "Objection, Your Honor, argument!"

Judge Desano was equally quick. "Sustained. The jury will disregard counsel's comment." The judge gave Gordon a scathing look but nodded his head slightly and said, "Continue, Mr. Gordon."

Gordon continued. "This is not a criminal trial but a political campaign . . . ."

Those ten words were all Gordon was able to utter before Judge Desano rapped his gavel soundly on the bench. The startled courtroom became silent.

"Bailiff, please escort the jury from the courtroom."

This time, Judge Desano did not order counsel to his chambers. When the jury had departed, he looked sternly at Gordon. He did not appear angry, but he had a determined look on his face, as if he had anticipated Gordon's continued defiance of his instructions. Gordon was still standing in front of the jury box, and Scott was standing at the prosecution table.

"Counsel, be seated," he said. Gordon returned to the defense table, and when both counsel were seated, Judge Desano continued. "Mr. Gordon, you seem to be determined to continue your contemptuous conduct. I fail to see how such conduct can benefit your client. As judge for this trial, I must ensure that your client receives a fair trial, so I will deal with that now and you and your contemptuous conduct later. You are relieved as counsel in this case."

Then, looking directly at the defendant, the judge said, "Mr. Harrison, Mr. Gordon will no longer be participating in this trial. The trial will continue with Mr. Nolan as your defense counsel."

The courtroom burst into a din of voices that prompted a series of raps by the judge's gavel. Several from the news media quickly departed for the door.

"Your Honor, may I be heard before you take such action?" said Gordon.

"Mr. Gordon, I have already taken the action. You are no longer counsel in this case, so you have no standing to be heard. Should counsel for the defendant, Mr. Nolan, wish to speak, he may do so."

Nolan looked at the judge. It was a look of bewilderment, followed by a long pause.

Finally, he spoke. "Your Honor, I don't think . . . eh . . . I don't think you can just so summarily dismiss primary counsel."

"Oh, but I have, Mr. Nolan. Do you have anything else you wish to say?"

"But I'm not a criminal lawyer."

"You are now, Mr. Nolan. Do you wish to finish with the opening statement, or reserve it until you are ready to present your defense? And Mr. Nolan, may I suggest you stand when you address the court. It makes the judge happy."

Nolan got to his feet but said nothing. He looked at Gordon, who was now seated. Gordon gave him no help, not even making eye contact. There was a long pause before the silence was broken by the judge.

"In fairness to you and the defendant, Mr. Nolan, I'm going to recess the court until 2 p.m. I believe you deserve some time to better prepare and to consider your options. And Mr. Gordon, when the court reconvenes at two, you are not to be within the bar. Of course, if you can find a seat elsewhere in the courtroom, you are welcome as a spectator. Court is now in recess."

•　　•　　•

At Savannah Law, Professor Leyton was watching the Harrison trial on the big screen TV at the Student Center. He was seated next to Dean Adams and was surrounded by four or five dozen students, some in chairs but most sitting on the floor wherever they could get a view. Many of the regularly scheduled classes had been canceled for lack of attendance. Most of the students had either gone home to watch the trial or were there in the Student Center.

When Judge Desano announced that he was removing Gordon as primary defense counsel, there was stunned silence then the deafening sound of students all talking at once and asking the same question of each other: *Can he do that?* As the cameras faded to the studio at WSAV-TV, the same question was waiting there for an answer. *Could he do that?* None of the studio's expert commentators were prepared for an answer.

Dean Adams turned to Professor Leyton. "It's been thirty years since I was in a trial, Fred. And I never saw a situation like this. What do you think?"

"This is déjà vu from my college days. Never in my wildest dreams would I have expected *another* law professor to get involved like this. My constitutional law professor at the University of Florida found himself in the same situation. He was assisting in a federal trial in Gainesville, a drug case with a law student as defendant. The prof was there to advise on some constitutional law issues, and, like Denis, he was not a trial lawyer. And, just as here, the trial attorney got thrown off the case for improper argument in the opening statement. Same scenario as this. Incredible."

"So a judge can do that?"

"Well, he did it."

"I mean, was it legal? Did it stand on appeal?"

"I'm racking my brain to recall. It happened before I was in law school, but I know it went all the way to the U.S. Supreme Court. And because one of our professors was involved, we all heard about it in our trial advocacy classes. It's the only case in which the Supreme Court has discussed the limits of argument in an opening statement. I can even recall the name of the case—*United States versus Dinitz*—but I don't recall the details of the decision. I do know the court made it clear that the trial judge can relieve a defense counsel for repeated violations. That's what has happened here. Max Gordon was warned several times. I don't think he can complain about Desano relieving him. But continuing the case with Denis as the only defense counsel? Now *that* may be a problem."

•   •   •

After Judge Desano declared the court to be in recess, Scott and Daniel headed for Daniel's office. It had been an exciting morning, but Scott was disappointed that Gordon was gone. He had looked forward to seeing him in action, even as opposing counsel.

"Daniel, do you think we are going to have to try this case again, even if we get a conviction? I'm concerned about Desano's ruling kicking Gordon off the case. Especially when Harrison now has to be defended by an incompetent law professor."

"I don't know, Scott. What choice did he have? Gordon kept defying him."

"Well, maybe he could have leveled a stiff fine, or threatened him with contempt."

"Maximum fine is $500, and he had already threatened him with contempt. And I expect after the trial is over, he may lock him up for twenty days—that's the max."

"Well, I'm still concerned," said Scott. "This is all new to me. The last thing I could have imagined when the trial started has already happened. Relieving the defendant's counsel is a pretty harsh sanction for mistakes in an opening statement."

"Those weren't *mistakes* in the opening statement. They were obviously deliberate. It may be an issue on appeal, but I don't believe it will be reversible. This issue was caused by the defendant's own counsel. Harrison fired his appointed defense counsel and hired Max and Nolan. Now he has to live with that decision."

Shortly after noon, Nick Cox returned from his murder trial for a lunch break and stopped in Daniel's office to see how the Harrison trial was going. Daniel told him about the morning events.

"Desano never forgets and never forgives," said Nick, slowly shaking his head from side to side. "Don't ever get on his bad side. He still believes Gordon was behind Escobar's escape. And he's probably right. Be thankful you don't have to deal with Gordon and his team now. But I do have some concern about what the Court of Appeals will have to say about booting him off."

Just as Nick left, Scott's cell phone rang. "I thought I might catch you—Desano always takes a lunch break about this time." It was Grady. "Saw you and Daniel on the news last night. Celebrities already. But what happened to Meg?"

"Hospitalized. Daniel was appointed about fifteen minutes before the trial was to start, and Desano wouldn't give a continuance. So Daniel and I have it now. Daniel had the voir dire, but I have the rest of the trial."

"Man, that's great. Clinic student prosecuting the son of the next governor. You and *the* Max Gordon, head to head, on TV—that's gonna be a TV classic. Every station in Atlanta picked up on it last night. I've set my TiVo for today."

"Not head to head with Max Gordon but with Savannah Law Professor Denis Nolan."

"Nolan? I don't know the guy. What happened?"

Scott briefed Grady on the morning's event, voicing his concern about Desano relieving Gordon.

"Got to admit that's quite unusual," said Grady. "I've never seen it done, but in the back of my mind somewhere, I do recall hearing about a case where the Supreme Court weighed in on it. The trial judge relieved the defense counsel from the case after he ignored a couple of warnings to quit arguing in his opening statement. You can find it if you are interested. I'm due in trial now—sorry, I've got to run. But I'll be keeping up with you on Atlanta TV."

Scott was indeed interested in searching for the case, but he had no time now, and, besides, what was done was done. Even if Desano had erred, he couldn't do anything to change it now. He would look for that case later; right now all he had on his mind was presenting his evidence.

•   •   •

Scott and Daniel entered the courtroom at 1:45 p.m. and found it packed. He noticed his old roommate, Jeff Swenson, in a center row. Jeff grinned and gave him a thumbs up. There were several other clinic students nearby. The front row seats were occupied by news media. The TV camera operator was busy walking around the courtroom taking readings with a light meter. Scott walked to the prosecution table, sat down, and opened his trial notebook. He would soon be calling his first witness, the first officer to respond to the robbery. He still had not heard from Richard Evans, who was to pick up Josh Johnson at the airport. This caused him some concern, but he knew planes from Atlanta were often delayed, and, fortunately, Josh would not be needed for two or three hours.

The defendant was seated alone and unshackled, under the watch of an armed deputy seated nearby. Scott wondered if his new defense counsel, Professor Nolan, was in a conference room practicing his opening statement or in the men's room throwing up. The latter thought brought a smile to his face.

As if he were reading Scott's mind, Daniel tapped Scott on the arm and signaled him with his thumb to look over his shoulder. "Nolan and Gordon are on the back row. Wonder what they are plotting?"

Scott turned. The two men were in a serious conference in the farthest corner of the courtroom. Gordon was doing the talking and Nolan, the listening. "Sneak," the former player, was now the coach. During his noon hour visit, Nick Cox had said he expected Gordon would stick around and do just that. There was obviously a big retainer involved, and he was not likely to forfeit it by leaving town. He would stay and put in the time. Nick also told Scott to expect Nolan to make a request for a continuance. If it was for an extended period, Scott might as well oppose it since Judge Desano was not in any mood to grant it and the jury had already been selected and sworn. However, if for a short period—a day or two—he shouldn't oppose it. In fact, he should support it. Upon appeal, the appellate court would likely find a denial of a short continuance to be an abuse of discretion. Scott agreed.

Nick was wrong. There was no request for continuance. And Nolan made no request to continue the defense opening statement. Judge Desano told Scott to call his first witness.

"The State calls Officer C. W. Furlow," said Scott. Furlow was the first officer on the scene after the robbery. He was followed by a detective and two members of the forensic team who took fingerprints. Nolan did not cross-examine any of the witnesses, and the trial was moving swiftly, throwing Scott's timetable off. Although he had subpoenaed Mr. Patel for the trial, he had informed him that he would not be called until Wednesday. With the jury being sequestered for the trial, he knew Desano would keep them in the courtroom until at least five, and probably later. Scott would have to find a way to fill in the time for the rest of the afternoon in case Josh did not get there soon.

None of the early afternoon witnesses had much testimony that would help the prosecution, but Scott knew that before he called them. These witnesses were for numbers only. The jury heard a lot about the work of the forensic team—especially fingerprint evidence—but nothing that connected the defendant to the crime.

At 3:30 p.m., Judge Desano announced that the court would take a twenty-minute recess. Without giving a reason, Scott asked if he could make it a thirty-minute recess. Any extra time would be helpful. The judge agreed. Court would resume at four. Surely Josh would be there by then.

He wasn't. Richard returned from the Savannah Airport with news that Josh did not arrive as scheduled. Richard had waited for the next incoming flight from Atlanta, and he was not on that flight either. Additionally, Delta advised Richard that Josh Johnson was not on any flight manifest for that day.

"I followed up with several calls to Josh's cell phone, but there was never an answer," said Richard.

"Damn," Scott muttered under his breath. He had counted on Josh concluding that day's testimony with a description of John Harrison holding a shiny revolver in the face of Vijay Patel. Instead, he would have to finish the day with a photographer, another detective, and a couple of neighbors who saw a strange car parked two blocks away, which was gone shortly after the robbery. Neither of the neighbors could identify the make, model, or color of the car. Useless evidence, except it added to witness numbers as well as further proof of a thorough investigation by hardworking detectives. That morning, Scott wasn't sure he would call these witnesses; now he would have to. He wasn't sure what Desano would do or say if he announced he had no further witnesses available for the afternoon, but he was sure he would be very unhappy.

The trial proceeded for the rest of the afternoon as expected, somewhere between uneventful and boring. The TV camera continued to roll, but there could be no question that the absence of fireworks to match the morning session was disappointing to the media.

After the second car-in-the-neighborhood witness, Scott announced he had no further witnesses available at that time, and Judge Desano recessed for the day. It was shortly after five. Scott wondered what the six o'clock news would report. Sure, there was the sensational surprise of one of the nation's most successful trial attorneys being dismissed by the trial judge. But as far as the evidence was concerned, it had been an unproductive day. However, with the defendant being the long-lost son of the leading Georgia gubernatorial candidate, the media would be there when the court opened Wednesday.

Richard promised to pursue the missing witness and, if at all possible, have him in the courtroom at nine in the morning.

Scott worried about the caveat, "if at all possible." He tried to be optimistic. If Josh testified and was followed by Patel, it would be a strong finish for the prosecution. For the defense, he expected Harrison to testify and deny even being in Savannah, but that was about all he expected from the defense, and he was confident that his two eyewitnesses would carry the day. Scott waited until the crowded courtroom was cleared, conferred briefly with Daniel, and went home.

Despite his youth and excellent physical condition, he was exhausted. He would go over his notes, practice his closing argument, and get a good night's rest. He was curious about what the local TV news programs were saying about the trial. And he wanted to check in with Jennifer. In fact, that was first on his agenda.

Jennifer was at her apartment. She was expecting her study group over at seven. She told Scott she had gone to the courthouse after her nine o'clock class.

"I got there and the bailiff said the courtroom was closed. No seats left. So I hurried back to the Student Center to watch it on TV. By that time, Max Gordon had already been relieved, and some talking heads were discussing what had happened. They kept running the video clip of his opening statement and your objections. They had several criminal defense attorneys commenting on the judge's action and speculating on what the appellate court will do if he's convicted."

"So what did they predict the appellate court would do?"

"They were all over the page. One seemed to think it depended on what took place when the judge called you and the defense counsel into his chambers. They were wondering if a record had been made of that session. Was the court reporter in there?"

"She was, and she made a record. But tell me, what's your opinion of the judge's action?"

"You expect a 1L to have an opinion on that? I was going to ask you that question."

"I think it will be OK, but it won't make any difference if we don't get a conviction. We only have two witnesses left to testify, and one is lost somewhere between here and Colorado."

"Oh, I'm sorry to hear that. We had a big crowd at the Student Center today. This trial—professor versus clinic student—is the only talk of the campus."

"Who are they pulling for?"

"Well, when it was between you and Max Gordon, they were cheering when you were objecting, and a big cheer went up when the judge ordered him out. But now, with you prosecuting and a Savannah Law professor defending, I don't know. How do you think Professor Nolan is performing?"

"Performing? He's hardly opened his mouth. He just sits there like his bottom is glued to his chair. I had expected some objections— had *wanted* some objections—but he's a spent balloon."

He could hear Jennifer's muffled laugh. They talked for a few more minutes about the trial and confirmed their date for Friday night. Jennifer said she planned to be at the trial in the morning. Scott told her if she arrived by eight-thirty, she should be able to get a seat.

After they hung up, Scott turned on his TV. The trial continued to be the prime local news of the day, and now that the famous Max Gordon was gone, the media was trying to stir up interest by focusing on the professor-versus-student story line. There was a clip of a reporter interviewing Senator Harrison, who was campaigning in Augusta. The senator was asked about the trial and the ejection of Max Gordon—and why he and Mrs. Harrison were not attending the trial of their son. He responded with a short statement that he did not want to contribute to the media frenzy and would have no comment at this time. He promised to fully answer all questions once the trial was over.

The final clip that Scott saw before turning off the TV was a short interview of Max Gordon by a reporter on the courthouse steps after Tuesday's afternoon session.

"Will you be at the courthouse Wednesday morning when the trial resumes?" the reporter asked.

"Professor Denis Nolan has the case for trial now," said Gordon, "but, yes, I'll be there, in the back of the courtroom where I was this afternoon. John Harrison is still my client for all purposes except for advocating his case before this jury. I intend to be as close to the trial as I can. If Nolan needs my advice, he knows where to find me."

"How do you feel about today's events?"

"In the words of Woody Hayes, 'There's nothing that cleanses your soul like getting the hell kicked out of you.' But despite this setback, we expect the jury to acquit John Harrison. At the end of this trial, he will be a free man."

About eight o'clock, Scott's cell phone rang. It was Jeffrey Swenson.

"Let me guess," said Jeff. "You're working on tomorrow's trial."

"There's a trial tomorrow?" asked Scott.

"There is. And my ex-roomy, Scott Marino, and his co-prosecutor, Judge Lawrence Desano, kicked some butt big time today. That was a thing of beauty to watch."

"Hush, Jeff, this line may be tapped. Besides, that kick in the butt was self-inflicted."

"Anyway, I didn't call to stroke your already-inflated ego. I called to give you a heads up. Did you get a good look at the spectators in the courtroom today?"

"Well, I saw you and some other clinic students. And some reporters. And I recognized a few local attorneys in the back."

"Did you notice anything unusual about the other spectators scattered around the room?"

"Can't say that I did. What are you suggesting?"

"I don't really know. There were three or four of them, young men, all dressed in suits and ties. And they all bore an uncanny resemblance to the defendant. Not exact, but same hair color, body shape, height. Really strange. I was curious, so I followed one out after the trial was over. Asked him where he was from. He said right here in Savannah. I asked, 'Law student?' He said, 'No, not a law student.' I asked, 'Relative of someone connected to the trial?' He said 'No.' I asked, 'What brings you to the trial?' He says, 'Just curious.' I said, 'My name is Jeff Swenson. And yours?' He says, 'I don't think it's any of your business,' and walks away. Of course, he was right, but I've decided to make it my business by calling you. That's all I know, but I don't believe that guy was there out of curiosity."

"Thanks, Jeff. I'll take a better look tomorrow. Will you be there again?"

"No, but I'll be watching on TV. By the way, how did Professor Nolan get involved in this? I didn't know he was a criminal trial lawyer."

"He wasn't—until Desano made him one. We'll see tomorrow if he's a fast learner. Thanks for the heads up."

CHAPTER 42
Wednesday, September 13

The courtroom was already packed when Scott and Daniel arrived Wednesday morning. It was twenty minutes before nine. Scott saw Jennifer seated in the middle of the third row, eyes down, apparently reading. Max Gordon was in his seat in a rear corner, in conference once again with Professor Nolan. Most of the news media and TV cameramen were in their usual places.

Scott briefed Daniel on Jeff's phone call from the previous night. He stood and surveyed the throng of spectators. Some were standing, some, seated, all talking. The room was unusually noisy.

"I see two or three that meet Jeff's description," Scott said, as he took a seat next to Daniel. "They are in different rows. I don't have a clue what they are up to. I'm just going to ignore them."

"Good. You have bigger fish to fry," said Daniel. He turned and looked toward the courtroom door and saw Richard approaching, alone.

"Couldn't locate Josh," said Richard. I called his cell every hour until 2 a.m. this morning, and I called again at eight this morning—six, his time. No answer and no voice mail. I also checked with Delta just fifteen minutes ago. He's not on any manifest today. Apparently, he just bugged out. I really misjudged him. I thought he was solid."

"That makes two of us," said Scott. "I spoke with him Saturday. I would have bet my Camaro he would show." Scott paused and bit down on his bottom lip. "Well, we'll just have to go with what we have. I'll call Patel and rest my case. If Josh shows, we can put him on in rebuttal."

"You are assuming the defendant is going to testify, or that the defense is going to put some other evidence on," said Richard. "You have only one witness who can ID the defendant, and that ID occurred with a loaded revolver in his face. And that was two years ago. They may just rest their case without putting on any evidence. Really wouldn't surprise me."

"You may be right," said Scott, "but that doesn't change anything. We still have only one witness—Patel. Let me know as soon as you hear anything on the whereabouts of Josh Johnson."

There were three sharp raps on the floor by the bailiff with the tall, tasseled staff, and the courtroom sprang to its collective feet.

"You may be seated," said Judge Desano. "Before we bring in the jury, Mr. Marino, are you ready to proceed with your next witness?"

"We are, Your Honor."

Professor Nolan then stood. "Your Honor, I have a matter to take up before the jury is brought in."

"And what might that be, Mr. Nolan?"

Nolan picked up a yellow pad and read from his notes. "I would like to have the defendant seated somewhere else in the courtroom other than at the defense table. There has been no evidence in this case to link John Harrison to the alleged robbery. We understand the prosecution has a single witness to ID the defendant as the robber. With the defendant seated next to me at the defense table, how can the witness fail to identify him? It's totally unfair and a violation of the defendant's due process rights to be placed where an identification is inevitable." Nolan put down his yellow pad.

"Do you have a response, Mr. Marino?"

Scott looked down at Daniel for some help, but Daniel was as surprised as Scott and offered no assistance.

"Frankly, Your Honor, this is news to me," Scott said, after slowly getting to his feet. "It would have been helpful had defense counsel given us notice so that we could research the law. This is the first I've heard of this 'due process' argument. Cases have been tried in courtrooms in this country for a couple hundred years with the defendant seated at the defense table throughout the trial. Counsel is free to argue to the jury the weakness of any in-court identification when the defendant is seated at the defense table, but we oppose the defendant being removed to the spectator section or anywhere else in the courtroom."

"Well, Mr. Marino, I'm not going to allow the defendant to be seated with the spectators. But I will allow him to be seated within

the bar and several feet from the defense table. Is that satisfactory
with you, Mr. Nolan?"

Nolan picked up his pad again. "Your Honor, would you
also allow some other persons—civilians—to be seated within the
bar? Except for the prosecutors, the defendant, and myself, all others
inside the bar are uniformed persons. It would still be inevitable that
the defendant will be the person identified if he is the only civilian
seated in this area."

"Fine. I will allow one other civilian. Do you have someone
who can fill another chair, Mr. Nolan?"

"Yes, Your Honor. There is a Mr. Troy Morrison already in
the courtroom. I'm sure he would be willing to come up."

Judge Desano looked at the crowded spectator section and
said, "Mr. Morrison, if you are in the courtroom, would you please
stand and identify yourself?"

A young man in a dark suit and red tie stood.

"Would you please come forward?" Judge Desano called
from the bench. "And, bailiff, please get a chair and place it about
ten or twelve feet from the defense table for Mr. Morrison."

Judge Desano faced the young man and asked, "Did you hear
what we were just discussing?"

"Yes, sir."

"Are you willing to be seated in that chair for the duration
of this trial?"

"Yes, sir."

"Very well." The judge then turned to a bailiff and said,
"Bring the jury into the courtroom."

It was all so clear now. Scott recalled Max taking the photo
of the defendant as he left the courtroom the previous Tuesday. He
knew that Max's team had used the photo to round up the "look-
alikes" to attend the trial for the purpose of fooling the eyewitnesses.
Those devious, scheming bastards. He wondered how much the
"look-alikes" were paid and just how much money these thugs had
at their disposal to hustle the system. Was this criminal conduct,
unprofessional conduct, or both? Jury tampering? Could he prove
it? Should he be objecting? Would Desano just tell him it's an open
court and any citizen can attend? Scott was pondering his options

while the members of the jury filed in. And before he could decide on a course of action, he heard Judge Desano's voice: "Call your next witness."

"The state calls Vijay Patel," Scott managed to say, as he gathered his thoughts to focus on the examination of his most important witness. After going through the usual preliminaries, he directed his questions of his witness to the evening of the robbery.

"Who was working in the store at that time?"

"I was the only person on duty. It was a slow night, and I was about to close. I had sent my only assistant home."

"What did you do after you sent your assistant home?"

"I turned off the outside lights and was about to lock the doors and begin my close-out procedure at the register. I had actually taken out my keys to lock up when a man entered the store. I waited behind the counter to accommodate him."

"Describe how the man was dressed."

"He was wearing dark sunglasses, Levi's, a dark pullover shirt, and a tan windbreaker."

"What did the man do?"

"First, he went to the beer cooler, opened it, looked in, and then shut it without removing anything. He turned and faced in my direction for a moment and then turned his head from side to side, like he was scanning the store. I couldn't see his eyes because of his sunglasses, but he must have seen me looking at him. He then turned back toward the beer cooler."

"After he turned back toward the cooler, what did he do?"

"He sort of disappeared behind the candy shelves. Those shelves have some tall displays on them, and I couldn't see him. I didn't see him again until he reappeared along the wall of big plate-glass windows that face the parking lot, walking with his head down."

"What did you observe him do next?"

"His path would take him up to the cash register, where I was standing. I expected him to ask for cigarettes or something else from behind the counter. Instead, when he got to within three or four feet of me, he pulled a pistol from his jacket and stuck it in my face."

"What type of pistol was it, Mr. Patel?"

"It was a snub-nose .38 revolver, I'm pretty sure. I used to own one like it. I bought it after I was robbed the first time."

"What happened after he stuck the revolver in your face?"

"He had a plastic bag, one like most grocery stores use, in his left hand. He said in a clear and strong voice: 'Place all of your cash in this bag. That includes all bills, coins, and rolls of coins.' I recall every word. That's exactly what he said. It was strange. I've been robbed three other times, and each time it was something like 'gimme all your cash' or 'put the cash in the bag and hurry.' This guy was different. He sounded very educated, and he was calm and methodical."

"What did you do?"

"I did exactly what he said. I put all the cash I had in his plastic bag. I expected him to order me to open my safe, but he didn't. He apparently saw my telephone on the shelf behind me, so he told me to turn around, disconnect the handset from the phone, and place the handset in the bag. That's exactly what he said. I recall every word. 'Turn around, disconnect the handset from the phone, and place the handset in the bag.' He spoke very slow, very deliberate."

"Did you do that?"

"I did. When I turned around, I expected my head to explode any second, but he never fired his weapon. He was still standing there when I turned to face him again. I placed the handset in the plastic bag with the cash and handed it to him. He didn't say another word—just ran out the back door."

"And what did you do then, Mr. Patel?"

"I looked out the front window, and I saw there was a car in the parking lot. It must have just pulled up, because it wasn't there when that man walked into the store. I wanted to go outside and call for help, but I didn't know if this car was connected to the robbery. It could have been a getaway car. I waited a minute or two and then went to the front door and opened it just a little to get a better view of the car. It had a military sticker from Ft. Stewart on it, and there was a man with a military haircut sitting behind the steering wheel. I took a chance and ran out and told him that I had just been robbed. He said, 'I saw it. I just called 911.'"

"Now, Mr. Patel, I want you to look around this courtroom and tell me if you see the man who held that pistol on you that night. Is he in the courtroom?"

Patel looked over at the two tables. At one was Daniel Mackay, and at the other was Denis Nolan. He looked over at the jury and then at the bailiffs, court clerk, and reporter. He looked at the defendant seated off to one side of the defense table and to Troy Morrison seated off to the other side. And then he gazed into the expanse of faces peering out from the rows of benches in the spectators' section. But he said nothing. Scott stiffened and breathed nervously.

Finally, Mr. Patel spoke. "Yes, he is."

"Would you point to him?"

The witness pointed directly at the defendant. "That's him, right over there, in the blue suit and red tie."

Scott heaved a sigh of relief, and the testimony from Patel continued. He told the jury how much money was taken and described the arrival of the investigators.

When Scott had finished his examination, Judge Desano turned to Denis Nolan for cross-examination. Nolan stood and picked up a yellow pad on which he had his notes and walked to the lectern.

"Mr. Patel, do you know the names of any other customers who entered your store on the day you were robbed?" asked Nolan.

"Not really. That was over two years ago, you know."

"Yes, I do know. And now, you can't recall any of them?"

"No, I can't."

"This man who entered your store—had you ever seen him before that night?"

"No."

"And today is the first time you have seen him face to face since that night?"

"That's correct."

"But you picked Mr. Harrison out of that photo lineup, didn't you?"

"Yes, I did."

"And that was almost two years after the robbery, right?"

"I believe so."

These last two questions puzzled Scott. When Harrison was represented by the Public Defender's office, his attorney, Sidney Ellis, had succeeded in having all reference to the photo ID suppressed. Why would Nolan ask those questions? Was this merely another display of Nolan's incompetence, or was it some ploy to prompt Scott to pursue the matter on redirect exam and risk a mistrial motion? Scott decided to just let it pass.

"And it has now been *over* two years since that robbery, right?" asked Nolan.

"Yes. Two years and four months."

Nolan dropped his yellow pad on the lectern and stepped to the side. "Now let me make sure I understand your testimony today," he continued. "Your testimony is that twenty-eight months ago, someone wearing dark sunglasses walked into your store, pointed a pistol in your face, and robbed you, and you haven't seen him again until today, but you can still identify him?"

Scott stood. "Objection, Your Honor. Compound and argumentative."

"Sustained."

"Would it surprise you, Mr. Patel, that I don't believe it possible for anyone to make such an identification after so many months? Do you expect the jury to believe your story?"

Scott was on his feet. "Objection, Your Honor. Counsel is stating a personal opinion. It's also a compound question and argumentative."

"Sustained. It is all that and more. The jury is instructed to disregard the last question—the last questions—by defense counsel."

Nolan remained standing. After a lengthy pause, he continued his examination without the help of his yellow pad.

"*Why* are you so sure that this is the man who robbed you?"

It was a terrible question. He should have stuck to the questions that Max had provided on the yellow pad. He would forever regret asking it. For a long moment, Patel looked intently at Nolan, who had moved to just a few feet directly in front of him. Patel turned and faced the jury before responding.

"Let me state why I am so sure. I looked at this man holding the pistol in my face, and I saw a person who appeared to have everything going for him—physically handsome, well-spoken, obviously well-educated—such a fortunate person. He looked like the son I never had but always wanted. Why would he be doing this? I was afraid, yes. He had the pistol pointed at me. But I also hoped that someday I would have the opportunity to identify him in court, like this court, this day. I was determined to remember every feature about him. As he stood there before me, he was just a few feet away." Patel paused and again faced Nolan.

"Even closer than you are now." And then, to the jury once more, he continued. "And the lighting was good. It was a short time, yes, but I made a careful study. I studied his height and his body size and shape. I studied the texture and color of his hair, the shape and size of his nose, his lips, his chin, his ears, the size and length of his neck, the complexion of his skin. The only thing I missed was his eyes because of his dark glasses. I have a good mind for recognizing and remembering people, and I stored every feature of this man in my mind so that, when the time came, I could recall it. I have seen that image in my mind every day since I saw him that night. It has remained unchanged. There is no question in my mind—there is the man who robbed me."

Nolan was stunned by the response. The courtroom had become absolutely silent during Patel's testimony and remained silent. Nolan stood, a totally frozen figure, facing Patel. Time passed slowly. Neither Nolan nor anyone else in the courtroom stirred.

Finally, Judge Desano asked, "Any further questions, Mr. Nolan?"

There were none.

Scott was quickly on his feet. "I have no redirect, Your Honor. The state rests."

Scott anticipated that the defense would make a motion for a judgment of acquittal, as is customary in criminal trials at the conclusion of the state's case, even if merely *pro forma*. He was prepared to argue the motion—even had a "Memorandum of Law" prepared for it and stashed in his trial notebook. No such motion was made. Nolan had not moved since Patel's testimony. He remained standing, a vacant look on his face, immobile since the devastating response to his "why" question. Only when Judge Desano announced that the court would take a twenty-minute recess before hearing the defense evidence did he move. Scott watched him as he walked to the back of the courtroom to confer with Max Gordon. An animated conversation followed. It was obvious that the coach was not pleased with his pupil.

When the court reconvened, the defense announced it would not be calling any witnesses. Scott was surprised as well as disappointed. He had looked forward to getting some questions answered, starting with the source of the defendant's hair piece. Not who purchased it, but who came up with the idea. Those questions and a dozen others, including what the defendant knew of the "look-alikes with the red ties" would remain unanswered.

Also not in evidence was just *who* the defendant was. No evidence at all was presented that he was the son of Senator David Harrison, as stated by Max Gordon during his flawed opening, and certainly there was nothing to justify Gordon's claim that the trial resulted from a politician "failing to keep his friends close and his enemies closer." There was not even a hint of political intrigue. Scott was sure the jury was as perplexed with the absence of this promised evidence as he was.

Judge Desano immediately called on the state to make its closing argument. Scott had not expected his closing to come before the afternoon session. He anticipated having the lunch hour or at least a short recess for last-minute preparations. The defense decision to put on no evidence was bringing the trial to a rapid close.

Scott rose to address the jury. Most of his argument went as he had rehearsed it. He gave the obligatory thanks to the jury for their service and the attention they displayed during the trial. He told the jury that the simple question to be answered is this: Is John Harrison the person who stuck the pistol in Vijay Patel's face and robbed him? He explained the proof required for the crime of robbery. Then he concentrated on the careful testimony of Patel, and he ended by exhorting the jury to bring in the only verdict that "speaks the truth"—a verdict of guilty.

Nolan's defense closing centered on the lack of evidence. He read from a prepared script. No gun, no recovered money, no forensic evidence to connect the defendant to the crime. "Mr. Patel says he opened the cooler. Where are the fingerprints?"

Scott expected this argument; he would have hammered on it himself if he were defending.

"This trial is based on a single eyewitness," continued Nolan. "A robber with a snub-nosed revolver, wearing dark glasses, robs this witness in a span of seconds. Two years later, he can identify him? Don't buy into that, members of the jury." The defense closing was a short, almost perfunctory, closing.

Scott's rebuttal would be even shorter. He picked up his yellow legal pad on which he had recorded most of Patel's response to Nolan's "why are you so sure" question and carefully and slowly read it to the jury. Scott then stopped and pointed directly at the defendant. "There is no question in my mind—*there* is the man who robbed me." With that quote, he ended his argument.

Judge Desano gave the jury their instructions, and the bailiff escorted them to the jury room to begin their deliberations. There was only the single charge of robbery to consider and not a great deal of evidence to sift through, but still it was unlikely the jury would have a verdict before the lunch hour. Judge Desano informed counsel that if the jury came in with a quick verdict, he would hold it until one-thirty. There was time for everyone to have lunch and then return for an update on the jury's progress.

Scott saw Jennifer in the middle of the mass of spectators leaving the courtroom. He caught up with her at the doorway.

"Jennifer, hold up."

She turned and looked surprised. "I thought I could sneak in and sneak out. I don't want to be a distraction."

"Distraction? My work is over. Now, I just have to wait on the jury. We can wait upstairs in Daniel's office."

It was a little after noon. Scott introduced Jennifer to Daniel, and they discovered they had some mutual friends. Scott just sat back and listened. He was still a bit wound up from the rush of adrenalin that had propelled him through the morning session.

Richard Evans entered, holding his cell phone. "I just got a call from Josh Johnson. You won't believe this. He was calling to ask what to do with his plane tickets."

"I believe it," said Scott. "Right now, I'll believe anything. I hope you told him where to stick those tickets. Did he say why he backed out?"

"He said he didn't back out. He was ready to come—he was looking forward to visiting Savannah again. He said he got a call on his cell phone from some guy in the Savannah DA's office, that the defendant was going to enter a plea and there would be no trial. The guy just thanked him for his cooperation and hung up. That was Monday afternoon. He didn't get my calls yesterday because he was guiding some East Coast dudes up the Blue River. That job came up suddenly. He didn't have his cell phone with him, and there's not much coverage there anyway."

Daniel and Scott looked at each other, stunned.

"That's impossible," said Scott. "A plea was never discussed, not by me, not by Grady, not by Meg—not by anyone in the DA's office. And no one besides me, you, and Grady even had Josh's phone number. He's either full of BS or deranged."

"Maybe neither," said Richard. "Did you give Josh's name, address, and phone number to the defense?"

"Yes, of course. I had to."

Richard just smiled at Scott; he didn't have to say a word.

"I'll be damned," said Scott. "First, the hair piece, then a courtroom full of defendant look-alikes, and now we find they eliminated our second eyewitness. Those rotten, deceitful bastards. I remember wondering why Gordon kept saying in his opening statement that we would have only one eyewitness. I thought he would have to eat those words. Now I know."

The room grew silent as they reflected on the latest act of perfidy by Gordon's team. The silence was broken by Jennifer.

"Scott, you said there 'was a room full of look-alikes.' Do you mean the young men in dark suits and dark ties?"

"Yes, dark suits and mostly red ties. Just like the guy Nolan called up to sit near the defense table. Jeff called me last night and said a half-dozen were in the courtroom on Tuesday. I saw them today."

"I saw them, too," said Jennifer. "One I knew—a recent SCAD graduate, Todd Ashby. I asked him what he was doing there. He said, 'Working,' and laughed. He said some guy saw him in Churchill's Saturday and offered him $500 a day to attend the trial, clean-shaven and in a suit. Todd's an interior designer. Flexible hours and slow month, so he took the job. He thought they were shooting a movie, and he was to be an extra. He was surprised to find it was a real trial—and with Senator Harrison's son. That was Tuesday, and he got paid as promised, so he was back again today."

"I'm a slow learner," said Scott. "I'm just now figuring out what we are dealing with—Max Gordon and his cartel of hoods, cheats, and liars. I would include Nolan in that mix, but he lacks their manipulative skill. Max and his team are pros. Nolan is just a super-incompetent lawyer. I'd really like to speak with Josh about that phone call. We just assume he is telling the truth—that may not be the case. Would anyone believe that Max Gordon would be involved in witness tampering?"

"Yes, Judge Lawrence Desano would," said Daniel, with a laugh. "That and more. I don't think he's through with Max. I think he's still planning a contempt citation. I'm surprised he didn't issue it yesterday."

"Scott, you may get a chance to speak with Josh," said Richard. "I told him the tickets were non-refundable and that he could just trash them. He said, no, he would use them anyway. He looked forward to coming. I think he plans to fly in today."

"Well, he's too late to help us with Harrison, but I would still like to speak with him. Try to contact him, and set up an appointment for tomorrow if he comes to Savannah."

Scott walked with Jennifer to the elevator. "Thanks for coming," he said. "Now, I would like to know if you have a read on the jury? What do you think they will do?"

"You really needed that second eyewitness. That would have sealed it. But Patel was a strong witness. I would convict, but who knows. They are probably wondering if the defendant is really Senator Harrison's son, and just what does politics have to do with it."

"But there's no evidence to connect any of that to this trial," replied Scott. "Nothing came out about any political connection. In fact, there's no evidence that John Harrison is even David Harrison's son. That was referred to only in the opening statement—and what Max Gordon said in his opening is not evidence."

"Yes, but all that is still whirling around in the minds of the jurors. Who knows what they will do with it." The elevator door opened. "Call me tonight, Scott." The door closed and she was gone.

• • •

At one-thirty, Scott and Daniel were seated in the courtroom, waiting word from the jury. TV cameras and the rest of the news media were in place, but the courtroom was not overflowing as it had been in the morning. John Harrison was seated alone at the defense table, a bailiff seated nearby. Nolan was in the rear corner conferring again with Max Gordon.

Judge Desano took the bench and announced that the jury was still deliberating. The prosecutors and defense counsel were free to return to their offices or anywhere else they wished to go to await the verdict, as long as they could be back in the courtroom within fifteen minutes of being contacted. Counsel were to provide the clerk of court with a phone number and an alternate number where they could be reached.

Scott and Daniel returned to Daniel's office to wait. At five-thirty, the clerk called them to return to the courtroom. Upon arrival, they found the TV cameras still in place along with most of the reporters. However, they were disappointed to learn that the jury had not reached a verdict.

Not a good sign, thought Scott. He had always heard the longer a jury was out, the greater the chance for an acquittal or hung jury.

"The jury foreman sent me a note," said Judge Desano, "asking that the jurors be allowed to go to their homes and return to continue deliberations in the morning. They don't want to go back to the hotel where they have been sequestered since Tuesday." He handed the note to the clerk for inclusion in the record. "I'm sure they have their reasons—they are not staying at the Hilton—but I don't plan on doing that. I'm going to send them to a nice restaurant then back to the hotel, to return here in the morning. I want counsel here at 9 a.m."

And with that announcement, Wednesday's court activities were over. Most of the day had been spent just waiting, but Scott was again surprised at how totally exhausted he was. Waiting for the verdict proved to be even more tiring than the trial. He went directly to his apartment. It would be another frozen pizza night.

Scott turned to the local news on WSAV-TV. The trial was the main focus. They replayed the testimony of Vijay Patel, and the camera zoomed in on Nolan as he asked his question, "Why are you so sure that this is the man who robbed you?" Then it zoomed in on Patel as he answered the question. The complete answer—every *why* detail—was captured on tape. And then once again, the camera was on Nolan as he stood in stunned silence, unable to speak. It seemed even longer, watching Nolan's silence on TV, than live in the courtroom. Then two of Savannah's top criminal defense counsel appeared on the screen. They were being interviewed, live, by a TV reporter in the station's newsroom.

Reporter: "Tonight we are pleased to have in our News 3 studio two of Savannah's top criminal defense attorneys, Jeff Brown and Charles Samarkos. Both have been watching the Harrison trial on WSAV-TV and have graciously agreed to appear and discuss the trial. We thank you for coming. Let me start my questioning with you, Mr. Brown. What's your impression so far of the case against Senator Harrison's son?"

Brown: "I'm impressed with how little evidence the prosecutors have. No forensic evidence and just a single eyewitness. A lone witness with a gun stuck in his face? That's what the state expects this jury to rely on for a conviction? I don't think so. However, the defense may have snatched defeat right out of the hands of victory during cross-exam of

the victim-witness this morning. That defense counsel—
the law professor—is not the first to ask a 'why' question
and get his head handed to him, but that was classic."

Samarkos: "At least half of the evidence any
prosecutor presents is always manufactured, so I don't
know why so little was produced for this trial. They must
have shut down their evidence factory for the summer. But
the real surprise so far is the bizarre defense put on by
Max Gordon. He wasn't defending just any old Joe; he
was defending the son of Georgia's next governor. And he
blows it. What was he thinking, bringing in a law professor
with no trial experience? That was mistake number one.
Then his stupid opening statement that got him relieved.
He was obviously baiting the judge. That may be a good
tactic in some courtrooms, but not with Judge Desano. No
doubt Gordon thinks he has a sure reversible error built
into this trial, but I don't think so. Judges always tend to
protect judges, and there's no way an appellate panel is
going to reverse Judge Desano on that decision."

Reporter: "Mr. Brown, do you agree with Mr.
Samarkos, that there's little chance for reversal based on
Max Gordon's dismissal?"

Brown: "I don't think it's going to be reversed
just because Max Gordon was relieved. That's not the
real problem. The problem is that once Max was off the
case, there was no adequate counsel for the defendant.
The professor, I'm told, is a property professor who's
never tried a case in his life. And it was obvious; he didn't
have a clue. Every accused is entitled to counsel, and this
defendant was tried without one. If he's convicted, I look
for a reversal."

Reporter: "The defendant did not testify. Did that
surprise you?"

Brown: "Not really. That was the only smart tactic
the defense exhibited in the entire trial. When the evidence
is this weak, you don't want your client on the stand. Why
give the prosecutors a chance to build their case on cross-

exam? The judge will instruct the jury that the defendant has no duty to testify, and if he doesn't, it's not to be held against him. It's been my experience that juries take that instruction seriously."

Samarkos: "It sure surprised me. He should have gotten on that witness stand, looked those jurors in the eye, and said, 'I swear I didn't do it.' I believe most jurors expect any innocent person to say that. They will indeed hold it against him, regardless of those jury instructions. So, I disagree with Jeff about putting Harrison on the witness stand. I wouldn't worry about cross-exam. I would have prepped him so well he could beat a lie-detector test. And remember, this wasn't a seasoned prosecutor; it was a Savannah Law clinic student."

Reporter: "You two have tried criminal cases all over Georgia. I'm sure our viewers would like to know your expectation of the verdict from this jury."

Brown: "The fact the jury has been out all afternoon without a verdict looks good for the defense. Or it could be a hung jury. But I never predict a verdict—juries are just too unpredictable. One thing I'm sure of is that the defense counsel is kicking himself in the rear tonight over that last question."

Samarkos: "From what he demonstrated in court, the defense counsel couldn't find his rear to kick." [Laughter from both attorneys.] "As I said earlier, the evidence is pretty slim. Sure, the prosecutor had lots of witnesses, but it was all show. I expect a not-guilty verdict."

Reporter: "Thank you both for joining us tonight. The jury will return for deliberations tomorrow morning, and when they have their verdict, WSAV-TV will be there, live."

Scott turned off the TV and called Jennifer. She was home and had seen the same interview.

"Not very encouraging," said Scott. "They expect a not-guilty verdict. And they say we didn't manufacture enough evidence—that we must have shut down our factory. That really burned me. How do they come up with such garbage?"

"Oh, Scott, that's just criminal defense lawyer prattle. And I don't think the long deliberation means anything either way. They don't have any real basis for that opinion. The only opinion that counts in this case is the jury's, and they haven't spoken. I would vote to convict, and I believe the jury will also."

That may have been a stretch, but she thought Scott needed a confidence boost. Jennifer sensed that Scott was tired, and they did not talk long. She reminded him that the first meeting of the Dean Search Committee was Friday afternoon. He said he had it on his calendar. Professor Nolan's role in the trial was not brought up. Jennifer's final words were, "Call me tomorrow as soon as the verdict comes in."

S cott and Daniel met in Courtroom K a few minutes before 9 a.m. Max Gordon and Denis Nolan walked in about the same time and took seats in the rear of the courtroom. The TV camera was in its usual spot, but the cameraman was missing, and the few reporters present were sprawled comfortably on the spectator benches, leafing through the morning newspapers. There were more bailiffs than spectators. The defendant was not present and would not be until the jury had a verdict or the court was called to order for some special purpose. Shortly after nine, Judge Desano sent the clerk to inform counsel that, like the previous day, they could leave the courtroom as long as they could be reached by phone and be back within fifteen minutes.

Scott and Daniel returned to Daniel's office to await the verdict. Minutes after their arrival, Richard walked in with news that Josh Johnson was present in the waiting room. He arrived Wednesday evening. He called Richard Thursday morning, and Richard picked him up at his motel.

"Invite him in," said Scott.

Josh, a tall, muscular man with a thick, unruly beard—the perfect picture of a Colorado fishing guide—entered. After the introduction and handshakes, Scott got right to the point.

"I understand you received a phone call informing you that the trial was off; is that right?"

"Correct," replied Josh.

"Male or female voice?"

"Male."

"Did he give a name?"

"No. Just said he was calling from the Office of the District Attorney in Savannah. Said there would be a plea and that I wouldn't be needed. He was off the phone before I could ask him what to do with my plane ticket. I got an unscheduled overnight job on the Blue River and was mostly out of touch by phone until I got back to

Breckenridge. That's when I called Richard and found out the trial was still on, but that I had missed it."

Scott looked down and saw a cell phone on Josh's belt. "Did the call come in on that cell phone?"

"Yes, it did. It's my only phone."

"Is the number that called you still in the phone's directory?"

"I suppose so. I haven't deleted it."

"See if you can find it."

Josh examined the phone and found the date and time the call came in, and the number. "Here it is—312-711-6722," he said.

Richard quickly got up and said he would check out the number. He was back in minutes. "It's a Chicago number, but it's a cell phone or unlisted, and I can't pull up the owner."

"Chicago. I think that's enough. That call was from Max or one of his cohorts."

Scott dialed the number for Judge Desano's chambers, and his assistant answered. "May I please speak with the judge? It's important."

Judge Desano was soon on the phone. Scott asked for an immediate meeting in the courtroom. He had an urgent motion to make.

"Urgent?" asked the Judge.

"Yes, Your Honor. It's urgent."

"It had better be *urgent*, counsel. Be in the courtroom in fifteen minutes."

Scott picked up the Savannah phone book from Daniel's desk and then turned to Richard and Josh and told them to follow him to Courtroom K. Daniel also followed Scott to the courtroom. The scene in the courtroom had not changed, just a couple of reporters lounging around. In a few minutes, the bailiffs entered with the defendant in tow. Max and Denis arrived just before Judge Desano entered and called the court to order.

"The prosecutor has requested this session. I understand you have a motion to make, Mr. Marino. You may proceed."

"Your Honor, we want to reopen our case to introduce evidence. We have an important witness who was unavailable until today. This is evidence the jury should have."

"Well, isn't that just dandy, Mr. Marino. The jury has been out deliberating since yesterday morning, and you now decide they need to hear the evidence. Tell me you are kidding. Or perhaps you are just proposing a new way of trying a criminal case."

"No, Your Honor. And I'm satisfied with the way criminal cases are *usually* tried. But this is not the fault of the state. This is the fault of the defense suppressing this evidence. I certainly realize that to reopen a case after the jury has begun deliberation is highly unusual, but I submit it is within your discretion. May I explain? I need to have a witness sworn."

"I'm all ears, Mr. Marino. This better be good."

Josh was called and sworn. He explained the details of the mysterious phone call exactly as he had explained it to Scott in Daniel's office.

"Do you have that cell phone with you?" asked Scott.

"I do."

"Would you please display the phone number that appeared on your cell phone when you received the call telling you there would be no trial, and read for the record that phone number, starting with the area code."

Josh read the number: "312-711-6722."

"That's all I have of this witness at this time, Your Honor."

"Any cross-examination, Mr. Nolan?"

Nolan remained seated and silent. He turned to look at Max in the back of the courtroom. Max refused to make eye contact. Obviously, no assistance was going to be available. There was a long pause, finally broken by Judge Desano.

"Mr. Nolan, for your information, the usual response is either 'No, Your Honor,' or 'Yes, Your Honor.' Now that's not too difficult, is it?"

Finally, "No, Your Honor" was heard from the defense table.

Scott stood again. "Your Honor, before dismissing Mr. Johnson, I request that he be allowed to keep his cell phone rather than introducing it as an exhibit. He needs it for his employment."

"Any objection, Mr. Nolan?" asked Judge Desano.

Again, Nolan remained seated and silent. But this time he did not bother to look for Max. And again the silence was broken by Judge Desano.

"Mr. Nolan, once again, the usual response is either 'No, Your Honor' or 'Yes, Your Honor.' Now, let's practice."

"No, Your Honor."

"Oh, much better, Mr. Nolan."

Scott was still standing. "Your Honor, I ask the court to take judicial notice that area code 312 is a Chicago area code, as can be readily seen from the front of this local phone book that lists area codes." Scott handed the phone book to Judge Desano.

"And suppose I do, Mr. Marino. So what?"

"Last Tuesday, Mr. Gordon was introduced as being from Chicago. We contend that this phone call, which prevented Mr. Johnson from coming to Savannah to be a witness, resulted from the action of defendant's counsel or his so-called team. There should be a remedy for such witness tampering. The jury should have this evidence. We ask that the jury be brought back into the courtroom and that Mr. Johnson be allowed to testify to what he observed at the crime scene."

"Now, wait a moment, Mr. Marino. All you have is an area code, 312. You haven't presented any evidence with regard to the owner of that phone number."

"True, Your Honor. We've tried to determine the name on the phone number, but it is either unlisted or a cell phone number that is not in the public domain. But adding this to the shady activity that we've seen from the beginning of this trial by the defense—a false hair piece and paid look-alikes seated around the courtroom during identification—it's obvious that this was just another deceptive trick by the defense. You may recall that during the defense opening statement, Mr. Gordon stated we would have only *one* eyewitness. At that time, we expected to have *two* eyewitnesses. But the defense knew we would have only one because they planned to notify Josh Johnson not to come. It will take us a couple days to get a warrant for the name of the phone owner of 312-711-6722. And then it will be too late. We need the jury to hear this witness now."

"Just what would this witness testify to, Mr. Marino?"

"He would identify the defendant as the robber. Our witness was in his automobile in the parking lot outside the store. He had a clear view of the robber."

"Those are serious accusations, Mr. Marino. If I had proof of that phone call coming from the defense, I would not hesitate to call the jury back in to hear your evidence. But your proof is far from sufficient. All you have is an area code. It raises my suspicion, but it's not sufficient to reopen this case after the jury has started deliberations. Your motion is denied."

Scott, Daniel, Richard, and Josh returned to Daniel's office. Josh spoke first.

"No question. That guy at the defense table in the blue suit and red tie is the guy who had the pistol pointed at the clerk. I got a good profile of him on my way to the witness box. No question. Sorry."

"Not your fault, Josh. There is evil in this world," said Scott, "and Max Gordon and his team are a trainload."

The phone rang. It was a bailiff from Courtroom K. "The jury has a verdict. Judge wants you down in fifteen minutes."

The courtroom was ablaze with activity when Scott and Daniel arrived. Apparently, the news media got the word the same time as counsel. The WSAV-TV cameraman was standing behind his camera, and reporters had returned to occupy all of the front seats in the spectator section.

The jury filed in, but none of the members looked at the defendant. Scott had always heard that an experienced attorney could foretell the verdict by whether the jury looked at the defendant when they entered or turned their eyes away, but he couldn't remember which clue matched which verdict. The anxiety that he felt before trial had left him when the trial got underway, but now it had returned with a vengeance. His stomach was churning; he wanted the process to speed up. It seemed that the jurors would never take their seats.

"Has the jury arrived at a verdict?" asked Judge Desano.

"Yes, sir," said the foreperson.

The verdict was delivered to the judge who examined it and passed it to the clerk to be read. The defendant was ordered to stand.

"We, the jury, find the defendant, John Harrison, *guilty* of armed robbery, as charged in the indictment."

As WSAV-TV's camera rolled, most of the news media rushed for the door. The few that remained observed but could not hear the lively conversation going on between the court clerk and Judge Desano. Then Judge Desano spoke.

"The defendant is remanded to the custody of the sheriff. I will be ordering a presentence report and will notify counsel of the date for a sentencing hearing. I want counsel to remain in the courtroom. I have a matter to be resolved."

The defendant was taken from the courtroom by two bailiffs, and counsel took their seats at their tables. Judge Desano looked sternly at Denis Nolan.

"Immediately after the verdict was announced, the clerk informed me of something very disturbing and very serious. I had agreed to allow counsel to depart the courtroom to await the verdict but to leave a phone number, and an alternate, where counsel could be reached. The clerk just reported to me that the phone number that witness Josh Johnson testified to as appearing on his cell phone, 312-711-6722, was one of the numbers provided by the defense. Mr. Nolan, would you like to address this matter?"

Nolan looked dazed, a look he had worn through much of the trial, and made no effort to respond. He turned to look at the back of the courtroom, just in time to see Max Gordon departing.

"No, sir," he eventually managed to say.

"There appears to be sufficient evidence of witness tampering in this case to turn the matter over to the local law enforcement authorities, and I will do that today. Mr. Marino, you and Mr. Mackay are to ensure that the district attorney is promptly notified. This court is adjourned."

The few members of the news media still in the courtroom stood and looked at each other in disbelief. They had a story that those who left early had missed. The guilty verdict would not be the only big story of the trial.

Scott and Daniel took the elevator upstairs to brief Nick Cox. He already had news of the guilty verdict and gave them both broad smiles and congratulatory handshakes. Broad smiles were rare from

Nick, and compliments even rarer. But he was lavish in his praise and anxious to hear about the phone call that had sidetracked Josh Johnson. If the investigation resulted in criminal charges, he vowed to handle the case himself.

Once the victory celebration in the DA's office was over, Scott drove home, stripped off his suit and tie, and got into comfortable clothes. He drove to the Library for lunch. There were a number of students still there who had been watching the trial on the big screen that Juri had set up in the Study Hall. Short news clips of the verdict were now being played every half hour. A couple of local attorneys were interviewed about the verdict and the mysterious phone call to the witness who did not appear.

Jaak and Juri had been glued to the TV throughout the trial, like most of the Savannah Law student body. Jaak saw Scott as he entered and grabbed him in a big bear hug. Turning to Juri, he said, "Lunch is on the house for this TV celebrity. Anything he wants, Juri. Never know when we'll need a good attorney. He looks famished."

Scott sat at the bar, ordered a sandwich, and discussed the trial with Juri and Jaak. Their conversation was frequently interrupted by congratulatory handshakes from Savannah Law students. His cell phone was also active. One call was from Grady Wilder, sending his congratulations. The verdict clip was also being replayed on Atlanta TV every half hour. A second call was from Jennifer.

"Hello, Big Shot. You were going to call me when the verdict came in. Where are you—being interviewed by Larry King?"

"No, I'm at the White House. Sorry, Jen, I was going to call . . . but I was famished. I'm over at the Library having a ham sandwich and listening to Juri's stale jokes. How about joining us?"

"Can't. Still getting ready for afternoon classes. And study group tonight. But save your appetite for tomorrow night. Dinner about six. That is, if we still have a date—and if your head can get through the door."

"Come on, Jen. I'm still just a country boy from Tennessee. And my appetite will be fine tomorrow night. Would you like me to bring something?"

"Nope, my treat. It's a celebrity roast. On second thought, yes, bring a good movie. And don't forget the Dean Search Committee meeting tomorrow at three."

Early Friday morning, Scott made a pot of coffee and spread the morning paper across his small dining table. By habit, he turned first to the sports page. The good news was that the Braves had finally beaten Philadelphia 4-1 Thursday night, after losing both games of a doubleheader Wednesday night. The bad news was that "Chipper" Jones was still being dogged by injuries, and it was unlikely the Braves would make the playoffs—the first time in "Chipper's" entire career. Then he turned to "Local News" and was surprised to find nothing about the trial. He soon realized that was because the article was on the front page, sharing space there with reports from Capitol Hill and Iraq. It occupied two columns and was accompanied by a photo of the defendant and Nolan as the verdict was read.

Harrison Found Guilty

In a highly publicized trial that saw the dismissal of a prominent defense attorney and allegations of jury tampering, a jury found John Harrison guilty of armed robbery.

Harrison, the estranged son of former Georgia Senator David Harrison, now in a tight race for governor in the November elections, faces the prospect of a lengthy prison sentence for robbing a Savannah convenience store clerk two years ago.

The media-intensive trial began Monday at the Chatham County Courthouse. Nationally prominent criminal defense lawyer Max Gordon had been retained to defend Harrison, but Gordon's opening statement for the defense Tuesday morning prompted Superior Court Judge Lawrence J. Desano to discharge him as Harrison's counsel.

Denis Nolan, the assistant defense counsel and a Savannah College of Law Professor, replaced Gordon.

The jury began deliberations Wednesday. When Thursday morning arrived without a verdict, the prosecution asked the court to allow it to bring in an additional eyewitness to the crime.

In a hearing outside the jury's presence, the witness testified that he had received a phone call telling him not to appear. Scott Marino, the Savannah College of Law clinic student prosecuting the case, argued that the call came from someone on the defense team. Judge Desano did not allow the jury to hear this testimony. But he turned the matter over to authorities for investigation of possible jury tampering.

Court observers could recall no similar incident in recent history in local courts. Roger Curlin, a reporter covering the trial for the National Law Journal, said it did not surprise him because of Gordon's reputation for trying criminal cases around the country "with a vade mecum of dirty tricks and an entourage of pernicious and disbarred associates."

The crime commonly known as "jury tampering" is a felony, punishable by imprisonment for not less than two nor more than ten years.

A local law-enforcement spokesman declined to discuss the case. But he did confirm the FBI had been called in because of the allegation of interstate use of the wireless phone system.

Scott was pleased to read that the FBI was joining the jury tampering investigation. Visualizing Gordon in a faded orange-colored jumpsuit brought a smile to his face.

•   •   •

The members of the Dean Search Committee, along with Dean Adams as ex-officio and the registrar, Deborah Channing, all arrived about the same time Friday afternoon. Name signs directed each member to their respective seats around the large conference table. Jennifer and Scott were seated on opposite sides. Ben Sterner, committee chair, called the meeting to order promptly at three. Sterner was a tall, broad-shouldered man in his late sixties. He still had a full head of hair, all silver and neatly parted. He was a prominent Savannah civic leader, an original member of the Board of Trustees, and one of the school's most generous benefactors. Scott saw from his manner and voice that he was a no-nonsense business executive with little tolerance for small talk and the idle chatter that so often precedes committee meetings. Other than having the members introduce themselves, he immediately got down to business.

"We have an important task with a tight timeline. We have twenty-seven applicants so far and will be accepting applicants for two more weeks. Our job is to complete the vetting process and send the best three names to the Board of Trustees no later than January 31. In order to do that, we must start culling right away. Ms. Channing has prepared and placed in front of you a folder with information on all the applicants to date. We can make short work of many, perhaps most. I believe you will find only a few who are truly qualified. Some of the applications are comical, including one from a disbarred attorney who claims his legal problems have given him great insight into the deficiencies of legal education."

Dean Adams interrupted. "Ben, please tell me he's not one of our graduates."

Before Sterner could respond, Jacqueline Hinesley, president of the Alumni Association, said, "Sorry, Dean Adams, I believe I recall him from my Legal Ethics and Professionalism class."

The committee members laughed, including Sterner. But Sterner quickly returned to the business at hand. "We must consider all applications and let them know promptly if they are, or are not, still in the hunt, so that they can move on with their career objectives. That will be my personal responsibility as chair. Your job is to make the decisions. Here's how we will proceed: after you have studied the candidates, we will take a vote by hand. An applicant who does not receive at least four votes to remain in consideration will be dropped and notified. Those who remain in consideration will be asked for additional personal information and references."

This was not exactly a democratic committee process, Scott thought. Ben Sterner personally set the rules of procedure and never inquired if the rules were agreeable with the other members of the committee. But it was perfectly acceptable to Scott. He liked the decisiveness of this no-nonsense leader. Sterner's rules went unchallenged, and the committee members went to work examining the material in their folders.

An hour and a half later, Sterner began the voting process. No secret ballots for him. This would all be by raised hands. He asked

Deborah to stand and tally votes. Out of the first seventeen applicants, five received four or more votes. A few received two or three, but most of the remaining, including the disbarred attorney "with great insight," received none. After each vote, Deborah would call out the results, even though the hands were visible for all to see.

Professor Nolan was the eighteenth applicant to be considered. When his name was called, a sudden stillness enveloped the members seated at the conference table, and there was complete silence. Then, as if on cue, each committee member began looking around at the others. Only heads moved. No arms moved. In a soft but decisive voice, Deborah said, "Zero votes."

Sterner stood for the first time since the voting started. "I trust all of you realize the confidentiality of all voting in this process, as well as the special sensitivity of the vote we just took. Nothing is to leave this room with regard to any particular vote. I will personally inform Professor Nolan that he is no longer under consideration, but the vote count will not be revealed."

With that, Sterner proceeded to the next applicant. The voting was completed shortly after five. Nineteen of the twenty-seven applicants had been deleted from further consideration.

As the committee members were departing, Jennifer told Scott that Marjory Hoffman and Jacqueline Hinesley were stopping at the Library and had invited her to join them. "Do you mind if I put dinner off until seven?" she asked.

"Of course not."

"Good. I'll see you at seven. And don't forget the movie."

CHAPTER 45

Scott did not forget the movie. What he forgot was to ask Jennifer for a recommendation. He had no idea what she had already seen, not a clue. As far as he could recall, they had never even discussed movies. Scott was not much of a movie fan. He preferred sports on TV, and, besides, his recreational viewing was limited by the demands of law school. He selected two: *The Departed*, with Jack Nicholson, and *Little Miss Sunshine*, with a cast he had never heard of.

Scott found a parking space on West Taylor almost in front of Jennifer's front door. When Jennifer opened the door, she was wearing a pair of tight jeans, a light blue, silk blouse, and a broad smile. Scott returned the smile and gave her a strong embrace and a passionate, lingering kiss.

Jennifer closed her eyes and breathed deeply. Then she took her lips from his and whispered, "Not now."

"I'll take that as a promise," Scott replied.

Jennifer just smiled and walked to the kitchen through a wide walkway that also held a dining table and chairs. "I'm still putting your victory dinner together. I stayed too long at the Library. Take a seat on the sofa, and turn on the TV while I finish in the kitchen. The lasagna is about out of the oven. You do like lasagna, don't you?"

"Does a *Marino* like lasagna? My mother invented lasagna."

"Good. This is chicken lasagna Alfredo, with shredded spinach. It's my mother's recipe and my dad's favorite—always served on birthdays and special celebrations. I made it a few days ago and froze it."

Jennifer was speaking loudly from the kitchen. Scott had turned on the TV and was searching for a ball game on WTOC-TV, the local Braves station. They were to play the Florida Marlins that evening. Jennifer's cell phone rang. It was on the table in the living room, next to the sofa.

"Would you get that, Scott?" Jennifer called. "It's probably Nicole. We have a study session at her apartment tomorrow morning."

Scott picked up the phone. "Hello . . . hello . . . Nicole?" There was silence from the other end but no disconnect. "Hello! Who's there, please?" There was no response, and Scott hung up and walked back to the kitchen.

"No one answered."

"I get a lot of those calls. Someone must have a number similar to mine. Clumsy fingers, I guess."

"You say you get a lot of such calls? How many is 'a lot'?"

"Oh, I don't know. About one a night recently."

"From the same phone number?"

"Just random calls, I suspect. None of the numbers were numbers that I recognized, and I didn't check to see if the same number was calling."

"Mind if I check?"

"Of course not."

Scott still held Jennifer's phone. He pulled up the calls she had received over the past two weeks, and yes, the number that had just called, 912-811-3160, appeared each day, and all were night calls.

"Did you ever return the call?"

"No. I just assumed they were misdialed calls. Until you just checked, I didn't know they were from the same number."

"Then I'll check it out." Scott turned off the TV and pressed the key to return the call. A mechanical voice responded. "Your call has been forwarded to an automated voice-message system. 912-811-3160 is not available. At the prompt you may record your message or hang up. Press 1 for . . . ."

"No answer, Jen. But it concerns me. I'll try to check the number out on the Internet tomorrow." Scott found a pen and copied the number.

"Dinner's about ready. Would you mind opening the wine?" Jennifer handed Scott a bottle of Chianti and an opener.

Scott was surprised. "I didn't know you drank wine. But I'm delighted you do—your family's lasagna recipe deserves it."

"There is a lot you don't know about me, Scott. There is a time and place for everything."

Scott just smiled and poured the wine into the two glasses on the table. Jennifer placed the lasagna and salad on the counter, and they served their plates. Jennifer turned off the lights in the kitchen, dimmed the light in the dining area, and lit two tall candles on the side of the table.

Just as she was seated and took her first bite of lasagna, she said, "Oops! I forgot the bread." She hurried to the kitchen and returned with the garlic rolls. "I need more practice at entertaining."

"You don't need more practice at cooking. This is perfect—and remember, I'm a lasagna expert."

"Thanks. I just follow the recipe. What movies did you bring?"

"*The Departed* and *Little Miss Sunshine*. Have you seen them?"

"No, neither one, but I've heard *The Departed* is great—Jack Nicholson, right?"

"And DiCaprio and Damon," said Scott.

"Even better!"

Scott was serious; he *was* a lasagna expert, and this rated with the best. The Chianti was the perfect complement.

Jennifer cleared the dishes, and they lingered at the table discussing classes, law school campus activities, and the trial. Eventually, Jennifer said, "Let's see the movie—I vote for *The Departed*."

"*The Departed* it is," said Scott, and they walked to the living room. Scott removed the movies from the video store bag. On the table beside the TV, Scott saw the VHS player and discovered his *second* mistake in renting movies that night.

He turned to face Jennifer, who had taken a seat on the sofa, and held up the DVDs and grinned. "Please tell me you have a DVD player."

Jennifer began to laugh. "No, I'm planning to put in a request for one at Christmas, but right now I'm in the VHS generation. I'm sorry; I should have told you."

Scott smiled and placed the movies back into the bag. "Now that *The Departed* has departed, any suggestions?"

"Yes. Let's just relax here on the sofa. I have a CD player and a great selection of CDs."

"Like what?" asked Scott. Not that it made any difference. He just liked the idea of the two of them "relaxing" on the sofa.

"Mariah Carey—all her latest. Kelly Clarkson, John Mayer, Céline Dion. But I've got plenty of others. What do you like?"

"All of them."

Jennifer loaded the CD, walked back to the dining area, and turned off the light. Then she returned and took a seat next to Scott on the sofa. They listened to Mariah Carey's "Hero" and "Without You." Then Céline Dion's unique, beautiful voice filled the room with "A New Day Has Come." The light from the two candles sent a soft, flickering glow into the darkened living room. Scott placed his arm around Jennifer and held her just as he had four weeks earlier on the same sofa, only this time she was not experiencing fear, just contentment.

When Céline began "My Heart Will Go On"—the theme from *Titanic*—Jennifer said, "That's an old one, but still one of my favorites." She reached for Scott's hand and said, "I feel like dancing."

He followed her from the sofa onto a nearby area of the wood flooring not covered by carpet. It was a perfect dance stage. Scott reached around her with both hands and held her close against his body. He felt the palms of her hands firmly on the back of his shoulders, her warm, soft cheek against his. It was easy and natural to follow the relaxing rhythm created by this sensational voice. They moved slowly, but their bodies were alive with the pulsating energy of each touch that brought them closer together. As the song was ending, Scott moved his hands lower and pulled her gently but firmly into him. Jennifer responded by looking into his eyes and smiling. Then she rested her head on his shoulder and joined in the song's lyrics, ever so softly.

When the last note was played, they were standing in the middle of their small dance floor, still warmly embraced in each other's arms. Scott tilted his head down, and they held their kiss until Jennifer took his hand and led him into her bedroom.

•   •   •

It was almost midnight when Scott left Jennifer's apartment. At the doorway, he held her close and gently kissed her again before walking out to his car. He did not see the figure of the man slouched down in the second vehicle behind his. The man had been waiting patiently.

Scott pulled out onto the one-way street and turned at the next intersection. As Scott's tail lights disappeared from sight, the man started his vehicle. He placed it in park, pushed a button to unlatch the trunk lid, and walked to the rear of the car. He made sure the trunk lid was unlatched. He did not want anything to delay him when he returned for he would be very busy. He then walked to Jennifer's door and knocked.

Jennifer had just returned to her bedroom when she heard the knock. It did not alarm her; in fact, she was delighted to hear it. Scott had returned—perhaps for the movies he left, or better, to give her another kiss. She opened the door to welcome him. It was not Scott. The man was wearing a ski mask and holding a hunting knife. Jennifer screamed as he closed the door, but no one heard her.

CHAPTER 46
Saturday, September 16

Scott's flag football team, the Pigdogs, had scheduled practice at nine for their ten o'clock game against the Strawberry Frogs. It was the first regular league game of the fall semester, and Scott had missed both practices earlier in the week because of the trial. By eight-thirty he was on the practice field, warming up and tossing the football around with another early riser.

The Strawberry Frogs, the first-place team in the spring semester, continued their winning ways, but the Pigdogs managed to keep the game close. The hard-fought game left Scott physically exhausted yet mentally exhilarated. To Scott, a good workout on the football field was the perfect way to refresh the body, mind, and soul during the constant grind of law school. After a leisurely hot shower and lunch, he would be ready to tackle an afternoon of studying. He was looking forward to the evening; he would be picking up Jennifer at six. They had made plans for dinner at the Six Pence Pub and a movie afterwards, this one in a theater.

He checked his cell phone for messages as soon as he arrived back at his apartment. There was one text message; it was not from Jennifer but from Nicole. "Please call me." Scott called right away.

"Jennifer didn't show up for our study group this morning," said Nicole. "I called her cell but no answer. Do you know where she is?"

"No, I haven't spoken with her this morning, but I know she was planning to be at your place for the study session."

"Well, I'll keep calling. I took notes and can bring her up to date with the group, but we need her input, too."

"We have plans for tonight, but if you don't catch up with her soon, give me a call."

"I will."

Nicole hung up, and Scott headed for his shower.

•   •   •

Scott was working on one of his two seminar papers in midafternoon when Nicole called again.

"Scott, I haven't been able to contact Jennifer. I've called several times. I'm over at her place on West Taylor now. Her car is parked nearby. She doesn't answer the door bell. She gave me a key to her apartment a couple of weeks ago. I think I should go in, but I don't want to do it alone. Could you come over?"

"Sure, Nicole. I'll be right there." Scott tried to respond casually, but he was immediately concerned. There were all sorts of possibilities to account for Nicole not being able to contact Jennifer. Most were no cause for alarm, but there were other possibilities. Her stalker was still out there, and that, added to those mysterious phone calls, heightened his concern. As he drove over to Jennifer's apartment to meet Nicole, he remembered that he had not tried to identify the mystery caller. He would check it out as soon as he got home.

Nicole was waiting on the sidewalk outside Jennifer's apartment. "Thanks for coming, Scott," she said. "I'm just concerned. It's not like Jennifer to not even call and say she was going to miss our study session."

Scott looked a few doors down the street and saw Jennifer's car in the same place it had been when he left the previous evening.

Nicole put the key in the front-door lock. As she tried to turn the key, she realized that it was *already* unlocked. Jennifer had not locked it when she left.

Scott and Nicole entered, and Nicole called in a loud voice: "Jennifer?" There was no response; she had not expected any. It was merely habit, a courtesy that a visitor instinctively makes when entering someone's home uninvited.

Scott found Jennifer's cell phone in the same place he had laid it. The answering machine was in its usual place in the living room. It displayed no messages. All was as he had last seen it. Even the bed was in the same rumpled condition, but he did not mention that to Nicole. Scott wondered if Jennifer had even slept in it. That observation worried him even more. He wanted to believe that she had gone for a walk, was visiting neighbors, or maybe her folks had surprised her for a visit. But then he recalled that her mom and dad had left Thursday for a ten-day cruise. And she would not have gone for a walk or visited neighbors for such a long time. He could come up with no explanation that diminished his concern.

Nicole saw the worried look on his face. "What do you think?" she asked.

"I don't know. Have you seen her handbag?"

"No, but I haven't looked for it. She probably has several, but the one she's been carrying recently is black leather—it's a big one."

Scott had seen it at the Library when Jennifer showed him the mace gun. It also carried her cell phone, wallet and keys, so it would be large enough to spot in the apartment, but neither saw it. It was there, hanging on an inside doorknob of a closet door; they just missed it.

"I'm at a loss," said Scott. "This is not like Jennifer. I'm to pick her up for dinner at six. Nicole, I don't like this. If she's not here at six, I'm calling the police."

"Yes, please do that, Scott. And would you call me, too?"

"Sure."

Scott returned to his apartment. He found the phone number 912-811-3160 on his nightstand. He ran it through the various Internet services for identifying phone numbers but found no listing. He paid one web site $9.95 on his credit card to find the owner of the number, but that also came up with a blank.

It was now four o'clock, and still nothing had been heard from Jennifer. He was fearing the worst. Of course, he had feared the worst from the beginning of this ordeal. And he felt helpless. Yet, if she had been abducted, he knew who to look for. He could wait no longer for Jennifer to just show up. Each minute that passed increased his fear. He had to act.

Marvin's Foreign Auto was less than a half hour away in Garden City and open on Saturday. He did not expect to find Craig there, but the shop owner may have his phone number and know where he lives. Maybe they had seen him recently.

Scott arrived at Marvin's just before 4:30 p.m. Cars were backed up, waiting to be serviced. The waiting room had three customers, and there was no one behind the cash register taking orders. He peered into the shop, looking for someone who might have a moment to answer his questions. After a few minutes wait, a stocky young man appeared with a job order to ring up. Scott waited until he finished at the cash register.

"I'm looking for Craig, the tow-truck operator." Scott regretted he had not noted the name of the towing company on the door of Craig's truck. He was relieved the young man did not respond, "Craig who?"

"You mean, *ex*-tow-truck operator."

"You know him?"

"Yeah, I know him. He owes us a couple hundred dollars for parts."

"Do you know where he is?"

"If I knew where he was, you can bet your sweet ass he wouldn't still be owing us. My boss sent me looking for him yesterday, when his bill got thirty days overdue. He's disappeared."

"When did you last see him?"

"A couple weeks ago. Came in with his hand bandaged. Said some bitch had slammed a door on him. He was pretty pissed."

"What do you mean, 'pretty pissed'?" As soon as he said it, Scott realized it was a dumb question.

"What do you think I mean? You speak English, don't you? He was angry. His arm was in a sling, fingers bandaged and as big as a mummy's head. He said something about having to empty his wallet at the emergency room at St. Joseph's. That's why he couldn't pay us. That's the last time I saw him."

"Do you know his phone number?"

"Nope. When he filled out his credit form for us, he gave a number, but it was a lie. No such number. Just like the home address he gave us. That was a lie, too. But we didn't find out until he stiffed us."

"I think he's done something really bad to a woman. That's why I'm looking for him. Do you have any idea where he might be?"

"Nope. And it won't be the first time he beat up on a woman."

"He's done it before?"

"According to him, that's his style. I heard him bragging out in the shop one night. 'No bitch crosses me! Three of 'em learned too late.' I ain't got first hand knowledge, just what I heard him say. But I believe him, because he's a real asshole."

"What was the name of the towing company he worked for? Maybe they have his home address and phone number."

"Right. They had it. I checked yesterday, but they said when they fired him, they accidentally wiped his personal stuff from their computer. But it was probably a bunch of lies anyway. Look, I gotta go, but if you find him, give me a call, would you?" And with that the man went back through the door into the shop area.

Scott drove back to Jennifer's place. Her car was still there. He rang the door bell. No answer. He went back to his apartment and called Nicole. No, she had not heard from Jennifer. He called Jennifer's house phone and cell phone every ten minutes, but there was no response.

At six o'clock, Scott called information and asked to be connected with the Savannah Police Department. He did not call 911 because he wasn't sure what he should say. Was it an emergency? To him it was; to a 911 operator, he was not sure.

He was connected to someone who identified herself as Sergeant Miriam Fisher. Scott said he wanted to report someone missing under strange circumstances.

"Is this a child or an adult?"

"An adult. Female."

"How long has she been missing?"

"Since this morning, at least."

There was a long pause. "I'll take the information. However, most people who are reported missing return safely in twenty-four to forty-eight hours. Are you the husband or a relative?"

"No. A friend."

"We prefer to take the information from a relative. Do you have the name of her husband or parents?"

"She's not married. And her parents are not available. They left two days ago for a cruise. I'm a close friend. She missed an important appointment with a female friend this morning, and she didn't show for a date I had with her at six. She's not in her apartment, and her car is parked and hasn't been driven all day."

Scott reflected on what he had just said and could see that it was not impressive. No busy police department is going to take action based on what he just reported. So he added what he hoped would be persuasive. "I believe she's been abducted."

"Abducted? What do you base that on?"

"A guy abducted her four weeks ago. I think it's the same guy. He's been stalking her."

"Who was he? Was he arrested? Was it in Savannah?"

"I only know his first name—Craig. It was in Savannah, but he wasn't arrested. It was not reported."

"Was Craig her boyfriend?"

"No, he was a tow-truck driver. He picked up her stalled automobile, and she went with him."

"And that was the abduction?"

Scott realized this was probably the most inane missing-persons report the sergeant had ever taken. He was desperate to make her understand that this was a critical situation that demanded swift action, but every response he was making made it sound like he was a loon.

"What can I do or say to make you believe me?" The desperation in his voice was evident.

"I believe you. And if you were reporting a missing child, I would issue an Amber Alert immediately. But you state this is an adult. There is no law that says an adult has to be where someone else says they should be. They can leave and disappear for any reason, or no reason. We have to respect everyone's right to privacy. However, I want you to give me the person's name and description, her address, phone number, nearest relative, and the last time she was seen. And any evidence you have that a crime was involved. We'll take whatever action is appropriate. You do understand that we have limited manpower, and the department has to set priorities."

Scott did not appreciate the mini-lecture but understood he probably deserved it. He supplied all the information he had, and then he drove to the Library. He was anxious, concerned, frightened—and helpless. He hoped Jaak would be at the Library; he would understand.

The Library was noisy and busy, but he saw Jaak as soon as he entered. Finally, some luck.

"Jaak, do you have a minute? I need to talk to you."

"Why sure, Counselor. We wondered where you've been. Jennifer was in with a couple of ladies last night. Let's go into the lounge."

Jaak led him into his lounge, and they took a seat at the poker table. "What's on your mind, Scott?"

"It's Jennifer. We had a date tonight. She didn't show. I'm really concerned."

"Did you two have a falling out?"

"No, no, Jaak; it's nothing like that. She hasn't been seen by anyone since last night." Scott then proceeded to explain all he and Nicole knew, as well as all he feared, and the mysterious calls that Jennifer had received on her cell phone.

Neither Scott nor Jennifer had ever mentioned to Jaak the two harrowing escapes Jennifer had experienced with Craig, nor the bloody headscarf left in her doorway. Jaak was hearing it all for the first time. He listened carefully, and his concern was evident.

"You did the right thing, filing that report with the police department, Scott. But I agree with you; they aren't likely to put that at the top of their priorities, especially on a Saturday night. They probably won't even take another look at it until Monday. Let's just hope she shows up by then. She has a lot of friends still over at SCAD. Maybe she just needed a breather for a few days and went to visit them. You tell me now, Scott, even if it embarrasses you, did you and Jennifer have a small spat—maybe you said something that hurt her feelings? Not intentionally, of course, but think hard." Jaak gave Scott "the look."

He couldn't have lied even if he tried. But of course, there was nothing to hide. "No, Jaak. I love that girl. I believe she loves me, too. She would have told me if she was not going to be there for our date. And she would have told Nicole. Her car is still there. I just know she did not leave of her own accord."

"You say you tried to find who was behind those nightly phone calls but couldn't. There was no listing that you could pull up on the Internet?"

"No, Jaak, and I'm pretty good at research on the Internet. Cell phones and unlisted numbers are still hard to find. There are businesses that specialize in collecting them now, paying big money for phone files, and in a year or so, those numbers will be searchable. But right now, they are mostly unavailable."

"Maybe. Maybe not. You said you saw Jennifer's cell phone in her apartment? Do you have it?"

"No, I left it there."

"I want you to get it and bring it to me. Right away."

Scott did not question why. He called Nicole and asked her if she could meet him at Jennifer's apartment with the key.

"Now?"

"Yes, now."

"I'm on the way."

As soon as Scott left, Jaak called his friend Malcolm. There was no answer, so Jaak left a message for Malcolm to call him ASAP.

Scott was soon back at the Library with the phone and the same worried look he had been wearing when he left.

Jaak took the phone from Scott and ushered him back to his lounge. "Did Nicole have anything new?" asked Jaak.

"No. She said she had called all of Jennifer's friends that she knew, and none of them had heard from her.

"While you were gone, Scott, I called a friend, Malcolm Zitralph. He's a retired detective now working for Verizon Wireless. If anyone can help now, it's Malcolm. Now you go home, and let me do the worrying. I'll call you when I have something. And if you hear from Jennifer, you let me know right away." He gave Scott his home phone number.

Scott went home, but he didn't leave the worrying to Jaak. He felt somewhat better after sharing his concern, but the length of time since Jennifer had been heard from was more troubling by the hour. He called her house phone several times, hoping to hear her voice, but the receiver was never picked up. And Jaak did not call. At midnight he went to bed, but he knew sleep would not be easy. It wasn't. After a couple of hours, he got up and started to read from a book that Daniel had loaned him, *The Innocent Man*. It was the latest from John Grisham. Unlike Grisham's other books, all novels, this one was a true story—of rape and murder. It wasn't something Scott found appealing at the moment. He put it away and tried again to sleep. His cell phone was next to him. He lay there for the rest of the night and early morning, dozing occasionally, his mind remaining alert for the phone to ring.

CHAPTER 47
Sunday, September 17

It was 8:30 a.m., and Scott had been up for over two hours hoping to hear from Jaak—or better, from Jennifer. He was making an unsuccessful attempt at studying when his phone rang for the first time that morning. It was a text message:

> Scott -- It's over. I'm with my parents at
> Hilton Head. I won't be back in school.
> Please don't come looking for me. Jennifer

Scott sat motionless and staring at the screen for several minutes. His mind was jumbled with images of Jennifer, both good and bad from the past four weeks: the terrifying tow-truck ride, Tybee volleyball, the visit to Hilton Head to meet her family, her warm body pressing against his as they lay in her bed just thirty-six hours before. As devastated as he was when he read the message, he took solace in knowing that she was alive and apparently well. He had feared the worst.

He would have to inform Jaak and Sergeant Fisher at the Savannah Police Department. But he hesitated. Something was wrong with that message. He had missed it when he first read it. He read it again. The first thing wrong was that Jennifer could not be with her parents. They were on a cruise and would be gone for ten days. And the second thing wrong was everything else—especially the words "It's over." It may have been sent by Jennifer, but it was not composed by Jennifer.

He looked at his phone to find the originating phone number. He knew it could not have come from Jennifer's phone because Jaak had it. The call came from the same mysterious number that he had tried to trace. He returned the call immediately. After four rings, he heard, "Your call has been forwarded to an automated voice message system. 912-811-3160 is not available. At the prompt you may record your message or hang up. Press 1 for . . . ." It was the same message he had heard Friday night. He called Jaak at his home.

"Jaak, I just got a text message on my cell. It says it's from Jennifer, but I don't believe it. Claims she's with her parents at Hilton Head, but her parents are off on a cruise. It's from that same mysterious number I told you about."

"Scott, I want you to take your cell phone to Malcolm Zitralph. He's working this weekend and didn't get my message until this morning. But there's good news. He has access to all the telephone records he will need to locate that number. I took Jennifer's cell phone to him a half hour ago. His workplace is on Abercorn Street. He says he can find the number *and* the cell phone tower that made the call. I'll call him and tell him to expect you. Meet me back at the Library, and we'll wait there for Malcolm's report."

Jaak gave Scott the Abercorn street address, and Scott left immediately. Sunday morning traffic was light, and he was there in minutes. The Verizon office was in a large multistory building. On weekends, its front doors were manned by a private security service. Scott stated his purpose, and the guard called Malcolm down to the entrance foyer. Scott introduced himself and gave his cell phone to Malcolm.

"I should have something soon," said Malcolm.

"Jaak said he would be at the Library. I'm going to meet him there," said Scott.

"I have his number. I'll call him there when I have what I'm looking for."

CHAPTER 48

Jennifer's wrists were still hurting, but the bleeding had mostly stopped. She could feel pain in her legs and back, and blood was still seeping from the gash on her right cheek, but she was *alive*. This was the second day of her ordeal. Despite the savageness of her abduction, she had survived, and she was determined to remain a survivor. But she did not underestimate the evil that she was facing. It was only one man, but he was delusional. Apparently, he had been planning this for many days. She had been thrown into the trunk of his car soon after being bound and gagged in her apartment. The ride in the trunk was half an hour or more. She had no idea where she was, or what roads were taken to get there. But she could recall clearly the sudden invasion into her apartment and the fierce struggle that followed. She did not go without a fight.

Her closet imprisonment began as soon as she arrived and had continued. She had been given only a single twelve-ounce bottle of water and two packets of cheese crackers. She remained bound at the wrists and locked in a small closet. The wrist binding, which included wire and tape, was removed only occasionally, when she was allowed to go to a small bathroom that opened only into the room with the closet. She was given a time limit for each break, and it was enforced by her captor, who was still wearing a mask.

She spent her second night in the same small closet, still tightly bound at the wrists. But she had been given a pillow and blanket for the first time. She had been warned not to attempt to leave the closet. The warning was unnecessary; she did not have the strength to attempt to leave. She had not been raped, which was about the last indignity left to be inflicted.

Even in her bound and painful condition, she was able to maintain some sense of time, aided in part by the fact that she had seen light coming through the louvered closet doors for several hours. She knew it was Sunday morning, perhaps nine or ten o'clock. Suddenly, the closet door opened, and there stood her captor. He held a sharp hunting knife in his hand—and for the first time, he was not wearing a mask.

CHAPTER 49

After delivering his cell phone to Malcolm, Scott arrived at the Library a little after 9 a.m. Jaak opened the door and greeted him.

"I'm making some hash browns and scrambling some eggs. How about joining me?" Jaak was holding a steaming mug of coffee in his hand.

"Thanks. My body could use that. Especially coffee."

The breakfast was ready in less than ten minutes. As they sat in the lounge eating, Jaak's phone rang. It was Malcolm, and he had some news. And some maps. He was leaving for the Library immediately.

As soon as he arrived, Malcolm spread a large map on the poker table. Jaak and Scott leaned over the map as Malcolm began a rapid explanation of cell phones and cell towers.

"This map pinpoints the cell phone towers within forty miles of downtown Savannah. I'm going to show you the movement of that cell phone, 912-811-3160, during the past couple of days. Late Friday afternoon and in the early evening, it was in this cell." He pointed to one of the many circled areas on the map. "Here's the cell tower, right off Victory Drive. Then beginning at 8:13 p.m., Friday, it was in this cell. The cell tower is right here, between East Gaston and Abercorn. Jaak says the young lady who's missing lived on West Taylor. So this is the closest tower. That phone remained stationary, in the same cell, until 12:09 a.m., Saturday."

"A call was made at that time?" asked Scott.

"No, no. We are tracing this phone without any calls being made. If cell phones are on, we can trace them. They are in constant contact with the nearest cell towers, and they emit signals—we call them pings—every few minutes, letting the network know where they are. We keep records not only of calls but also of the pings. Not all of them, but some of them. This phone was moving pretty fast for the next half hour or so. Look, I've traced the path on the map by circling the location of cell phone towers as they picked up the signals. See, it's moving northeast, and it appears to be on State Road 21 going into

Effingham County. First, it's picked up by the West Gwinnett Tower, then Chatham City, then Dean Forest Road, then the tower here on Augusta Road, near I-95."

Malcolm was pointing with a table knife. Scott followed the path of the cell phone as Malcolm spoke, but the names of roads and places along its path were of no interest to him; he wanted to know where the phone was *now*.

"Next, we see activity at two towers along State 21. Then, after it passes through Rincon, the vehicle apparently turned right, onto State 275. That's Ebenezer Road. The next tower is here, just past the railroad, and the final tower is here, near the intersection of the road that leads to McIntosh Power Plant on the Savannah River. The phone has been in that cell, stationary, ever since it stopped traveling. That was around 1 a.m., Saturday morning."

"So you know the location of the phone from those pings?" asked Jaak.

"Not the exact location, no. That cell has almost a two-mile radius, and without some triangulation data to other towers, which I don't have, I can't pinpoint its location, except it's somewhere in the radius of that cell. I've worked out there a couple of times. It's a rural, sparsely populated area. That's where the phone was when Scott got his text message, and it hasn't moved. At least it hadn't moved when I left the office. And if it stays there, we can eventually find it. But it might take a search party."

"Do you know the owner? Whose cell phone is it?" asked Scott.

"I can tell you, but I want you to be aware of something important. *Very* important. What I've done is a violation of Verizon's company policies. Privacy rights and all that stuff. The correct way to do this is for law enforcement to get a warrant. That would take hours, maybe days. I can and probably will get fired for this. Pretty hard to keep secret someone rummaging through Verizon customer records. That's OK; I can handle it. But you should also know, it's criminal. I don't know offhand whether it's a state or federal crime— probably both. And if you guys know about it and take action on it, you're going to be just as guilty as I am. So, do you really want to know?"

"Yes, I want to know. But, Scott, cover your ears," said Jaak.

"Not on your life, Jaak. I'm in this, too."

"OK," said Malcolm. "You may be as surprised as I am, but the phone is in the name of Denis Nolan."

"Professor Denis Nolan?" both Jaak and Scott asked at the same time.

"The one and only. Our poker chump. And last week's inept TV star. I checked the data carefully. His phone. No question. And that explains the cell tower over on Victory Drive Friday afternoon. He has a big home on Victory Drive."

"Denis Nolan—holed up on the Savannah River," said Jaak.

Frightening thoughts went through his mind and Scott's at the same time. Thoughts of what Denis might be doing—and thoughts of what they would do to Denis if they found him. There was a period of silence as each tried to think of the next move. Malcolm was the first to speak.

"Jaak, do you remember at the poker game a couple of weeks ago, Jimmy saying he had been hunting on Howard Nolan's property on a high bluff on the Savannah River?"

"I do, Mal. I think you've hit it. Nolan's place would be within the grid of that last cell tower. Jimmy knows exactly where it is."

Jaak had Jimmy on the phone almost immediately. And, sure, he knew where it was. Jaak explained the circumstances, and Jimmy insisted on guiding them to it.

"I'm going armed," said Jaak. "I don't know what we'll find. You sure you want to go?"

"Why, sure. I haven't been in a good firefight since I left Nam. I'll bring my Remington 700."

"You do that, Jimmy, but we're not looking for a firefight. Just want to be prepared. All I'm bringing is my 1911A1—only weapon I own."

"You can't go to a firefight with a pistol. I'll bring you a rifle. I've got a half dozen. Y'all ready to go?"

"Yes," said Jaak. "Malcolm wants to stop at his house and pick up his service revolver, but it's on the way. We can meet you in forty-five minutes."

"OK," said Jimmy. "Let's meet in the parking lot right in front of Jerusalem Church, the old Salzburger Church at the end of Ebenezer Road. You know where that is, don't you?"

"Sure. We'll be there," said Jaak.

"I'll drive," said Scott. "My Camaro's right outside."

CHAPTER 50

Professor Denis Nolan hovered over Jennifer. He had a knife in one hand and a rifle in the other. Framed in the doorway of the closet, he was a terrifying image. He knelt down and cut the bindings, freeing her wrists. He then helped her up and out of the closet.

Jennifer saw a large dining table filled with breakfast items: milk, orange juice, scrambled eggs, bacon, and various breads. Even though her fright had suppressed her hunger, the food was a welcome sight.

"Patty, I want you to join me for breakfast. I prepared it for you."

It was strange, surreal, bizarre—"*Patty*." This professor, this man, this monster, had known her for a month. Sponsored her on the trial team and the Dean Search Committee. Walked with her on the beach. Bound her, violently threw her into the trunk of his car, and brought her here to languish for days in a cramped closet. *Patty?*

"Sit down. I want you to enjoy your meal," he said with a big smile.

Her eyes were watering from the bright sunlight streaming in through the windows. Her mind was groggy, confused. It was difficult to think. Where was she? Through the window, she saw a forest of tall oaks, festooned with Spanish moss. Nothing was moving outside, and the familiar sound of city traffic was missing. Wherever she was, it was not Savannah.

She sat down but did not speak. Nolan sat directly across from her. He no longer held the knife, but the automatic rifle, of a style Jennifer had seen only in movies, was now strapped to his back. He was still smiling, obviously wanting her to speak.

"How do you like our place?" He gestured with his hand, pointing around the room. It was decorated as a lodge, with an array of mounted deer heads, fish, and birds on every wall. "It was my dad's favorite place, his retreat. It's ours now, Patty."

"*Ours?*" And once again, "*Patty.*" The pain from the injuries to her wrists, legs, and face remained, but her mind was clearing somewhat. His words, however, remained baffling. She did not respond to his question.

"I want you to be comfortable here—and every place we live. I know this will work out. It must. Patty, you are all I have now. I waited for your response. I knew you would say 'yes.'"

He was delusional; the conversation, such as it was, was absurd. As the minutes passed, her mind slowly began to function with some clarity. The pieces were coming together. She recalled the conversation with Max Gordon at the party—Nolan's obsession with Patty Hearst and her abduction by the Symbionese Liberation Army. *She* was Patty, and *he* was the Symbionese Liberation Army. The rifle strapped on his shoulder was his prop for the storyline with which he was obsessed. There were many pictures of Patty Hearst and her captors holding automatic weapons in their hands or strapped across their shoulders. According to Gordon, Nolan had movies—several movies—of actual footage of the SLA in action. And now he was acting it out. The words "Stockholm syndrome" echoed in her mind. Yes, he was attempting to control her by making her so utterly dependent on him that she would become emotionally attached to him. This psychotic man was manipulative and cunning—and very dangerous. But she would never be *his Patty*.

"I can see that your eyes are saying yes, aren't they? But you have not really responded with the words I want to hear. Remember our walk on the beach when we shared our two goals in life? First, I would be dean at Savannah Law. And then, we would spend our life together. I've lost the first. Ben Sterner called me Friday. That was the most hurtful call I have ever received. He said I did not receive enough votes from the committee to remain a candidate. But I knew already. It was the trial. I saw you there. You came to see me, and I will always cherish that, Patty. We won. The jury said we won. But TV and the newspapers changed the verdict. How can they do that? I could not believe what they wrote in the paper. Those were stressful days, but we won. The judge said we won. But the newspapers . . . the newspapers lied. They told lies about me and the trial. But you knew the truth. I know you voted for me, didn't you, Patty?"

Nolan's voice was rising, and his eyes were darting as he faced Jennifer across the table.

"You did, didn't you, Patty? The committee. You were there. Tell me you voted for me! I have to know!" His voice became louder and sharper.

Jennifer could feel the danger building. She searched the table for an object to focus upon. She could not look at him. She was both terrified and traumatized.

He jumped suddenly from the table. Instantly, he was at her chair and spun it around to face him. He then reached for her throat and placed his hands around her neck in a firm strangle hold. "Tell me! Tell me that you voted for me! Now! Tell me now!"

"Yes!" Jennifer screamed. "Yes! I did!"

Immediately, he removed his hands and became still. He had a look of repentance. "Of course. Of course. I never doubted you. I'm sorry. I'm so sorry."

He took his seat again. He opened a small metal pill container, removed a tablet, placed it in his mouth, and swallowed. She recognized the container. She had seen it when she visited his office. He had pulled it from his desk, claiming he needed to take an "aspirin" for a headache. Then, as now, she knew it was not aspirin, but it was a drug of some kind—perhaps amphetamine, perhaps a tranquilizer, perhaps worse. Jennifer knew her life was in imminent danger. Her silence was unraveling whatever sanity he possessed. Her survival, she knew, depended on keeping him calm. She must respond enough to keep him in a positive mood.

"We have enough food for a week, maybe two. Do you like it here, Patty. I gave you a pillow last night. Were you comfortable?"

"Yes. Very comfortable."

"You can sleep with me tonight, Patty. Would you like that?"

She saw the danger of leading him on. If she said yes, he would be expecting her in his bed, and when that did not occur— and *it would not occur*—his reaction would be unpredictable but likely brutal or deadly.

"I was quite comfortable last night, thank you. I will be pleased to just stay there again. But without the wrist bands."

"Wrist bands? You had wrist bands?"

"Yes."

"Oh, yes. They were put on to protect you. You should not leave the house. You are safe here. Come over here, Patty, to the window."

Nolan got up and walked to the window and motioned for Jennifer to join him. She felt she had no alternative. He was pointing to something outside the window.

"See that fence? It will protect us. No one can get through that fence. Should they come to take you away, they will regret it. No one can harm you now, Patty."

Nolan patted the rifle sling that stretched across his shoulder. "This is an M2 carbine. It's automatic, much more deadly than an M1 carbine. The magazine holds thirty rounds. My dad taught me how to use it when I was twelve. He served in the Army in Korea, a radioman. He told me radiomen were armed with carbines, but they were M1 carbines. He always wanted an M2, the automatic kind. When he built this house by the river, he bought one. We came out here often, my dad and I. Almost every weekend, all through high school. I was homeschooled, you know. We had targets over by that big hickory tree." Nolan pointed out the window to a large tree beyond the fenced area.

"We would stand beside the fence and take turns shooting. I was a pretty good shot, but I never was as good as my dad. I never was as good at anything as he was . . . never." Nolan shook his head slowly and walked away from the window.

Jennifer remained, viewing the tall fence that surrounded the house. It was a chain-link fence with two strands of barbed wire about six inches apart at the top, which made the fence at least seven feet tall. She could see a hinged metal gate. It had a chain wrapped around the bars near the handle. She did not see the lock, but she knew it was there. She was in a compound, a stockade, overseen by a madman.

Nolan moved into the living room and was standing near a mounted, antlered deer head.

"Come join me, Patty. This is the first deer I ever killed. My dad was real proud of me. It was the happiest day of my life. Yes, my dad was so proud. I was fifteen. These woods were full of deer back then. Still are, but I never go hunting now. Would you like to go deer hunting, Patty? We can, you know. It's our place now—all the way to the river. I'll show it to you this afternoon. We can walk all around our land. We have almost five hundred acres. I'll bring my carbine. I'll protect you. No one will harm you."

Jennifer had followed Nolan into the living room but had said nothing. She took a seat in an oversized chair and watched Nolan as he spoke.

"I wish I had a TV for you, Patty. My dad never allowed us to have TV out here. And no telephone. But I have a cell phone we can use when we need to. I called your friend Scott this morning and left him a text message. You were sleeping so well, I did not wake you. But it was from you. I just wrote, 'I have gone away; don't come looking for me.' Are you pleased I did that, Patty?"

Jennifer was not sure if this was good news or bad, but she felt a response was necessary to keep his mood stable.

"Yes, fine."

"I feel tired. I think I will lie down. I must bind your wrists again so they can't harm you." He walked to a wall shelf that contained tape, wire, and pliers. "Come over here, so I can help you."

"I'm fine; that's OK. You go lie down." She was surprised she could even respond, but she was certain it would not appease him. It didn't.

"Come, Patty. Don't be difficult. This is for your safety."

How delusional, how surreal, she thought. If he would just lie down, go to sleep. At least, she would be safe for a while, and maybe she could find his cell phone. She must not let him bind her wrists again. She would be even more helpless, if such were possible. Besides, her wrists were lacerated and hurting. Her body was still sore from the cramped ride in the car trunk following the violent struggle in her apartment. And her face was throbbing from the cut on her cheek, though it was no longer bleeding. No, she must not let him bind her wrists again. She did not move from her chair. They were exchanging stares.

Nolan began to walk toward her with the wire and pliers in his hand. Jennifer could only stare; she could not move. And even if she could, there was no safe place to go.

As Nolan began to walk toward her, they both heard the sound of approaching vehicles. Nolan ran quickly to the front window and looked out.

"They are here! Reporters, liars! I knew they would come! They destroyed me, but I will not let them harm you, Patty."

He unstrapped the carbine from his shoulder and rushed to the dining area. He reached in the top drawer of a cabinet, removed a magazine and placed it in the carbine. Jennifer had not noticed that the carbine had not been loaded. But she knew now that this madman had an automatic weapon and thirty rounds of ammunition. It was a deadly combination.

Nolan opened the front door and rushed outside. Jennifer could see him through a window, taking a position behind a concrete-block pump house, about four feet high. He was quite visible to Jennifer but could not be seen by the three men approaching. They had parked their two vehicles about a hundred yards from the fenced compound and were walking slowly towards the house. The pump house was just a few yards from the fence. They were walking into a trap set by a psychopath armed with an automatic rifle.

Jennifer did not recognize two of the men, but Jaak was clearly visible and in the middle of the group. They were walking slowly, side by side, about ten feet apart, on the right side of the road that led to the compound's gate. The area did not have dense underbrush—just a few scattered saw palmetto bushes underneath a thick canopy of oak and other hardwood trees. The ground covering of dry leaves produced a loud crunching sound as they walked. She could see that Jaak was armed with a rifle. One of the other two men had a rifle, and one was carrying a handgun. They were glancing from side to side, but it was obvious that they were unaware of the deadly trap they were about to enter.

But it was clear to Jennifer. She opened the front door, pointed to the pump house, and screamed, "He's there! With a rifle!"

As if on cue, Nolan opened fire with a burst from his M2 carbine. Jimmy was hit and went down. Jaak and Malcolm hit the ground, rolled a couple of times, and then returned fire in the direction of the pump house.

Scott, the only one unarmed, had been instructed by Jaak to remain in his vehicle while they scouted the fenced compound, and he reluctantly did as instructed. He watched from behind his steering wheel as the three men moved slowly toward the house, into the trap. The burst of gunfire was as unexpected by Scott as by the others. He watched as Jimmy went down and Jaak and Malcolm hit the ground. He saw just a head peering from behind the concrete wall of the pump house, and then, immediately after the burst of fire, he saw the head disappear. Then the head appeared again, and there was another burst of gunfire. This was the first time he actually saw the rifle. The shooter disappeared again behind the safety of the concrete blocks but not before Scott got a good view of him. There was no doubt; it was Nolan. He was now crouching safely behind the pump house.

As if by instinct, Scott started his Camaro and turned onto the dirt roadway. He braced himself and gunned it. A ton and a half of "wheeled steel," with its 190-horsepower engine, roared down the roadway toward the gate. Jaak and Malcolm watched as the thundering beast passed them and crashed into the gate. The chain link fence was no match for the massive projectile. The steel posts broke at ground level, and the wire was forced to the ground. But the vehicle did not stop. It careened forward, slamming into the concrete blocks of the pump house, where it finally came to rest.

Nolan had heard the roar as it headed toward the compound and directly at him. He ran toward the front door of the house to escape and, in doing so, presented a clear target to Jaak and Malcolm. Both shot at the same time.

Nolan fell near the doorway. Jaak ran forward, leaping over the collapsed fence, fully intending to finish off Nolan if he moved. He did not move; blood was now coming from his mouth and his chest.

"You bastard," Jaak muttered under his breath. Then he called to Malcolm. "He's down—down for good. Go see about Jimmy."

By this time, Scott had climbed out of his wrecked Camaro, momentarily dazed from the impact. His face and arms were peppered with superficial cuts from flying glass, but his seatbelt held and saved him from serious injury.

Jaak stepped over Nolan's body and threw open the front door. With Scott right behind him, he rushed to find Jennifer, who was staring out the window, as if frozen in place. She had observed it all from the window.

Scott embraced Jennifer, and she began to weep. She felt cold and was trembling. He walked her over to the sofa, while Jaak searched for and found a blanket. Scott wrapped the blanket around her and continued to hold her close. She continued to cry softly, finding release from the terror that she had experienced during the past day and a half.

Jaak hurried back outside to make sure that Nolan was, indeed, down for good. Finding him with no signs of life, Jaak ran over the recently destroyed fence to where Malcolm was tending to Jimmy, who was conscious but seriously wounded. He had been hit in the thigh and losing blood fast. Malcolm had already cut through Jimmy's trousers, found the wound, and was applying pressure to stop the bleeding when Jaak came to assist.

"Keep the pressure on that wound, Jaak," said Malcolm, "while I call 911." He placed the call from his cell phone, and when the operator came on, he said, "We've got two people down with serious gunshot wounds." He then gave directions to their location. He stayed on the phone until he was assured that medics were on the way.

"I think most of the bleeding has stopped," said Jaak, "but I hope they get here soon. He's lost a lot of blood."

Malcolm needed to make another very important phone call. He dialed 411 and asked the operator to connect him to his party.

Meanwhile, Scott had retrieved a first-aid kit from his thoroughly demolished car, and returned to the house. Jennifer declined Scott's offer to treat her injuries and, instead, took the kit into the small bathroom.

Scott went outside. He could see Jaak tending to Jimmy and called out, "Do you need any help?"

"No, help is on the way. You see about Jennifer."

Scott went back into the house but kept watching from the window for any sight or sound of an emergency vehicle.

Malcolm's phone call was to Carl DeBickero, a friend at the Georgia Bureau of Investigation in Statesboro. Malcolm had worked with Carl on many occasions while serving as a detective with the Savannah Police Department. They were long-time friends. The nearest GBI regional office was in Statesboro, only forty-five miles away, in Carl's territory.

Serious, violent crimes such as these—an abduction, aggravated battery, and a homicide—are the types of crimes GBI agents handle. The GBI enters upon request from sheriffs, DAs, superior court judges, and other such officials, not from private citizens. But Malcolm wanted them in—and fast. The death of a law professor so recently in the news caused by what could be deemed a "vigilante group" was not something Malcolm wanted to leave to local authorities on a Sunday afternoon. Not when he might be accused of being one of the vigilantes. There are ways to "get invited" into an investigation, and Malcolm was sure his friend could arrange it. Carl was soon on the phone, and Malcolm explained the situation and gave his location.

"We can take the investigation," said Carl. "We have good relations in Effingham with the sheriff and local chiefs. I'm senior duty agent this weekend, and I'll handle the investigation myself. You and all the uninjured witnesses stay right there. I'll call the sheriff, get him to invite us, and let him know I'm on the way. His men may get there before I do, but that's OK. They will just secure the area until I get there with my forensic team. Just stay cool. How's the girl?"

"I don't know. I'm still in the woods and haven't even gotten to the house."

Malcolm turned to Jaak. "How's the girl?" Malcolm had never met Jennifer and had momentarily forgotten her name.

"Pretty shook up," Jaak said. "She's been through hell, but she's going to be OK."

"Carl, she's had it rough, but she's going to be OK. We'll be right here."

"I'll be there within the hour," said Carl.

Deputies arrived at the same time as the medics. The same cell phone tower that had been the key to locating Jennifer was now the key to the emergency response. A medic went into the house to check on Jennifer, but she declined treatment, stating that she was OK.

After Jimmy and Nolan were placed in the emergency vehicles, Malcolm and Jaak went into the house. By this time, Jennifer had finished tending to her wounds and soothing her red eyes with a cold cloth. When she returned to the den, Malcolm and Jaak were there, talking with Scott. She smiled at them and sat down on the sofa next to Scott, resting her head on his shoulder.

As promised, Carl was at the compound in less than an hour. A forensic van arrived soon afterwards. A search warrant had already been signed, thanks to some expedited measures begun by Carl before he left his office. The investigation promised to be thorough. They searched for drugs, ammo, shell casings, additional weapons, letters and writings, computers, and more. They swiped the hands of all four: Scott, Jaak, Malcolm, even Jennifer, with dilute nitric acid to prepare for gunshot residue tests. Later they would go to the hospital and do the same to the hands of Jimmy and Nolan. They confiscated and tagged Nolan's phone and each weapon used in the shootout. They found Nolan's tin "aspirin" container, which was still on the kitchen table, and the tape, wire, and pliers used to bind Jennifer's wrists, and tagged and bagged all of it. They took dozens of photos inside and out and samples of the blood wherever they found it.

Carl made a call to the hospital and determined that Jimmy had been admitted with serious but not life-threatening wounds. He would be interviewed later. He also learned that Nolan was dead. Carl turned to Jaak and Malcolm.

"I have good news and bad news. The good news is that your friend, Jimmy, is going to make it. The bad news is that Denis Nolan is dead."

Jaak and Malcolm were pleased to hear the good news about Jimmy. And they already knew that Nolan was dead. But "bad news"? Perhaps Nolan's death was "bad news." They would not get the pleasure of seeing him brought to justice in court for his crimes.

Neither Jaak nor Malcolm responded to Carl's report. They had agreed before he arrived to answer questions honestly but not to volunteer anything. Malcolm expected that his rummaging in the Verizon files would be discovered and that he would be fired. Whether criminal charges would follow, he wasn't sure, but he did not regret his action. During his service as a police detective in Savannah, he frequently had the personal satisfaction of solving a crime. Several times, his work had prevented a more serious crime. But nothing had given him satisfaction like today. If he was fired, even charged and convicted, so be it.

Jaak was disappointed and concerned that Jennifer had refused to be seen by the medic. Though she insisted that her injuries were slight, Jaak thought otherwise. He wanted to get her to a hospital, but now they had no transportation. Scott's vehicle was totally wrecked, and the other vehicle belonged to Jimmy, who had been evacuated, along with his car keys.

Jaak phoned Juri and gave him directions to the scene. When he arrived, Jaak insisted that Jennifer go with Juri to the emergency room at Candler Hospital in Savannah. Jennifer did not resist; she knew he was right.

The three men remained at the scene, waiting for Carl to give his approval for them to leave. Malcolm called his wife, Nancy, and she was soon there to drive them back to Savannah when Carl gave his OK. He released them about three o'clock.

During the ride back, they recounted each step in their adventure. Nancy drove, shaking her head as they worked through the rescue, step by step.

"Malcolm, you are grounded for a month," she said.

Malcolm just laughed. He was enjoying the after-action critique.

Jaak placed a call to Juri. "What's your news?"

"I took her to the emergency room at Candler. She was dehydrated, and she needed butterfly stitches on her cheek. Plus, a tetanus booster. And they put bandages on her wrists. She wanted to go home, but the ER doctor said she really should stay overnight. He told her that sometimes after an experience like she had, there's a delayed reaction. When he learned that she lived alone, he was adamant that she spend the night at the hospital. She's to be given a sedative to make sure she sleeps. She was doing OK when I left. She had me call her friend Nicole, who came right away."

"Can you think of anything she needs now?" asked Jaak.

"No, Jaak. She's fine. The hospital, or Nicole, will make sure that she has what she needs. Is your poker game on tonight?"

"No. I think I'll take a shower and go back to Springfield and visit Jimmy. Call the guys, and let them know what's up. I'm on my way home now."

After dropping Jaak off at home, Nancy drove Scott to Candler Hospital. When he located Jennifer's room and knocked, Nicole opened the door. Scott could see Jennifer in her bed, bandages on her cheek and wrists. Jennifer smiled when she saw Scott in the doorway. He walked over to the bed, bent down, and kissed her lightly on the lips.

"I'll be leaving now," said Nicole, "but I'll be back later tonight." She closed the door as she left.

Scott pulled a chair close to the bed and took Jennifer's hand in his.

"I'm so glad you're here," said Jennifer.

"I love you, Jennifer . . . from first sight I have loved you"

Jennifer squeezed his hand and closed her eyes. She could sleep now.

THE END

EPILOGUE

Monday's paper had a front-page story of the shoot-out and rescue.

Law professor killed; his hostage rescued. GBI Investigation continues

Denis Nolan, a professor at Savannah College of Law, died during a shootout Sunday. Nolan who had taken a female law student hostage, was killed by friends of the hostage during a rescue effort near Rincon, police said. He was the son of the late Howard Nolan, a prominent Savannah business and civic leader.

According to the police report, Nolan abducted the student from her apartment early Saturday morning and imprisoned her at a house he owns on the banks of the Savannah River in Effingham County.

The investigation of the abduction and rescue led police to piece together the following account.

Early Sunday morning the abducted student used a cell phone to contact a friend, Scott Marino, a fellow law student at Savannah College of Law. She told Marino that she had been taken hostage and where she was. Marino was with Jaak Terras when he received her call. Terras immediately contacted two friends, Malcolm Zitralph of Savannah and Jimmy Exley of Springfield.

Marino drove Zitralph and Terras, who were armed, to rendezvous with Exley, who knew the location of Nolan's house. As the party approached the house, Nolan opened fire with an automatic weapon. In the exchange of fire, Nolan was killed and Exley was seriously wounded.

"The quick action of these four men likely saved the life of the student," said Carl DeBickero, the GBI agent in charge of the investigation.

DeBickero reports that the investigation is still underway, but he believes it is unlikely that any charges will result since the shooting appears to be justified.

The name of the student is being withheld by this newspaper because of privacy concerns.

When Jaak arrived at the Library Monday morning, Juri was seated at a table with a cup of coffee and the front page of Monday's newspaper spread before him. Jaak stood reading over Juri's shoulder about the rescue.

"Quite a weekend, eh, Jaak?" said Juri.

"You might say," replied Jaak, as he sat down next to Juri. "Malcolm said we could count on DeBickero, but I wondered how it would play out in the paper. The report says the call went straight from Jennifer to Scott, giving her location. Nothing was reported about Malcolm rummaging through Verizon's files to locate the phone number and the cell towers. I think Malcolm's job is going to be OK. And I don't believe anybody's going to question our vigilante activities. The one thing missing from the article is Scott's storming the compound in his Camaro, giving us a clear shot at Nolan. Scott saved Jennifer, no question. And lost his prize Camaro."

"He's going to need some transportation. Maybe we ought to help him with it," said Juri."

"Yes, a Camaro. A 1984, eight-cylinder Z28."

• • •

Three weeks later, the newspaper ran the following two articles in its local news section.

Investigation of law professor's death closed

No criminal charges will be brought against the four men involved in the September 17 shooting death of a Savannah law professor who abducted a female law student.

According to GBI Agent Carl DeBickero, the investigation into the death has been concluded. "The facts established that the shooting of Denis Nolan during the rescue efforts was clearly justified," DeBickero said.

Bonaventure memorial dispute ends

The death of Denis Nolan on September 17 has brought to an end the long-running dispute over the building of a large memorial in Bonaventure Cemetery.

The Department of Cemeteries refused to grant a permit for the immense walk-in memorial that Nolan wanted erected on the large family lot in Bonaventure. The memorial was designed to have an Egyptian obelisk that would have towered over all other monuments in the historical cemetery. Nolan had hired legal counsel to fight the department's decision.

Nolan's closest relative, Mrs. Goodwin Tuck, an aunt who lives in Covington, Georgia, said plans for the extensive memorial and tall obelisk have been dropped.

As Scott was reading the newspaper that morning, the phone rang. The caller identified himself as a salesman at Dan Vaden Chevrolet. "Mr. Marino," he said, "we have a special order for you here at the dealership, and it's ready for pick-up."

"A special order?" Scott inquired.

"Yes—a 1984 Camaro Z28."

Obviously surprised, Scott said, "I know nothing about that."

"Yes, I'm aware of that. It's from someone who insists on remaining anonymous. The title is free and clear in your name. I have the keys; just call for me when you get here."

Scott was sure that he knew who the anonymous donor was, and he knew that someday he would repay him.

• • •

The day after Scott picked up his Camaro, another newspaper article caught his attention. It was accompanied by the photo of a man he recognized, although he had seen him only once.

Local man arrested for rape and assault

Craig E. Muldrabe, 34, of Savannah, was arrested last night after a police chase that began in midtown Savannah and ended with his capture in Port Wentworth.

Police said they charged Muldrabe with burglary, rape, and attempted murder of a 25-year-old woman. The woman was reported to be a former girlfriend who had obtained a restraining order against him last summer.

Muldrabe allegedly broke into the apartment of the woman, raped her, and then stabbed her multiple times after she called 911.

When officers arrived on the scene, Muldrabe sped away in a black Camry, police said. The 12-mile chase ended when Muldrabe crashed his vehicle just inside the city limits of Port Wentworth. He is presently being held without bond in the Chatham County jail.

This newspaper is withholding the victim's name because of its policy not to identify rape victims. She was reported to be in serious condition.

Scott called Jennifer immediately. She had not seen the paper, so he read the article to her. Both were grateful—and relieved—at the news that her tormentor was now in jail. They agreed it called for a celebration. Jennifer promised to make chicken lasagna Alfredo, and Scott promised to bring a couple of movies. Both knew he would forget, and they would end up on the sofa listening to Jennifer's CDs. And, of course, they would feel like dancing . . . .

End of Epilogue